Invaded

MELISSA LANDERS

HYPERION

LOS ANGELES   NEW YORK

First Hardcover Edition, February 2015
First Paperback Edition, February 2016
1 3 5 7 9 10 8 6 4 2
FAC-025438-15319

SUSTAINABLE FORESTRY INITIATIVE
Certified Chain of Custody
Promoting Sustainable Forestry
www.sfiprogram.org
SFI-01054
The SFI label applies to the text stock

This book is set in Bembo.
Designed by Tyler Nevins

Library of Congress Control Number for Hardcover Edition: 2014035000

ISBN 978-1-4231-8526-0

Visit www.hyperionteens.com

For L'annabes of all ages.
Keep your eyes on the stars.

PROLOGUE

Cara frowned at the starched gray duffel bag at Aelyx's feet. It was identical to the one he'd brought to Earth last fall when he'd traveled from L'eihr to stay with her for senior year.

"We only have a few minutes," he said, taking her hand in both of his.

She glanced out the spaceport window to the ship that would jettison Aelyx back to Earth—without her, this time—while she continued on to his planet. A shiver of anxiety skated down her spine. The exchange wasn't supposed to happen like this, without Aelyx there to guide her. As much as she wanted to go home, that wasn't an option. The Elders had made their demands painfully clear. Her chest tightened and heat prickled behind her eyes, but she refused to cry. Repairing the alliance between their worlds could save the human race.

That trumped a broken heart.

She summoned a smile and met his silvery gaze. If they had only one minute left, she'd make it count. "I love you."

The corners of his lips quirked in a grin. "Show me."

"I've been trying to show you for days," she said suggestively. "You'd think on a ship this big, we could find someplace to be alone."

Her lame joke didn't deter him. "Do it."

"Right here?"

He checked over both shoulders to ensure no one was watching. "Go ahead. It's safe."

They'd kept her ability to use Silent Speech a secret, but Aelyx made her practice every day. It didn't come easily. Communicating with her mind was more grueling than advanced trig.

"But it's our last minute together," she objected. "Don't I get a break?"

"No." He took her face between his palms. "Show me."

Of course she couldn't deny him, not when she knew how good it felt to experience his emotions, to know on a cellular level how much he loved her.

"Okay."

Closing her eyes, she pulled in a deep breath and released the tension in her shoulders. Aelyx used his thumbs to lightly brush her temples, helping her relax and reminding her to clear her thoughts. That was the hardest part—banishing her inner voice.

She rested a hand over Aelyx's heart, feeling its rhythmic beat against her palm while she focused on the rush of sentiment she felt for him in the moment—attraction, respect, adoration, and, more than anything, need. She let the feelings multiply until she couldn't contain them any longer, and when she opened her eyes, she channeled her passion through his wide pupils and into the consciousness beyond.

He felt it—his expression left no doubt. He closed his eyes for a moment as if to savor the sensation, then locked gazes with her. *That was amazing,* he communicated. *You're getting better.*

"Now it's your turn," she said.

Aelyx tapped her forehead. *Ask me the right way. From up here.*

"Slave driver."

You'll thank me one day.

Cara heaved a sigh and restarted the process of clearing her mind. When she was ready, she gazed through Aelyx's pupils and formed two simple words in her brain: *Your turn.*

But nothing happened.

Try again, he encouraged.

She did—three more times—but without success. For whatever reason, she could share her emotions with Aelyx but never her words. But on the bright side, she didn't get the headaches anymore.

He caressed her cheek. *Be patient and keep practicing. Ask Elle to help you while I'm gone. She should teach you to block your thoughts as well as share them. I trust her, but don't tell the other clones about your progress . . . especially not the Elders.*

Just as she opened her mouth to reply, the steely travel band around Aelyx's wrist buzzed, alerting him that it was time to board. They shared a desperate glance before he pulled her mouth hard against his.

It didn't take long for the kiss to transform from benign to scorching—it never did. The signature tingles only he could summon danced across her chest. Cara crushed their bodies together, clinging to his broad shoulders like she could stop him from leaving if she got close enough. But it didn't last. Just as she captured his lower lip between her teeth, he groaned and broke away.

"I have to go," he murmured, tilting their foreheads together. His wristband buzzed again, a final warning before it would heat against his skin and cause him physical pain.

She pushed his chest, refusing to break down. "Hurry. Before it burns you." She smiled and added, "I don't want anything making you that hot unless it's me."

With a grin, he grabbed his duffel bag and jogged across the metal grating that led to the boarding corridor. When he reached the doorway, he stopped and shouted, "I almost forgot. I built a new blog for you, to replace the one Syrine deleted. Same login and password as before."

"Thanks," she called with a wave. "You're pretty awesome . . . for an alien."

He laughed as he backed into the corridor, leaving her with five final words.

"Actually, *you're* the alien now."

CHAPTER ONE

Subscribe [Archive] [Recent Entries] [About Me]

Invaded

MAY THE SOURCE BE WITH YOU

MONDAY, DECEMBER 24

I'm Dreaming of a Beige Christmas.

Happy Holidays, earthlings! Welcome to INVADED, your exclusive sneak peek into my one-woman invasion of planet L'eihr. I don't know how 597,350 of you found my new blog so quickly, but I'm glad you're here. Pull up a chair, kick off your boots, and grab a steaming mug of *h'ali* (the closest thing to hot chocolate on this sugar-hating spaceship).

It's Christmas Eve, and if the stars align—not to mention the intergalactic transmissions—you should see this maiden post by morning. It's an icy absolute zero here in space, but we should arrive at my balmy home away from home by lunchtime.

I have to say, it's a little weird being one of only two people on this vessel to celebrate Christmas. My new friends think it's crazy to believe that God's spirit impregnated a virgin, but they think it's totally logical to accept that a Sacred Mother birthed six gods and goddesses who created L'eihr from meteor dust and starlight. Because that's a lot more feasible.

But I digress. L'eihrs celebrate the birth of their deities each spring, but instead of exchanging presents, they fast for two days to bring them closer to the Sacred Mother by way of collective suffering.

Talk about *bah humbug!*

To all my friends and family back home, guzzle some eggnog for me, and while you're at it, choke down some fruitcake, too. You'd be surprised how much I miss that stuff . . . and you. Always you, dear readers.

Merry Christmas and Happy New Year!

Posted by Cara Sweeney

No comments had posted, but that didn't surprise Cara. Sometimes there was a twenty-four-hour delay sending and receiving electronic data from the L'eihr ship stationed above Earth's atmosphere. Still, that wasn't too shabby, considering how many galaxies those poor bytes had to travel.

She pushed aside her brother's laptop and set her com-sphere on the polished cafeteria table, where Mom and Dad would soon join her for Christmas dinner, hologram-style. Her life felt like a futuristic holiday special: *A Very Virtual Christmas.* If only she could summon some digital decorations for the ship's sterile, empty dining hall. It was as festive as a death-row prison cell in here—bare gray walls, rows of meticulously parallel metallic tables and benches, dead silence, and nothing illuminating the darkness but the computer's backlit screen.

At three in the morning, not a creature was stirring, not

even a *harra*, the L'eihr equivalent of a mouse. But instead of nestled all snug in her bed with visions of Reese's Cups dancing in her head, Cara was running on Midtown time, day versus night, waiting for the "phone" to ring. As she often did during these quiet moments, she wondered what Aelyx might be doing in Manhattan.

It'd only been a week since the L'eihr Elders had sent him back to Earth to help rebuild the alliance, but it felt like a year. Aelyx was the reason she'd left Earth in the first place— so they could build a life together on the L'eihr colony. She never imagined she'd be alone when she glimpsed her new home for the first time.

Well, not literally alone.

Her brother, Troy, was here to serve as a human mentor, but truth be told, he was a real horse's ass—the kind of guy who would point and laugh at her misery instead of warning her not to touch a flesh-eating alien plant . . . assuming those existed on L'eihr. She hoped they didn't.

The sound of dragging footsteps turned her attention to the doorway, where Troy shuffled into view sporting unlaced combat boots and the same rumpled military fatigues he'd worn to bed last night. He yawned loudly, not bothering to cover his mouth, and used both hands simultaneously to scratch his chest and butt.

Yep, that was her mentor. She was *so* screwed.

"They call yet?" he grumbled, taking the seat across from her.

Cara slid an extra nutrient packet at him. "Merry Christmas to you, too."

7

Instead of answering, he rubbed one eye and plucked his offering from the table. He loved those protein bars, though Cara couldn't understand why. They smelled and tasted exactly like boiled cabbage.

"Merry Christmas," he said eventually. Then followed it with, "Dorkus."

Flipping him off didn't seem very "yuletide gay," so she rolled her eyes instead. "When are we supposed to shuttle down?"

"Dunno."

She rested her chin in one hand and sighed.

Their transport had reached the L'eihr solar system hours ago, but for reasons she wasn't privy to, the Elders had held off on shuttling them planet-side. Cara had a raging case of cabin fever—or starship fever, as it were—and if she had to listen to Troy's chronic snoring one more night, she'd smother him in his sleep. He'd insisted on bunking with her while Aelyx was on board, because God forbid she got lucky for once, and he'd refused to leave her side ever since.

She narrowed her eyes at him. "I hope you don't think we're sharing a dorm at the Aegis." Or on the colony, or wherever they ended up.

She expected him to cop an attitude, but he dropped his gaze into his lap. An emotion she couldn't place darkened his features. It looked a lot like guilt, which didn't make sense. Troy was too self-absorbed to feel guilty.

"What's going on?" she asked. "There's something you're not telling—"

She was interrupted by the buzzing of a thousand hornets

inside her skull, her com-sphere's irritating-but-effective way of alerting her to an incoming transmission. Cringing, she snatched the gadget into her fist and whispered her password against its cool metal shell.

Mom's and Dad's six-inch holograms flickered to life beside her nutrient packet while Troy hopped onto the table and slid across its slick surface to occupy the spot next to her.

"Merry Christmas!" Mom called, waving from her seat atop Dad's lap. They had settled on the magnolia-festooned living room sofa, and Dad wore a jolly red sweater that clashed with his orange hair. It was a cornucopia of tackiness, but Cara had never beheld a more beautiful sight.

If she listened closely, she could just make out Bing Crosby's buttery voice crooning "I'll Be Home for Christmas," which was kind of ironic, considering. She returned the greeting along with Troy, then held up her nutrition bar. "Did you finish dinner? I thought we could eat together."

"Oh," Mom said, "we got takeout from the Szechuan place down the street." Her cherry lips curved in a smile, but she couldn't hide the sadness in her voice. "Didn't seem right, cooking a big meal for just the two of us."

Cara wilted and tossed aside her packet. "I hate these protein bars anyway."

"I can barely see you," Mom said. "Why are you sitting in the dark?"

Troy pulled his laptop closer and adjusted the settings to brighten the screen. "They're pretty frugal with energy here."

"Good for them," Dad piped up. "Now lean in so I can get a closer look." Cara and Troy obeyed, pressing their cheeks

9

together to let Dad scrutinize them. Dad nodded in approval until his gaze settled on Troy. "When're you going to cut that hair, Rapunzel? I can't believe your CO lets you wear the uniform when you look like that."

Troy's hand darted to the loose black curls—identical to Mom's—that brushed the tops of his shoulders. His hair was almost long enough to wear in a low ponytail like the L'eihrs did. Wrinkling his brow, he argued, "When in Rome . . ."

"Get a trim," Dad said, then turned his attention to Cara. A grin broke out across his face. "Pepper, I can't get used to the sight of you in that L'eihr getup. You remind me of those little fan girls who wear costumes and dye their skin brown."

"L'annabes," Mom supplied with a soft snort.

"Yeah, that's it."

Self-consciously, Cara smoothed down the front of her tunic. She couldn't get used to wearing the uniform, either, or pulling her auburn waves into the same low braid every day. She missed her jeans and scoop-necked sweaters, not to mention her leather riding boots and double-barrel curling iron.

But saving Earth was worth the sacrifice. And so was Aelyx.

Clearly Dad's thoughts traveled on the same wavelength. "You hear from Aelyx lately?"

"He called a couple days ago," she said. "He's staying with the ambassador in Manha—" She cut off as a miniature white ball of fur pattered into the hologram and hopped onto Mom's lap. It looked like an overgrown hamster. Cara extended a finger. "What's that?"

Mom cuddled the fluffball against her cheek and made

smoochy noises at it. "Say hello to your new baby brother, Linus. He's a German-Malty-Doodle-Poo." Then she spoke directly to her furbaby. "Who's Mommy's little sweetums? You are! Yes, you are!"

What in the ever-loving hell was a German-Malty-Doodle-Poo?

"We adopted him from the shelter," Dad explained, not sounding pleased. "I think your mother's got Empty Nest Syndrome."

Mom elbowed him in the ribs while Cara exchanged a puzzled glance with Troy.

"But I'm allergic to dogs, remember?" Cara said. "What happens when we come home to visit?"

Mom waved a dismissive hand. "That won't be for ages."

"Uh, actually . . ." Troy began, then stopped to clear his throat. "I'll be home sooner than I expected. Colonel Rutter's calling me back to Earth. I got orders yesterday."

Cara almost sprained her neck whipping around to face him. *"What?"*

Troy took a defensive tone. "I only came to L'eihr because of the student exchange program, and now they're saying it's over. The other two humans won't come because they're scared. The Marines want me to report back to—"

"When?" Cara demanded.

He couldn't meet her gaze. "Two weeks."

Cara wiped her sweaty palms on her pants. No, this couldn't be right. The Marines had agreed to station Troy here for two years, until the original exchange students— herself included—returned home. If he left now, she'd be alone. The only human on a planet full of mankind-loathing L'eihrs. She had exaggerated on the blog when she'd referred to her "friends." Only one clone aboard the transport gave her the time of day, and that was Aelyx's sister.

Troy was undeniably a horse's ass, but he was *her* horse's ass, and she loved him. There had to be a way to keep him with her. He could go AWOL. What were the Marines going to do, court-martial him from Earth?

"No," she told him with a firm shake of her head. "You can't go. The program isn't over. I'm still here, and . . ." *I need you.*

"But that's the thing," Troy said. "You're an official colonist now, not an exchange student. When the year's over, you're staying on L'eihr. Like, forever."

"Pepper," Mom said tentatively, "if you're not happy there, you can come home with your brother."

A light *ding!* chimed from Troy's laptop as the incoming electronic data began delivering comments to Cara's blog post.

Subscribe [Archive] [Recent Entries] [About Me]

Invaded

MAY THE SOURCE BE WITH YOU

Ashley said . . .
So jealous. Seriously, I wanna go. Take me to your leader!

Eric said . . .
Glad to hear you're safe—FOR NOW—but you're an idiot for leaving Earth over some guy, especially after he poisoned our mothereffing water!!!

Tori said . . .
E has a point. Come back, culo. I miss you.

Cara tapped the touchpad and closed her Web page before any more discouraging remarks popped up. She'd committed to this life, and she wasn't turning back.

A shrill *yip!* forced her attention to Mom, who held Linus over one shoulder and patted his back, burping him like an infant. It was official—Cara had been replaced by a German-Malty-Doodle-Poo. In two weeks, she'd lose her brother, and once they landed on L'eihr, she wouldn't have a friend in the world.

This was the worst Christmas ever.

"This is the best Christmas present ever!" A L'annabe danced from one foot to the other, nearly slipping on the icy sidewalk while Aelyx autographed her copy of *Squee Teen*.

"Not a problem." After scrawling a quick signature, Aelyx returned the girl's magazine.

She stared at his glossy eight-by-ten photograph and sighed dreamily while her friend thrust a copy of *Fangasm* at him and asked, "Did you and Cara really have a secret wedding? 'Cause that's *sooooo* romantic!"

"Excuse me, miss." A young national guardsman named Sharpe extended one palm toward the girl. "I need you to step back."

She nodded and obediently retreated a pace, joining a dozen other girls, each dressed in mock L'eihr uniforms, their hair fastened into low ponytails. The only threat they posed was admiring Aelyx to death. But while he found his guard detail overzealous at times, he was grateful for their presence. His last visit to Earth had ended in an attempt on his life, and he wished to return to Cara with all his parts intact.

"No," he told the girl, forcing a smile. "Humans and L'eihrs can't legally wed." He added with a wink, "Yet."

"Oh, gods," groaned Syrine, his former best friend. Emphasis on *former*. They'd barely exchanged ten words since she'd tried turning Cara against him on the transport. Syrine shoved him aside and jogged up the front steps leading to the penthouse apartment they shared with the L'eihr ambassador. Two armed guards followed her inside.

"You should probably wrap it up," Private Sharpe whispered. "You're exposed out here."

A frigid gust of wind stung the back of Aelyx's neck, sending a shiver across every inch of his flesh. He'd never felt winter's bite until his travels to Earth, and gods willing, he never would again after this mission ended. A warm fireplace beckoned from upstairs, and Sharpe didn't need to ask him twice.

"Just one more," Aelyx said to the girls, eliciting a chorus of disappointed moans. He was poised to sign his name when a sudden movement in his periphery caught his eye.

Glancing to the side, Aelyx noticed a uniformed guardsman approaching quickly from an armored Hum-V parked at the curb, his boots loudly crunching over the salt and slush that carpeted the street. A pink scar stood in contrast against the man's ivory forehead, his brown eyes fixed straight ahead at no one in particular. Aelyx scanned the soldier's jacket but found no name tag.

Why didn't he have a name tag?

When the soldier broke into a jog, Aelyx's body tensed, his instincts on high alert. Before a question could form on his lips, the man drew his pistol and aimed it over Aelyx's heart. In a voice colder than morning frost, the man rasped, "This is from the Patriots," and pulled the trigger.

Adrenaline surging, Aelyx reacted, but not quickly enough. As he dodged right, a deafening crack pierced his eardrums and two hundred pounds of force knocked him to the frozen asphalt. A cocktail of screams, shuffling boots, and counterfire flooded his senses.

It took Aelyx a moment to realize that not only was he alive, but that Sharpe lay atop him. Aelyx freed himself and propped on one elbow in time to see the rogue gunman tear down the street and vanish between two townhomes. Several guardsmen followed in pursuit while the rest of their unit scrambled to secure the area.

Sharpe rolled onto his back with a deep groan and asked, "You all right?"

Aelyx patted his chest and moved his arms and legs in a brief inventory. "Yes." A glance at Sharpe revealed a wet patch of blood slowly spreading across the outside of his shoulder. "But you're not."

Sharpe followed Aelyx's gaze to the wound before he gave a frustrated grunt and rested his head on the ground. "Just a scratch. But it's gonna sting when the rush wears off."

Up close, Aelyx realized for the first time how young the man was, likely no more than twenty. They might even be the same age, which surprised him. Sharpe's bravery and quick reflexes rivaled that of a seasoned warrior. "You took a bullet intended for me."

Sharpe shrugged his good shoulder. "Part of my job."

Aelyx couldn't help smiling at the boy's stoicism. They could use more like him on L'eihr. "Well, thanks for doing it so thoroughly, Private Sharpe."

Sharpe chuckled, then grimaced in pain and extended his opposite hand. "Call me David."

CHAPTER TWO

Cara fastened her five-point harness, wincing when the seat-belt strap brushed the sensitive inoculation scar on the inside of her wrist. Judging by the quarter-size lump beneath her skin, she wouldn't catch a single sniffle on L'eihr, which suited her just fine. The last thing she needed was an alien stomach flu. L'eihrs were smarter, faster, and stronger than humans, so their viruses could probably melt steel. After buckling her clasp, she nestled back against her seat beside Troy, who hadn't said a word since they'd boarded the shuttle five minutes ago.

When Elle padded through the doorway and settled in the row of seats facing them, Troy's posture stiffened and he tucked his black curls behind both ears—not much of a reaction, but enough to make Cara suspect he was crushing on Aelyx's sister. This didn't come as any great shock. With her mile-long lashes and delicate features, Elle was a natural beauty. Plus, she had a nurturing spirit, which probably accounted for her position as medic aboard the ship. But Troy's timing was terrible. Elle's *l'ihan* had been murdered in China a few weeks ago, and she mourned him in her own quiet way.

Troy drummed his fingertips against his thigh. "Can't wait to feel the ground beneath my feet again," he said, mostly talking to Elle. He released a shaky laugh and bounced one booted heel against the floor. Poor guy, he had it bad—totally alien-whipped.

"Mmm," was her only reply. She secured her seat belt and turned her silvery gaze to Cara. As soon as their eyes met, Cara felt the girl's voice inside her head asking, *Can you really hear me?*

Cara froze in panic. No one was supposed to know she could communicate this way.

Aelyx told me, Elle went on. *But I didn't believe it.*

"Yeah," Cara said, sending an unspoken message in the tone of her voice. "I'm ready to get off this ship, too. Space travel makes me nauseated."

"I hope you don't mind," Elle told Cara, "but I asked the Elders to assign us to the same room." Then she added privately, *Aelyx told me to watch over you until he returns.*

"That depends." Cara winked. "Do you snore?"

"Sometimes," Elle confessed, not understanding the joke. "But Eron used to say it was endearing." She bit her lip and studied her folded hands, her expression heavy with grief.

Everyone fell silent after that, electing to stare out the side windows into the blackness.

Moments later, two final passengers joined them and the door hissed shut. Cara flicked a quick glance at the clones, then did a double take.

"Hello, *Cah*-ra."

The young leader, Jaxen, took the seat directly across from her, extending his long legs until the tips of his boots touched hers. He peered at her intently and smiled while his sister, Aisly, lowered beside him and greeted Cara with a nod.

Cara pulled back her feet and offered a hasty grin. His presence caught her off guard. Jaxen and Aisly were members of The Way, L'eihr's governing body, so why hadn't they shuttled down with the Elders?

Jaxen continued to study her while fastening his straps. "Aisly and I volunteered to escort you to the capital." It was like he'd read her mind, though Cara was pretty sure L'eihrs couldn't do that.

Aisly tipped her head and scanned Cara's face—not in a disdainful way, more like how a visitor at the zoo would observe an exotic animal behind the glass. Cara figured she should get used to the scrutiny. Individual races had ceased to exist on this planet, and with her pale complexion, blue eyes, and copper hair, she would stand out like a joke at a funeral.

"On Earth," Aisly said, "a year equals one planetary rotation around your sun, correct?"

Cara nodded, feeling the rumbling engines vibrate the bottom of her seat. The shuttle separated from the boarding corridor with a slight lurch, and a thrill of exhilaration shot through her. They were finally leaving the transport.

"Then that would mean I'm seventeen years old, like you," Aisly told her, then nodded at her brother. "And Jaxen's twenty-one."

"Twenty-one?" Cara wrinkled her forehead in confusion, trying to remember what Aelyx had told her about the old L'eihr breeding program. Geneticists had played God for too long and bred the life out of themselves, so they backtracked, cloning citizens from the archives. But that policy had gone into effect twenty years ago, and it took nine months to grow a baby inside the artificial wombs. "I thought the oldest clones were nineteen."

Jaxen's smile never faltered, but his words turned frosty. "I suppose Aelyx told you that." He didn't give her a chance to reply. "Our population is small, Miss Sweeney, but I can guarantee that your *l'ihan* hasn't met every clone on the planet."

Whoa. Clearly she'd touched a nerve. She tried to make light of the misunderstanding. "I'm sure it's an innocent mistake. Despite what Aelyx thinks, he doesn't know everything."

Nobody laughed. Tough crowd, these L'eihrs.

Jaxen and Aisly locked eyes in a private conversation, so Cara quietly cleared her throat and faced the window to her right.

The shuttle came about and gained speed, and within minutes, empty space gave way to distant pinpricks of light. The air was colder near the window, but Cara leaned in and searched for the swirling blue nebula Aelyx had described to her a couple of weeks ago. *Every time you see it, I want you to think of me,* he'd said. *I'm going to mend that alliance in record time, and soon we'll stand together and watch the L'eihr sky from our colony.*

She couldn't find the nebula, but she noticed twin moons and then the muted blue planet that would become her new home. A wide expanse of ocean wrapped around the globe, interrupted by a single tan continent and a sprinkling of tiny islands. Thick clouds obscured her view as the shuttle jettisoned into the atmosphere. Once their craft broke through the haze, rows of beige-capped mountain peaks greeted her, jutting proudly against a sky the exact shade of slate. At their base, a placid sea stretched to the horizon and kissed the rising sun.

Cara faced the opposite window to take in forests of majestic redwood-size trees, their silver leaves sparkling like quartz in response to the morning rays. Her eyes widened to absorb it all. She tried to find some hideous flaw in the landscape to prove that Aelyx had exaggerated the magnificence of his world, but every atom in her body sang with its beauty.

As the shuttle descended, she could make out a settlement in the distance. She quickly identified the capitol building based on its position at the heart of the city. Offices, apartments, shops, and dormitories splayed out from the humble three-story structure like satellites in orbit, each as neutral as the next. It seemed that architecture, like every other aspect of life on L'eihr, focused on practicality over aesthetics. The small city reminded Cara of how the ancient, sandy-colored ruins in the Middle East might have looked in their prime.

When she turned toward the other window, she caught Jaxen observing her reaction. He held her gaze for a few beats and leaned forward as far as his restraints would allow. "What do you think?"

As soon as Cara found her voice, she told him, "It's spectacular."

"I think so, too," he said. "This is the smallest of the five precincts, but it's my favorite."

"For good reason," Aisly added. "Everything important is here: the academic and scientific archives, the genetics labs, the cultural galleries."

"Not to mention your government," Cara said. The tiny capital reminded her of Washington, DC. "Do all ten members of The Way live here?"

"Yes and no." Jaxen gestured out his window toward the city. "We rotate living in different precincts and shuttle to the capital when we need to convene. It allows us to oversee the local governments while ensuring each region's needs are fairly represented."

"Except Alona," Aisly said. "The head Elder always resides at the capital."

"Kind of like our president in Ameri—" A sudden dropping sensation made Cara gasp, and she glanced outside to see the shuttle touch down in the shorn beige grass outside the capitol building.

Once her heart quit thumping, she scanned the open courtyard, noting a cluster of silver-leafed willow trees and shrubs near a side entry. At this early hour, there was only one L'eihr in sight: a middle-age guard standing at attention near the front entrance. Cara's eyes darted to the *iphal* holstered to the man's side. It was a handgun of sorts, but with the power to stop a victim's heart with a concentrated pulse of energy.

Welcome to L'eihr. Start anything and we'll end you. Have a nice day!

Cara unbuckled her harness and waited for the dozen passengers ahead of her to de-board. Then she followed her brother down the shuttle steps and paused to draw her first breath on an alien world.

The air was warm and humid—slightly heavier than she'd expected, smelling faintly of bitter citrus. It was an oddly pleasant scent, especially compared to the exhaust fumes she'd grown accustomed to on Earth. The gentle morning sun warmed her shoulders, a sensation she hadn't felt in weeks. Until this moment, she hadn't realized how much she'd missed the feel of sunlight on her skin. The main transport had provided ultraviolet lamps to encourage vitamin D production, but they couldn't replicate the breeze that stirred loose wisps of hair against the back of her neck. She'd missed that, too.

Right away, she noticed Earth's vibrant color spectrum didn't exist here. Aelyx had once compared L'eihr to Midtown in winter, when the few remaining leaves had shriveled and turned brown. It was a fair comparison, but much less dreary. These tan leaves glistened with an opalescent sparkle that made Cara want to string them together and wear them around her neck.

She observed a great stone wall in the distance, hugging the rolling hills until it disappeared behind a multistory apartment complex. She wondered what was on the other side and why they bothered with walls when shuttles could easily fly over them.

"A credit for your thoughts," said Jaxen, studying her again with a smile.

"A credit." Cara laughed at his spin on the American expression. "Guess my pennies are worthless here."

Jaxen held up his wrist. "Your nano-chip will track your credits, among other things." He strode to the doorway and gestured for her to follow. "Come here and I'll show you."

Cara glanced at her inoculation scar. She'd forgotten that in addition to a thousand vaccines, the medic had implanted a data chip beneath her skin.

Jaxen pointed to a light switch–size box affixed to the outside wall. "There are stations like this everywhere—even inside your quarters. Hold your wrist under here, like this." When he demonstrated, a beam of light danced over his flesh. "The system will scan you for personalized notifications."

Cara extended her arm, palm up. Seconds later, a woman's soft voice ordered, "*Cah*-ra Sweeney, please report to the first Aegis at your leisure."

Impressive. They'd even programmed the system to speak English for her.

"The first Aegis is ours," Troy said, pointing to the complex by the city wall. "It's the closest school to the capital. Students from the other four campuses have to take the air train to get here."

"What train?" Cara asked.

He pointed to a set of metallic pillars she hadn't noticed before. Her gaze followed them upward to a monorail track.

"And *at your leisure* really means *now*," Elle advised her.

"I'm staying at the Aegis?" Cara asked, a little disappointed. "Not the colony?"

Jaxen drew back in surprise. "No. The colony is on the other side of the world and still under construction."

"The other side of the world?" But the entire population of L'eihr lived here, divided into five small precincts on a continent half the size of Canada. There was nowhere else to go except . . . "On an island?" She didn't say *marooned*, but that was what came to mind.

Again, Jaxen seemed to have tasted her thoughts. "Yes, but don't worry. The intent is to allow colonists the liberty to form a unique society, free from our influence . . . to some extent."

Cara supposed that made sense, though she wondered to what "extent" The Way would interfere.

Jaxen turned to Troy and Elle. "I have sensitive matters to discuss with Miss Sweeney. I'll deliver her to the Aegis shortly. You're free to go."

Troy hesitated, but Jaxen's word was law, and the tone of his dismissal left no room for negotiation. Once Troy and Elle had strode out of sight, Jaxen led the way down the same path, motioning for Cara and Aisly to follow.

"Is everything okay?" Cara asked while glancing at the pavement beneath her boots. It had a slight bounce to it, like shock-absorbent indoor track. She hopped on the balls of her feet and grinned, realizing she'd always have a spring in her step.

Aisly shot her a curious glance and they began at an easy stroll. "Yes. We only wanted to give you a proper welcome."

A soft *whoosh* sounded from above, and an air train jettisoned into the city at lightning speed. Somehow, it managed the job with barely a breath of wind. Cara craned her neck, marveling like a child as another train passed above her. Even higher, sky lanes directed a few shuttles to and from the city, though she had no clue how their pilots avoided midair collisions without visible boundaries.

"I imagine this is difficult to process," Jaxen said.

Cara laughed dryly as her gaze darted from one unfamiliar object to the next. "I need another pair of eyes."

"It was the same for me," Jaxen said, "my first time on your world."

She whipped her head around. "You've been to Earth?"

"Many times. I love your people—you possess such passion and creativity, the traits L'eihrs have lost over time." Jaxen brushed aside an overgrown dandelion seed. At the contact, the thing flitted away like a jellyfish. "I can't wait to return and explore other human cultures. I've never traveled much farther than the ambassador's residence in Manhattan."

"That's where Aelyx is now." A glance at the tan and gray trees lining the walkway brought a question to mind. "He told me there's no green here because your plants don't use photosynthesis. So what would happen if I brought a maple from Earth? Would it be compatible with your sun?"

"Irrelevant, as The Way would never allow it. Destroying an ecosystem is easier than you think." Then with a slightly haughty tone, he added, "Earth's current predicament should've taught you that. It's a shame that such a dynamic race can't be trusted to care for their own planet."

Cara took her tongue between her teeth, literally biting back a scathing response. *You forgot about the* sh'alear, *jerkwad. The clones didn't hesitate to meddle with our ecosystem when it suited them.*

"Your cheeks are flushing," he said, as if this greatly amused him. "I've made you angry. See? Such passion. I envy you."

Cara gestured at the trees and blatantly changed the subject. "So how do they derive nutrients if not from the sun?"

"From the air." He reached over her head and plucked a leaf from its branch, then handed it to her.

"That's right, like Spanish moss. Aelyx told me." She rubbed the leaf between her fingers. It felt light and spongy, and when she brought it to her nose, she recognized the citrusy scent. "This is what I smelled when I stepped off the shuttle."

"*Ilar* trees," Aisly said. "They're fragrant."

"And plentiful," Cara said, scanning the landscape. *Ilars* were everywhere. Their branches even loomed over the stone wall surrounding the city.

"Only in this precinct," Jaxen told her. "In the marshlands to the south, you'd find shallow-rooted trees that absorb nutrients through their scaly bark."

"They're ugly," Aisly said with a flick of her wrist. "The most beautiful trees are in the mountains. At that altitude, they have to grow higher to find nourishment, and their leaves are twice the size of your hand."

Cara gazed to the west, recalling the quartz forest she'd admired from the shuttle. Now she couldn't see anything beyond the great wall. "What's on the other side of that?"

Jaxen's eyes darted to the stonework. "We've kept the majority of our landmass in its natural state. The wall protects wildlife from our influence." He pointed overhead at a flock of spotted birds resembling doves. "Except those that fly."

"Or climb," Aisly added darkly.

They were quiet until they reached the Aegis grounds, and then a nervous flutter tickled Cara's chest. Suddenly she wanted the walk to last longer. She wasn't ready for her first day of school.

"You won't start classes until tomorrow," Jaxen said.

Cara paused for a moment and studied him. On the surface, Jaxen resembled the others of his kind—tawny skin and silvery eyes. He wore his light-brown hair in a ponytail, his athletic frame concealed beneath the standard uniform. But there was something different about him. Maybe he had unique abilities. That would explain his position on The Way.

"Can you read minds?" she asked.

He laughed at her. "No, but I can read expressions, and your translucent cheeks tell me you're afraid."

Cara couldn't deny it, so she turned to survey her surroundings. The Aegis reminded her of the community college back home—a large boxy dormitory opening to a courtyard, half a dozen scattered outbuildings, and multiple trails that led into a thicket of woods. She leaned forward and squinted, bringing an obstacle course into focus.

Aisly followed Cara's gaze. "That's where you'll take your physical conditioning class."

Cara groaned inwardly. Even in another galaxy, she couldn't escape PE.

"But don't worry," Aisly continued. "The instructor will adjust your target time to compensate for your inferior respiratory system."

Awesome. Add to the equation Cara's inferior human brain, and after Troy left, she'd be the most worthless person on the planet. Quite the downgrade from her previous title of Midtown High valedictorian.

"Do you go to school in this Aegis, too?" she asked. From what she understood, children stayed in their local Aegis from birth until the end of their twenty-first year, when they received a job assignment and moved to the occupational barracks. But surely any L'eihr gifted enough to be appointed to The Way wouldn't take classes with the rest of the students.

"We do now," Jaxen said. When she waited for him to elaborate, he didn't.

The three of them climbed the front steps leading to the dormitory, and Aisly extended her wrist for the scanner. In response, a pair of metallic doors hissed aside to allow them into the vacant lobby. Cara braced herself for an icy burst of air-conditioning, but a cross breeze from open windows along the adjacent corridors brushed her skin, reminding her that the temperature here hovered around seventy year-round. The next sensation to reach her was the warm, welcoming scent of baking bread. Her stomach growled in response.

"Must be breakfast time," she mused. That would explain the absence of students.

"Yes," Aisly said. "Our morning staple here is *t'ahinni*. It's made from *larun*, which is a flat—"

"Flatbread," Cara finished. A bittersweet smile curved her

lips. "I tried re-creating it on Earth for Aelyx, but I never got it right."

From there, they whisked her to the headmaster's office and outfitted her with a supply of clean uniforms and a palm-size tablet.

"Bring this to each class," Jaxen said. "All the texts and essays you'll need are preloaded and translated into English."

Even after his demonstration, Cara didn't understand how to use the device, but she kept quiet for fear of looking stupid. She'd ask Elle to explain it later. Next, Jaxen and Aisly escorted her to her room, which was near the lobby on the first floor.

Jaxen paused outside her door. "Is it still your intention to remain here permanently, as Aelyx's *l'ihan?*"

Cara nodded, even though "remain here permanently" sounded so . . . permanent.

"Excellent," Aisly said. "Then we can resolve the issue of your citizenship."

Cara's stomach dipped. Just because she'd left Earth didn't mean she wanted to sever all ties to her people. "Can I have dual citizenship?"

"Absolutely," Aisly promised. "But the process remains the same. In order to become a citizen, you have to hold a *Sh'ovah.*"

A *Sh'ovah*? Why did that sound familiar?

Cara searched her memory. When nothing came, she turned to Jaxen for clarification, but by the time their eyes met, the answer hit like a cannonball to the gut. It sounded familiar because several months ago she'd written a blog post about the rite of passage: *You swear an oath to the Sacred Mother, and then all your peers stand in line and smear mud on your naked body to symbolize your union with Her. Mazel tov!*

All the blood in Cara's face went south, settling somewhere in the vicinity of her socks. She'd have to stand before her new classmates in her birthday suit? And let them cover her with mud? There had to be another way.

"*Cah*-ra," Jaxen said, "we don't sexualize nudity here. I promise the sight of your body won't faze anyone."

So maybe the clones wouldn't leer, but surely they'd gawk at her pasty skin and the freckles peppering her butt. Why couldn't they give her a pass, just this once?

"If you're having second thoughts . . ." Jaxen trailed off, his voice heavy with implication.

Before she had a chance to change her mind, Cara blurted, "I'll do it."

"This isn't a choice to make in haste," Aisly warned. "Becoming a citizen means accepting and supporting our customs and following The Way in all things. We're not a democracy."

Cara knew that. She and Aelyx had spent hours debating the differences between their governments. Minor offenses such as mouthing off—just a matter of time for her—would result in the electric lash. When she considered the penalty for other crimes, her mind wandered to the brushed chrome *iphal* holstered to the capital guard's hip. This place was no utopia, but if she wanted a life with Aelyx on his planet, she had to abide by his people's rules and respect their culture, even if she didn't agree with it. Cara stiffened her spine. She was a lot of things, but a coward wasn't one of them.

"I understand," she told Aisly. "And I agree."

"Then I'll tell the others," Aisly chirped. "I know The Way will be pleased."

Jaxen pressed two fingers to Cara's throat in the standard farewell. "We'll schedule your *Sh'ovah* for next week." Ducking down to meet her height, he added, "As they say in your country, *sleep on it.* There's no shame in changing your mind."

Cara returned the good-bye and pulled her hand free. "I won't change my mind."

Chapter Three

Aelyx watched the L'eihr ambassador sweep a wrinkled hand across the surface of the dining room table, knocking the newspaper to the floor. It landed face-up and revealed a mocking headline: *HALO Denies Attack on L'eihr Youth.*

"Humans Against L'eihr Occupation," Stepha said through clenched teeth while he glared at Director-General Kendrick. "On my planet, we would have terminated those savages after their first rebellion—rooted them out like the cancer they are." In a rare display of emotion, he slapped both palms on the glossy mahogany. "How many of our young must die before you assume control of your people? Or perhaps this alliance isn't a priority for you. In which case, we'll return to L'eihr on the next transport."

The ambassador's final words chilled Aelyx to the core. Without L'eihr technology to decontaminate Earth's water supply, the planet would cease to sustain life within a decade. But the release of that technology hinged on the alliance, and everyone in the room knew it. Even Syrine looked nervous, and she despised humans.

"I can assure you," Kendrick said, shifting in his seat, "there's nothing's more important to the World Trade Organization than this alliance. We've partnered with the milit—"

"Whatever you're doing, it is ineffective." Stepha sat back in his chair and folded his hands, resuming his usual monotone. "Negotiations cannot continue while our safety is threatened."

Kendrick scratched the back of his neck, then splayed both hands in a gesture of helplessness. "Ambassador, there's nothing to negotiate. The world's leaders have voted unanimously— they'll agree to an alliance on your terms."

In other words, *We're at your mercy.* Aelyx didn't want to take pleasure in the supplication of humanity, but a smooth negotiation process meant he could return home to Cara. He couldn't deny feeling a rush of excitement at the news.

Stepha considered the director-general's words, then slowly stood from the table and collected his com-sphere. "Before we can proceed, I must confer with The Way."

Kendrick stood, too, nodding in assent as Stepha made his way to the master suite in sluggish, labored strides. Aelyx considered offering the director-general a cup of coffee, but the man's dewy forehead and labored breathing said he was anxious enough without the aid of a caffeinated beverage.

"Can I get you some water?" he asked instead.

"No, thanks." Kendrick used his phone to point toward the foyer. "I need to make a few calls myself. Think I'll step outside for a minute."

"I'll walk you to the door," Aelyx offered, since Syrine had chosen to remain seated and ignore the man.

The two strode to the front entrance, and when Aelyx opened the door, a pair of familiar faces greeted him— Colonel Rutter, head of the L'eihr security detail, and David, who waved a friendly hello. Kendrick scooted past the soldiers, and Aelyx stepped aside to let them in.

Colonel Rutter nodded his gray head and greeted Aelyx with a curt, "'Mornin'." He removed his camouflage winter hat, and David did the same, revealing a crop of shorn blond hair. Rutter glanced around the open living area, acknowledging Syrine with a dip of his head. "Is the ambassador here?" he asked. "I need to talk to all three of you."

"He's in a conference, but you're free to wait." Aelyx led the way to the living room and gestured for his guests to sit on the sofa. He noticed that while Rutter wasted no time in making himself comfortable, David remained standing, one arm folded against his lower back, brown eyes scanning the room to take in every detail. Aelyx had never met a human youth so dedicated to duty.

"How's the shoulder?" Aelyx asked him.

"What?" David asked with a smile, pointing to his upper arm. "This mosquito bite? I'll be fine once the stitches come out. It takes more than a .22 to bring me down. Your shooter didn't know squat about guns, otherwise he'd have used a .45 to double-tap it. That's how a real man gets the job done."

Syrine made a disgusted noise and launched up from her dining room chair. She stomped over to David and jabbed her finger toward his nose. "You deserve the extinction you've brought upon yourselves. Look at what happened to Eron. 'Real men' tortured him for hours before they allowed him to die." She raked her gaze over David's uniform, glaring at the pistol holstered to his waist. "Violence is what feeds you. Your kind isn't worth saving."

Aelyx caught Syrine's gaze and chided her. *David risked his life for me. If he were extinct, I would be dead. Not all of them are dangerous or—*

She squeezed her eyes shut, refusing to hear him.

"I'm sorry about your friend," David said quietly. "It wasn't right, what happened to him. We're trying really hard to find the guys who did it."

A single tear rolled down Syrine's cheek. She scrubbed it away with her fist and kept her gaze trained on the carpet. "Thank you for protecting Aelyx," she whispered. Then she turned and padded quickly to her bedroom.

Aelyx and David shared an awkward glance while Colonel Rutter buried his face in the newspaper.

"Well," David said. "Now I feel like an asshole."

The colonel muttered, "She's not gonna like what we came here to tell her."

"Which is . . . ?" Aelyx asked.

Colonel Rutter tossed his newspaper onto the coffee table. "I'm assigning Private Sharpe as your personal bodyguard." He pointed in the direction of Syrine's bedroom. "For both of you. I'd like him to move in, maybe sleep in the guest room. That way you'll have around-the-clock protection with another half dozen guards patrolling the outside hallway."

"Surprise," David said with a smile. "I'm your new best friend."

The casual term didn't sit well with Aelyx. His best friend was Eron, whose ruined body lay in a cold storage unit as he awaited his final journey home. But Aelyx forced himself to return the smile. "I'll talk to Syrine. Don't worry; she'll get used to you."

He'd just begun to lead David to the guest suite when his com-sphere buzzed to life in the signature frequency that told him Cara was calling. In that moment, the outside world ceased to exist. Aelyx rushed to his bedroom and locked the door behind him. He knelt beside his expansive king-size bed and spoke his passkey, then rested the sphere atop his comforter.

That first glimpse of her face warmed his blood and made his heart swell. She sat cross-legged atop her cot in the Aegis, her fiery orange hair gathered in a low braid, her blue eyes bright with excitement to see him. If he leaned in close, he could barely detect the adorable freckles that dotted her nose.

Sacred Mother, he missed her so fiercely he ached.

"*Elire.*" Or *beautiful warrior*, as he'd nicknamed her. An automatic smile spread over his lips. "How did you know I needed you today?" He hadn't even realized it himself.

She shrugged, then winced and rubbed her arm. "We're on the same frequency, I guess." Then she rotated her shoulder, clearly in pain.

Aelyx tried to check her for injury. "What's wrong? Are you hurt?"

"You could say that. I feel like I've been stuffed in a pillow-case and trampled by elephants." When he waited for her to go on, she rolled her head to the side in a tentative stretch. "I started your sadistic alien PE classes this week. I barfed twice today on the novice course, and that was an improvement over yesterday. Maybe by next week I'll upgrade to dry heaving."

Aelyx tried not to laugh. He supposed the calisthenics routine would seem rigorous to a human unaccustomed to high-intensity interval training. "Ask Elle to grind some *h'esha* root for your tea," he said. "And soak in a hot jetted bath. It'll help diffuse the lactic acid in your muscles."

"Maybe you missed the part about me being trampled by elephants."

"Well, I know something that'll make you feel better." Aelyx stopped himself and glanced at Cara's hologram, making sure she was alone. "Is anyone with you?"

"No, Elle's still at supper."

He lowered his voice and told her the newest development in the alliance negotiations. "Stepha's talking with The Way now. With any luck, I could be home before you graduate to vomiting on the intermediate course."

"Really?" Her face lit up. "Fingers cross—" The *hiss* of her door interrupted her, and Cara's gaze darted to the front of her room. She lowered her auburn brows and shouted, "Get out! Go on! You'd better hope I never catch you!"

What was that all about?

When she returned her attention to him, she huffed an

angry sigh. "That was Vero. The little monster's been sneaking in here to pee on my pillow. He hates me."

Vero. Aelyx released a sigh of his own. He missed his house pet, a fiercely loyal animal, though certainly not without quirks. "Vero's breed is territorial," Aelyx explained. "Once he identifies you as part of the pack, he'll stop marking your bedding." But in order for that to happen, the clones in the Aegis would need to accept Cara as one of their own. "Better tell the house caretaker to change the settings on your touchpad so Vero can't get inside."

Cara nodded, but she didn't recover her earlier cheer. She slouched and traced imaginary patterns on her blanket. "I can tell the clones don't want me here. Most of them won't look at me, and the others make this sign when I walk by." In demonstration, she touched her thumb and pinkie together. "What does it mean?"

"Uh . . ." He didn't want to give her the literal translation— *fornicate with a h'ava beast and kill yourself with fire.* "It's our version of the middle finger."

"That's what I was afraid of."

"Give it time," he said. "You're unfamiliar to the clones and they don't understand you yet."

"I know." She stared at her hands and shrugged. "My *Sh'ovah* is in a few days. Maybe that'll help. I hear they're supposed to think of me as a sister after that."

Aelyx paused as a pang of guilt settled low in his belly. For a L'eihr, nothing was more sacred than *Sh'ovah.* Younglings looked forward to that day for well over a decade, until the

Elders deemed them worthy. He should be there with Cara to celebrate her union with the Sacred Mother, not here, stuck on Earth, squabbling with politicians. "I'm sorry to miss it. Who's your sponsor?"

"Elle."

"Good." At least it wasn't that *fasher* Jaxen. "She'll take her duties seriously."

Cara's door hissed open again, and Elle's voice called, "Come on. It's our turn to sanitize the kitchen."

Aelyx missed a lot of things about home, but cleanup detail wasn't one of them. "You'd better hurry," he told her. "If you're late, they'll add an extra day."

Cara didn't need further convincing. After a wave and a quick "Love you," she disconnected and disappeared from view.

Aelyx remained kneeling for several seconds, as if to hold on to the warmth of her smile. Only when he heard the echo of voices from the hallway did he relinquish Cara's ghost and rejoin the others.

Stepha had finished conferring with The Way, and he rested opposite Director-General Kendrick on a plush leather armchair while Colonel Rutter and David sat beside each other on the sofa. Tension clung to the air like mist, each man silent but speaking volumes through his rigid posture. Aelyx dragged a dining room chair near the coffee table and took his seat, then used Silent Speech to ask the ambassador what he'd learned.

Did they approve the alliance? he asked Stepha. *Can we return home?*

When Stepha replied, a hint of confusion colored his thoughts. *No. Human deference isn't enough. The Way wants the general population on Earth to support the union between our worlds.*

But why? Aelyx asked. *That doesn't make sense.* The purpose behind the alliance was to recruit human colonists and integrate on L'eihr, infusing fresh DNA into the populace. Already, thousands of healthy young humans had submitted applications, eager to begin life anew on the colony. It was just a matter of screening them for mental wellness and superior IQ, then finding willing matches among the clones. What did it matter whether or not the rest of Earth's population approved?

It is not our place to question The Way, Stepha told him. *Only to follow—*

Follow The Way to glorify Mother L'eihr, Aelyx finished. *I understand.* Though he didn't understand at all.

"On the first day of spring," Stepha announced to the group, "as a symbol of rebirth, The Way will join Earth's leaders here in an alliance ceremony. Our scientists will then provide you with the solution to neutralize the algae blooms burgeoning in your oceans." He pulled in a deep breath and clarified, "But this is contingent on your control of human violence. Any further attempts on our lives will terminate all relations between us. Your people must support the partnership between our worlds in order for us to move forward."

So not only was Aelyx trapped here for another three months, but he had to avoid acts of violence, too? It was impossible. Human extremists didn't support the alliance—they believed L'eihrs had poisoned the water supply in an effort to enslave humanity. Not only were they wrong, but they didn't know about the algae blooms, nor that the problem was spreading. The only way to win them over was to tell the truth about their dying planet, which he'd been expressly forbidden from doing.

The director-general rubbed his jaw. "Sounds like we have some serious public relations work ahead of us."

"That was the purpose of the student exchange," Colonel Rutter said. "It was going fine until . . ." He trailed off, and all eyes shifted to Aelyx.

Until the L'eihr students were caught tampering with the crops and one of them was murdered for it. Coincidentally, Syrine chose that moment to emerge from her bedroom and join them.

Aelyx addressed the group. "What can we do to help?"

"How about a multicity PR tour?" the director-general suggested. "We can identify the hot spots of extremist activity and send the L'eihrs there to do good deeds on camera, then broadcast it nationwide."

"I guess it's worth a shot." Colonel Rutter nodded in consideration. "With a constant security detail, of course."

"Of course," the director-general agreed. "We'll treat this like a presidential reelection campaign—nobody without security clearance will get anywhere near the L'eihrs. We'll even screen the participants in each photo op to make sure no one poses a threat. A few months of kissing babies and shaking hands should be all we need to turn the public's opinion in our favor."

Syrine drew back, curling her upper lip in disgust.

"Kissing?" she screeched. "With *humans*? That's a—"

The ambassador caught her eye and instantly silenced her with a stern private message. Aelyx didn't need Silent Speech to understand what was transpiring between the two of them. Stepha's narrowed gaze and Syrine's darkening cheeks said it all.

After a few moments, she forced a grin that wouldn't fool a blind man. "A wonderful idea. I will gladly participate."

"Then we're agreed," said the director-general. "I'll have my staff make the necessary arrangements and book your first appearance. We'll want to get the ball rolling right away, so go ahead and pack a suitcase."

"Cool," David said with the only genuine smile in the room. "We're going on tour!"

"We?" Syrine turned to Aelyx for clarification.

David is our personal bodyguard, Aelyx told her. *He'll be living with us for the rest of our stay on Earth.*

Bleeding Mother. Syrine didn't bother disguising her distaste for the young man. *Why couldn't The Way simply give us a dozen lashes with the* iphet *instead?*

"How exciting," she said aloud, then faced their new bodyguard. "I can hardly wait."

Chapter Four

Invaded

MAY THE SOURCE BE WITH YOU

Friday, January 16

What the FAQ?!

It's *Sh'ovah* Day, and what better way to celebrate my impending L'eihr citizenship than to feed your inquiring minds? Without further ado, here are the most frequently asked questions this week:

Sarah in San Marcos asks: *Are there really no sweets on L'eihr? Can we send you a Hershey's care package?*

Thanks, Sarah, that's so SWEET of you. Hardy-har-har. To answer your question: yes and no. Natural sugars don't exist here, and my nutrition counselor won't let me have candy from the transport. He claims I'm an addict and that my body is going through detox. Maybe he's right. You don't want to know what I'd do for some Pixy Stix.

Tori in Midtown (my paranoid BFF) asks: *Why aren't you posting any pics? I want to see for myself that you're okay. How do we know you're the one who's writing all this stuff?*

Step away from the *National Enquirer*, my friend. I'm not preggers with an alien baby or being held here against my will. The L'eihrs have requested that I don't share photos or video of their home without prior approval. And how do you know this is me? I'll prove it: in seventh grade, you burped really loudly in Social Studies, and I took the blame so you wouldn't be embarrassed in front of Jared Lee. You're welcome for that, by the way. Also, lay off the onions.

Dixie in Columbus asks: *How do you get news on L'eihr? Do you watch television?*

Great question! Nope, there are no TV shows or movies here. News is delivered to our com-spheres, and we're expected to listen to the updates immediately. Think of a com-sphere as the ultimate iPhone. It emits a frequency only I can hear, and if I ignore my sphere, it'll keep pestering me until I answer it.

Okay, guys, that's it for now. I need to get ready for my *Sh'ovah*. Just think: the next time I post to this blog, I'll be an official L'eihr citizen! Isn't that awesome?

Posted by Cara Sweeney

"Psh," Cara whispered. Getting naked in front of aliens wasn't her idea of awesome, but whatever.

She closed her laptop and crept to the door as quietly as possible to avoid waking Elle, who snored softly from the top bunk. Eron had been right when he'd called the sound "endearing." Elle slept on her tummy with both hands tucked beneath her chest, snuffling like a child. It was such a cute contrast to the businesslike way she directed Cara from class to class during the daytime.

Cara slipped into the hall and tiptoed to the community bathroom, pleased to find it vacant. Privacy was a rare delicacy in the Aegis, and she needed a few moments to herself today.

She snatched a microfiber towel from the shelf and blotted her face. Her impending *Sh'ovah* had her perspiring like a linebacker, but whether on Earth or in another galaxy, high school was a battlefield. Cara never let anyone see her sweat.

After wiping down the back of her neck and the crooks of her elbows, she balled up her towel and chucked it into the waterless purifying chute, where ultrasonic waves and infrared technology would decontaminate it.

Cara fingered the lapel of her stiff white ceremonial robe. A quick glance over one shoulder showed she was still alone, but she knew from experience the bathroom wouldn't remain vacant once the sun rose in a few minutes. So without wasting another second of rare solitude, she dropped her robe to the floor and regarded her naked body in the reflective wall opposite the showers.

Right away, she noticed a slight roundness to her lower abdomen—that troublesome spot no amount of crunches would flatten. She sucked it in, and from there, her gaze moved from ankles to thighs, noting the smooth, polished effect she'd achieved last night from scrubbing her skin with a mixture of oil and salt procured from the kitchen. Her ivory complexion glowed, and with any luck, it would reflect the high-noon sunlight and blind all her guests.

She loosened her ponytail and pulled her auburn strands forward to see if they'd cover her breasts, but no dice. With a frown, she secured her hair with the jeweled clasp Elle had given her as a sponsor gift, then donned her robe as the first yawning clone shuffled in, rubbing the sleep from her eyes.

Cara didn't know the girl's name. She hated to admit it, but most of the clones still looked the same to her. *"Mahra,"* Cara said, shrinking back at her own loud echo. She hadn't learned many words yet, but she could manage *hello, good-bye,* and *sorry, pardon my ignorance.*

The girl paused, taking in the circular bronze emblems that adorned the shoulders of Cara's ceremonial robe. They were symbols of the Sacred Mother, L'eihr itself, and the stark white of the fabric represented the purity of heart with which Cara would pledge her fealty to the planet. Funny how white stood for virtue no matter which galaxy you inhabited.

The girl pursed her lips in hesitation, and after scanning the room as if to ensure they were alone, she offered a curt "Wel-come," in broken English before striding to a nearby toilet enclosure. It wasn't much, but that quiet greeting was more than Cara had received from her schoolmates since she'd joined their ranks.

Maybe this *Sh'ovah* was a good idea after all.

Another girl strode into the washroom, and she was one of the few clones Cara recognized. She carried herself with more arrogance than the rest, and her mouth was always pinched in a scowl. Her name was Dahla, and she'd been the first to give Cara "the finger."

Cara tipped her head in a greeting and waited for the girl to do the same. But Dahla tossed back her ponytail and strode toward the toilets, making sure to bump Cara's arm extra hard when she passed.

"Open your eyes," Dahla said in English. "Clumsy human."

Refusing to be baited, Cara held her head high and returned to her room. She reminded herself of what Aelyx had said. Everything would be all right. The clones simply needed time to get used to her.

She clung to the remnants of that confidence hours later, when Troy's knuckles rapped on her bedroom door. "Elle isn't here," she told him. Cara suspected that most of his visits were really covert missions to cozy up to her roommate.

"Good," Troy said. "'Cause I want to talk to you alone." He flicked a glance at her robe and took a step back, eyeing her warily, as if she might detonate if he got too close. He wrinkled his nose and extended one index finger. "Are you naked under there?"

Cara wrapped the lapels more snugly across her chest and tightened the belt at her waist. "Don't be such a prude. I'm more covered up now than all the times you've seen me in a bathing suit." Thank God that only L'eihr citizens could attend her *Sh'ovah*. She'd die a thousand deaths if Troy saw her naked. But to complete her ruse of boldness, she added, "There's nothing obscene about the human body. You're only ashamed because our society taught you to be."

He folded his arms and focused over her shoulder, taking an abrupt interest in her room. Not that there was anything remotely interesting in there. Bare gray walls and minimalist furnishings made up her décor, consisting of a bunk bed and a cabinet that looked like a cross between an armoire and a refrigerator.

"I can't have a conversation with you while you're naked," Troy complained. "It skeeves me out."

"Then come back later."

"I can't. It'll be too late then."

"Too late for what?"

Puffing in exasperation, he turned to face her. "Too late to talk you out of this citizenship stuff. You don't belong here, Pepper. This place is . . . uh . . ." He deliberated over his next choice of words, then leaned in and confided, "Intense." While she shook her head, Troy hitched a thumb toward Aelyx's vacant room a few doors down. "Listen, I know you like this guy—"

"Love," she corrected. "I love this guy."

"Right." He flashed his most condescending *whatever* face. "But you've got nothing in common. It won't last."

Cara gripped her waist. "Just because you change girlfriends before your gum loses flavor doesn't mean my relationship is doomed to fail."

"It's basic statistics." His blue eyes flashed to hers. "You know what the divorce rate is for teens?" Without giving her a chance to guess, he announced, "Three times the national average."

"The national average is fifty percent, Einstein."

"Then you have a one hundred and fifty percent chance of breaking up. Even higher if you take into account that you're from different worlds. That brings it to"—he counted silently on his fingers—"like, four thousand percent."

Poor Troy. What he lacked in brains he made up for in . . . well, something other than brains. "I found my match," Cara said. "Why should I be penalized because I'm young? Besides, it doesn't matter, because I'm not getting married."

Matrimony didn't even exist here. L'eihrs declared a *l'ihan* and that was that. Zero drama.

"You promised to stay here and be with him for life. It's the same thing, minus a piece of paper."

She couldn't dispute that, so she adopted a new tactic. "It's none of your business."

"Wha—" He blinked at her in silence for a few beats. "You're my sister!"

She couldn't dispute that, either—she didn't want to. She'd always wished Troy would take an interest in her life. It was a shame he'd waited until now to play the role of protective big brother. In less than a week, he'd be gone again.

They'd never been touchy-feely types, but Cara rested her fingertips on his forearm. "I don't expect you to understand, but I expect you to support me."

That seemed to get through to him. "Fine. When things don't work out, I guess you can catch the next transport to Earth."

Cara sighed. If he didn't believe her, nothing she said would change his mind. She told him good-bye and slid the door shut.

Elle returned from the medical lab right before lunch-time, greeting Cara with a smile and a *l'ina* sandwich. Vero, who rode atop Elle's shoulder, greeted her with a beady-eyed glare and a growl, flicking his long tail like a cat to show his displeasure.

"Ve-*ro*!" Elle warned the creature.

With his racoonish gray paws, Vero covered his eyes, rem-iniscent of a toddler who knew he'd done wrong. He peeked out from between his tiny digits and howled *aaaeee-oooo* at Cara. It sounded like *haaaate yooou*, which was probably what the little pillow-pisser meant.

Cara shot daggers at her deceptively cute, fuzzy nemesis, using her eyes to warn him away from her bed. She took the sandwich from Elle, but when she brought the flatbread to her lips, the meat's smoky aroma made her stomach lurch, so she set it on her desk and pushed it aside. "Thanks, but I'd better save it for later."

Elle whispered a L'eihr command to Vero, and the animal leaped onto Cara's desk and began nibbling on her discarded sandwich. While brushing a few bits of fur from her shoulder, Elle said, "You're nervous."

Cara didn't deny it.

"L'eihrs aren't conditioned to feel scandalized by nudity," she said in that no-nonsense way of hers. "Most of us were raised in this Aegis since birth. Imagine all the times we've seen one another's bodies. Yours is no different."

An arch of Cara's brow told her otherwise.

"All right," she conceded. "You have a navel and we don't."

"Plus pale skin, orange hair, and freckles." Cara patted her thighs. "And flab," which the clones didn't possess, thanks to their freakish obsession with exercise.

"I give you my word that—"

Before Elle could continue, Vero screeched a litany of complaints from the bottom cot, where he'd just crouched over Cara's brand-new pillow.

"No!" she and Elle cried, each thrusting out one palm in mirrored desperation.

51

It was too late. Vero finished his business and chirped something that sounded exactly like *owned! owned!* Then he ran to the door, high-fived the keypad, and scurried out into the hall before they could catch him.

"Happy *Sh'ovah* Day to me." Cara held her pillow at arm's length and carried it to the sanitation bin in the hallway. Farewell, pillow number seven.

After washing her hands in the restroom, she returned to Elle, whose shrugging shoulders said, *I'm sorry,* while her twitching lips said, *This is funny as hell.* Cara's mouth curved against her will. It was the first time she'd seen her roommate laugh, and the snickering was infectious.

"It really *is* a simple ceremony," Elle assured her with a comforting pat on the hand. "I'll lead the way, and you'll follow right behind me. Once the head Elder delivers her speech, The Way will begin your Covering."

"Smearing mud on me, you mean?"

Elle clucked her tongue. "You make it sound so base. It's not muck from the ground, *Cah*-ra. The *valeem* is like your holy water. It's imported from the third precinct, where the ground is rich and fertile. They use only the purest soil, and it's blessed before the ceremony."

Pure soil? Cara was pretty sure that was an oxymoron, like *sanitary landfill* or *jumbo shrimp*. "And everyone's been through this, right?"

"Every single one of us," Elle promised. A wistful smile enlivened her face, and she fell silent for a few moments, as if reliving a cherished memory. "I was fifteen—older than most of my friends when they crossed over, but the Elders wouldn't recommend me until I'd demonstrated patience. It was the happiest day of my life."

Despite her fear, Cara couldn't deny feeling a tingle of anticipation. It made her think of her many-greats grandmother O'Shea, who'd left Ireland for America. Just like Grandma O'Shea, Cara would rebuild her life on a new world, and this was the first step in bringing that future to fruition. She could do this—become a L'eihr—and help cement the alliance between two planets.

"Are you ready?" Elle asked.

With a firm nod, Cara answered, "Born ready."

When they reached the open doors leading to the courtyard, Elle walked in slow, measured strides into the brightness of day. To Cara's surprise, she didn't hesitate to fall into place, her bare feet moving across the spongy sidewalk. She trained her eyes on the back of Elle's head instead of the continuous rows of uniformed teens in her periphery. Soon, the soft tickle of grass replaced pavement, and Elle stopped, reaching out for Cara's hand.

To their left, the clones stood at attention like a battalion receiving orders, backbones stiff, arms held rigidly by their sides as they stared through her. The Way had positioned themselves on Cara's right, all ten leaders standing erect, clad in cloaks of deepest brown, their expressions more lively than she'd ever seen. Clearly, this was a happy occasion for them, if not for the clones. They formed a semicircle around a waist-high brass trough that seemed to absorb the sunlight instead of reflecting it the way other metals did.

When she peered inside, she didn't find the black, gritty

sludge she'd expected. The *valeem* appeared claylike—a smooth burnt-orange porridge that bore a slight resemblance to half-baked pumpkin pie filling. Occasionally, a lazy bubble would disrupt the soup and burp to the surface, filling the air with the seasoned sweetness of cloves.

The ancient Alona drew a breath and asked in English, "Who guarantees this girl's integrity?"

"I guarantee it," Elle replied. She extended their linked hands toward Alona, and with flawless timing, released her as the old woman claimed Cara's fingers.

Alona's grasp was cool, but stronger than Cara had anticipated, and she remembered that while the Elders seemed as frail as baby's breath, they were only in their fifties.

Alona delivered a message to the assembly in L'eihr while Elle quietly translated. She told the story of the Sacred Mother, who'd loved this majestic planet so fiercely, she'd sacrificed her immortal body by splitting herself into half a dozen equal pieces, each one forming the six gods and goddesses of L'eihr. Her "children" went on to create the topography, oceans, animals, and intelligent beings that populated the world. And just as the Sacred Mother had surrendered her body and spirit to give life to the planet, in turn, each citizen was expected to devote his or her existence to the betterment of L'eihr. It was a beautiful story with parallels to many of Earth's religions, and the similarities made Cara feel closer to home.

"*Cah*-ra Sweeney, *l'ihan* to Aelyx of the first Aegis," Alona spoke. "Do you join your fate with the Sacred Mother—freely, of your own choosing, and without duress?"

Cara cleared her throat. "Yes."

"Will you devote your existence to the advancement of L'eihr?"

"Yes."

"And will you submit to The Way in all matters, without fail?"

Cara hesitated. Submission wasn't really her cup of tea, but she knew any further delay would insult her leaders. Without waiting another second, she licked her lips and sealed her fate. "Yes."

"Then let me be the first to welcome you, sister." Alona's clouded gray eyes sparked alive. Although the woman hadn't initiated Silent Speech, a trickle of emotion leaked from her gaze—one of pure hope. Alona believed that Cara would lead others to the colony, that they'd join their societies and bring the spirit of humanity to the clones. Cara didn't know whether to feel flattered or terrified. It seemed The Way had some serious expectations of her.

Alona raised Cara's hand into the air, and in flawless synchronization, the entire assembly shouted, "Welcome, sister!" in the militant voices of their native tongue.

The old woman's eyes shifted to Cara's robe, a silent message that the time had come to bare it all. Cara glanced at Elle for confirmation, hoping she'd say, *Just kidding! Did you really think you'd have to get naked?* then laugh and clap her on the shoulder. But, of course, she didn't say those things. She nodded and took her place in line behind The Way.

Cara brought ten trembling fingers to her waist and fumbled with the belt tie. After three tries, she worked the knot free and untangled its ends, then brought both hands to her lapels and clutched the stiff fabric like a security blanket. Suddenly she realized she didn't know what to do with the robe once she'd shed it. Let it fall to the ground? Sling it over one arm? She glanced at Alona, who seemed to understand.

"I'll hold it," she whispered, extending an arm.

If Cara was going to do this, she'd do it right. Taking a deep breath, she peeled back the lapels of her robe and pulled her arms free, then handed the garment to Alona and faced the sea of clones, staring through them as they'd done to her.

Instantly her cheeks burst into flames, her entire body flushing so red hot, she expected to see fire shoot from her fingertips. A light wind brushed her naked flesh in places she'd never felt the breeze before, but the oddest sensation of all was the pressure of five hundred curious gazes. The attention crackled over her like static electricity—invisible but very real.

Alona used her free hand to dip into the trough. She cupped the thick liquid and then poured it over Cara's left shoulder, where it trickled downward to coat her arm. It was warmer than she'd expected, and her muscles relaxed in response. The next Elder repeated the process on the other side, and when Jaxen's turn came, he scooped two handfuls of mud and spilled them across her lower abdomen, essentially creating a dripping bikini. It was an oddly chivalrous act, and she thanked him with her eyes.

Elle heaped two layers of mud over Cara's chest, kindly concealing "the girls" from view, and then the first group of clones approached. But instead of cupping a handful of *valeem*, the six of them dipped their index fingers just deep enough to coat the tips. They passed her quickly, not bothering to meet her gaze when they tapped their nails against her chest.

It didn't take a sociologist to interpret the message: they would participate in the ceremony, but that didn't mean she was welcome. On and on it went, each group of six offering the least required of them by their leaders.

Cara's skin felt tight and tingly in a way that had nothing to do with the clay beginning to dry across her body. She dug her fingernails into her palms and lifted her chin as she completed the rite of passage that marked her transition into adulthood. Once the last clone had marked her, Cara wrapped a dark blanket around her shoulders and waited for Alona to dismiss the assembly for the *Sh'ovah* feast.

But just as Alona drew a breath to make the announcement, a deafening whistle sounded from above. The entire group turned their gazes skyward, where a tiny ball of flame—a meteorite, perhaps—streaked the beige clouds. Quickly, the flame drew nearer and the shrieking became so loud it stung her ears. It didn't take long for the assembly to realize that the object was headed right for them, and bodies scattered in all directions while voices screamed and shouted commands Cara couldn't understand. She clutched her blanket and bolted for the protection of the Aegis wall, barely reaching it when a crash boomed from behind.

Once she'd reached a safe distance, she turned and surveyed the damage, surprised to discover that the only casualty of the fiery impact was the steaming vat of mud. Orange *valeem* lay in puddles around broken bits of metal, and in the heart of the debris rested a softball-size orb. From where Cara stood, it didn't look like a meteorite. She could swear she saw colored lights twinkle from its surface, but before she could get a better look, Jaxen removed his cloak and draped it over the sphere. The Elders glanced nervously at one another and then commanded the students to go inside.

From all around her, the clones murmured in confusion but did as they were told. Cara filed inside with them, casting occasional glances over her shoulder at the lump beneath Jaxen's cloak.

What was that thing? And why was he trying to hide it?

CHAPTER FIVE

"Look, more L'annabes. They're lined up around the block." David pointed out the rear passenger window at the Omaha convention center, where Aelyx had spent the last several hours guest lecturing to university students about the physics of space travel. "You have more groupies than the Rolling Stones ever did, you lucky bastard."

The armored SUV hit a bump in the road, sending a dozen rifles clanking against their owners. If Aelyx wanted to venture beyond the hotel, this was his only option. He hated living like this, in constant fear of attack. "It's not as glamorous as you think," Aelyx said, shielding his eyes from the setting sun. "The attention gets annoying after a while."

"Yeah, you poor baby." David rolled his eyes. "*Annoying* doesn't describe that model I busted trying to sneak into your room last night." His lips curved in an appreciative grin.

"*Flexible*, maybe. Can't have been easy to squeeze inside the maid's cart like that."

Aelyx laughed. "You're more human than I gave you credit for."

"Oh, come on," David said with a light elbow nudge. "Tell me you wouldn't have been a little bit stoked if she'd jumped out of your closet."

"Not in the least," he assured David. "Cara's the only one I want."

"Mmm." David nodded at Aelyx as if they were members of a secret club. "Once you go human, you never go back, huh? I'll bet our girls are firecrackers compared to L'eihr chicks. I mean, no offense, but they seem kind of frigid with that empty stare. Not like Earth girls—especially redheads. Man, I love me some gingersnap action."

Aelyx thought he'd mastered English slang, but he had no clue what David was saying. However, he got the distinct impression that his new friend was much more experienced than he was when it came to women. Aside from what Aelyx had gleaned from the Internet, he didn't know much about the mechanics of intimacy. Of course, he couldn't admit that to a human male. Eron would have understood, but not David.

David must have misinterpreted Aelyx's silence as anger. "Did I go too far with that 'frigid' comment? Sorry, man. I'm an idiot. Sometimes I can't shut up."

"No, I'm not offended. You've got it wrong, though." In the years since The Way had weaned his generation off the hormone regulators, the clones had wasted no time in pairing off and doing what came naturally. Caught off guard, the medics had rushed to ensure that each student was outfitted with a contraceptive implant before any unauthorized breeding occurred, an offense punishable by death. "Our females are willing."

David glanced at his comrades to ensure they weren't listening, then leaned in close. "So, what's the difference?" he whispered. "You know, between Earth girls and L'eihr girls? Does everything work the same?"

Aelyx tried to think of an answer that wouldn't betray his limited knowledge of either race. He'd never gone further with a clone than an occasional *sh'ellam*, their equivalent of a kiss. He told David a deceptively innocent truth. "L'eihrs and humans are biologically identical."

"Well, sure," David said over the whirring of the tires. "But there must be *something* . . ."

"No," Aelyx lied, then immediately changed his mind. He couldn't believe he hadn't thought of it before. "Actually, there is a difference. If L'eihrs are using Silent Speech, we can share each other's sensations."

"No way," David breathed out in awe. "Feeling yours *and* hers at the same time? That must be awesome."

Yes, Aelyx imagined it would be. With any luck, Cara would feel ready someday, and he'd actually get to find out.

After that, David gazed silently out the window, no doubt wishing his brain were capable of Silent Speech, while Aelyx wondered how he'd survive until the spring. He wished The Way would allow him to tell humans some measure of the truth. That would accomplish their goal of finding support for the alliance and allow him to return to Cara. But the request he'd submitted to his leaders had gone unanswered, leaving him bound to silence.

When the armed convoy arrived at the hotel and David ushered Aelyx into their suite, the ambassador greeted them at the door.

"I've held dinner for you," Stepha said, leading the way to the dining room, where small white cartons of takeout waited. "Was your speaking engagement successful?"

Nodding, Aelyx scanned the living area for Syrine. She should have returned from her visit to the children's hospital by now. "Is Syrine joining us?"

"No," Stepha told him. "She returned from her outing and went straight to bed. She isn't feeling well."

"What's wrong with her?" David asked. "I thought L'eihrs had super immunity or something."

Stepha shrugged and dipped a serving spoon into a carton of fried rice, a rather casual response considering David was right. Between Syrine's natural immune system and the inoculations she'd received prior to leaving L'eihr, she shouldn't fall ill.

Aelyx turned his gaze to her bedroom door and wrestled with the urge to go to her. A month ago, he wouldn't have hesitated, but that was before she'd betrayed their friendship. He owed her nothing.

He grabbed a container of chicken and served himself while unwanted memories haunted him—six-year-old Syrine sneaking him supper after he'd been lashed with the *iphet* and sent to his room; eleven-year-old Syrine using her gift as a spiritual healer to lessen his grief when the old house pet had died.

She had been there when he'd needed her.

Aelyx threw down his fork and stood from the table. Curse it all, Syrine wasn't forgiven, but he had to know she was all right. "I'm going to check on her."

"Thank you, brother." Stepha grinned in a way that told Aelyx this had been a test, and he'd passed. "I'm certain you will help her in a way I cannot."

When Aelyx knocked on her door, she didn't respond, so he opened it a crack and peeked into her room. The purple bruise of twilight filtered through the window, making her seem even smaller as she curled into a ball atop her bed. She'd hugged a pillow to her chest, and tears welled in her eyes. Seeing her like this made Aelyx's heart heavy.

He shut the door behind him and sat on the edge of her bed. "You're missing dinner."

It seemed to take extra effort for her to draw a breath. "I'm not hungry."

Aelyx extended a hand toward her and drew back. He didn't need to touch her to know she didn't have a fever. "What happened today? Did someone hurt you?"

She shook her head against her pillow.

"Talk to me," he pressed.

When she met his gaze, a plump tear spilled free and plunked to the mattress. "Do you know what my 'good deed' was today?"

"To visit the children's hospital."

"No. To visit *dying* children in the hospital," she clarified. "There's a program that gives them one final wish, and their wish was to spend the day with me." She scoffed and repeated, "Me. They could've had anything they wanted."

Aelyx offered a sad smile. "I'm glad you were able to give them that gift."

"I did my best," she said, her breath hitching. "I told them stories about our Voyagers and the strange worlds they've discovered. Their favorite was the swamp planet where the trees are sentient. They loved hearing how the branches tangle with one another to pass along messages and songs."

"That's one of my favorites, too."

"And I told them the old legend—how some say ancient L'eihrs were abducted and transplanted on Earth to form the human race." She lowered her voice and confided, "I've never believed it, but I told the children we were related. They seemed to like that."

"I'm glad you were able to bring them happiness." Aelyx chose his next words with care, not wanting to add to her unease by sounding accusatory. "Do you still believe that their kind isn't worth saving?"

For a long time, she didn't answer. When she did, her voice was a strangled whisper. "It's not fair. Eron's killers will live on while these younglings are doomed to die."

"No," Aelyx agreed, "it's not fair."

Syrine covered her face with both palms. "Nothing makes sense here. I want to go home."

"I do, too." He pulled back one of her hands and waited

until she looked at him. "But not until we secure the alliance. Don't you agree?"

She didn't say yes, but judging by the way she averted her gaze and hugged her pillow tightly, Syrine had learned a lesson today. That was enough for Aelyx. He stood to return to his supper.

"Wait," she called as he turned the doorknob. She propped herself up on one elbow and hesitated to speak. Just when Aelyx thought she might apologize for her behavior last month, she sighed and lay back down. "Thanks for the talk."

Aelyx gave a tight nod. "You would do the same for me."

CHAPTER SIX

"Aelyx isn't answering."

Cara stuffed her com-sphere beneath pillow number nine and resisted the urge to jut out her bottom lip. She always called Aelyx before he went to bed—it was the only time they were both awake and she had a minute to spare. By the time she finished all her classes, extra duties, and barf-inducing exercises, she'd fall into a coma until morning. Now she understood why the L'eihr crime rate was so low. Everyone was too exhausted for shenanigans.

The top bunk shifted above Cara's head, and Elle's dainty four-toed feet dangled into view. After a long yawn, she said, "Perhaps his sphere is malfunctioning. It happens sometimes. I've had mine refurbished twice."

"I could try reaching him on Syrine's sphere, but she'd probably chuck it out the window before taking a call from me." Cara caught herself rubbing her cheek, where Syrine had once slapped her.

"I'm no help to you there." Elle hopped to the floor and joined Cara on the bottom bunk, where she sat cross-legged, her loose hair spilling over both shoulders. She looked so human first thing in the morning. "She hasn't spoken to me since Eron asked me to be his *l'ihan*."

"Oh, that's right." Cara had forgotten the two were once besties. "You loved the same boy." Few friendships could withstand the dreaded BFF love triangle. Cara knew firsthand. "My best friend started dating my ex as soon as we broke up. They snuck around behind my back for weeks and made me feel like an idiot. We're speaking again, but it's not the same."

"Friendships evolve," Elle said clinically. "And often fade. It's the natural order of things." And just like that, their girl-talk ended. "Let's get to work. We don't have long."

Cara groaned. She didn't want to practice Silent Speech anymore. What was the point? Her mind was physiologically different from the L'eihrs, so she'd probably never master the art.

"Are you getting headaches again?" Elle asked.

"No, but between this and my classes, I go to bed each night feeling like I've given birth from my brain."

"Think of your mind as a muscle," Elle lectured. "It will—"

"Grow stronger with use," Cara parroted. Since resistance was futile, she might as well cooperate. "Okay. Same drill as before?"

"No. Let's try something new." Elle shook back her hair and leaned forward to meet Cara's gaze. "Show me how you feel, then use your words to tell me what we're having for breakfast."

Cara completed her first task in less than a minute. She noticed it didn't take as long as it had last week to channel her frustration into Elle's mind. In that respect, she'd improved. But when she tried to say *t'ahinni*, Elle heard nothing.

"Don't be discouraged," Elle said. "You're making progress. I understand your emotions more clearly than before. You feel defeated, but also curious." Her forehead wrinkled in thought. "And you're suspicious, but I don't know why or of whom."

Cara lowered her voice to a whisper. "Something's been bugging me. You know that meteorite everyone's been talking about—the one that crashed my *Sh'ovah*?"

"What of it?"

"It wasn't a rock. I'm pretty sure it was man-made." Aside from Cara, no one had caught a glimpse of the object. "I saw metal and lights, then Jaxen covered it with his cloak."

Elle considered for a moment. "I've observed reflective matter in space debris, some of it metallic. Could that explain what you saw—sunlight glinting off the mineral deposits?"

"I don't think so." But Cara couldn't be certain, and that's what drove her crazy. "Why would Jaxen bother to hide a worthless chunk of rock?"

Elle's troubled expression showed she agreed, though she didn't say so. "Can you summon the image and share it with me?"

In theory, that was a great idea. In practice, however . . .

"I've never tried that."

"The process is similar to sharing emotions. Close your eyes and form a picture in your mind. Wait until it's clear before you connect with me."

Cara did exactly as her roommate instructed, but it didn't work. No surprise there. If she wanted answers, it seemed she'd have to find them herself. No surprise there, either.

"*Cah*-ra Sweeney."

At the sound of her name, Cara glanced up from her tablet at the science teacher who stood at the front of the classroom glaring at her. He'd spent the last thirty minutes speaking L'eihr, so she'd decided to catch up on a few chapters of history—clearly a mistake.

She set her tablet in her lap. "Yes, Instructor Helm?"

"You just missed my demonstration of *h'ylo* reproduction." He shook a fuzzy brown thing at her that looked like a rotten kiwi. "What captivating topic has lured you away from my lecture?"

Jaxen and Aisly, along with every other student on the long wooden bench in front of Cara, turned to study her. Most of them couldn't speak English, but Helm's disapproving tone must have said enough to pique their interests. Dahla seemed especially pleased as she smirked from her assistant's place beside the instructor.

Cara wiped both palms on her tunic. Truthfully, she'd been reading her favorite thesis, a brand-new one that argued L'eihrs were the descendants of humans, not the other way around. If you asked her, the evidence was compelling. The only reason L'eihrs clung to the original legend was because they'd rather amputate all eight toes than trace their lineage to Earth.

"I'm sorry," she said. "It was an essay."

"On?" Helm demanded, gripping his waist with one hand.

Cara glanced at her tablet and read aloud, "'The Primate Connection: A Thesis—'"

"'Regarding L'eihr Lineage,'" Helm finished. "Written by a scholar named Larish. He argued that L'eihrs are related to your ancients, who in turn evolved from animals."

"Exactly," Cara said. "Humans and L'eihrs share ninety-eight percent of their DNA with chimpanzees. Earth scientists believe we all descended from a single ancestor and developed differently over millions of years. But on L'eihr, you have no close primates. It's as if you were dropped here by an alien race. You evolved differently from humans, but that's mostly due to organized breeding and—"

"A fascinating theory," Helm interrupted. A tiny muscle twitched in his jaw. "Are you in humanities class now?"

Cara cleared her throat. "No, sir."

"And will Larish's dissertation help you with my exam tomorrow?" He pointed to his white-rimmed instructor tablet, where he kept his lectures and testing materials.

"No, sir."

"Then perhaps you should make use of your translator and focus on the subject at hand."

Cara nodded, willing herself invisible.

But understanding the language didn't help her absorb

Helm's lesson. His words—*genetic port, reverse micro-sequencing, inverted bioethnicity*—had no context for her. It was like trying to decipher gibberish. Cara hated to admit it, but she didn't belong in this class. She needed to take a massive step back and master the prerequisites of L'eihr science. Too bad she'd have to join the preschoolers to do that.

An idea came to mind.

Maybe she should request a rotation working in the Aegis nursery. She'd pick up some basic concepts that way, and besides, she felt sorry for all those motherless kids, taken straight from the artificial wombs to a quasi-orphanage. They were so darned cute, and she wanted to snuggle the toddlers when their caretakers weren't looking.

After class, she jogged to the headmaster's office to fill out a rotation request and then double-timed it to the novice obstacle course, relieved to discover she'd made it there before the fitness instructor. The man had a name, but Cara preferred to think of him as Satan. He loved making her suffer. *Pain is good*, he'd told her. *If no hurt, you do it wrongly.* Satan didn't speak very good English, but he was fluent in whoopass. He wore his ponytail extra tight and probably flogged himself for fun.

"Sweeeeeney."

Speak of the devil, and he shall appear . . . from behind a climbing wall. She hadn't beaten him here. Fabulous. That meant an extra lap. At least no one would be around to watch her stumble over the balance stones and yack in the bushes. The other clones had long ago graduated to proficient courses.

"Today we try new technique," he said, rubbing his

75

massive palms together. "Make you win time and move to intermediate course." He patted his tunic pocket. "I fasten *t'alar* on your shoulders. Make you fast."

Unless he had a jet pack in there, she didn't see how that was possible. "Is the *t'alar* an antigravity device?"

"No." He dug into his pocket and pulled out a simple black strap. Then he smiled in a way she didn't like at all. "Is *motivation.*"

That didn't sound good.

"Human lung," he continued, "it hold less air, yes? But still the body do great things when provoked." He lumbered over to her and snapped the *t'alar* across her shoulders like a handgun holster. "You run course, and I watch from above." He pointed to a small platform built into the trees. "To keep time. When you need boost, I do this." Then he clapped his hands loud enough to make her jump.

At first, Cara didn't understand. But when a jolt of electricity ricocheted down the length of her spine, she yelped and nearly wet herself. The *t'alar* was a torture device? Holy crap, he really was the devil! "You're going to make me run faster by *shocking* me?"

Satan shrugged. "Eh, we try." Without giving her a chance to reason with him, he pointed at the climbing wall. "Now begin," and he followed with a *clap.*

Zzzttt!

Another sharp current shot through Cara, and she lurched toward the wall like a marionette that'd had her strings pulled too hard. "Oh my God," she whimpered as she grabbed the first hold. "This is so messed up." But she didn't stop. After reaching the top, she scaled down the other side and set off at a sprint the instant her feet touched solid ground.

The balance stones came next—two dozen round slabs set one stride apart in zigzag fashion, each designed to tilt thirty degrees in all directions. She leaped onto the first stone with her right foot, crouching low to distribute her weight, then immediately jumped to the second and third. With each rapid leap to and fro, she made her thighs do all the work and kept her arms extended for balance. She didn't hesitate or second-guess herself like before. She cleared her mind and let her body take the wheel. Before she knew it, she'd reached the last stone and jogged around the bend toward the impact bags.

Zzzttt!

Correction: she *sprinted* around the bend toward the impact bags, veering left when the first body-shaped target came into view. With a savage war cry, she tensed her shoulder and collided with the sack. The force of the blow knocked aside her target, and Cara dodged to the right before it had a chance to bounce back. This was her favorite part of the course. She pictured each target as a sneering professor or a haughty clone, knocking the snot out of each one until her anger dissolved. When she reached the last bag, she hit it extra hard in honor of Satan. He must have known, because he zapped her again.

She squeaked in pain and felt a sudden burst of energy— just enough to propel her into a run and carry her through the mile-long endurance track. After that, she breezed over the hurdles and approached the final obstacle: the cord maze, also known as the tangler. She barely had the strength to lift her head, let alone grip the overhead ropes and maneuver her way, monkey-bar–style, to the other side. She stood with her boots rooted to the ground, staring at the finish line in the distance.

So close, yet so far away . . .

Zzzttt!

Stifling a sob, Cara jumped up and grabbed the thick cord with both hands. She pumped her feet to create momentum, then swung forward to grip the next section of rope. Though the material was coated for maximum traction, she felt her fingers slipping with fatigue. But each time she slowed, a jolt of electricity stirred her adrenaline. She forced herself onward, drawing on power she didn't know she possessed, until she reached the other side.

She wasted no time in barreling toward the finish line, head down, muscles burning, heart pounding as she drove her legs harder and faster. When she crossed the threshold, she heard Satan yell, "Sweeeeeney! You make most excellent time—top twenty in whole Aegis!"

Cara bent at the waist and gripped her knees, fighting for breath. Her stomach heaved, and she lost her breakfast in the bushes. But damn if she didn't feel like a rock star.

Satan climbed down from the tree and removed her *t'alar* harness, then gave her a hearty smack on the back. "Eat plenty *l'ina*," he said with pride. "And make much rest. Tomorrow we meet at intermediate course."

"Sleep"—pant-gasp-wheeze—"*l'ina*"—pant-gasp-wheeze—"got it."

Cara waved good-bye to Satan and dragged her rubbery legs toward the main building. The cafeteria would serve lunch in fifteen minutes, which meant she had to shower and dress in ten.

Her body gave her a second wind by the time she reached the courtyard. She noticed Troy there but didn't bother to wave. He was engaged in a game of sticks with a couple of jerks named Odom and Skall. They usually hung out with Dahla, who was watching the game from the opposite side of the lawn.

Each boy gripped a wooden staff and circled his opponents, waiting for an opportunity to knock one another to the ground. Players weren't allowed to strike the left side of the body, and they could only hit below the waist. They didn't wear cups, either. Only the hard-core L'eihrs played sticks, and Troy was surprisingly good at it. He deflected each attack with lightning speed and struck back twice as hard, keeping Odom and Skall on the defensive.

Cara moved in closer.

Troy had pulled his black curls into a ponytail, and sweat dripped between his bare shoulder blades as he twirled his staff. Typically, Cara didn't pay much attention to her brother's body—because, *ew*—but she couldn't help noticing how much he'd bulked up on L'eihr. He was seriously ripped, holding his own against the two largest clones in the Aegis. Even when Odom and Skall teamed up against him, Troy left them limping in pain, whacking one in the gut and the other in the thigh. Without hesitating, he swept his staff behind both men's ankles and knocked them to the grass.

Cara summoned enough strength in her noodle arms to

applaud her brother. "Woo-hoo," she called while clapping wildly. "Go, Troy! You kicked—"

In a flash, something solid hit the backs of Cara's knees, and she fell, hard. When she opened her eyes, she was staring at the beige sky and struggling to breathe. After blinking a few times, she pushed up on her elbows and realized Skall had used his stick to flatten her.

Dahla broke into hysterical laughter while Skall jumped to his feet. They pointed at Cara, clearly teasing her in their native language. A few onlookers joined in mocking her, and she half expected her brother to laugh the loudest.

But Troy was not amused.

His eyes narrowed and his nostrils flared. He threw down his staff and charged Skall without warning, planting his shoulder in the clone's midsection. For the second time, Skall landed on his ass, but this was no game. Troy used the side of his hand to slam Skall's windpipe, leaving him coughing and retching in the grass.

Odom rushed to his friend's aid, but Troy stopped him with an expression that said, *The Marines taught me how to pull a man's nuts through his throat. Want a demonstration?* Odom backed away, and Skall glared at Cara while he rubbed his neck. His message was also clear: *Your brother won't always be here to protect you.*

"Let's go." Troy helped her to standing and brushed loose bits of grass from her uniform. Then he wrapped an arm around her shoulders, leading her up the front steps and into the Aegis lobby. When they reached Cara's door, Troy held her at arm's length and inspected her for damage.

"You all right?" he asked.

"Yeah, just got the wind knocked out of me." She knew Troy wouldn't like it, but she gave him a hug.

As she predicted, he squirmed away. "Gross, Pepper. I'm all sweaty." He sniffed the air a few times. "And you smell."

She glanced down the hall into the lobby, where Odom, Skall, and Dahla had just stalked inside. "Do you think they'll tell the headmaster?" L'eihrs didn't tolerate fighting, and she didn't want Troy whipped with that awful electric lash.

"I doubt it." Troy stretched and flexed his fingers. "If he snitches, he'll have to admit that he hit you. He'll keep his mouth shut—or his eyes shut, or whatever, since that's how they talk." He started to say something more, but Elle joined them, and Troy stood a few inches straighter and tightened his abs.

Elle didn't spare him a glance. "Why haven't you showered yet?" she asked Cara in a rush. "The headmaster called a house meeting in the dining hall. You can't be late."

Cara checked her pocket to make sure she hadn't lost her com-sphere. "I didn't get an alert."

"You didn't?" Elle seemed surprised at that. "The message transmitted a few minutes ago."

Cara shook her sphere and listened for the rattle of loose parts. "Maybe it's broken." That would explain why she hadn't been able to reach Aelyx. "Did the headmaster say what's wrong?"

Elle cupped her mouth and whispered as if the message were too shameful to speak aloud. "It's Instructor Helm. His tablet has gone missing—he believes someone stole it."

"Whoa," Troy said. "That's a heavy accusation. Don't they execute people for theft?"

Elle seemed to notice him for the first time. She scanned his sweaty chest and took a step back. "Yes, but there hasn't been an execution in many generations. Our people know better than to steal."

"I'm sure he left it somewhere and forgot." Cara pressed a palm to her keypad. "I need to grab some clean clothes."

"Me, too." Troy nodded good-bye to Elle, but she ignored him. Poor guy.

Elle rushed to the cafeteria, and Cara hurried into her room to gather a towel and a uniform. She stuffed her comsphere beneath her pillow for safekeeping, but in doing so, she heard it *click* against another object. She used her fingers to explore, feeling cool, smooth metal. She lifted her pillow and a breath locked in her throat. There, on her mattress, rested a white-rimmed tablet.

Instructor Helm's tablet.

Oh, *fasha.* She was toast.

The pillow slipped from Cara's fingers as she realized what this meant. Helm's tablet hadn't accidentally materialized on her bunk. Someone had planted it there to frame her. For a *capital* crime. Dahla had assisted Helm in his lecture today, which had given her access to his tablet. But Cara had barely exchanged ten words with the girl. She couldn't hate humans *that* much, could she?

Cara sank onto the mattress, wondering what to do.

If she returned the tablet to the headmaster and told him the truth, he might believe her, but then again, he might not.

She could use Silent Speech to project her feelings of fear, but not to proclaim her innocence.

Maybe she should wipe the prints from Helm's device and return it to his classroom. The clones and instructors had assembled in the cafeteria, so it could work if she hurried. But what if a latecomer caught her in the act? She'd look guilty as homemade sin inside Helm's lab with his stolen tablet in her hand. And what about video cameras? She didn't know if L'eihrs recorded activity in the hallways like at Midtown High.

One thing was certain: she couldn't leave the tablet here. Whoever had planted it would lead the headmaster to her room. Cara grabbed her blanket and used it to wipe down the glossy screen and the metallic backside, hopefully erasing her fingerprints. She wrapped it in a clean towel and stepped into the hallway, still unsure of what to do.

In a daze, she glanced past the vacant lobby and toward the cafeteria. Maybe instead of returning the tablet to Helm's class, she should leave it in the bathroom or shove it down the sanitation chute.

Wait, the sanitation chute . . .

Of course! Why hadn't she thought of that before? It would take days before anyone discovered the tablet, and even then, no one could link it to her. She scrambled toward the nearest sanitation door and tugged the handle.

"Hello, *Cah*-ra."

She flinched, nearly dropping her bundle, and whirled around to find Jaxen approaching from the other end of the hall.

Double *fasha*.

Jaxen's smile fell as he surveyed her. "Are you all right?"

Cara clutched the evidence to her chest and stepped away from the chute. What were the odds she could get rid of Jaxen and ditch the tablet before the assembly began?

At her silence, he bent to meet her height, and studied her closely. "Your pupils are dilated, your cheeks are pale, and I can see the pulse racing at the base of your throat. What's wrong?"

Those odds? Zero. Even if she chucked the tablet, Jaxen would remember this encounter and suspect she'd done something shady. She didn't have a choice. She had to tell the truth and hope for the best.

"I'm beginning to worry," he said. "Perhaps I should summon a medic."

"No!" Cara extended one hand, stopping just shy of touching him. "I need your help. I think I'm in trouble."

"What kind of trouble?"

"First, promise you'll listen before you make up your mind. I'm not a liar—I swear it."

Jaxen didn't hesitate. "I promise. You can trust me."

Cara swallowed hard and unwrapped her bundle, revealing what lay inside. "I found this under my pillow. I didn't take it. Someone must've put it there to make me look guilty."

Jaxen's brows rose up the length of his forehead. "Who would do that?"

"Who wouldn't?" she asked. "Half the Aegis wants me gone."

He glanced at the sanitation chute and back to her. "And you were about to destroy it?"

"Yes," she admitted. "I didn't know what else to do. I was afraid no one would believe me."

For the next few moments, Jaxen said nothing. Then he held out his palm. "Give it to me. I'll turn it in to the headmaster. That will settle the matter."

"But what'll you say when he asks where you found it?" L'eihrs couldn't lie through Silent Speech.

Jaxen took the tablet from her. "The headmaster doesn't question me. I answer to none but Alona."

Cara averted her eyes and thanked him. She hadn't expected him to believe her.

Using an index finger, Jaxen tipped up her chin. "You're welcome. I want you to come to me if this happens again." His touch made her uneasy, but she held still. "Do you understand?"

"Yes."

"Good." He released her and gestured toward the cafeteria. "I'll take care of this. Go shower and calm yourself."

As he strode away, Cara tried to pinpoint why her stomach was still turning somersaults. She'd discovered the tablet in plenty of time and had managed to dodge a potential death sentence. She should feel ten pounds lighter, not weighed down by dread.

It wasn't until she reached the showers that the reason for her unease became clear: she now owed Jaxen her life, and deep down, she knew he'd ask for something in return. But what would he want from her, and when?

CHAPTER SEVEN

"I'll bet it was Jaxen." Aelyx climbed into bed, nearer to Cara's image. He wished he could pull her safely beneath the covers and wrap her in his arms. "It's too convenient that he came to your rescue at the last minute. Why wasn't he in the dining hall with the assembly?"

"I don't know." Cara sat cross-legged atop her own bed, finger-combing her loose red waves of hair. "But Jaxen likes humans. He doesn't have a motive to hurt me. I mean, I don't really trust him, but—"

"Good. You shouldn't." Jaxen wanted Cara for himself—Aelyx had felt it weeks ago when he'd engaged in Silent Speech with the bastard. What better way to win Cara's affections than to become her savior? Aelyx wasn't there to intervene, and no one would question a member of The Way. "I don't know him well, but there's something—"

"Different about him," Cara finished. "Yeah, I get that,

too." She twisted her hair behind her head and pinned it in place. "Which Aegis did he grow up in? Nobody here knows."

Aelyx shrugged. He didn't want to talk about Jaxen anymore. "You need to recalibrate your keypad so only you and Elle can get inside."

"I did."

"Try again. And make sure you're never alone." Jaxen would certainly try to put Cara in his debt again. "You need a constant alibi—someone like Elle who can use Silent Speech to confirm your innocence."

Cara began chewing her thumbnail. "I knew living here would be an adjustment, but I wasn't expecting anything like this." With a sigh, she pulled her pillow into her lap and curled around it. "I mean, a constant alibi? Is this my life now?"

"No." Aelyx couldn't let her think that way. His greatest fear was that she might change her mind and return to Earth. "This is only temporary. Once we're on the colony, everything will change. You'll see."

"I hope you're right."

"I understand how you feel," he said. "I'm under constant guard. They don't even let the L'annabes near me." Not that he objected to that decision. "Every day it's a new city, but I don't get to see much. Syrine and I just sit in our hotel all night."

A shadow passed over Cara's face. "So you spend every spare minute together?"

Before he could answer, Syrine knocked twice and opened the bedroom door, bringing with her the smell of charred beef from the kitchen. She announced in their native language,

"Our *l'ina* is ready," before noticing Cara's hologram and switching to English. "Oh, I'm sorry. Hello, *Cah*-ra. How are you enjoying L'eihr?"

"It's fantastic," Cara said tightly.

Syrine backed out of the room and told Aelyx she'd keep his plate warm until he was finished with his call. Once she left, Cara turned her glare on him.

"Syrine made *l'ina* for you?" she asked.

"If you can call it that," he said. "She does the best she can with local ingredients . . ." He trailed off when he realized Cara had interpreted Syrine's words. "Hey, your L'eihr is improving!"

"Since when?"

He didn't understand. "Since when is your L'eihr improving?"

"Since when," Cara said as if he were obtuse, "does she cook for you?"

"I don't know." Aelyx counted the nights since Syrine's visit to the children's hospital. "For the past two days, I suppose." She'd insisted on serving him *l'ina* both nights in an obvious effort to "extend the olive branch," as humans said. He'd forced himself to choke down her meals in the interest of rebuilding their friendship, but it wasn't easy.

"Why does she do that?" Cara asked.

"It's a peace offering. Either that, or she's trying to kill me," he teased. "Her cooking is only marginally better than yours."

Cara sputtered, unable to speak, until her mouth dropped into a pink oval and held there.

84

What? Had he said something wrong? Cara loved to joke about her horrible culinary skills. "You said your flatbread could end life on Earth."

She didn't laugh as he'd expected. Redness rose in her cheeks, continuing all the way to her hairline. She clenched her jaw and ground out, "I've got to go," then disconnected. He tried to summon her again, but she denied the transmission.

Great bleeding gods, what had he done?

Aelyx didn't pretend to comprehend the workings of the human female mind. He closed his eyes and replayed their conversation, which seemed to have gone awry when Syrine announced dinner was ready. Could that be it? Was Cara threatened because another female had offered him a meal? That seemed ridiculous, even for a human, but what did he know?

He decided to ask David.

Aelyx found his bodyguard in the living area, sitting by an open window on a chair he'd dragged over from the dining room. An icy breeze swirled through the penthouse as David used a magazine to fan a light haze of smoke outside. Smiling, the boy nodded toward Syrine in the kitchen and whispered, "At least she didn't set off the fire alarm this time."

Syrine peeked her head through the doorway and caught Aelyx's eye. *I'll bring your l'ina to the table. I think I finally got it right!*

Aelyx smiled, to match her excitement, while his heart sank. Judging by the smell, she hadn't "gotten it right" at all.

David tried to hide a chuckle. "I don't know whether to pity you or hate you."

"Hate me?" Aelyx asked as he took a seat in front of the coffee table. "I should share my supper with you. Then you'd know where to direct your loathing."

"Yeah, last night's dinner looked like charcoal briquettes," David said. "But damn, man. Look how many chicks fall at your feet." He listed them on his fingers. "You've got Cara waiting on L'eihr; Syrine busting her cute little butt in the kitchen; and on any given day, a hundred groupies sending you their panties." He pointed to a postal delivery crate, piled high with envelopes and packages. "And I'd know—I screen the mail."

"Really?" Underwear as a form of correspondence? Human behavior truly confounded him sometimes. "Thanks for reminding me why I don't read fan letters." Aelyx hooked a thumb toward the kitchen. "As for Syrine, we're friends. And barely that."

David stopped waving his magazine, his face brightening. "You sure?"

"Completely." Aelyx tapped the side of his head. "We communicate from here, remember? She thinks of me as a brother. I'd sense it if she felt differently."

"Huh. You don't say . . ." David tipped his head, appraising Syrine as she crossed the room with a plate balanced on her forearm and utensils in both hands.

Aelyx recognized the glazed-over look in his friend's eyes. "Save your efforts," he whispered. "She hates humans."

David continued watching her as a crooked grin tugged at his mouth. "That's because she doesn't know me yet. Just wait till I unleash my charm."

The boy's unfailing confidence reminded Aelyx of why he'd wandered out here. "Can I ask you something? You seem to know a lot about females."

"Yeah," David said with a smirk. "And the first thing I can tell you is they don't like being called females. Just say *girls.*"

"Okay, then. Girls." Aelyx took the plate Syrine offered and thanked her. "I think Cara's angry with me, but I'm not sure why." He used his fork to poke at a chunk of blackened meat. "She kept asking why Syrine was cooking for me. Could that be it?"

David snorted a condescending laugh, making Aelyx regret that he'd asked. "Are you serious?"

"Yes."

"Of course she's mad." David softened his tone and pointed at the mail crate. "Dude, women send you more than lacy thongs. You got six marriage proposals and a dozen abduction requests last week. Your girlfriend is on another planet while you're here—surrounded by horny chicks—and now the girl you're *living* with is making you dinner. Can you blame Cara for feeling insecure?"

Aelyx hadn't thought of it that way, but when he considered David's argument, he guessed he understood how Cara felt. But she didn't have any competition for his heart. How could he make her see that?

"It doesn't help that Syrine's beautiful," David added with a grin at the object of his unrequited infatuation. "She'd make any girl jealous."

Syrine rolled her eyes and locked gazes with Aelyx. *Does it really upset Cara that I prepare meals for us? What an odd reaction. How else does she expect us to eat?*

Aelyx tried to block his thoughts, but a swirl of malodorous steam wafted up from his plate and turned his stomach. Unbidden, his distaste flowed into Syrine's mind.

Oh, gods. Her eyes flew wide. *You hate my supper! You've only been eating it to appease me!* Without giving him a chance to explain, she grabbed the plate from his lap and retreated to the kitchen, muttering something about ordering takeout.

David let out a low whistle. "You may not know much about girls, but you're an expert at pissing them off. What just happened?"

Aelyx threw his hands up in frustration. "I was honest."

"Ouch," David said, then sucked a breath through his teeth. "That's the second thing you need to learn about relationships. Telling the truth is overrated."

In a way, Aelyx agreed. If he'd lied to protect Syrine's feelings, he would have spared both of them the awkwardness to follow. But deception tended to compound his problems. The conspiracy to end the alliance had cost Eron his life.

David was wrong. In Aelyx's experience, the truth was *under*rated.

"I'd better go talk to her," Aelyx said.

"Good luck." David resumed fanning smoke out the window. "Oh, and by the way." He glanced at the postal bin. "You should read those. I mean, some of the letters are creepy, but you get nice ones, too." He shrugged. "It could make good PR for you to reach out to your fans while we're still on tour."

Aelyx supposed that David had a point. "I'll go through them later."

He made his way to the kitchen and found Syrine elbow-deep in a suds-filled sink, not washing or rinsing dishes, just staring at the bubbles. When she didn't move, he cleared a spot nearby and sat on the countertop.

"These are primitive appliances," he said, pointing one booted toe at the stove. "And unfamiliar ingredients. You did a far better job than I could have. I've never managed to prepare anything more sophisticated than toast."

She replied with a grunt and snatched a washrag from beside him.

"The meat here is dense," he said. "It cooks differently."

"Not *that* differently," she finally replied, scrubbing an item beneath the water's surface.

"But all skills take time to master." He used a comparison to make her understand. "Would you expect Cara or her brother to braise a flawless roast in our Aegis kitchen?"

Syrine scoffed. "Of course not. They're human."

"You're missing the point. If cooking makes you happy, then keep practicing. But don't do it for me."

She stared into the sink. "I thought it would be a nice gesture. Maybe I shouldn't have bothered."

"You know what *would* be nice?" he asked. "A simple apology for what happened on the transport. That's all I want."

When she grumbled something unintelligible that definitely wasn't an apology, Aelyx gave up and left the kitchen. Syrine surprised him by following close behind, wiping her sudsy hands on her pants.

"I'll help sort your stupid fan mail," she said, avoiding his eyes. "But I won't touch their disgusting undergarments."

He shook his head in bewilderment. Why couldn't she just say she was sorry?

When they rejoined David in the living area, he'd settled on the opposite end of the room, reading his magazine while cool air from the open window cleared the haze. He peered at both of them from above *Sports Illustrated*. "Everything okay?"

In typical fashion, Syrine ignored him and dragged the postal crate into the living room, where she dumped its contents onto the area rug.

"We're going to sort the mail," Aelyx explained. "And we've nominated you as Keeper of the Thongs."

Syrine snickered and lifted a large padded envelope from the heap.

"Uh, hold on." David sat upright and tossed aside his magazine. "I just remembered something."

"This one's heavy," Syrine said, giving it a shake. The clink of metallic pieces jingled from inside the envelope. "No satin or lace in here. I'll take it."

Palms forward, David shouted, "No, wait! I forgot to pre-screen this batch. I always let the bomb-sniffing dogs—" He cut off when Syrine tore open the top of the envelope.

After that, everything happened in an instant.

David bolted off the sofa and grabbed the envelope from Syrine's hands. His combat boots squeaked against hardwood as he raced to the open window and hurled the package outside. Half a second later, a deep *boom* sounded from the street, and the windowpanes along the front of the penthouse rattled. David clutched the wall and panted for breath while Aelyx and Syrine shared a blank stare.

Nobody spoke, aloud or otherwise. Aelyx's mind raced to process what he'd witnessed. He blinked a few times to make sure he hadn't imagined it, but nothing had changed except a new acrid scent on the breeze.

Had Syrine actually opened a bomb?

Her thoughts must have matched his own. *Did that really happen?* she asked.

Yes, I think so.

Still in a fog, Aelyx walked to the window and leaned out, squinting at the pavement several stories below. He couldn't recall which city they were in, but the streetlights illuminated bits of shrapnel littering the sidewalk and confirmed what he wished he could deny. If the sender of that letter had accomplished his goal, those jagged metallic fragments would be embedded in Aelyx's skull. Syrine could have died tonight, simply for opening his mail.

Thank the Mother for David's quick thinking—and for the National Guard's decision to block off the street to foot traffic, or someone could have been hurt when David threw the envelope outside.

The guard detail in the hallway shouted muffled commands and then began ramming the front door. David ran to let them in while Stepha shuffled into the living room, clad in his bathrobe and rubbing his eyes with one fist.

Aelyx froze when he realized the ramifications of this

attack. He recalled what Stepha had told the director-general: *Any further attempts on our lives will terminate all relations between us.*

Bleeding gods, no.

In the wake of Eron's murder, this was mankind's second chance. Once The Way discovered the truth about the bomb, they would abandon the human race to their fate. Cara's people would die—billions of innocents, wiped out as if they'd never existed.

"What was that noise?" Stepha demanded, scanning the suddenly crowded room. "It woke me from a dead slumber."

Aelyx's first instinct was to lie, despite his previous conclusion that the truth was underrated. But no matter how hard he tried, he couldn't summon an explanation to erase the evidence scattered across the street.

David's arms trembled as he stood at attention, addressing his commanding officer. "Sir, the girl got ahold of a fan letter before I had a chance to screen it—from the looks of it, a homemade shrapnel device." His voice cracked, and he paused to draw a calming breath. "I assume full responsibility. I shouldn't have brought in the mail before inspecting it."

All eyes turned to Syrine, who remained kneeling on the rug among hundreds of multicolored envelopes. "You saved me," she whispered to David. "You took the bomb in your own hands." She shook her head in disbelief and repeated, "Right into your own hands."

"Let's go," the commander barked, snapping his fingers. "Everybody out. I want the hotel evacuated." He ordered one of his men to contact the bomb squad, then told David to remain with "the aliens" until they'd reached the safe house.

"But I'm not dressed," Stepha objected. "And I need my sphere."

"Sorry, Ambassador. It'll have to wait." At the commander's signal, a pair of soldiers surrounded Stepha and half escorted, half dragged him into the hallway.

Aelyx's hopes lifted as he took Syrine's hand and followed. Without a com-sphere, the ambassador wouldn't be able to contact The Way. Between now and the time they returned to the suite, Aelyx would have to convince Stepha not to make that call.

"In your own hands," Syrine repeated for the tenth time. She shifted on the safe-house bed, peering at David like she expected antlers to spring from his temples. "You could have lost both your arms and bled to death. Do you know that?"

David broke formation long enough to pinch the bridge of his nose. He sucked in a loud breath and exhaled slowly. "It's my job to protect you. If I'd blown my head off, it would've served me right for being so stupid." He threw a pleading glance at Aelyx before resuming his sentinel at the door.

"It's all right," Aelyx said, handing Syrine his pillow. "We're safe—no harm done." He spoke extra loud for the ambassador's benefit. "Why not close your eyes and practice your *K'imsha*?" The meditative art had often helped her cope with emotional upheaval. If she'd made greater use of it on Earth, she might have avoided her breakdown last month.

In an unusual move, she glanced at David as if seeking his input.

"Definitely," David said with a nod that nearly dislodged his camouflage hat. "Do that kismet thing."

"*K'imsha*," she corrected.

"Right. You should do that."

"Okay. I'll try." But as soon as she placed a pillow beneath her knees and lay back on the bed, she sat up and announced, "I can't. My mind is spinning."

David hung his head while Aelyx turned to Stepha, who sat on the other side of the room brooding in his fluffy robe.

"Ambassador," Aelyx said cautiously. "As Syrine has pointed out, Private Sharpe saved both our lives, at great risk to himself."

"Indeed." Stepha pulled his lapels together, covering his spotted pajamas. "And as I pointed out in the car, Private Sharpe has my gratitude." He lowered his brows and asked, *What is it you wish to say to me, brother?*

Since Aelyx couldn't lie, he figured he should get to the point. *I'm concerned that The Way will misinterpret tonight's events and prematurely call us home.*

There's nothing to misinterpret, Stepha said. *This marks the third attempt on your life.*

Actually, the fourth, but who was counting? *We're safe . . . because of a human. Would The Way leave him to die?*

Perhaps, Stepha said. *Or they may recruit him for the colony and let the rest of his kind face a well-deserved extinction. Regardless, they will hear of this, and soon.*

Aelyx sensed the ambassador's resolve and knew he couldn't dissuade him. It was time to change strategies. *Then*

I request an audience with The Way to plead my case. It's my right as a citizen.

Absolutely. Stepha's certainty was clear—he didn't believe Aelyx's petition would sway the Elders. *We can summon them now if you like. We'll speak in our native tongue—the human soldiers won't understand. Do you have your sphere?*

Aelyx kept his sphere in his pocket at all times, and the ambassador knew it. He produced the object and held it up, giving his answer.

Initiate contact, Stepha ordered. *Enter priority code One to ensure they assemble right away.*

Aelyx did as instructed, then set his sphere on the bed-side table and leaned back against the headboard he shared with Syrine. Of the six people in the room—three L'eihrs and three human soldiers—she was the only one whose anxiety matched his own. Her chest rose and fell far too quickly, the restless jiggle of her feet shaking the bed. He took her wrist and pressed two fingers against the pulse racing through her veins.

"Look at me," he whispered. When she did, he asked, *Are you all right?*

Instead of speaking, she bared her consciousness to him. It didn't take long to identify the problem. The bomb scare had done more than frighten Syrine; it had dredged up memories of the day Eron died, when she'd escaped the French guard and fled to her shuttle. Aelyx visualized her actions as if he were there, feeling the pounding of fear in her heart as she ran into the woods, the sting of tears behind her eyes, the suffocating grief of losing Eron, the only boy she'd ever loved. In the weeks that had passed, she'd grown more secure on Earth. Tonight's attack had shattered all that.

We'll never be safe here, she told him. *I want to go home.*

Close your eyes, he said. *Practice your* K'imsha.

He helped her lie flat and watched as she steadied her breathing. She must have succeeded in her mental exercise, because minutes later, her pulse slowed and she fell into a sleeplike trance.

"Is she okay?" David whispered.

Aelyx shrugged. "For now." He wasn't sure about the next time.

Soon after, his com-sphere called to him in the signature high-pitched frequency that announced a message from The Way. Aelyx moved off the bed and whispered his passkey while walking to the other side of the room. He sat in the vacant chair beside Stepha and placed the sphere on the desk in front of them.

Ten bodies flickered to life in miniature form—Jaxen and Aisly sitting in youthful contrast against eight withered Elders. Alona held up two fingers in the standard greeting and spoke for the group. "How can we assist you, brothers?"

Stepha returned the greeting. "When last we spoke, you informed me that an additional attack on our youth would terminate alliance negotiations. It grieves me to report yet another attempted murder."

"Attempted?" Alona asked. "Are you saying the assassins were unsuccessful?"

"Thankfully, yes." Stepha indicated the soldiers standing guard by the door. "Aelyx and Syrine are unharmed. A young guardsman—"

Alona cut him off with a flash of her palm. "Then we shall overlook it."

Stepha's jaw went slack, mirroring Aelyx's shock.

Alona hadn't conferred with her fellow Elders—she'd made up her mind in an instant, without hearing Aelyx's pleas for mercy. This was the response he'd hoped for, but it made no sense. In his eighteen years on L'eihr, The Way had never overlooked a crime.

"I beg your pardon?" Stepha said.

"The young ones are safe," Alona replied. "Negotiations shall continue." She effectively dismissed them by asking, "Do you require further assistance?"

"Uh . . . uh," Stepha stammered. "No."

"May the Sacred Mother watch over and protect you." She lifted two fingers and ended the transmission.

Aelyx and the ambassador shared a look of utter confusion.

Much like his close call with the letter bomb, Aelyx wondered if he'd imagined the entire exchange. Not that he was complaining, but why would L'eihr continue to tolerate acts of terrorism, especially if all they wanted was fresh genetic material? Human DNA was easily acquired, as were colonists.

Aelyx couldn't help wondering if The Way wanted more from mankind than they'd originally claimed. And if that were the case, what did his people truly stand to gain from this alliance?

Chapter Eight

Babies weren't as stinky as Cara remembered. From the top end, they smelled halfway decent.

She buried her nose in a toddler's honey-brown curls and pulled in a sweet breath. The little guy gripped his bedrail and bounced in place, flashing a gummy smile while reaching out to her with his eyes. His thoughts were jumbled, but Cara felt his fascination with her bright orange hair, which he desperately wanted to capture between his fingers. The tiny clone was heart-meltingly cute, not to mention bright. This nursery assignment wasn't so bad. Maybe Cara could handle kids of her own someday . . . like in a couple of decades.

"*Cah*-ra," Elle called from the next crib. "Stop smelling that boy and come help me. This one's sick." She peered down the back of the child's pants and recoiled in disgust. "From both ends."

Cara covered her nose as the stench wafted in her direction.

Never mind about the hypothetical kids. She'd let Troy carry on the Sweeney line. She glanced at the head caretaker for guidance and received an encouraging nod from the old woman.

"Poor little guy." Cara pressed a hand to the boy's forehead. No fever. "Do we need to quarantine him?" The Aegis had strict policies regarding contagious bugs, which made sense, considering the number of kids who lived in close quarters here.

"If it's viral, yes. If it's bacterial or food-borne, no." Elle plucked something from her pocket that looked like a long white spoon wrapped in plastic. "I won't know until I analyze his stool."

Oh, gross. Cara did *not* need that visual.

Poor Elle looked ready to hurl, despite her medical background. Her new position as Constant Alibi meant she accompanied Cara everywhere, even to the bathroom for midnight pit stops. But diaper inspection was above and beyond the call of duty.

"Sorry to get you dragged into this," Cara said, stripping the baby's clothes.

"Not a problem." Elle dipped the collector tool into the baby's diaper. "I needed a rotation in the nursery to complete my medical training." She grimaced while sliding a cap over her sample. "I couldn't avoid it forever."

"Not a fan of kids, huh?"

Elle lifted the baby to the nearby basin and tapped a foot pedal to fill the sink with warm water. "I don't dislike young-lings. I simply have no experience with them."

"None?" Cara removed the boy's dirty sheets and dropped them in the sonic purifier bin. "You never had to babysit?"

Elle laughed, though Cara didn't see what was funny. "Not everyone is suited to work with small children."

Well, sure. Kids were annoying, but if L'eihrs wanted to imitate the human method of reproduction, they needed to learn to care for their young. "Aren't they shutting down the artificial wombs?" Cara asked.

"Our geneticists disabled the wombs months ago." Elle dodged splashes while she washed the baby with all the confidence of a pig at a bacon festival. "Haven't you noticed the absence of newborns?"

"Here, let me." Using her hip, Cara nudged Elle aside and finished the job. "So there won't be any more babies soon? Won't that create a weird generation gap?"

"Not really." Elle opened her medic bag and inserted the spoon tool into a testing device, then sanitized her hands. "The oldest clones are nearly twenty. Next year they'll leave the Aegis for their designated work dormitories, and when they find approved *l'ihans*, we'll deactivate their fertility suppressants."

Cara grabbed a towel from beneath the sink. "What suppressants?"

"The nano-chip beneath your wrist," Elle explained, "also halts your ovulation. When you're approved to breed, I'll scan your wrist and reverse the settings."

Approved to breed? What was she, a prize heifer? "What if I don't want kids?"

Elle handed over a cloth diaper and wrinkled her brow. "Why wouldn't you want to pass on your gifts? Once the child is born, you won't be burdened with it."

Cara had to focus on diapering the baby before he got sick again, but as soon as she secured his hind end, she held him close and whirled to face Elle. "Are you telling me nothing will change—you'll pop out your spawn, then hand them over to the Aegis?"

Elle drew back, lips parting in offense. "You make it sound so sinister. I enjoyed growing up in this Aegis with my peers. I never felt deprived of anything." She patted the baby clutched in Cara's arms. "If you wish to house your offspring, perhaps you'll be permitted to do so on the colony. I've heard they hope to model a more humanistic lifestyle there."

Cara relaxed her death grip on the infant and shuffled to the changing station to dress him. So, assuming she decided to have kids, and assuming The Way approved her request to "breed," she *might* be allowed to keep her children? That was twisted, no matter how Elle tried to spin it.

A small voice whispered, *Maybe Troy's right. Maybe you don't belong here*, but she shook that thought out of her head. It didn't matter—she probably wasn't having kids anyway.

Elle read the results of her test sample and smiled. "Excellent news, it's a food-borne illness." She ruffled the infant's hair and told Cara, "You dress him and replenish his electrolytes while I alert the nursery kitchen staff." Then she violated the Constant Alibi rule by leaving the room.

"That's all right," Cara said to the nearly naked bundle in

her arms. "I can go ten minutes without getting in trouble." She stroked his soft, chubby cheek with one finger. "Can't I, little guy?"

He responded by vomiting down the front of her tunic.

Soft laughter sounded from nearby, and the head caretaker hurried over to take the baby. The woman's face was heavily lined but gentle, her smile a beacon of sunshine in an otherwise bleak afternoon. Unlike most of the older generation, she had life in her eyes, that spark the others had lost. She reminded Cara of her late Grammy O'Shea, so from that moment, Cara dubbed the woman *Gram*.

"You're not a real caretaker until you've been christened in this way," Gram said in a thick accent. With a gentle hand, she pushed Cara toward the hall. "You'll find clean tunics in the washroom."

When Cara had wiped down her chest with a damp cloth and changed clothes, she returned to the nursery. She scanned the vast room for Gram, beginning with the transparent cribs, pressed flush against one another with see-through dividers so the babies could socialize. From there, she turned her gaze to the various stations—specialized places for feeding, changing, bathing, intellectual stimulation, open play, and even physical contact. Centuries of research had taught L'eihrs the precise amount of touch a child needed to maximize brain development, and caretakers didn't dole out a minute longer than necessary.

Cara noted the absence of swings, cradles, and rocking chairs. L'eihrs were big on "self-soothing" and didn't want the babies to grow dependent on motion for comfort. There were no newborns here at the moment, but according to rumor, they cried a lot for the first two months, then kind of gave up the fight. Thinking about it made Cara's heart ache. It wasn't right, breaking a person's spirit fresh out of the package like that.

"Here, Miss Sweeney." Gram waved her over to the front window, where the afternoon sun filtered inside and bathed a pair of infants lying face-up on a floor mat.

Cara strode across the nursery, still searching for her sick baby. She eventually found him at one of the feeding stations, suckling clear fluid from a plastic sack attached to the wall. She motioned toward him. "I can feed him his electrolytes."

Gram appeared confused at first, but then understanding dawned on her face. "Oh, no, Miss Sweeney." She shook her head as if Cara had proposed a blood sacrifice. "We never hold the children while they feed. It's important they don't associate food with comfort."

Just add this to the list of *Top Ten Reasons Why L'eihr Is Whack-a-Doodle.* "But food *is* comforting," Cara said. The scent of Mom's gingerbread still had the power to transport Cara to her happy place. And nothing took the edge off an awful day like a few squares of dark chocolate.

"That may be true on Earth," Gram said, "but here, food is fuel for our bodies. Nothing more. Our meals nourish us, and while we might enjoy the experience, it's not meant as a form of pleasure or a means of finding solace."

Maybe if L'eihr food weren't so tasteless, Gram would feel differently.

But the woman was wrong about L'eihrs not finding solace through familiar foods. During the exchange, Aelyx had lit up every time Mom made roast for supper—not because of its nutrients, but because it tasted like *l'ina*. Each bite had nourished him in a way that had nothing to do with protein. That's why Cara had flipped out when Syrine waltzed into Aelyx's bedroom to announce she'd cooked his favorite supper. There was love in a good meal—not that Cara had ever produced what she'd call a *good* meal, but still.

Cara kept those observations to herself while turning toward her sick baby. "But he's not feeling well. He could use an extra cuddle, don't you think?"

The smile on Gram's face said, *Silly human*, but she conceded the battle. "You may hold him once he's drained the supplement bag."

While Cara waited, she knelt on the mat and smiled at the pair of infants, their tiny legs kicking out, fists balled, eyes wide and peering at the dust motes dancing in the sunlight. She noticed they shared identical features—their lips slightly asymmetrical, the same cleft dimpling both their chins.

"Are these twins?" Cara asked. She hadn't met a pair of identical clones until now. Aelyx had said the geneticists never used the same archive twice in a generation.

"You're very observant," Gram answered. "These were the last younglings incubated in the artificial wombs."

"But why two? Are they gifted?"

"You could say that." Gram stared into empty air and zoned out, the ghost of a grin on her lips. "I remember the last clone from that archive. He grew up in this Aegis. Such a gentle boy, always smiling. The others gravitated toward him—he was a friend to everyone. Empathy was his gift."

From the way Gram spoke about the boy in past tense, Cara wasn't sure whether he'd moved to the work dormitories or if he'd died.

"I believe you met him briefly during his stay on Earth," Gram continued. "His name was Eron."

The hair on the back of Cara's neck prickled, and she glanced around the room to make sure Elle hadn't returned. The last thing her roommate needed right now was to meet the double reincarnation of her dead *l'ihan*. Cara tried to imagine how she'd feel in the same situation, but she couldn't wrap her mind around it.

Cara gazed at the baby nearest to her. "I can't believe this is Eron."

"He's not," Gram said, her chrome eyes lingering on the child. "This is Mica." She stroked the other infant's arm. "And this is Ilar." She delivered a pointed look. "Eron is dead. We can generate new offspring from that archive, but they will be shaped by their own experiences. Each clone's path is distinctive. The young man you and I knew as Eron is gone forever."

Naturally, Elle chose that moment to rejoin them. The word *Eron* moved silently on her lips while she blinked in confusion. Moments later, the pieces must have clicked into place, because she glanced back and forth between the twins, the color gone from her face. Her throat worked as she swallowed, her eyes welling, her grief forcing its way to the surface. But in true Elle fashion, she stuffed down her emotions and stubbornly set her jaw.

"Elle and I should go," Cara said to Gram. "Maybe tomorrow we can work with the older children." *Away from the nursery and reminders of Eron's crooked smile.* "I'd like to learn some basics of science with them."

"Of course," Gram said. She might have been talking to Cara, but she regarded Elle when she spoke. "You can't move ahead until you face what impedes you."

Definitely a message for Elle—but one best pondered from the privacy of their room. Cara pushed off the mat and gave her roommate a gentle tug. Elle stiffened at the bodily contact, but she didn't complain when Cara linked their arms and led the way out of the nursery. Instead of the main elevators, they took the secondary stairwell on the far end of the Aegis and made their way down to the first floor.

They let the echo of their boots fill the silence, Elle deflecting each of Cara's glances in a message that she didn't want to talk. Cara recognized that avoidance tactic. She'd used it years ago, when Mom had begun her second round of chemo and Dad stopped coming home from his hospital visits. Then Troy had snuck off to join the Marines, snapping Cara's last tether to normalcy. Her friends had known better than to ask if she was okay.

But when they reached their hallway, it was Cara's turn to fight for composure. Sitting in the middle of the floor was Troy's luggage: two military-issue duffel bags and a black trunk with SWEENEY, USMC stenciled on the lid.

Cara's boot soles clung to the floor. Until now, she'd managed to block out Troy's departure date in hopes that he wouldn't abandon her this time.

Troy's door hissed aside and he hauled another bag into the hallway. Then the *real* blow came—a cold shot to Cara's chest that made it hard to breathe.

He'd cut his hair.

Troy's loose black curls were gone, replaced by the standard military "high and tight." She remembered his words to Dad on Christmas morning, *When in Rome.* . . . In Troy's camouflage uniform and buzz cut, dog tags clinking together against his chest, not a trace of L'eihr remained on him.

Troy's eyes widened when they met hers. He stood stockstill without saying a word.

"What's the matter?" Elle asked.

Of course Elle wouldn't understand. L'eihrs didn't form family bonds. Genetics only tied them together as strongly as whatever friendship they formed, if any. She and Aelyx were more like buddies than brother and sister.

"It's fine," Cara said, keeping her gaze fixed on Troy. "Go ahead. I'll meet you in a minute."

Troy took abrupt interest in his bootlaces, crouching to retie the left one. "Hey," he finally said. "Glad I caught you."

Glad I caught you. That implied he would have left without saying good-bye if their paths hadn't crossed.

"Aw, come on, Pepper." Still bent low, he scrubbed a palm over his fuzzy head. "Don't look at me like that."

How should she look at him? With a smile and an easy wave good-bye?

At her silence, he pushed to standing. "I don't have a choice. Sooner or later I have to go." His blue eyes bored into hers. "Because I don't belong here. Neither of us does."

"I can make a life on the colony," she insisted. It tasted like a lie, but she had to keep believing.

"Come home with me," Troy said. "There's nothing for you to pack. You know everyone misses you, especially Mom."

His offer tempted her more than she wanted to admit, but she shook her head. "I can't." The L'eihrs had almost called off the alliance after Eron died. She was the one who'd convinced them to try again. "The alliance is too important."

"Plus, you're in love, right?" Troy mocked her with his tone. "You're staying here because you've found The One."

"That, too." She wrapped both arms around herself and tried to blink away the moisture blurring her vision. "Either way, I can't go."

Troy turned his face aside and swore loudly. He splayed his hands. "The Marines issue orders, not suggestions. What do you expect me to do, just tell them no?"

A lump formed in Cara's throat, but she swallowed it and refused to make a sound. He'd leave, no matter what she said. There was no use begging.

"What?" he pressed. "What am I supposed to do?"

"I don't know," she choked out. She'd made the decision to join this fledgling colony, but Troy hadn't. She had no right to ask him to stay.

Troy cursed again and braced himself against the wall, letting his forehead *thunk* against the stucco. For several seconds, he fell silent. Then he made a sudden move for one of his duffel bags. Cara sniffled, preparing to watch him grab his luggage and bolt for the lobby.

But he didn't.

Troy unzipped his bag and rummaged inside until he found his com-sphere. He mumbled his passkey and connected with his unit on Earth. When his commander picked up the line, Troy heaved an aggravated sigh. "Sorry, sir. I missed my transport. I'll have to catch the next one in a couple weeks."

While Cara listened to her brother mutter excuses and apologies, hot tears leaked down her cheeks and made her blind. A few of her classmates passed in a sodden blur, but she didn't care whether they shook their heads and called her an emotional fool. Let them think what they wanted. She wasn't alone—at least for now—and that was all that mattered.

Troy shoved his sphere into his duffel and stood, gripping his hips. "I hope you're happy. He'll have my ass when I get back."

Cara didn't wait another second to lock both arms around his neck. She buried her wet face in his shoulder and took in his scent of cinnamon Altoids and shaving cream. Knowing he'd push away soon, she filled her lungs with him and held it in.

"All right, all right." He gave her a few token pats on the back and made a show of glancing at the clones passing them in the hallway. "The ladies are going to get the wrong idea. If I'm stuck here for two more weeks, I might as well make the best of it."

Laughing, Cara released him and used her tunic to blot her eyes. "I'd hate to hurt your game, Casanova."

"Oh, I got game!"

She shrugged. "You *smell* gamey, so there's that."

He shot her the bird and palmed his keypad. Together, they dragged all his luggage back inside, and then Cara gave him her extra nutrient packet.

"Thanks." He nodded his approval and yanked her braid. "Dorkus."

Cara beamed at the insult. She never thought it could sound so sweet. "Any time."

Inspiration struck that night, and she uploaded a new blog post. She knew Troy wouldn't read it—he never visited her site—but she didn't care. She had a message of hope to share with siblings across the universe.

Subscribe [Archive] [Recent Entries] [About Me]

Invaded

MAY THE SOURCE BE WITH YOU

WEDNESDAY, JANUARY 12
Big Brothers: Life Beyond the Wedgie

Unless you're an only child, you are doubtlessly aware of the varied forms of sibling torture: the noogie, the wet willy, the towel snap, and the ever-maddening "I'm not touching you," in which a spit-laden index finger is held one millimeter from your nose. Friends, I'm no stranger to a good pantsing. I quit wearing drawstring shorts after my brother tugged down my Umbros in front of the entire youth league soccer team. But I'm here to tell you there is life beyond the swirlie. You may not believe it now, but sibling tormentors actually grow up and even become—dare I say it?—useful!

Nonsense, you say?

Just keep reading.

My brother is a United States Marine. (OOH-RAH!) He joined the service two years ago, and I haven't seen much of him since. But when he found out the L'eihrs picked me for the exchange, he volunteered to come here and learn the culture so he could serve as my mentor. In the past two weeks, he's taught me:

• How to change the pitch setting on my translator earpiece so my professors sound like helium-huffing Oompa Loompas. Alien teachers are a lot less intimidating when they're channeling the Lollipop Guild.

• Which bugs NOT to squash. There's an insect here whose self-defense mechanism is secreting a stench that makes skunk musk smell like Chanel No. 5. My brother discovered this the hard way when he whacked one in the lobby and the whole Aegis had to be evacuated. He could have let me make the same mistake, but he didn't.

• That despite years of jackassery, he cares about me. That might sound cheesy, but it's true. My brother claims he volunteered for this position so he could be the first human to travel at light speed, but I think there was a lot more to it. He's proven that whether in Midtown or on L'eihr, he won't let anyone torture his kid sister. Only *he* gets to do that. And I kind of love him for it.

So to all of you back home, hug your siblings tonight—and not so you can tape "Kick me!" signs to their backs.

Posted by Cara Sweeney

Chapter Nine

Aelyx never expected to become so good at cheating death. As a child, he'd resented his assignment as translator, a seemingly dull occupation. He'd wanted a position in the genetics labs, or perhaps aboard the voyager shuttles, cataloguing new planets and unfamiliar species. He'd craved adventure and discovery. Who would've guessed that his job manipulating mere words would result in so many assassination attempts?

The most recent attack had been rather creative. After the bomb squad had swept and secured the building, Aelyx and his pseudo-family had returned to their suite and settled at the dining room table for supper. Syrine had abandoned her interest in cooking—thank gods—so they'd resumed their habit of ordering takeout. She'd just brought a spring roll to her lips when David stopped her and asked who'd ordered the meal.

Syrine had assumed Aelyx placed the order. Aelyx figured it'd been Syrine. The ambassador insisted he hadn't called for delivery—he didn't even like Szechuan. David boxed up the dinner and sent it to a government facility, where it'd tested positive for strychnine. Since then, Aelyx had taken it upon himself to learn how to cook.

Again, Stepha had reported the crime to Alona, and again, she'd pardoned the act, citing *no harm, no foul.* It was as if she didn't care whether Aelyx lived or died. She'd even gone a step further, insisting they double their efforts to reform his and Syrine's reputations and endear them to HALO members. Now Aelyx had a government-appointed crisis communications specialist and an image consultant named Blaze.

An image consultant! As if a trendy haircut would fix everything.

But strangest of all, HALO continued to deny responsibility for the attempts on his life. Nothing made sense anymore. It was as if he'd fallen down the rabbit hole in that popular children's story and landed in an alternate dimension . . . in which he had an image consultant.

"Damn, I'm good," Blaze said as she added a dollop of sticky goop to his hair. She had one of those faces that made it impossible to guess her age, but she pinched his cheek like a grandmother. "Of course, it's not hard making you pretty, is it, hon?"

Gods, kill me now.

"Are we done?" Aelyx gestured toward the living room, where his next interview was set to begin. This time the government had flown Cara's parents to Kansas City to participate. Or at least that's where Aelyx thought he was. He tended to lose track these days.

Blaze patted his chest. "Knock 'em dead, hot stuff."

On his way to the living room, Aelyx crossed paths with Sharon Taylor, the journalist who'd conducted his exchange program interviews in the fall. Clad in her signature pink suit, she devoured him with her gaze while a predatory grin curved her mouth.

"Aelyx," she practically purred. "You look delish, honey." She twirled one finger toward his head. "Love what you did with the hair. The ponytail was hot, but this is edgier. My audience is going to eat you up with a spoon and fight each other to lick the bowl."

He tried to hide his annoyance. "Thanks for accommodating us on such short notice."

"Oh, please!" she cried with a wave of her red-tipped fingers. "I should be thanking *you*." She indicated for him to sit on the sofa with Bill and Eileen Sweeney while she picked her way over wires and around crew members to the adjacent armchair.

Eileen threw her arms around Aelyx's neck before his backside had met the sofa. She brought with her the scent of lilacs and a warmth that he'd missed more than he had realized. She took his face between her palms. "It's so good to see—"

"Hands off," Sharon interrupted. "You'll make his skin shiny."

Eileen obediently released him while Bill extended a hand

for a firm shake. If the man harbored any ill will against Aelyx for stealing Cara away from her home, he didn't let it show. Bill's eyes gleamed with the respect Aelyx had regularly seen there, even if he hadn't always deserved it.

"We miss having you at the house," Bill said. "Now that you're gone, there's no one to organize the canned vegetables by dietary fiber content."

"Or rearrange the plates in the dishwasher," Eileen added.

Aelyx had missed them, too. When he'd lived with the Sweeneys, it was the first time he'd felt like he belonged to a family. "I'm glad we have this chance to—"

Sharon cut him off with a clap. "Everyone ready?" She pulled a gold pen from her breast pocket and pointed it at them. "I have dinner reservations at six."

"Charming as always," Bill muttered under his breath.

When the cameraman flashed the signal, Sharon began. "Good evening, America. I promised you an interview with a special guest, and, boy, am I about to deliver! I'm joined tonight by our favorite L'eihr exchange student, and my sixth sense tells me he has big news to share." Crossing her legs at the ankles, she angled her body toward Aelyx. "So tell me: does this big news involve a secret wedding?"

Aelyx played the part of a reluctant celebrity, relaxing his posture and favoring Sharon with a good-natured chuckle. "Now, Ms. Taylor, you know humans and L'eihrs can't legally wed."

"Besides," Bill coolly interjected, "Cara's too young to get married."

"But not too young for interplanetary travel." Sharon arched a brow. "An unaccompanied minor jetting off to a foreign galaxy? Not many parents would approve of that."

Aelyx didn't say so, but Cara's parents *hadn't* approved. In the wake of Eron's death, The Way had given them no say in the matter.

"She wasn't unaccompanied," Eileen said with a smile that didn't reach her eyes. "Her brother was with her, and Aelyx's leaders. We knew they would take care of our little girl."

"Mmm." In that one simple utterance, Sharon made her judgment clear. "You're very trusting, aren't you?"

Bill ground his teeth but nodded with a grin. The PR specialist had explained that parts of the interview had to appear harsh, or it wouldn't seem genuine. Sharon would ask a few uncomfortable questions, but when the hour was done, she'd surrender her footage to the government, who would edit the material in their favor.

"And Aelyx," Sharon went on, "there's some negative chatter about you and the other two exchange students. Wasn't it discovered that Eron"—she touched her chest—"God rest his soul, tampered with the water supply? When they searched his bedroom, they found contaminated water samples and all kinds of strange equipment."

"That's not true," Aelyx said. "Those analytics were sanctioned by your government."

"Then why don't you tell me what *is* true?"

He hesitated, wanting desperately to do what she'd asked. But The Way still hadn't responded to his request. Without their approval, he was compelled to remain quiet.

"Oh, come on," she crooned. "I can tell it's weighing on you. Go ahead and get it off your chest." Smiling in anticipation, she tapped her pen against one knee. "Confession does wonders for the soul."

Even if Aelyx believed in souls, he would doubt that Sharon Taylor possessed one. However, he began to take her suggestion seriously. The first step in earning forgiveness was honesty, and he couldn't mend human-L'eihr relations by continuing to lie. If the PR specialists disagreed, they would simply cut the footage later. Stepha wasn't here, so there was no one to stop him.

"A confession," he said. "All right. My friends and I have been accused of many things—among them, blighting local crops and poisoning the water supply." Taking a deep breath, he leaned forward and rested both forearms against his thighs. "One of those allegations is true."

Sharon's eyes brightened and she nearly dropped her pen. "Which one?"

"The first. We used parasitic seedlings to stunt the crop growth in Midtown, Bordeaux, and Lanzhou."

Eileen gasped beside him while Bill's lips parted. Aelyx offered an apologetic glance before dropping his gaze to the carpet.

"Why would you do that?" Sharon asked.

"Because humans and L'eihrs have more in common than you think," Aelyx said. "Stubbornness, prejudice, fear of the unfamiliar—my generation feels these emotions, too. We couldn't understand why the Elders wanted to ally with humans. And because we opposed the alliance, we contrived to sabotage it." The admission felt good, as if an invisible weight had lifted from his shoulders. "It was a decision we made together in secret, but we agree now it was a terrible mistake. We were wrong about mankind."

"What changed your mind?"

"Basically, I came to know humans on a personal level. The more time I spent here, the more I learned that the criminals dominating your news stories are a misrepresentation of your kind." Aelyx dipped his head and glanced into the camera. "And I fell in love. I wasn't expecting that."

"Ah, yes," Sharon said, drawing out the words. "With Cara Sweeney, your host student. I saw sparks fly at every interview, but you both denied the rumors." She paused as if waiting for a response.

"We wanted to keep our private lives to ourselves."

"Hmm." She shook her head and pointed that damned pen at him. "So many lies, Aelyx. So many secrets. How do we know you're telling the truth now?"

"Because I have no reason to lie. I want to make up for what I've done—to help repair the damage I've caused so we can join together and—"

"Where is Cara?" Sharon interrupted.

Aelyx stared at her for a few beats, trying to discern her motive behind the asinine question. Sharon knew full well where Cara was. The whole world knew. "At this very moment? I imagine she's in her cot, dreaming of hot fudge sundaes and debate tournaments."

"Isn't it true," Sharon asked coldly, "that the other two

human exchange students refused to leave Earth because they feel threatened?"

"I haven't spoken with them, so I can't say. But breaking the contract was their prerogative. The Elders would never force—"

"Cara was valedictorian of her class," Sharon cut in. "Why would she leave now, four months before the end of the school year?" Sharon's assistant handed her a piece of paper. She glanced at it and set it facedown on the sofa. "My records show that she failed to earn the credits she needed to graduate. I find it odd that such a dedicated student would simply walk away from her diploma, especially since her exchange wasn't scheduled to begin until next fall."

Aelyx fought to maintain a calm expression. "You're forgetting an important detail."

"Which is?"

"Cara and I fled her home because a riotous mob stormed the property—hours after the Patriots of Earth tortured and killed my best friend. We escaped in my shuttle and joined the main transport while her father stayed behind to distract the crowd." Aelyx nodded toward the man. "He barely survived the attack."

Bill spoke up from the other end of the sofa. "He's right. Where are you going with this?"

Sharon ignored him. "But why not send Cara home the next day? It didn't take long for the military to end the riots."

Aelyx didn't have an answer for that. In truth, Cara *had* wanted to return to Earth, but The Way insisted on sending her to L'eihr to punish him. It was one of their nonnegotiable conditions for continuing alliance talks in the wake of Eron's murder.

"Isn't it true," Sharon went on, "that you kidnapped Cara to avenge your friend's death—an eye for an eye, a life for a life? Maybe she refused to serve out the exchange, and you couldn't bear the thought of losing her. There's a thin line between love and obsession. Did you force her to leave with you?"

Aelyx sat bolt upright. "Of course not! I could summon her on my com-sphere right now and she'd tell you herself."

"It's true," Eileen said. "We talk to her almost every—"

"Maybe," Sharon interrupted. "But I imagine she'd say anything if she were scared enough."

"This is ridiculous, even for you." Aelyx should have known better than to listen to this relentless shrew. "Cara will visit Earth in the spring. Until then, the topic is closed."

A chilling smile uncurled across Sharon's lips. "Not quite." She pointed her pen at the television. "A new witness has come forward. I think we deserve to hear his side of the story."

One of the production assistants angled the television toward Aelyx and began attaching various cords to it. Then, like an image from a nightmare, Marcus Johnson's smug face appeared onscreen, the caption below claiming, MIDTOWN ATTACK VICTIM TO SUE L'EIHRS FOR DAMAGES.

Aelyx's body tensed and flashed white-hot. Victim? The last time he'd seen Marcus, the boy had broken half of Cara's ribs and fractured her skull. Marcus was no victim, though Aelyx would welcome the opportunity to rectify that.

"Marcus," Sharon said, "you were the last person to see Cara Sweeney before she disappeared. Tell us what happened."

Marcus pressed his lips together and raked a hand through his shaggy brown hair as if traumatized. "I was patrolling the woods with my girlfriend and my buddy Eric. We saw the alien dragging Cara toward his ship. She tried fighting him off, but then he stunned her with this laser thing, and she just kind of froze up, like this." He grimaced, tongue lolling aside, looking every bit like the imbecile he was. "Then we jumped in to help her."

"And that's when Aelyx attacked you?" Sharon asked.

Marcus hung his head and nodded. "He grabbed my shotgun and used it to bust my knee. The doctors say I'll never get full use back. I lost my lacrosse scholarship—that's why I'm suing the L'eihrs. They should have to pay for what he did." Marcus seemed to remember the other characters in his lie. "He shot Eric. Brandi got away, but she's real shook up. She might need therapy."

Brandi needed therapy, all right. Anyone who would mate with Marcus Johnson was certifiably insane. Aelyx spoke while he still had the chance. "Ask Marcus why he was patrolling the woods with a firearm. He and his fellow Patriots were hunting me." Eric had tried saving Cara, but he would never swear to it and face the Patriots' retribution.

"So you admit to attacking Marcus?" Sharon said.

That's when the head of PR stepped in, literally pulling the plug on the interview. His nostrils flared as he jerked each power cord from the main extension. "Check your footage at the door and get out," the man said to Sharon. "This isn't what we agreed to. I don't know what you were thinking, but your career is over."

Sharon ordered her crew to obey, and in twenty minutes they were gone without another word. Aelyx sat back and drew a deep breath, puzzling at how quickly the interview had spiraled out of control. Thank the gods it hadn't aired live.

He was still thinking about it later that night as he plotted ways to keep Stepha from finding out. But in order to do that, he'd have to avoid using Silent Speech with the ambassador, which alone would be suspicious. Aelyx was tired of politics, public relations, and lies.

He just wanted to go home to Cara.

"You're thinking about *Cah*-ra, aren't you?" Syrine peered through his open doorway to where he lay, stretched out on his bed. "I can tell by the moronic look in your eyes."

Aelyx turned his head. "Oh? Like the way you looked at our bodyguard tonight at supper?" He used a high-pitched voice to mimic her hilarious attempts at flirty banter. "I made iced tea, David, sweetened just the way you like it. Shall I pour you a glass, or would you rather lick each drop from my naked flesh?"

She gasped, whipping her head to check over both shoulders. Not that David spoke L'eihr. "Shut up, you *fasher*!"

Aelyx smiled. This was fun. He twirled a lock of hair around one finger and batted his lashes. "Oh, David, you took that bomb right into your hands. Is there anything *else* you'd like to get your hands on?"

She rushed inside and proceeded to beat him with an extra pillow. He couldn't help laughing. "Guard my body, David," he squeaked. "It's all yours!"

"You idiot!" She pummeled him until feathers floated in the air, but she didn't deny her attraction to the boy. There was no point. Aelyx had sensed it during Silent Speech the morning after the bomb scare.

"I told you," Aelyx chortled, scooting aside to dodge a knee to his ribs, "he feels the same way. You should talk to him." A tryst could be a good distraction for Syrine. "Maybe you can lure him to the colony." He was joking, though. He knew she'd never take it that far.

Syrine made a disgusted noise from the back of her throat. "I'm not one of your hedonistic humans. Perhaps I can't help my body's reaction to him, but I can control whether I act on it—which I won't!"

Aelyx used his pillow to whack her midsection. "Why fight it? You know you want him." All teasing halted when Aelyx's com-sphere summoned him for his nightly call with Cara. He made a reach for his bedside table. "Okay, enough," he told Syrine.

Understanding flashed in Syrine's eyes and a maniacal smile uncurled across her lips. She made a lightning grab at his sphere, beating him to it. "Is this what you want?" With an evil sneer, she dangled the sphere within his reach, then jerked it back. "To talk to your *l'ihan*?" Now it was her turn to mock him in a low, breathy voice. "Oh, *Elire*, I love you so! I want to make a thousand half-breed babies with you, my fiery-haired goddess!"

"Give it here," he ordered, trying to take it by force. "This is the only time she can talk."

Syrine hit the mattress, giggling and making kissing noises. "When can we start practicing, *Caaaah*-ra?"

When he couldn't pry the sphere from Syrine's fingers, he shouted his password and untangled himself from her limbs so Cara didn't get the wrong idea. Cara's image appeared upside-down on the ceiling, the far wall, the floor, as she jerked across the room with each of Syrine's movements.

"What the hell?" Cara asked.

Syrine finally surrendered the sphere. "Hello, *Cah*-ra. Aelyx is simply dying to talk with you."

Cara settled in cross-legged miniature atop Aelyx's bedspread, taking them both in—Syrine sprawled out beside him and shaking with laughter, a few feathers in her hair, pillows strewn about. But this game wasn't funny anymore. Syrine didn't understand human jealousy or how easily seeds of doubt could take root in Cara's mind.

"It's true." Aelyx addressed Cara but threw a sharp look at Syrine. "I can't wait to tell you about Syrine's new lover."

Syrine pushed upright. "You wouldn't."

"I would."

"But you started it!"

"And I'll finish it."

Syrine heeded his warning and left the room without another word. She did, however, sneak in a dirty glare at him before pulling the door shut.

"Did I interrupt something?" Cara brushed off a bit of lint from her tunic in a carefree gesture, but she couldn't disguise the irritation in her voice. "Because I can call back tomorrow if you'd rather finish your pillow fight."

"It's not like that." Aelyx swept the feathers to the floor and hid the evidence, though he'd done nothing wrong.

"I don't know," Cara said, staring into her lap. "Syrine seems to spend a lot of time in your bedroom . . . when she's not cooking for you."

"I cook for myself now." Though he chose not to tell her why. The government had gone to great lengths to cover up news of the bombing, and if Cara knew about the constant attempts on his life, it would only add to her worry. "Syrine and I were roommates in the Aegis, remember? We're just starting to mend our friendship. I wish you'd trust me."

Cara didn't reply, but the color staining her cheeks betrayed embarrassment or shame, he couldn't tell which.

"*Elire*," he said softly, "look at me."

She peeked at him through her lashes.

"You're the only one I love. I've shown you. You've felt my emotions, the way I care for you so deeply it hurts. Do you remember that feeling—how strong it was?" When she nodded, he asked, "Do you think that's changed in the last few weeks?"

She shook her head. "You're right. Syrine's just a friend, and logically, I get that. But I'm in a weird place right now. I feel like an egg with a crack in my shell, and I don't know how to hold it together."

He wasn't sure he understood, so he told her, "I miss you."

That seemed to get through to her. Her face broke into a sad smile. "Me, too. More than you know. When something weird or funny happens, I look for you because you're the first person I want to tell. But then I remember you're not here, and it stings." She rubbed her chest to show him. "Every single time."

"I miss touching you," he said, extending a finger as if to caress her cheek. "It's strange to think the feel of your skin ever made me uncomfortable. Now it's all I want."

Her smile brightened. "Know what I miss most about you?" In her excitement, she didn't wait for his answer. "Your smell."

"My what?" That wasn't what he wanted to hear. He'd hoped she missed touching him, too. "That doesn't say much about my kissing skills, does it?"

"You don't need to worry about that. You've got skills." She bit her lip, then added, "Mad skills."

That was better. Aelyx felt himself sitting a bit taller. "But still, my scent? Of all the things to miss about me . . ."

"It's amazing. Sweet and spicy with a dash of something else, like the way the woods smell after a long rain." She closed her eyes and inhaled, going dreamy. Her door hissed open, but she paid no heed to whoever entered her room. "I used to wonder if all L'eihrs smelled like that, but it's just you. I wish I had one of your shirts to sleep in. Then I could pretend you were with me."

"Oh, God," groaned a male voice from her room. "Excuse me while I puke and die." When the male strode into view, it took Aelyx a moment to identify him as Cara's brother. Troy had practically shaved his head. He shot Aelyx a glare and sneered, "Hey, *Alex*."

Aelyx ignored the jab. "Did you really miss your transport?" Instead of responding, Troy shoved half the contents of a nutrient pack into his mouth.

"Um," Cara said, "he sort of missed it accidentally on purpose."

Of course he did. *Humans.* "Well, I suggest you don't miss it again. The Patriots think you're being detained against your will, and my crisis communications specialist wants you to set the record straight."

"Your crisis communications specialist?" Cara said.

"Don't ask."

"No worries," Troy said. "If I miss my ship again, I might as well stay here, because my CO will put his boot down my throat."

"Then I'll make sure you forget," Cara said, poking her brother in the arm.

Troy flicked the side of her head, but something poignant and bittersweet passed between them. It only lasted an instant, but Aelyx noticed. Until now, he hadn't realized the intensity of their sibling bond, and he suddenly understood why Troy had "accidentally on purpose" missed his transport home. Cara must have been struggling to adjust to Aegis life more than she'd let on during her nightly calls. She was keeping things from him, just like he'd hidden the latest attacks from her.

The knowledge put a damper on the rest of their conversation, and after they disconnected, Aelyx felt the need to do more. He kept imagining how Cara would feel when her brother left on the next transport. Aelyx couldn't be there to comfort her, but if he hurried, he might be able to send her a package on the same ship that would carry Troy to Earth. That way, she'd have something from home to soften the blow.

But what? Flowers wouldn't make it past customs and Cara's nutrition adviser wouldn't let her have chocolate. Human females loved faceted rocks set into jewelry, but the practice was so absurd that Aelyx hated to patronize it. He needed a gift that would speak to the heart. Unfortunately, he had no experience in that area.

Once again, he decided to ask David for advice.

He stepped into the hall, finding the penthouse still and silent with nothing illuminating the darkness but a sliver of light leaking beneath the door to David's room. Avoiding the creakiest floorboards, Aelyx crept down the hallway and knocked softly on David's door. When he didn't respond, Aelyx knocked again.

Nothing.

"David?" Aelyx whispered, turning the knob and slowly stepping inside. "Are you awake?" He scanned the room, taking in the neatly made bed, wooden dresser covered in sports magazines and loose change, and a small pile of dirty laundry on the floor. But no David.

Aelyx was about to leave when a *clink* sounded from the far end of the room, drawing his eye to the bathroom door, which stood slightly ajar. Through the few inches of open space, Aelyx could see part of David's reflection in the bathroom mirror. Under any other circumstance, Aelyx would have respected the boy's privacy and left, but what he saw in the mirror made his eyes widen and rooted his feet to the floor.

Below the hem of David's T-shirt sleeve, a blue elastic band tightly encircled his bicep. Lower, in the bend of his arm, David sank a hypodermic needle into his vein and pressed the plunger with his thumb. Milky fluid disappeared from the vial into his arm, and David tightened his fist, giving a hiss of pain.

Aelyx was no stranger to injectables—he'd used nutrition supplements many times on Earth before he'd learned to tolerate the local food. The act of self-administering medication didn't shock him in the least. What Aelyx found alarming was the fact that David had used a L'eihr injectable. There was no mistaking the short, sleek design, nor the symbols printed in gray on the vial.

Why was David using L'eihr medication, and where had he gotten it?

When David finished, he removed the blue elastic band and rubbed his arm to restore circulation. Then he opened the door and met Aelyx with the unmistakable open-mouthed expression of a person caught doing something wrong. They both stood there for a moment, staring at the other, David clearly calculating how much Aelyx had seen and grappling for a way to explain it.

Aelyx didn't know why, but he felt the need to disclaim, "I knocked twice, but you didn't answer."

"Uh, yeah." David kneaded his arm, his gaze flicking up and down in a warning that a lie would follow. "Sorry about that. I should've warned you . . . I've got diabetes, so, you know . . . injections and stuff. It sucks." He quirked a smile and laughed without humor. "I've got track marks, but I promise I'm not a junkie."

David might've had diabetes, but humans dispensed their own medicines for that. He wouldn't need a L'eihr syringe to inject insulin. Aelyx liked David—had come to think of him as a friend—but he couldn't risk his or Syrine's safety by turning a blind eye to what he'd discovered.

"I'm going to give you one chance to explain," Aelyx said. "Because I owe you my life. But if you lie to me again, the next person I talk to will be Colonel Rutter." He tried to sound nonthreatening, but he meant every word. "Do you understand?"

David blanched. It was the first time Aelyx had seen him show weakness. A few seconds passed before he nodded. "Can you keep a secret?"

"Depends on the secret."

"This job," David said as he moved past Aelyx to shut the bedroom door, "of protecting L'eihrs? It comes with perks. But no one can find out, especially not my CO or Colonel Rutter. At best, they'd stick me behind a desk. At worst, they'd give me a medical discharge."

Aelyx folded his arms and kept some distance between them. "Why?"

"I have a genetic disorder," David said. "It's degenerative and incurable. My dad had it, too."

"Had it?"

"He died when I was a kid."

"Oh." Aelyx knew what that kind of loss could do to humans. He offered a sympathetic nod. "I'm sorry."

"Thanks." David took a seat at the foot of his bed and gazed at his folded hands as he spoke. "I always knew I was a carrier, but I hoped the disease would skip over me like it did with my grandpa. But then I started showing symptoms a couple years ago." He glanced up at Aelyx, delivering an urgent look. "The military doesn't know. I went to private doctors for all my treatments, because I didn't want a discharge. I know it sounds stupid, but I kept thinking I could beat this."

"It's not stupid," Aelyx said. His instincts told him David was being honest, and he felt a compassionate tug for the boy. "Sometimes there's power in positive thinking."

"And even greater power in L'eihr drugs."

Now Aelyx understood what David meant about receiving perks. "What are you taking?"

"Honestly, I don't know." David studied the inside crook of his elbow, where his most recent wound had begun to scab over. "It's something experimental. Diseases like mine don't exist for you guys because of breeding, or something like that."

"Selective reproduction," Aelyx said. "Genetic disorders died out thousands of years ago, because the people carrying those anomalies weren't permitted to pass on their DNA." He'd always considered it a logical practice, but it occurred to Aelyx that David wouldn't be alive if his ancestors had been banned from reproducing.

"Whatever's in this stuff makes me feel like Superman." When David glanced up again, his face was full of optimism. "I think it's working."

Aelyx hoped so. But if David had tried so hard to hide his disease, how did a L'eihr discover it, and who'd acquired the drugs from the transport?

David must have seen the question on Aelyx's face. "You're wondering how I got the meds," he said.

"And who gave them to you." Frankly, Aelyx didn't know many L'eihrs who cared enough about humans to put forth the effort.

"I met one of your leaders when he came here for a World Trade meeting," David said. "Young guy—looked kind of like you, but taller. Real friendly. He's crazy about humans."

A young male member of The Way? There was only one possibility and Aelyx didn't like it. "Jaxen?"

"Yeah," David said, wrinkling his forehead. "That sounds familiar. You know him?"

"Not really." *Just well enough to distrust any drugs he would give me.* But as much as Aelyx wanted to warn David, speaking against The Way was treason—punishable by death. Besides, if David's condition was fatal, the experimental medication couldn't make it much worse.

"Anyway," David said, "he was real observant. I couldn't hide anything from him. I had the shakes one day and he noticed." David held up a hand in demonstration, making his palm tremble. "The guy came right out and asked what disease I had. I denied it at first, but when he said he could help me, I came clean."

"He must have liked you." Or wanted something.

David shrugged. "I guess so. He asked if I was interested in joining your colony."

"And are you?"

"I'm thinking about it," David said. "I lost my mom last winter, and I don't have any brothers or sisters, so there's not much keeping me here."

Aelyx sat down beside him. "I hope you'll go."

"Yeah?" David seemed pleased to hear it. "So we're cool?"

"Completely."

"And we can keep this between us?"

"Yes and no," Aelyx admitted. "I'll try to control my thoughts, but I can only hide so much during Silent Speech."

"But you can't silent-talk to Colonel Rutter or my CO, right?"

"Right."

"Then I'll be okay."

For the next few beats, they sat in awkward silence, both fidgeting with their hands and staring at their boots. Finally, David cleared his throat and forced a smile. "So, did you need something?"

Aelyx raised one brow in question.

"When you came in here," David said with a teasing grin, "and caught me shooting up."

Oh, right. He'd wanted advice on what to send Cara on the next transport. It seemed so trivial now, compared to David's troubles. "It's nothing."

"Out with it." David bounced up from the bed and crossed the room to lean against his dresser. "It's about Cara, right?"

"How'd you know?"

Another shrug. "You only come to me with girl problems. I don't know why you think I've got all the answers, though. It's been a long time for me, my friend."

"A long time since . . . ?"

"I got laid." He laughed casually, not the least bit embarrassed to discuss something so intimate. "I should be asking *you* for tips."

David's unabashed honesty gave Aelyx the confidence to admit his lack of experience. "My tips wouldn't get you far. I've never . . . well . . . ." He felt his face heating. "You know."

David's blond brows shot up his forehead. "Never? Not even with Cara?"

Aelyx shook his head. "She said it was too soon."

"Ouch." David sucked in a sharp breath while pushing off the dresser, then clapped Aelyx on the arm. "Tough break, man. But she's got to be crazy about you. Otherwise she wouldn't have left Earth, right?"

"I'm worried she's having second thoughts," Aelyx confided. "I want to send something to make her feel better."

"Let me guess—you came to me for gift ideas?"

"Got any?"

"That's the thing," David said. "Girls like stuff that comes from the heart—something only you can give them. It has to be personal. I can't tell you what to buy, or she won't think it's romantic."

Aelyx considered that. *Something only I can give her . . .*

"Maybe a mushy letter," David suggested. "Or glue your

picture in a locket so she can wear it over her heart, or some crap like that. Whatever makes her feel closer to you."

That gave Aelyx an idea, and he found himself smiling when he imagined Cara's reaction. She would love it. More importantly, he hadn't needed David to tell him what to send. "I know just the thing."

Chapter Ten

Cara made several key discoveries over the next week, mostly involving her brother. She learned the reason he loved those nasty cabbage-flavored protein packets was because they reminded him of sauerkraut, which he'd grown fond of during a brief assignment in Germany. During a game of truth or dare, Troy confided that a servicewoman called Melanie Maloney had broken his heart, and that he'd lost his best friend in an ambush two years ago. He showed Cara the scar on his left calf from a friendly fire incident he'd never told Mom and Dad about, and he confessed to watching *The Muppet Christmas Carol* when he was homesick during basic training.

It was like Troy had this whole other life, and she'd never known him until now. Cara spent every spare minute glued to her brother's side. She'd even convinced Elle to let Troy bunk with them for his last week on L'eihr. His snoring kept them awake, but Cara didn't mind. Who needed sleep?

At that moment, he slept flat on his back with one arm hugging a pillow against his chest and the other arm resting beneath his head where the pillow belonged. His metal dog tags hung over his cot and stirred with the breeze from the open window, creating a light tinkle.

God, she was going to miss him.

Cara tried reminding herself that she could go home to visit every year, but twelve months seemed like forever with multiple galaxies stretched between them. She wished they could get back all the time they'd wasted on Earth, holed up in their bedrooms watching Internet videos or texting friends who hadn't lasted beyond the school year.

The room alarm interrupted her moping in three long, buzzing bursts that rattled her teeth and vibrated the furniture. Cara flipped back the covers and stood, then tugged Elle's arm. The alarm wouldn't stop until they'd both scanned their nano-chips and reported awake. Troy didn't have a chip, so he grumbled a curse and stayed beneath his blankets, scratching himself like a typical guy.

Elle thrust her wrist beneath the scanner affixed near the door, and in response, the system replied in L'eihr, "Elyx'a of the first Aegis, you have no notifications."

Cara followed suit, expecting to hear the same message in English. "*Cah*-ra Sweeney," the computer said, "return after your morning meal and await further instructions."

Cara made it halfway back to her bunk before she absorbed

the message. "Wait. What?" She'd never had a notification before. She turned to Elle, who didn't appear to understand it, either.

"That's odd." Elle pulled off her nightshirt without a care for the male in the room. "But I wouldn't worry. It's probably an administrative matter."

"Maybe I'm getting a new com-sphere," Cara said. Her transmissions were getting through to her parents and Aelyx, but she kept missing alerts, like the emergency assembly the headmaster had called last week. She'd reported the issue to the devices department, who in turn had promised to look into it.

"I hate to leave you alone, but I have to attend classes." Elle unfastened her ponytail and ran a comb through her hair. "Troy, can you stay with her today?"

Troy pushed onto his elbows and glanced across the room, then went slack-jawed at the sight of Elle's bare chest. "Holy God!" he shouted, blocking his view with one hand. "You could've warned me!"

Elle laughed and refastened her hair at the nape of her neck. "You humans are amusing. Such a prudish view of your own bodies."

He peeked through his fingers. "Are you saying it wouldn't bug you if I strutted around here buck naked?"

"Whoa." Cara held up one finger. "It would bother *me!*"

"Go ahead." Elle swept a permissive hand toward Troy's cot. "Yours wouldn't be the first male reproductive organ I've seen. They all look the same to me."

Troy threw a pillow on his lap while trying not to ogle Elle's boobs. "I'd better stay put for a few minutes."

Gross. This was why siblings shouldn't share a room. Cara gathered a towel and a clean uniform, deciding to make a run for the showers before she saw something that would scar her for life. But when she reached the communal washroom, she wished she'd stayed behind.

"Look," Dahla said in flawless English, glancing at Cara from the enzyme mouth-washing station. "It's our resident chimpanzee."

Odom spat his enzyme rinse into the sink and jutted out his bottom lip, then made a weird growling noise in his misinterpretation of monkey chatter.

Refusing to let them intimidate her, Cara strode toward the shower. "Chimps don't sound like that. And besides, you have just as much of their DNA as I do." She glared at Dahla and flashed her best *f-you* grin. "Sister."

The girl's eyes turned to slits. In one massive step, she blocked Cara's way until they stood toe-to-toe. "A handful of sacred mud doesn't make us sisters. You're an insect, and when the alliance fails, no one will even notice the extinction of your race."

"Don't you mean *our* race?" Cara asked sweetly. "You know, since your ancestors are from Earth."

Dahla's hands clenched, but Odom pulled her aside and communicated something in Silent Speech, probably a warning that the consequences of a fistfight weren't worth it. The two gave her the L'eihr middle finger and stomped away.

When Cara had finished washing, she returned to her room, pleased to find Troy alone and fully clothed, lacing up his combat boots.

"I'm starved. You ready?" Troy patted his belly. "By the way, you missed a call from Mom. She said Tori's going to sneak away tomorrow to talk to you."

"Really?" Cara perked up as they made their way toward the cafeteria. It had been too long since she'd heard her best friend's voice.

"*Alex* called, too," Troy said with an eye roll. "I told him to get a life."

"You'd better be joking."

"Nope. When you didn't answer your sphere, he tried mine." Troy led the way inside the dining hall and grabbed a tray. "Total stalker."

"You dillhole!" she hissed. "He's worried about me because of what happened with the tablet."

"Whatevs." Troy dumped a ladleful of ground meat over his flatbread. "Just say the word and I'll introduce you to a couple of my friends. They're jackasses, but at least they're not stalkers."

Cara grabbed the ladle and positioned her plate near the steaming vat of meat. She hated *t'ahinni*, but her muscles would ache for protein once she joined Satan on the intermediate course in a few hours.

She'd just sat down opposite her brother when Dahla swooped in and lifted Cara's plate from the table. "Thank you, *sister*," she sneered, then took her ill-gotten breakfast to the table she shared with her friends.

"You gonna put up with that?" Troy asked.

Cara remembered all the times Aelyx had turned the other cheek during his portion of the exchange at Midtown High. She could be mature about this. "I like to think of it as being the bigger person." But on her way to fetch another serving, she strode by Dahla's table, licked her finger, and dipped it in the little thief's *t'ahinni*.

Maturity was overrated.

After breakfast, she and Troy had just slid their plates into the sanitization chute when shouts drew their attention to the other side of the dining hall. Dahla had fallen to the floor in convulsions and lay on her side moaning in pain. She lurched, and the breakfast she'd stolen came back up.

Elle and her medic friends rushed to Dahla's side and assessed her while someone called for help. Soon the kitchen supervisor came out to investigate, and Cara moved closer to see if the girl was okay. Dahla was a total jerk, but Cara hated to see anyone suffer.

After pricking Dahla's finger with a handheld machine, Elle frowned at the screen. "She has poison in her blood, a neurotoxin from the *h'urr* blossom. She'll be all right, but we'll have to cleanse her system."

Odom pointed at Cara and loudly announced, "The human put something in Dahla's food. We all saw her."

Cara froze.

Everyone at that table confirmed it, and without bothering to ask for Cara's side of the story, the supervisor ordered her to report to the headmaster's office. Her first instinct was to stay and defend herself, but Troy tugged her elbow.

"Come on," he whispered. "You don't want to be here if things go south."

When Cara glanced around and noticed all the hostile glares, she understood. She was a scapegoat, and with emotions running high, it wouldn't take much for her classmates to turn on her. Probably best to hang out with the headmaster and wait for tempers to cool.

They'd barely taken a dozen steps when Aisly intercepted them in the lobby.

"Where are you going?" Aisly asked, gesturing toward Cara's room. "You're supposed to report to your quarters so I can fetch you for our outing."

"What outing?"

The girl grinned and leaned in as if sharing a secret. "Jaxen will be back momentarily with our shuttle. Then we have a surprise for you." Her chrome eyes twinkled and she bounced on her toes, reminding Cara of a child eager to present a gift to her parents.

There was something odd about Aisly. On the outside, she resembled the other clones, maybe a few inches shorter than most of the girls. However, much like Jaxen, she seemed almost human, but with an icy edge that made her every bit L'eihr. Cara sensed another difference in the siblings, but the answer lingered just beyond her grasp, making her wonder for the hundredth time what gifts they possessed that had earned their positions in The Way.

"I can't go. I'm in trouble," Cara said. Or at least she thought she was. She kept forgetting that Jaxen and Aisly trumped the headmaster by about a thousand steps on the hierarchical ladder. "Maybe you can talk to the headmaster for me."

"What did you do?" Aisly asked.

Cara explained everything, making sure to mention all the times Dahla had bullied her. "I didn't put anything in her breakfast. As much as she hates me, I wouldn't be surprised if she poisoned herself to make me look guilty. It's easily cured, so she wasn't risking anything."

"I'd believe that," Troy said.

Aisly studied him for a moment, then abruptly asked, "Did you poison her?"

"*What?*" he cried, hand flying to his chest. "Me? Why would I do that?"

She shrugged. "To avenge your sister."

"I had nothing to do with it," Troy told Aisly. "I wouldn't poison anyone, especially in a place *like this.*" His last words were charged with contempt.

Aisly picked up on it, defensively folding her arms. "A place like what, exactly?"

"A place where the punishment could get me whipped or killed."

Aisly peered at them both as if trying to see inside their heads.

"I. Didn't. Do it," Troy forced out through gritted teeth.

"He's telling the truth," Cara said. "Troy didn't touch her food. Besides, it's possible the toxin got into her system some other way."

Aisly didn't appear convinced, but she told Cara to wait for Jaxen at the courtyard landing pad while she stayed behind to resolve the incident with the headmaster. "I'll meet you there shortly," she added before striding toward the administrative offices.

"What a bitch," Troy muttered under his breath after Aisly had moved out of earshot. "Wherever it is they're taking you, I'm going, too. I didn't get an invite, but I don't care."

"Fine by me."

On their way toward the front doors, Vero crossed Cara's path and gave her the animal equivalent of the evil eye. *Aaaeee-oooo,* Vero howled, pumping his tiny raccoonish paw in the air. Indecipherable as it was, Cara knew his impassioned rant reflected the sentiment of nearly everyone on the planet.

"Yeah," she said, striding out the front door. "I hate you, too."

Cara squinted against the sun's glittering reflection as she jetted over the sea at speeds so fast she could barely lean forward in her seat. As it turned out, her big surprise was a visit to the colony, a sneak peek of sorts to help her explain the lifestyle to prospective humans who might settle there.

To her left, Jaxen piloted the small four-person shuttle, while Troy and Aisly sat together in the back. Judging by the charged silence filling the rear of the craft, neither was thrilled with the seating arrangements, but Jaxen had insisted Cara take the copilot position because it offered the best view.

And, boy, was he right.

"Look there," Jaxen said, slowing down and pointing out Cara's window. "A pod of *maru.*"

She pressed her fingertips to the glass and gazed at a family of shimmery white whale-like creatures slicing through the water by using their oversize flippers as wings. She thought she spotted a baby among them, but the shuttle sped past in a flash, and they were gone.

"Wow." She tried to turn in her seat to face Troy, but velocity held her still. "I wish you could see this," she called to him. "It's amazing."

He answered with a grunt.

"I could slow down," Jaxen offered, "but I don't want to lose daylight. It'll be nearly dusk when we arrive at the colony."

"What's the time difference between the colony and the main continent?" Cara asked.

"About six hours." Jaxen pointed out her window again. "There's *Allahn*, one of our ancient societies."

"Oh!" This was Cara's favorite part of their journey. She loved catching glimpses of the L'eihrs' ancient ruins.

She turned her gaze to the island, trying to form a mental snapshot of its crumbling temple. The sandy stonework reminded her of a cross between the Parthenon and the pyramids of Giza. She'd learned in humanities class that the ancients had occupied these islands before discovering the continent. Here, they'd battled over trade routes and fertile fishing waters, even invading one another to impound slaves, much as humans had done. Jaxen explained that without weather controls in place, storms would have eroded the structures several millennia ago.

"And their greatest foes," Jaxen said as the shuttle approached a larger island, "the *Ellohi*. They were a terrifying force. If they perceived a threat, however slight, they launched a preemptive attack. Very proactive."

"I've read about them." If Cara's memory served, the *Ellohi* were relentless warriors who'd sought to dominate the sea, Roman Empire–style. "According to your legends, they're the ones who were supposedly abducted by aliens and scattered across the universe, right?"

"Yes, if you believe that."

She slanted a glance at him. "I don't."

"That's right," he said with a smile. "You're a fan of Larish's theory—that our ancients were abducted from Earth and transplanted here."

"It's the only thing that makes sense," she told him. "First of all, our people have to be related, because the odds of two genetically identical species existing in this universe are zero."

"Agreed," he said.

"Okay. So now that we've established that, why would anyone think ancient L'eihrs brought blue eyes to Earth when brown-eyed humans existed for thousands of years before that mutation? Where do they think brown-eyed humans came from? And as for L'eihr mono-ethnicity, I assumed it was because your people had been around longer, but really, I think it had to do with your ancestors being abducted from a single nation."

Jaxen glanced at her with a grin. "You don't need to convince me, *Cah*-ra. I realized Larish's thesis was valid before he'd even written it. You and I are descended from ancient humans, as are countless other societies throughout galaxies we've yet to discover."

His concession surprised her. According to Aelyx, only a handful of L'eihrs believed they were related to mankind. "But Aelyx said—"

"Gods on fire," Jaxen swore. "I'm tired of hearing about the nonsense Aelyx told you."

She thought she heard Troy snickering from the backseat.

Cara quietly cleared her throat. "But aren't most L'eihrs ashamed to admit their connection to Earth?"

"I don't see why," Jaxen said. "If anything, our shared lineage proves the superiority of the L'eihr race. We're younger than mankind, and yet we've managed to evolve beyond you."

Cara suppressed an eye roll. "You're leaving out one key piece of information."

"And what's that?"

"Larish wrote that the abducting aliens probably gave technology to your ancients when they left them on L'eihr." While the human race was still mastering written communication and domesticating animals, the L'eihrs were beginning to experiment with solar power. The rest of their advances were achieved through organized breeding, which the aliens had probably helped with, too. "You had a head start."

Jaxen gave a haughty laugh. "I admire your competitive spirit, *Cah*-ra. You and I are alike in that way."

"It's not a contest or anything," she said with a shrug. She just didn't like the L'eihrs acting superior all the time. "But it explains a lot."

He took his eyes off the controls and watched her for a long moment, the way a dieter stares at the last cookie. "I do love mankind. Despite their shortcomings, they've managed to produce a few fine specimens. Quite fine."

After that, the mood shifted. Cara stared out her window and took in the aquatic sights, but Jaxen tainted the experience. He felt too near, his knee resting inches from hers, his elbow brushing her sleeve, and she couldn't wait to get off the shuttle and away from him.

When they arrived at the colony an hour later, Jaxen smiled as if nothing had happened. "Behold—your future home!"

He slowed the shuttle and circled the island so Cara could take in the entire settlement. She glanced out the window, heart fluttering as her spirits lifted.

The miniature town was adorable, reminiscent of a theme park in the way narrow streets and pathways connected each structure, all compacted within the span of a hundred acres. An ancient temple crumbled near the beach, but instead of the sandy-colored rubble, they had imported blocks of gray stone from the continent, so the buildings within town resembled those at the capital. Cara imagined they'd done so for the clones' benefit, to make them feel at home.

"It's still a work in progress," Jaxen said, drawing Cara's attention to empty plots and slabs of slate. "Think of this as the skeleton. We'll flesh it out later with landscaping and recreational areas." He pointed to a flat expanse of land in the distance. "And we'll plant the first season's crops for you."

Crops. That probably meant The Way intended for the

colony to sustain itself. Cara didn't know the first thing about agriculture, but that was okay. They'd recruit people with a broad range of talents. She liked the idea of existing independently of the continent.

"What kind of animal is that?" she asked, pointing to the north beach, where hundreds of small creatures dragged their bodies onto the sand. They had sleek tan skin and flippers with a single talon at the end, which they used to gain traction. Cute, in a freaky-deaky sort of way.

Jaxen leaned aside to peer out her window. "Ah, the *mahlay*. They come here to lay their eggs because the rich soil beneath the sand keeps the ground a few degrees warmer than other islands. Don't worry. They won't bother you."

Cara turned her attention to a cluster of apartment-style buildings that resembled the Aegis. The grouping sat at the center of town, with each road and pathway leading back to it. "And what's that?"

"We call that the Living Center," he said, hovering above one of the buildings to give her a closer look. "We tried to blend human and L'eihr cultures, so colonists will reside in family units as opposed to occupational barracks. Each unit will contain basic sleeping quarters and a living room, but you'll dine together in the main hall and share communal washrooms."

"Family units?" Cara asked. "Does that mean children will live with their parents?"

"Yes. Younglings will spend their evenings in the family unit and their days in the Aegis, to ensure developmental consistency."

Cara released a breath. "That's good. Otherwise, you won't get many humans here."

"We understand your attachment to your offspring."

There wasn't room to land the shuttle in town, so Jaxen touched down on the beach. Once the thrusters died, Cara exited the craft and stretched her stiff back and legs. She'd become unaccustomed to sitting still for so long, thanks to Satan's PE class.

Right away, she noticed a dampness in the air that made her skin feel sticky, and it seemed several degrees warmer here than on the continent. She supposed the temperature difference made sense, considering the island's position near the equator. L'eihrs only controlled their weather systems enough to prevent destructive storms.

Troy hopped down from the backseat and pointed to a thicket of tall taupe trees and leafy underbrush. "Be right back," he whispered. "Gotta drain the lizard."

Laughing, Cara faced the softly crashing waves and let the ocean breeze caress her face. She shielded her eyes from the sun, which hung low on the horizon. Beautiful as the L'eihr sunset was—with smudges of salmon and gold contrasted against a slate sky—it couldn't compete with Earth's cotton candy dusk. But the air here smelled sweeter than the beaches of home—an unpolluted mixture of salt, sun, and a scent that reminded her of pine. Sharp-beaked winged animals dove, kamikaze-style, into the surf to spear fish. That, at least, was familiar.

Hugging herself, Cara gazed into the heavens and mentally recited Aelyx's words: *Soon we'll stand together and watch the L'eihr sky from our colony.* An electric charge passed through her. They were really going to do this—build a life here. She could picture it: barefoot strolls on the beach under a tri-moon glow, weekends spent fishing and gathering shells, nights in Aelyx's arms, falling asleep to the sound of distant waves.

This was paradise. They didn't even have to worry about hurricanes.

Jaxen surprised her by capturing a loose lock of hair and tucking it behind her ear. "What are you thinking?"

Not wanting to encourage his casual touches, Cara moved away. "I'm imagining what a typical day would look like."

Aisly strode to Jaxen's side and answered for him. "Much like your days now. You'll scan for updates, engage in physical conditioning, eat in the dining hall. But instead of classes, you'll report to your assigned vocation."

Cara didn't like the sound of that. "We won't be able to choose our own jobs?"

"No." Jaxen kicked aside a chunk of driftwood and began walking over the dunes toward town. "Our method of optimal placement in the workforce is too efficient to abandon."

Paradise just lost a point.

Troy emerged from the bushes, zipping his fly. He nodded toward the ancient ruins. "Are they going to leave that temple standing?"

"It's not a temple," Jaxen said, staring into the rubble. "It's a tomb. Or it *was*."

"For a warrior queen and her consort," Aisly added. "Killed in battle. Their bodies lay undisturbed until recently."

That sounded cryptic. "They didn't tear it down for the colony, did they?" Cara asked.

"No. The remains were exhumed and relocated decades ago." Jaxen pointed ahead and quickened his pace. "Hurry. We don't have much sun left."

As they strode onward, something needled at the back of Cara's mind—a warning bell of sorts—but she couldn't put her finger on the problem. She scanned storefronts and offices as she passed, finding nothing amiss. In fact, the apartment complexes were homier than she'd anticipated, complete with benches along the sidewalk and the beginnings of a swimming pool in the courtyard. The L'eihrs weren't big on leisure time, so she knew this was a concession for them.

"Can we go inside?" Cara asked. She wanted to see the living quarters she'd share with Aelyx.

"No," Jaxen said. "They're not finished. All you'd find are stairs and plumbing."

"Too bad." She gazed up and down the vacant street, half expecting a tumbleweed to blow down the center of town. "I'd love to get a sneak peek at . . ." She trailed off, finally realizing what had been bothering her.

It was the streets. They didn't exist at the capital because citizens shuttled from place to place or took the air train. But now that Cara looked around, she noticed the absence of landing pads, too.

"Wait," she said. "Where will our shuttles land? And why are there streets here?"

Jaxen and Aisly shared the briefest of glances, just long

enough for Cara to get the impression they were hiding something.

Recovering quickly, Jaxen offered a placating smile. "In keeping with human customs, we've begun the manufacture of small motorized vehicles for your use on the colony."

"Cars?" Cara asked.

"Powered by the sun," Aisly added. "Like everything else here, so you won't need to worry about fuel dependency."

Cara noticed they didn't answer her first question. "Where will we keep our shuttles?"

After a moment of hesitation, Jaxen admitted, "You won't have them."

"At all?"

"No."

Paradise lost another point. No, make that a dozen points. Because without shuttles, the colonists were trapped here— powerless, isolated, and utterly dependent on the continent to travel any farther than the beach.

Paradise morphed into prison.

Troy clearly understood her concern. He didn't say any- thing, but he whistled the theme to *The Twilight Zone* and used his index finger to make twirling motions toward his head.

"What if there's an emergency?" Cara asked.

Jaxen didn't miss a beat. "You'll have com-spheres."

"But a com-sphere won't fly me off this island."

Drawing a deep breath, Jaxen brought both his hands together as if in prayer. "Listen, *Cah*-ra. I give you my word: The Way means you no harm. But you have to admit that human colonists have a history of rising up against their founding nations. This is more to protect our society than anything else."

Cara didn't buy it. What did he think the colonists were going to do, wage war with a few shuttles and a handful of alien coconuts? No, this was a deal breaker. Human beings weren't wayward children who needed to be managed. She wouldn't live inside a cage, even if it did resemble one of those fancy resorts her family could never afford to visit.

"Then I'll have to reconsider my decision to stay here," Cara said, opening the door for negotiation. "This is a sticking point for me. Can't you spare a few—"

An earsplitting shriek interrupted her and tore everyone's attention skyward, where a ball of fire streaked into the atmosphere. Cara recognized it at once—it was identical to the "meteorite" that had crashed her *Sh'ovah*. This time she narrowed her eyes and focused on the sphere, checking for any detail that might give her a clue to its origin. But all she could discern was flame. It picked up speed and barreled into the ocean with a mighty splash, making her wonder how many other spheres had crashed in these waters. She didn't care what The Way said; that thing was man-made. The repeat appearance confirmed it.

Troy verbalized what she was thinking. "Was that a satellite? I've heard of small ones falling out of orbit."

Jaxen and Aisly exchanged another loaded glance.

"No," Aisly said. She strode to Troy's side and smiled up at him. Staring deeply into his eyes, she crooned, "It was only lightning. There's a storm coming, don't you think?"

While Cara scrunched her brows in confusion, Troy's face went all dopey and he nodded in agreement. "Yeah," he said, turning his gaze to the cloudless sky. "We should head back to the shuttle before it rains."

What had just happened?

Jaxen turned to Cara and cupped her cheek in his palm. When she tried backing away, he took her face between both hands and peered at her, softening his focus as if to use Silent Speech.

Oh, God. She had a feeling she'd just discovered the siblings' hidden talent.

Cara didn't know if it would work, but she blocked her thoughts the way Elle had taught her during one of their practice sessions. She cleared her mind of everything but her default safe image, which happened to be a red kickball. While Jaxen tried connecting with her consciousness, Cara summoned that ball, envisioning its textured surface, its rubbery scent, the springy feel of it beneath her fingers.

"*Cah*-ra," Jaxen said, low and smooth as melted chocolate. "You don't need to worry. You'll find happiness here."

Red ball. She focused with all her might. *Bouncy red ball.*

Jaxen's breath stirred against her lips, and for a moment, she feared he might kiss her. But he released her face and stepped back, studying her with a confident grin.

He thinks it worked. Cara decided not to give him any reason to doubt it. She faked a dazed expression to match her brother's, then lied her ass off.

"I'm not worried."

CHAPTER ELEVEN

"Impossible," Aelyx said. "Mind control only exists in legends. There has to be a logical explanation." He hadn't spent much time with Cara's brother, but Troy struck him as the less intelligent of the two—by leaps and bounds. "Perhaps Troy really thought a storm was coming."

Elle dipped her head into view from the top bunk. "That's what I said."

"Well, you're both wrong." Cara's eyes narrowed, sending Elle darting out of view. "Troy's not the sharpest knife in the drawer, but he's smart enough to know when it's raining. You weren't there—I was. And I'm telling you that Aisly used a Jedi mind trick on my brother, and Jaxen tried the same thing with me. You can choose to believe it or not, but that's what happened. And I'll tell you another thing—I think The Way knows what they can do, and that's why they keep them around."

"I don't see how it's scientifically feasible," Aelyx said.

"Neither do I," Cara conceded. "But I don't know how shuttles fly or how transports jump through wormholes, and those things happen. Until I met L'eihrs, I thought telepathy was impossible. If you can communicate with your minds, it's not that big a stretch to assume you can do other stuff with your minds, too."

Aelyx supposed she had a point, but he still didn't believe it. "Does Troy remember anything helpful?"

Cara poked the top bunk to get Elle's attention. "Tell him what Troy said when we got home last night."

"I asked where they'd been all day," Elle said. "Troy told me they'd flown to the colony, but they'd cut short the trip because of rain. He did appear a bit stunned, but he always looks that way when I undress for bed."

Cara leaned forward, her voice urgent. "But it never rained yesterday—not one drop. Explain *that*."

Troy probably needed his head examined, but Aelyx didn't say so. "Where is he now?"

"In the washroom."

"Has he shown any odd behavior since then? Experienced hallucinations or—"

"No, he's fine," Cara said. "And Jaxen's pretending that nothing happened, like he never grabbed my face and tried to brain-rape me."

Aelyx didn't know what to say. None of it made sense.

Cara pinched her finger and thumb together. "He came this close to kissing me, too."

"*What?*" Aelyx's vision went spotty, and he damned near

fell off the bed. "Why didn't you say that to begin with?"

"Oh, sure," Cara said. "I tell you Jaxen can brainwash people and you don't care. But I mention an almost-kiss and *that*'s what gets your attention?"

Precisely. Aelyx doubted Jaxen's alleged mental powers, but he had no trouble believing the son of a motherless *f'exa* would try to seduce Cara. Aelyx wanted her by his side, far away from Jaxen's influence. "Maybe you should come home with your brother."

"And risk the alliance?" she said, reminding him of what was at stake. "Being here is one of the conditions, remember? I can't come back until spring." She chewed her bottom lip and fell silent awhile. When she spoke again, she kept her gaze fixed on her blanket. "Listen, what do you think about . . . maybe . . ."

"Maybe what?" he prompted.

"Defecting from L'eihr and living on Earth after the alliance is sealed." She peeked through her lashes. "The colony isn't all it's cracked up to be. I know Earth isn't your favorite place right now, but you might grow to like it someday. Right?"

Aelyx tried not to betray the chill that gripped his stomach. If Cara refused to remain on the colony, they couldn't be together. He supposed he could eke out a life on Earth, but humans would have to stop trying to murder him first. As much as they enjoyed killing one another, he imagined his odds weren't very good. And breaking his vow to The Way would mean severing ties to his heritage. He'd never be permitted to return to L'eihr, not even to visit. He loved Cara, but he loved his people, too.

"It's not that simple," he said. "Can't you . . ." What? *Try harder? Lower your expectations?* He didn't know what to ask of her, or even if he had any right to.

She shook her head blankly, probably struggling to make similar requests of him. "They want to trap us there. We won't be free to come and go as we please."

"But you're not free to come and go now," he told her. "You can't take a shuttle and fly it to the spaceport, then simply walk aboard an Earth-bound ship. You have to apply for passage and wait for approval. The colony will be no different."

"You don't understand."

Elle's head appeared again, upside down, from the top bunk. "You don't know what you're asking of him," she said to Cara. "I can't believe you're willing to quit so easily. The *Cah*-ra Sweeney I've come to admire wouldn't give up without a fight."

In an act of surrender, Cara turned up her palms. "What am I supposed to do? Jaxen's part of The Way. He's like everyone's boss—times ten. You should've seen how he snapped his fingers and suddenly I was off the hook for that poisoning incident. Nobody questions him."

"But even he has a superior," Elle said. "Why not appeal to Alona?"

"Wait." Cara raised one orange brow. "I can do that?"

"Of course you can," Aelyx told her. "It's your right as a citizen."

She speared him with a glare. "It's not like they gave me a handbook at my *Sh'ovah*, you know."

Despite the tension, Aelyx found himself smiling. Gods, he loved this girl—her humor and passion, her temper and heart. She filled empty spaces inside him he'd never known were vacant. He simply couldn't lose her. With one finger, he reached out to trace the curve of her face. "Please keep fighting."

She nodded but didn't meet his gaze. "I'll try."

Aelyx left her with an extra-firm "I love you" and disconnected to dress for the day. He didn't like the dejection in Cara's voice, but he hoped the gift he'd sent would cheer her up. He tucked his com-sphere inside his back pocket before striding into the living room.

Ordinarily, now was the time he'd peel off his clothes and climb into bed, but Aelyx had special plans this evening. At his urging, the military had facilitated a meeting between him and the HALO leader, Isaac Richards—a heavily guarded meeting set in a public location, per Isaac's paranoid request. Stepha had refused to attend and "acknowledge that cretin's existence," but Aelyx didn't mind going alone. He'd finally secured permission to share the truth about Earth's water crisis with Isaac. Once the lead Patriot understood the gravity of terminating the alliance, surely he'd cease the assassination attempts he continued to deny.

Or at least that's what Aelyx hoped.

"Time to suit up," David said, holding forward a Kevlar vest. He seemed ready to go in his camouflage jacket and matching hat, semiautomatic weapon slung across his shoulder. Maybe it was nothing, but David seemed more tired than usual, with dark circles shadowing his eyes. "Colonel Rutter's not taking any chances with your precious alien hide."

"What about you?" Syrine demanded from her spot on the sofa. "Are you wearing one?"

David pounded one fist against his chest, giving a hollow *thunk*. "Yes, ma'am."

"Good," she snapped, as if irate with herself for caring. Which was probably the case. "It won't protect against a head wound, though." And with that, she snatched a magazine from the coffee table and pretended to read it. Aelyx decided not to tell her it was upside down in her grasp. More fun to let her discover that on her own.

While Aelyx shrugged out of his sweater and donned the bulletproof vest, David took a seat on the sofa's armrest. "I don't know," David said, leaning down to read over Syrine's shoulder. "My mom used to say my head was hard enough to stop a bullet."

A disdainful sniff was her only reply.

"But I think stubbornness is kind of hot." When David plucked the magazine from Syrine's hands and turned it right side up for her, Aelyx's chest shook with silent laughter. "Don't you?" the boy murmured near Syrine's ear.

In a flash, she threw down the copy of *People* and retreated to her bedroom. The slamming of her door soon followed.

Aelyx chuckled while fastening the Velcro straps at his sides. "What was it you said the other day?" He tipped his head aside, pretending to think. *"Soon she'll be wrapped around my pinkie finger? You sure about that? Because it looks like she'd rather wrap her hands around your throat."*

David frowned at Syrine's door. "She's going to be a tough nut to crack."

Not really. David didn't know it, but Syrine was already cracking. Aelyx had felt her conflict deepening through Silent Speech, even when she'd tried to block it. Her attraction to their bodyguard had grown each day, along with disdain for her weakness. She'd spent more and more time sequestered in her bedroom practicing *K'imsha*, but all the meditation in the world wouldn't harden her heart against the human.

Aelyx pulled on his sweater and grabbed his wool overcoat. "Just unleash that irresistible charm you're always bragging about."

"I did. Turns out she's immune to it."

They walked into the hall, where half the guard unit waited to escort Aelyx to his meeting. Together, the entire group made their way down two flights of stairs and then filed into the armored vehicle idling at the curb. Once he and David settled into their customary seats in the back row, it occurred to Aelyx that for the first time, he could offer his mentor some romantic advice.

"It's not you she hates," Aelyx whispered. "It's mankind in general. I think your strongest chance of winning her over is to show that you're different."

"Stop acting human?"

"Basically, yes." At his friend's sigh of exasperation, Aelyx explained one of the reasons behind Syrine's prejudice. "Her host student relentlessly pursued her during the exchange. He cornered her in the hall, groped her legs under the dinner table—even hid a camera in her bedroom. So when you compliment her beauty or engage in typical human mating rituals, you're—"

"Coming on too strong," David finished. "And reminding her of that doucher."

"Exactly."

"Huh." A hopeful grin pushed up the corners of David's mouth. "I just need to tone it down a little."

"And show that you're different," Aelyx repeated. Syrine's feelings had first sparked alive when David put his life at risk to save her from the letter bomb. She'd never before considered humans capable of self-sacrifice, and he had proven her wrong. "That's the most important part."

David nodded thoughtfully. "I can do different."

After that, David chewed the inside of his cheek and fell into an introspective trance, so Aelyx turned his gaze out the window to watch the miles pass in a dark blur of frosted brick and salted asphalt.

They left the city and traveled into the suburbs, eventually stopping at the entrance to a defunct strip mall with only one functioning business—an Italian bistro at the far end. The National Guard had secured the parking lot in the form of barricades and armed patrols at the periphery. When the driver of their Hum-V rolled down his window and presented his identification, two soldiers dragged aside the plastic barrels blocking the way, allowing them to pass.

Colonel Rutter met Aelyx as soon as he stepped onto the

sidewalk. "We paid the owner to close down the place," the colonel explained while directing Aelyx toward the bistro. "We've swept the inside, and it's cleaner than a preacher's pickle."

David snickered from nearby but went instantly stoic when the colonel's gaze landed on him.

"Due to the . . . uh . . ." Rutter began, still watching David, "*sensitive* nature of your discussion with Richards tonight, I'll be inside with you, and Private Sharpe will help patrol the perimeter." He dismissed David, who saluted his superior and jogged away to join the guards stationed at the parking lot entrance.

"Did you bring the equipment I requested?" Aelyx asked.

Rutter lifted a small duffel bag. "Got it right here."

"Is Richards already inside?"

"Yep," the colonel said. "He's clean. Searched him myself." With a devilish smirk, he added, "Extra thoroughly."

Aelyx didn't really want to know what that entailed, but he hoped it involved a painful body cavity examination. Nobody deserved it more than Isaac Richards.

A comforting burst of dry, warm air greeted them in the restaurant, followed closely by the tangy scent of marinara sauce. Aelyx removed his coat, glancing around the dining room to survey his surroundings. A polished oak bar claimed the side wall, and behind it stood twenty or so round, linen-draped tables, each adorned with a repurposed wine bottle holding a tapered candle. But only one candle flickered with light, casting shadows over the folded hands of the man seated behind it.

Isaac stood when he noticed Aelyx, and he nodded his

brunet head in a greeting. Aelyx studied his foe while striding toward him. In his tweed jacket and khaki pants, bifocals teetering on the tip of his nose, Richards looked more like a university professor than the commander of a xenophobic civilian army. The man didn't offer his hand to shake, but that was all right. Aelyx didn't want to touch him anyway.

"Thank you for meeting me," Aelyx said. He gestured at three small glass jars atop the table, each filled with clear liquid collected from opposite ends of the country. "And for bringing your water samples."

After placing his duffel on the floor, Colonel Rutter took a seat at the next table, giving them the illusion of privacy. Isaac lowered to his chair and motioned for Aelyx to follow suit. "I did so against my better judgment," Isaac said. "But I couldn't resist. I admit your message had me intrigued."

"This won't take long." Aelyx found it difficult to maintain eye contact with the seemingly innocuous man. While Richards began sipping his coffee, memories of Eron's death pushed their way to the front of Aelyx's mind—specifically how the Patriots of Earth had proudly claimed responsibility for the murder.

Isaac must have sensed it. "Before we begin," he said, "I want to say that I regret what happened in Lanzhou. I don't have much control over individual chapters, and I didn't sanction violence against that boy."

Aelyx didn't much care for semantics. Whether or not Isaac had called for Eron's death, he'd facilitated the group protest that brought together thousands of extremists in Eron's town. Isaac had to have known bloodshed would ensue.

"I won't lie," Isaac continued. "I still want your kind off my planet."

Aelyx laughed without humor. "Now *that* I believe."

"But I don't kill children."

"I'm not a child."

Isaac brought the cup of coffee to his mouth and watched Aelyx over the rim. He set the cup atop its saucer with a light *clink*. "No, you're not. But I have a son your age, so I guess that's how I see you."

Aelyx didn't like this. He didn't want to hear that Isaac had a family, or any humanizing elements about his life. The man had fostered an organization that fed on fear and paranoia. They'd tried to kill Aelyx many times. That was all he needed to know.

Roughly, Aelyx unzipped the duffel bag at his feet and pulled the microscope and glass slides from inside, then set them on the table.

"What's all this?" Isaac asked.

Aelyx unscrewed the first jar and used a sterile dropper to squeeze a few beads of water onto the slide. "I knew you wouldn't believe me unless you saw this with your own eyes." He flipped on the scope's light and peered through the eyepiece to bring the sample into focus under heavy magnification. "Look in here and tell me what you see."

Isaac slid the scope across the table and did as Aelyx asked. "I don't know," he said. "A bunch of green blobs joined together in strands."

"They're algae blooms," Aelyx explained. "And you'll find

them reproducing at an exponential rate in every single one of these samples."

Isaac's answering shrug said he didn't understand.

"I didn't poison Earth's water, but it's tainted all the same." Aelyx removed the slide and repeated the process using liquid from the second jar. "Years ago, our Voyagers introduced your scientists to L'eihr nanotechnology. Human scientists began experimenting with our particles without pondering the consequences, and they released a nano-fertilizer that leaked into the Atlantic and Pacific oceans, thus—"

"Wait," Isaac interrupted. "In English, please."

While Aelyx tried to rephrase the occurrence in simpler terms, Colonel Rutter offered from the next table, "We screwed ourselves, right up the tailpipe. And unless L'eihrs give us the technology to fix it, we're all dead in less than a decade."

Isaac removed his glasses and rubbed his eyes. "You can't expect me to take your word for it."

"Of course not," Aelyx said. "Feel free to bring in someone you trust to substantiate the findings. I'll wait."

Isaac excused himself to make some calls and returned thirty minutes later with a scientist from the local HALO chapter. The man brought his own microscope, slides, and water samples and set them up on the opposite side of the bistro. After inspecting the droplets, he conferred privately with Isaac and left.

When Isaac rejoined their table, his skin had paled a few shades. "All right. Assuming I believe you, what are we going to do to fix the problem?"

"My leaders have the technology to neutralize the algae blooms," Aelyx said. "But they won't deliver it unless our people form an alliance."

"Of course they won't." Isaac stared into the first jar of water. "They'll use this to get whatever it is they want from us." He glanced up and demanded, "And what is that, exactly?"

At one time Aelyx had thought he'd known. But not anymore. He folded both arms on the tablecloth and dodged the question. "Let's be honest. My people have the means to defeat you, easily. If The Way wanted you dead or enslaved, you would be. If we wanted your land or your DNA or your women, we would already possess them."

The tightening of Isaac's jaw showed he agreed.

"After the Patriots murdered Eron," Aelyx continued, "I fought for your kind. I begged The Way to give you another chance. Now you have it, and you won't stop trying to assassinate me."

"Whoa, there." Isaac flashed a palm. "I already told you I had nothing to do with that."

"Maybe not you specifically, but when you preach hatred, how do you expect your followers to respond?" Aelyx delivered a stern warning. "If one of them succeeds in killing me, there'll be no one left to plead your case. There will be no alliance and no solution to the water contamination."

"What is it you expect me to do?"

"Support the alliance," Aelyx said. "Publicly."

Colonel Rutter added, "Without mentioning the water crisis. If you do, there's a military prison cell with your name on it. We don't need riots and hoarding on top of everything else."

"How am I supposed to justify a sudden change of heart?" Isaac asked. "I've been battling this alliance for two years. I'm still against it. My members will think you brainwashed me."

Aelyx pushed the microscope across the table as a grim reminder. "I'm confident you'll think of something."

Isaac gazed into his coffee as if the answer might drop from the heavens into his cup. Seconds ticked by, turning to minutes.

"Think of your son," Aelyx pressed. "Without this alliance, he won't live to see thirty. And it won't be an easy death. Have you ever seen what dehydration does to a man? His lips will crack. His muscles will cramp and his head will throb. If he's lucky, his heart will fail before his skin begins to—"

"Enough!" Isaac pushed away from the table, his chair loudly scraping against the floor. "I'll do it. But if your leaders don't hold up their end of the deal, there will be war. I swear it."

Colonel Rutter bristled at the threat, but Aelyx waved him off. "I'll get the technology myself if I have to," Aelyx said. "But I can't help you if I'm dead."

Isaac snatched his coat off a nearby chair. "None of my people will touch you. I'll make sure of it."

Before he charged toward the door, Aelyx called, "Wait," and handed him the first jar of water. "If you ever doubt what I've told you, look at this sample beneath a scope and see how quickly the blooms multiply."

Isaac took the jar, careful not to make contact with Aelyx's skin, then stuffed it inside his jacket pocket and wiped his hand on his pants as if he'd touched filth.

What a bastard.

"Well, that didn't go too badly," Colonel Rutter said after Isaac had left. He stood and clapped Aelyx on the back. "Now all we have to do is keep you alive till spring." Gathering his supplies, he beamed and said, "Easy peasy."

When Colonel Rutter returned Aelyx to the hotel an hour later, the penthouse was crowded with politicians and publicists—none of them smiling. Confused, Aelyx made his way into the room, then stopped short when his gaze landed on the television screen. Someone had paused the program, but he recognized it at once. His own image stared back at him from a hotel sofa he shared with Cara's parents.

Somehow the botched interview with Sharon Taylor had aired.

Stomach dropping, Aelyx glanced around the room for an explanation. He grew cold when he noticed the ambassador glaring at him from the dining room table. No doubt, Stepha would punish him for this.

"What happened?" Aelyx asked.

"She leaked the whole thing," the PR specialist said. "We're not sure how she did it, but I assume she was wearing a hidden camera and transmitting the footage offsite."

"So it's . . ."

"Everywhere. And the response isn't pretty. HALO leaders are already calling for your arrest."

The room exploded in simultaneous conversation as everyone bickered over who to blame and what to do next.

Colonel Rutter's voice carried over the crowd. "Simmer down. We've got backing from Isaac Richards now. Whatever the damage from that interview, we'll call a press conference and have him put out the flames. This isn't the end of the—"

Stepha raised a hand and silenced the colonel. "It's late. We will continue this discussion in the morning." A few objections arose, but Stepha insisted that everyone leave, even David, who begrudgingly agreed to wait in the hallway. Within minutes, the room cleared until only Aelyx and Syrine remained.

"I'm sorry," Aelyx said. He doubted it would help, but he meant every word.

The ambassador showed no sign of emotion. "You know what has to happen."

Aelyx could only nod.

Stepha led the way into the living room, where he settled in his armchair and instructed Aelyx and Syrine to take the sofa. Right away, Aelyx noticed the *iphet* resting on the coffee table and his shoulders clenched of their own volition.

"I haven't administered a Reckoning since I accepted the post of ambassador," Stepha said. "I find the task demeaning." He wrinkled his nose. "And I loathe the smell. It reminds me of my own childhood indiscretions."

Syrine shifted beside Aelyx on the sofa and wrung her hands. She'd nursed him through his first Reckoning at age six. Afterward, she'd empathized with his pain so acutely she'd vomited her breakfast. Aelyx wished Stepha would dismiss her. She didn't need this anxiety.

"Stepha, please," Syrine whispered. "Aelyx is repentant. Perhaps you can spare him the *iphet*. The Way doesn't have to know you waived his penalty. I won't tell anyone."

Aelyx expected the ambassador to chide her for suggesting such a crime, but he didn't. Instead, Stepha studied them for several minutes, never initiating Silent Speech—just watching. When at last he spoke, his voice was eerily calm. "I'm not going to administer a Reckoning." He leaned forward and took the *iphet* in his hands, then turned it over, inspecting the deceptively delicate wiry rod attached to its handle. He held it toward Syrine. "You are."

Syrine brought a hand to her breast. "Me?" She shook her head so fiercely her ponytail escaped its clasp. "I can't! Please, if you consid—"

"I believe you mistook my order for a request." Stepha tossed the *iphet* onto the table, where it rolled toward the sofa. He locked eyes with Aelyx but chose to speak aloud. "Do you see how your insubordinate actions have corrupted this girl? In defense of your treachery, she has proposed a lie by omission—seeking to deceive The Way, whom she has sworn to obey in all things. Do you see how your poor example has led her astray?"

"Yes," Aelyx said, offering a silent prayer to the Sacred Mother that Stepha would reconsider. Syrine didn't deserve this. "And I'm deeply sorry."

"In the end, rebellion hurts us all." Stepha showed no signs of relenting. "Syrine will deliver your Reckoning and share in your anguish, to teach you that everyone suffers when you defy The Way." Without moving an inch, he glanced at the *iphet*. "She will administer twenty strokes."

"Twenty?" Syrine cried. "But that's a dozen more than—"

"Twenty-five," Stepha corrected. "You may begin at your leisure."

Syrine clenched her fists, but she didn't argue. Aelyx knew her well enough to imagine she was punishing herself for adding five lashes to his penalty. He couldn't let Syrine assume the blame. This wasn't her fault.

He claimed the *iphet* and handed it to her. When their eyes met, he said, *Don't be afraid. I've been through this so many times I barely feel it anymore. You won't hurt me.*

Of course she knew he was lying, but she nodded and took the handle in her trembling fingers. Aelyx showed her how to power it on, then removed his shirt and knelt in front of the sofa, resting his folded hands atop the cushion.

"I'm ready," he told her.

She positioned herself behind him, her breaths coming in shallow gasps. She began to speak but must have thought better of it, because the next thing Aelyx knew, she'd struck him directly between the shoulder blades.

Aelyx tasted the electricity before he felt it, but the sting quickly followed. His muscles clenched, skin burning as the stench of singed flesh filled his nose. She struck again and then again in quick succession. Sweat beaded across Aelyx's brow. His lungs ached to cry out, but he gritted his teeth and refused to make a sound. He wouldn't burden Syrine with the knowledge of his pain.

On and on it went. The sickening *zap* of the lash echoed against the high ceilings, punctuated by Syrine's wet sobs. Once she reached twenty strokes, Stepha told her to stop.

"Are you contrite, brother?" Stepha asked.

Aelyx couldn't speak, so he nodded. He'd never felt so contrite in his life. Black spots danced in his line of vision, and he knew he'd never make it back to his room. With limbs weaker than onionskin, he pushed away from the sofa and lay on the carpet, letting the air flow freely over his lacerated back.

After the ambassador retired to the master suite, Syrine knelt by Aelyx's side. She dabbed medicated salve on his burns and whispered "I'm sorry" a hundred times. He wanted to tell her this wasn't the kind of apology he'd wanted, but those dancing black spots merged into one, and he surrendered to oblivion.

The next morning, Aelyx awoke facedown on his bed, unsure of how he'd made it there. He squinted against the early sunlight and discovered Syrine on the floor beside his mattress, fast asleep with an open bottle of salve in hand. Before he had a chance to whisper her name, she blinked awake, as if sensing him.

She sat up and flashed a palm, her eyes reddened by tears. "Don't move. I added another layer to your *fahren* wrap an hour ago. I need to wash it off."

Syrine rushed to the bathroom and returned with several damp towels. When she placed the first on Aelyx's back, he held his breath and braced for the pain, but all he felt was warm moisture. He relaxed at once.

"Okay?" she asked, blotting his skin. "Is this too hard?"

"I barely feel a thing. What did you do to me?"

While removing the dried salve from his back, she whispered, "I gave you two analgesic injections and a healing accelerant. The *fahren* wrap is cosmetic, so you won't scar." Those medicines were hard to find on Earth. "Where did you get all of that?"

"Easy," she said. "I liberated the medic kit from Stepha's suite after he fell asleep."

Grinning, Aelyx glanced at her over his shoulder. "I truly *have* corrupted you."

Syrine didn't return his smile. Her eyes welled with fresh tears as she dried his skin and smoothed on a final layer of ointment. "He never said I couldn't heal you. Technically, I haven't disobeyed him."

When the treatment was complete, Aelyx sat up and faced her. *Thank you. I'm sorry you had to do that—any of it. I shouldn't have put you in that position.*

Syrine gaped as if he'd told her the Sacred Mother wore combat boots. *You're apologizing to me?*

Yes, it was my fault.

No. She shook her head and burned a glare into his skull. *Don't say that. I hurt you, not only last night, but months ago on the transport. And I never said I was sorry. Now I'm saying it: I'm sorry.*

After last night, Aelyx didn't need to hear it anymore. He held out a hand. *I just want my friend back.*

Tears spilled down Syrine's cheeks as she took his hand in both of hers. She gave him a watery smile. *I never left.*

Chapter Twelve

"No crying," Troy ordered. "You promised."

Cara dabbed at her eyes with her tunic sleeve. "Who's crying?"

"You are, dorkus."

"Nope, not me." Tears didn't count unless they spilled over, so she hadn't violated their deal. "Must be something in the recycled air."

Troy had wanted to say good-bye at the Aegis, and when Cara begged to tag along to the spaceport, he'd agreed on one condition—no sniveling. He'd said it was hard enough leaving her behind, and he didn't need one more reason to feel like crap.

"Well, get it in check," he said. "Or I'll have Jeeves take you back early."

The capital guard who'd shuttled them to the spaceport—whose name was Aloit, not Jeeves—pointed to the station manager and gave Troy a command in L'eihr. Troy looked to Cara for an interpretation.

She translated for him. "You need to turn in your orders and get a travel band."

"Impressive," Troy said with an appreciative nod.

"I know, right?" Cara never imagined how quickly she'd pick up the language. Cultural immersion really worked.

That didn't mean she wanted to stay. Her decision to leave Earth was starting to feel like a knee-jerk reaction, and she would stow away inside Troy's duffel bag if she could. She wondered if The Way had sensed it. That would explain why they'd sent a guard instead of a mere pilot to shuttle her to the transport.

"Okay. I'll make it quick." Troy backed away by slow degrees as if the two of them were tethered at the waist by a bungee cord. Cara could tell this was hard for him, and she suddenly regretted dragging out their good-bye. She should have given him a clean break at the Aegis like he'd asked.

"Take your time," she said, hitching a thumb toward the spaceport window. "I love the view from up here." To make it easier on him, she turned and strode away.

Once she reached the window, she darted a glance over her shoulder and found Troy making his way to the transportation official, orders in hand. Aloit had joined two other middle-age guards in browsing goods for sale along the vendors' corridor.

"Huh," Cara said to herself. "Shopping." She hadn't considered that. Maybe she should send home some presents with the credits she'd earned from all those nights sanitizing the kitchen. If she hurried, Troy could stuff the gifts in his bag and deliver them once he arrived on Earth. But just when she'd taken two steps in the other direction, her com-sphere buzzed to life. She rushed to a quiet corner to answer it, careful to keep Troy in sight so she could wave him over when he was done.

After whispering her password, she set her sphere on the floor and sat cross-legged facing it. The floor's steely panels chilled her bottom, so she pushed to her feet and crouched low, hugging her knees.

Tori's upper torso appeared in miniature from Mom's kitchen table. Cara smiled so widely it hurt. If anything could make this day bearable, it was a call from her best friend.

Tori's ebony eyes beamed against skin the precise shade of toasted caramel, her jet-black hair cut in a meticulous bob that followed her jawline. She still had that familiar spitfire in her gaze, the kind that warned a zinger was coming. "You're in the fetal position," Tori quipped. "I would be, too, if I were on Planet Freak."

Cara laughed, drawing a few glances from nearby crew members. "I was literally freezing my ass off. I'm at the spaceport saying good-bye to Troy."

"Good," Tori said. "Now get on board with him."

Cara figured her friend couldn't talk long, and she didn't want to waste one minute arguing for the hundredth time about the exchange or listening to a litany of complaints about L'eihrs. "You know I can't do that, so drop it and tell me how much you miss me."

Tori answered with her middle finger, a strangely welcome sight.

"Are you okay?" Cara asked. "Is it safe to be at my house?" Tori and Eric had joined HALO before they'd understood the Patriots' violent nature. Since then, they'd had to pretend not to associate with Cara's family or face the same "accidents" that had befallen those who openly supported the Sweeneys.

"Safe and sound." Tori's face broke into a grin. "You're not gonna believe this."

Cara noticed Troy scanning the room for her, so she stood and waved to get his attention, then crouched low again. "Believe what?"

"Isaac Richards is backing the alliance."

"Right," Cara said with a snort. "And I'll ride a unicorn back to my gingerbread dorm."

"I swear it on my *abuela*'s grave." Tori raised one hand in oath. "He said the L'assholes have more to offer than he thought. We should still be careful, but no more protests or he'll disband our chapters."

"You're serious?"

"As cancer." Tori bit her lip and considered for a moment. "Guess that's not really serious anymore, since the L'eihrs cured it, but still. Yeah, totes serious."

"Huh." Maybe someone had filled in Isaac on the water crisis. "Did he say what?"

Tori shrugged. "Technology, cures for more diseases. Stuff like that." When Troy approached and took a knee by Cara's side, Tori offered a quick wave. "Anyway, after Aelyx confessed to that stuff with the crops—"

The silvery band around Troy's wrist buzzed loudly, startling them all. "What the hell?" he asked as he stared into his palms.

Cara understood what it meant—she had less than five minutes with her brother. "We've got to go," she told Tori. "Try back tomorrow, okay?"

When Tori's image vanished, Cara took her brother's wrist and explained the boarding notification system. "You get two warnings. After the third buzz, it'll start to burn, and it won't stop until you cross the gate around that corner." She nodded into the distance at the metal ramp that led to the main transport. "It's sadistic, but you're guaranteed not to miss your flight."

He glared at his wrist and then back at her. "Another example of why we don't belong here."

Instead of arguing, Cara used a method of redirection she'd learned in the nursery: linking their arms, towing him toward the gate, and changing the subject. "Thanks for staying the extra couple of weeks. I hope I didn't get you in too much trouble."

He eyed her suspiciously but played along. "I'll live."

"Do you know where you're stationed next?" She hoped the military would keep him stateside this year. Mom missed Troy something fierce when he was away, and a German-Malty-Doodle-Poo was no substitute for a son. Or a daughter, she thought with a pang of guilt.

"No." He steered them around a cart of luggage. "My orders are to report to the L'eihr guard unit in Manhattan. No telling where they'll send me after that."

"Manhattan?" Cara squeezed his arm and bounced on her toes. "You might get to see Aelyx when he's done with his tour."

Troy rolled his eyes and faked a giddy voice. "I'm all tingly in my pants just thinking about it."

She laughed and poked at him some more. "Make sure you give him a big hug from me."

"Okay, shut up." They'd reached the base of the boarding ramp, so Troy dropped his duffel and shook free of Cara's grasp.

Her shoulder cooled at the hasty separation, so she rubbed her upper arms, resisting the urge to force a hug on her brother. She knew what he was doing—pulling away and preparing for the inevitable.

"When will I see you again?" she asked.

He dropped his gaze to the tips of his boots, which meant he didn't know.

Maybe in April, when she returned home for the big signing. "They have to let you come to the alliance ceremony, right?"

"The Marines don't *have* to let me do anything, Pepper. That's not how it works."

"Oh." She didn't know what else to say. This was it—the end of the line. The tears she'd fought so hard to block started to push back. A slow pressure built inside her chest while her eyes began to tingle, but she dug a thumbnail into her palm. *No crying!* She would not leave her brother with a depressing mental image to replay while he sat alone inside his ship's chamber.

Troy looked as if he was struggling for the right words, too. He opened and closed his mouth three times before offering a broken, "Uh, listen . . . I just wanna—"

The travel band cut him short with a threatening *buzz*.

"That's your last warning." Cara straightened her spine and faked her best smile, not too bright but warm enough to seem genuine. "You should go."

Troy didn't move.

"Really," she said. "If you see Mom and Dad, tell them I'm fine and I'm having fun. Don't mention the electric shock thing I wear for PE. They won't understand." She nudged him and joked, "And tell our baby brother, Linus, I can't wait to meet him."

Troy still didn't move. Instead, he swallowed hard, his body rigid and his feet glued to the platform.

Cara had to focus like mad to keep her voice steady. "It's okay. I'll be fine, promise."

He gave a slow nod but remained in place. "You're tough. I know that. But it's not—"

Before he could get another word out, his eyes flew wide and he shook his wrist while howling in pain. "Son of a bitch!" He jumped in place, then turned and bolted toward the transport without another glance in her direction. His boots rattled the metal grating, obscenities trailing behind him like a noxious cloud as he turned the corner and ran out of sight.

Leave it to Troy to say good-bye in style.

Cara's chest heaved with silent giggles. The burns weren't lasting—it was more of a mind trick than anything—but she'd never seen her brother more motivated to board a flight. He'd even left behind his duffel. She picked it up and hauled it to a nearby crew member who was sorting crates by the cargo hold.

"Excuse me," she said in L'eihr. "My brother left his bag. Can you take it to him?"

The man said yes but told her to wait a moment, then dug through bins and boxes until he pulled a large padded envelope from the pile. He handed it to her. "This is for you."

Cara's heart fluttered when she glimpsed Aelyx's name above the return address. She hugged the soft package to her chest, torn between ripping it open right there and waiting for the privacy of her room at the Aegis.

In the end, impulsivity won the battle.

She crossed the spaceport, back to the spot where she'd answered Tori's call. There, she leaned against the wall and ran her finger beneath the envelope seam. When she peeked inside, she found a gallon-size Ziploc bag filled with something dark. She spotted a scrap of paper and pulled it free.

Wear me.

"Wear me?" she mumbled, separating the Ziploc seal. Why had Aelyx sent clothes from Earth? He knew she couldn't wear anything but the standard uniform. She removed an extra-large gray T-shirt, puzzled until a familiar scent reached her—warm and sweet and spicy. Like a drug, it rushed her senses and made her go fizzy all over. She would recognize that luscious smell anywhere. It was his. She dropped the envelope and brought the shirt directly to her nose, then huffed it like the junkie she was.

Oh, man, it was better than chocolate.

She sucked in breath after breath, closing her eyes and pretending Aelyx was there with her. She could almost feel his lips at her throat and the satiny tickle of his hair against her cheek. It was a nice fantasy until she opened her eyes and found Aloit and the other guards staring at her in disbelief.

Cara didn't bother trying to explain. She rubbed the shirt over her neck and chest like a perfume stick, then stuffed it back inside the Ziploc bag and sealed it tight to hold in the eau de Aelyx. She was *so* sleeping in that shirt tonight.

Two hours later, Cara stepped inside the Aegis and hung a left toward her room. The headmaster had given her a day-long reprieve from classes for "emotional distress" in the wake of Troy's departure. She planned to bang out a quick blog post, then spend the rest of the day outside, maybe practicing the spinners, the trickiest obstacle on the intermediate course.

She'd just opened her door when Vero padded by and skidded to a halt, doing the animal version of a double take. He peered at her in silence, wide black eyes boring into her skull while his nose twitched like a rabbit's. He didn't screech gibberish or dart inside her room to pee on her pillow.

That wasn't like him.

Intrigued, Cara waited to see what he'd do next.

Vero crept an inch toward her and paused, crept forward again and paused, repeating the dance until he reached Cara's boots. Nose twitching, he sniffed her pants in rapid huffs, moving up to her knee and then across to the package in her right hand. He took in the scent and pulled back, then released the most heartrending whine Cara had ever heard, exactly like a dog that missed his master.

"Aww," Cara said, putting it together. "You smell Aelyx on me, don't you?"

Vero eyed the envelope as if he thought Aelyx were inside it. To dispel any doubt, she pulled out the clear bag so the animal could see there was nothing to fear.

"See?" she said. "It's just a shirt."

He backed toward the lobby, darting glances between Cara and the T-shirt, his tiny face contorted in confusion. His whine turned into a deep, throaty *ah-woo* of despair.

Poor Vero. She'd totally mindfreaked the little bugger with Aelyx's scent.

"Sorry, hon. I know how you feel. I miss him, too."

After Vero hightailed it to the cafeteria for his ritual post-lunch scavenging mission, Cara walked into her room and stopped short. Troy's bunk looked so empty stripped of its linens that she had to avert her gaze before the tears started falling.

Forget the blog post; she needed to get out of here.

After tucking Aelyx's envelope beneath her pillow, she grabbed a towel so she could make it to the intermediate course between PE classes. She didn't want an audience, and she especially didn't want Satan to spot her practicing. She hoped to impress him by mastering the spinners on her own.

Slinging the towel around her neck, she jogged across the courtyard to the courses, then slowed her steps and peered through the trees, making sure to stay hidden. She crept within view of the spinners and ducked behind a tree, disappointed to find them already populated by a class of freshman-age clones.

"*Sh'ot*," she muttered under her breath. She hadn't gotten here in time. But maybe if she hung out for a while, she'd have fifteen or twenty minutes to herself when the classes changed. She might even learn a new technique by observing the group of students racing toward the rotating disks. Cara knelt in the underbrush and studied the clones' tactics.

Just as the first one broke into a sprint, a shriek sounded from the sky.

Cara's pulse quickened. She didn't have to gaze into the heavens to know a fiery orb was about to rain down upon them. The clones noticed, too, stopping on the track and pointing toward the flames. Satan jogged into sight and produced his com-sphere, probably to report the occurrence to the capital. Cara tried to estimate the orb's trajectory. If she was right, it should land in the woods, about a quarter of a mile from her current position.

A delicious idea came to mind.

Nobody knew she was here. If she snuck away and got a head start, she might be able to reach the object before The Way sent a shuttle to retrieve it. She didn't waste another second pondering her next move.

After tiptoeing out of sight, she sprinted in the direction of the burning trail, hurtling over fallen logs and ducking beneath low branches. The whistle grew louder as she ran onward, and soon a crash boomed in the distance, followed by a thin plume of smoke. She increased her speed, barreling toward the black wisps that clouded the air.

In minutes, she'd reached the source of the impact—a slight crater in the forest floor with steam wafting up from within, smelling slightly of sulfur. Cara made her way to the site with tentative steps, then crouched down to peer inside the hole.

That thing was man-made, all right.

It was slightly smaller than she remembered, more like a baseball than a softball, but she recognized the twinkling lights scattered in haphazard increments across the orb's brassy surface. Each light flashed independently of the others in no discernible pattern. Cara couldn't imagine what the sphere could be. Maybe an intergalactic message in a bottle?

"What are you?" she asked the object.

That's when it replied.

Cara gasped and scrambled backward, flailing to remain on her feet. Holy crap, had that thing actually beeped at her? She neared the crater and peered inside again just in time to watch the orb wriggle free from the ground and drift slowly upward until it hovered in the air with a barely perceptible hum. Another sound caught her attention, coming from the sky. The shuttle was almost here.

Cara acted quickly, reaching behind her neck to see if she still had her towel. Luckily, she hadn't lost it during the sprint. She inched forward and threw her towel over the twinkling orb, then wrapped it up to protect her hands from its heat and jogged back the way she'd come. If the capital guards had any sense—which they did—it was only a matter of time before they saw her boot prints and tracked them to the Aegis. Then they'd sweep the building and she'd have to surrender her prize.

She had an hour, maybe two, to figure out what this thing was.

Chapter Thirteen

Aelyx had never seen anything like it. The golden orb didn't appear L'eihr-made, but perhaps The Way had invented something new and was testing its functionality above the atmosphere. If that were the case, maybe a few defective units had fallen to the ground.

"Speak to it in L'eihr," Aelyx suggested. "Give it a command and let's see if it responds."

"Good idea." Cara cupped one hand around the floating sphere and drew it nearer to her face. "Reveal your message." She spoke with a heavy American accent, but clearly enough to understand.

Lights flashed once in unison, and after an audible hum, a distorted computerized voice responded in a series of garbled words Aelyx didn't recognize. Cara's wide eyes reflected his own shock. Neither of them had expected the gadget to attempt verbal communication. He wondered what it meant.

"What are you trying to tell me?" Cara asked it in L'eihr. "I don't understand."

The voice slowed and took on a feminine tone, then spoke another series of words. Aelyx still didn't recognize the language, but it was obviously different from the first. When Cara didn't answer it, a series of clicks emanated from the orb, followed by a few guttural utterances that sounded like bastardized Latin. It seemed the sphere was going through a database of languages in an effort to connect with Cara.

Only one kind of device would do that.

A lump of dread rose in Aelyx's throat, but he maintained a calm facade. "I think I know what it is."

"Really?" she asked over the sphere's increasingly rapid discourse. "What?"

"Before I say, I want to get a second opinion from Syrine. Be right back."

He found Syrine sitting cross-legged on the living room rug playing a game of backgammon with David, who lay stretched out on his side, propped on one elbow. They both wore easy smiles as they baited each other with what David referred to as "trash talk." Aelyx had to call Syrine's name twice before she noticed him. When she threw a quick glance in his direction, he waved her over.

"Just a minute," Syrine said. "I've almost got him beat."

"In your dreams." David rolled the dice and gave a victory whoop. "I'm catching up."

"Not quickly enough," she taunted.

"Sy-*rine*!" Aelyx shouted.

Now he had her attention. *What is it?* she asked privately.

I need you to see something, he told her. *It's important.*

She nodded vigorously and turned to David, pointing at their game. "I've memorized the board, so I'll know if you've moved any pieces while I'm gone."

David flashed a mischievous grin. "I'm going to take you down, firecracker. And when I do, it'll be fully legit."

She pushed to standing and hurried to Aelyx's side, two spots of pink rising high on her cheeks. Aelyx led her into his bedroom and closed the door behind her, then pointed to Cara's hologram. The sphere was orbiting Cara's head now, continuing to spew undecipherable messages and flashing brighter than the ball he'd seen in Times Square last month.

Syrine knelt at the foot of Aelyx's bed and squinted at the object. "What is that?"

Aelyx caught her eye and used Silent Speech to explain. *Cara said they've been falling from the sky—three that she's seen so far. It's sending her messages in a variety of unknown languages, over and over like it's feeding from a central—*

"Uh, hello," Cara interrupted. "Out loud, please."

Syrine ignored her, holding Aelyx's gaze as her jaw dropped. *Does The Way know?*

Aelyx nodded. "But they've been hiding the orbs from the population, claiming they're meteorites."

"Then it's probably not one of ours," Syrine said aloud. "If it were, the Voyagers would claim it."

Cara growled in frustration and caught the orb inside her blanket, where it wrestled for freedom. "Okay, what is this thing? It's starting to piss me off."

"It's a probe." Aelyx pulled in a deep breath and let it out in a whoosh. "I'm almost certain of it. And like Syrine said, I don't think it's one of ours."

"A probe?" Cara asked. "As in *I'ma disrobe you, then I'ma probe you?*"

Aelyx didn't understand the reference, but he imagined she was thinking of a medical tool. "No. A device used to gather data. Our Voyagers have used them in the past to explore unsafe environments, but those were elemental collection devices. Nothing as elaborate as this." Nothing that spoke. He'd give anything to understand what it was trying to say.

"So who sent it?" Cara asked.

That was the million-credit question.

"Are you sure there's no way it's yours?" Cara grew flushed with anger. She finally gave up fighting the blanketed orb and simply sat on it. "Maybe the Voyagers sent them out, and now they're coming home. That would explain why they're falling all over the place."

Aelyx shared a knowing look with Syrine. "Maybe," he said, though he had little doubt the object was foreign.

Cara must have heard a noise from outside the Aegis, because she slid off the orb and darted to her window. "The guard's here," she said. "That didn't take long."

Blinded by its blanket, the sphere knocked against the top bunk a few times before drifting about the room like a clumsy ghost.

Cara chased it down and tucked it football-style beneath one arm. "They can have it." Narrowing her eyes, she spoke to the orb. "You're a pain in my ass."

Syrine suggested, "Take it outside to the guard without letting the clones see it."

"I agree," Aelyx said. "If the clones catch you with something like this in your room, it'll fuel more rumors."

"That's the last thing I need." Cara secured the blanket tightly around her bundle and said good-bye, then disconnected, leaving Aelyx and Syrine staring at each other in concern.

What worried him most was that The Way had hidden the probes' existence. That implied a threat, or at least the fear of one. Aelyx had studied the Voyager logs to learn of other beings, but he'd never heard of a society advanced enough to create an interactive probe. Clearly these aliens existed—the glittering orb was proof.

So were the senders friends or foes?

Cara made sure no part of the probe was visible when she stepped into the hall, but even though the passing clones couldn't see the object, its bleeping and blabbering drew a few curious gazes. To muffle the noise, she loudly hummed the first tune that popped into her head—"Jingle Bells," which drew twice the curious gazes and a few open sneers from Dahla and her friends.

After jingling all the way through the lobby, Cara rushed outside and scanned the capital guards, hoping to spot the one in charge. She didn't identify him, but she did find Satan locking eyes with the headmaster.

Satan was a nice guy, in his own sadistic way. If she had to confess to smuggling an alien-made spyball into the Aegis, he was the person to talk to.

"Psst," she called from the front stoop. When he glanced in her direction, she skipped down the steps and waved him over to the only private spot available, the corner formed between the steps and the side of the building.

While Satan strode to meet her, Cara summoned her best innocent face: wide eyes, head tipped downward, pouty lower lip. She'd have to deliver an Oscar-worthy "stupid human" performance in order to pull this off. Fortunately for her, most L'eihrs already thought she was dumber than a bag of hammers.

"I'm glad you're here," she whispered to him. "I need your help."

"What is matter, Sweeeeeney?"

"I was walking in the woods a little while ago, and I heard a crash. When I went to check it out, I found this." She pulled back enough blanket to reveal a flash of brass and twinkling lights. At once, Satan's chrome eyes widened. "I thought it was pretty," she continued, "so I brought it back to my room, but now it's flying around and crashing into walls. I'm afraid it's going to break something." She made an extra-pitiful face. "Can you take it for me?"

"Others in Aegis, they see this?" He licked his lips nervously and tucked the blanket back in place.

"No. I'm the only one."

He took the probe from her and gripped it with about ten tons of force. "Stay for moment," he instructed. "I must find Jaxen."

Oh, no. She'd managed to dodge Jaxen since their trip to the colony. A gab session with L'eihr's resident brainwasher was the last thing she needed today. "I told you everything I know. Can I go back to the nursery?"

"Stay," Satan repeated, then jogged away without another word.

Damn.

Jaxen wouldn't be fooled by her innocent act. He'd know she brought the probe back to her room to study it. She should've just taken the device out the back door and released it into the wild.

It didn't take long for him to find her.

Jaxen pinned Cara with an amused look. "You brought it here because you thought it was pretty? If you're so taken with pretty things, I can direct you to the wildflower conservatory."

There was no point in trying to deny what she'd done, but her instincts warned her to plead partial ignorance. If it weren't for Aelyx, she'd never have guessed the orb was a data-gathering machine. "Look," she whispered, "you and I both know that's no meteorite. So why don't you tell me what it is."

"Sure." Jaxen's patronizing tone didn't fill her with confidence. "But not here. Let's talk in my chambers."

Alone with Jaxen inside his bedroom? No thanks. Cara matched his lie with one of her own. "Actually, I'm late for my shift at the preschool. They need me to help run the water diffusion experiment."

"Oh?" he said with an arched brow. "I thought the headmaster relieved you of your duties today."

Double damn.

"Well, technically I don't *have* to be there, but I wanted—"

"Excellent. Right this way, then."

He turned and strode inside the Aegis, and with an inward groan, Cara followed him to his room on the second floor. She kept scanning the halls for Elle, hoping to form an exit strategy, but with classes in session, the dormitory was empty. Her last hope was to find Aisly inside the room. But when Jaxen pressed one palm to his keypad, the door hissed open and revealed a vacant bedroom much like hers, only with the cots laid side-by-side instead of bunk-style.

He swept a hand toward the left cot, indicating for her to sit. The door closed with an extra-loud *hiss*, as if sealing her fate as well as the exit. She settled at the end of the bed, as far from the pillow as possible. It seemed too intimate near the spot where Jaxen rested his head at night.

To her relief, Jaxen remained standing. He gave her as much space as the small chamber would allow, folding his arms and leaning against the side wall when he began. "You're a smart girl, *Cah*-ra."

That was debatable based on her decision-making skills today. But whatever. She'd take it.

"I'm confident you can piece together the purpose of that sphere for yourself," Jaxen said. For the briefest of moments, she thought she saw a flicker of fear behind his gaze. "Did you understand anything it said to you?"

She wished she had, especially after seeing his reaction. "No. Not even close."

"Good." His shoulders sank an inch as he relaxed. "That's probably for the best."

Cara wondered if this was going to turn into one of those *Scooby-Doo* endings, where the bad guy loses his mask and confesses everything. Only in this version, the "meddling kids" would wind up with their memories erased. She decided to go for it. She might as well learn as much as she could and hope to retain it later by blocking her thoughts.

"Why?" she asked. "Because it would've transmitted my responses back to whoever sent it? And who is that, by the way?"

Jaxen ignored both her questions and posed one of his own. "Why are the governments of Earth concealing the full extent of the water crises from its citizens?"

Cara puckered her brow because he already knew the answer. "If people found out our water would be unfit for drinking, they'd start hoarding it. Prices would skyrocket. Looting and riots would break out, maybe even wars for the rights to clean rivers and natural springs. Humans don't have the best track record when it comes to rational behavior."

"Precisely." He moved from the wall and took a seat on the opposite cot. "Sometimes for the greater good, a governing body must keep its citizens ignorant of danger."

If Jaxen was trying to compare Earth's impending apocalypse to the probes raining down on L'eihr, he'd missed two major points. "L'eihrs are nothing like humans and your world isn't dying. Big difference."

She expected him to argue, but he studied her in silence,

taking the time to unclasp and resecure his long hair at the base of his neck. Then, in an abrupt move, he darted from his cot to occupy the seat beside her. The mattress shook with his added weight, tipping her nearer to him until their thighs touched. She wanted to scoot away, but she was already at the end of his bed.

"I've always liked you, *Cah*-ra," he said. "You've intrigued me since the day we met."

"Um." She leaned away as much as she could. "I didn't mean to."

He took her hand and pressed a thumb over the vein in her wrist, then swirled his fingertips lightly over her sensitive skin. Cara realized what he was doing. This was the L'eihr version of a kiss, in which they measured each other's pulse in an effort to make it rush beneath their lover's touch.

"But your inquisitive nature," he murmured, "is a danger to you in this case."

As respectfully as she could, Cara pushed away his hand, making sure he knew her spiked pulse had nothing to do with attraction. "This makes me uncomfortable." She scooted a few inches to the right until half her bottom hung off the mattress. "I have a *l'ihan*."

Clear disappointment dragged down the corners of his mouth. "As do I."

This was news to Cara. "Who is she?"

"In some ways, my perfect match." He sighed, then added, "And yet . . ."

Before he could finish, the bedroom door hissed open and his sister strode inside, stopping short when she noticed them together on the edge of his cot. Aisly didn't speak, but her expectant glance said, *What is* she *doing here?*

"*Cah-*ra discovered the emissary probe that crashed nearby," Jaxen explained. He left Cara's side and joined Aisly, where they engaged in a few beats of silent conversation. Aisly didn't seem alarmed, probably because she assumed her brother would pluck the memories from Cara's head. The girl pulled a mirror from her bureau drawer, along with a small bottle filled with clear liquid.

If Jaxen wouldn't reveal any details about the probe, maybe his sister would. "What can you tell me about the aliens who sent it?" Cara asked.

Aisly didn't respond. She flipped open the lid to her bottle, then tipped back her head and squeezed two drops into each of her eyes.

Cara had never seen clones do that. "Is something wrong with your eyes?" she asked.

"No." Aisly blinked a few times and blotted her cheeks with a handkerchief. Maybe it was Cara's imagination, but Aisly's irises seemed a darker shade of silver now. "Simple allergies." Aisly glanced at her brother. "You'll soon forget."

In other words, destroy this memory, too. Cara didn't know for certain, but she doubted the clones suffered from allergies, not after all those years of meticulous breeding. So what drug was inside that bottle?

Jaxen sighed again and motioned for Cara to stand. He seemed wearier of the mental cleansing than Aisley was. Must be rough screwing with so many heads.

This was it—time to summon her focal image. While

she crossed the room and stood before Jaxen, Cara imagined herself in the gym at Midtown High, surrounded by red dodgeballs. She fell so deeply into her fantasy that she could smell the pungent reek of sweat and hear the squeak of sneakers against the waxed wood floor. She scooped an imaginary ball into her hands and repeatedly bounced it, listening to the echo reverberate off the gym walls. When Jaxen took her face between his palms and peered into her eyes, Cara pictured him standing defenseless on the half-court line. A wicked grin curved her mouth. She was going to nail him, right in the beanbags.

The pretend ball felt tight beneath her fingers, overinflated for maximum impact. She drew back, tensed all the right muscles, then threw the ball with a mighty heave, making sure to follow through and hit her target. The ball flew from her grasp and connected with Jaxen's dangly bits with a satisfying *thwack*, and he doubled over before sinking to his knees.

Take that, you mind-warping asshole.

Cara had focused so intently on blocking her thoughts that she didn't notice when Jaxen pulled away. A loud throat-clearing snapped her to attention, and she found herself staring at the wall.

Uh-oh.

She'd missed his entire message. What had he tried pushing inside her head—to forget the probe and Aisly's eyedrops or to forget their entire encounter?

"I'm a little confused," Cara said, rubbing her temples and glancing back and forth between the siblings. "I came in here to ask you something, but now I can't remember what it was."

Aisly smiled sweetly. "You must be tired from waking up so early to take your brother to the spaceport."

"Do you need me to escort you back to your room?" Jaxen asked.

"No, I'll be fine." Cara shook her head and laughed dryly. "Guess I need a nap. Sorry to bother you."

"Any time," Jaxen told her.

She held up two fingers in a L'eihr good-bye and returned to her room, but not for a nap. She spent the rest of the afternoon talking to Aelyx about what had happened while intermittently huffing his shirt. After what she'd endured, she needed the comfort.

That night as Cara and Elle lay beneath their covers, Cara whispered, "Hey, can I ask you something?"

"Of course."

"Do L'eihrs get allergies?"

"Allergies?" Elle asked.

"Yeah, you know, reactions to pollen and mold. Itchy, watery eyes, cough, runny nose. Things like that."

"No," Elle said, confirming Cara's suspicions. "Anyone with a hypersensitive immune system would have been barred from reproducing thousands of years ago."

"You're a medic," Cara said. "What reason would someone have to use eyedrops?"

"They wouldn't." Elle sounded confused, which made two of them.

"That's what I thought."

The hiss of their door opening interrupted their conversation, and Cara pushed onto her elbows, heart thumping as she scanned the darkness for the intruder.

Ah-woo, came a low whine.

Cara pressed a relieved hand to her chest. It was only Vero. "Our keypad's messed up again," she told Elle, then pointed a warning finger at Vero. "If you pee on my pillow, I'll choke you with your own tail."

He crept to the foot of her cot, then extended one paw and lowered his head to the floor.

"Ooh," Elle whispered in awe from the top bunk. "He's showing deference. This means he sees you as his pack leader."

Yeah, right. Or he was trying to trick her into leaving her pillow undefended.

"It might have something to do with Aelyx's scent," Elle said. "He followed Aelyx everywhere—idolized him completely. As Aelyx's mate, Vero would consider you an alpha by association."

It was an interesting theory. Cara patted her mattress. "Come on, boy. It's okay."

After a while, Vero found the courage to climb into bed with her, scooting nearer by slow inches. Just when Cara started to think it *was* a trick, he curled up against Aelyx's T-shirt and rested his head on the mattress, purring sadly.

"You poor thing," Cara whispered. Slowly, so as not to startle him, she lowered her head to the pillow. A few minutes later when Vero's breathing began to slow, Cara extended one finger and petted his arm. His shorn fur was baby-soft, his delicate skin warmer than she'd anticipated. He surprised her by curling his little digits around her finger and tucking her knuckles beneath his chin.

Aww. Vero was a cuddler.

Even though he smelled kind of like wet dog, she enjoyed the contact, so she scooted close enough to feel his warm breath against her cheek. They snuggled that way for the rest of the night, united by their love for a boy in another galaxy.

Chapter Fourteen

Cara awoke the next morning to a dead bird in her bed and a pair of not-yet-dead snakes in her boots. Luckily, her screams of terror brought Vero back to her room to finish his breakfast. Within minutes, the reptiles lay on the floor, relieved of their heads.

Not the best way to start the day. Especially for the snakes.

For reptiles, they were actually pretty—with shimmery hides and dozens of delicate antennae extending along the length of their spines. The bird was lovely, too, featherless with opalescent cream-colored skin that caught the faint glow from the window. Still, Cara preferred not to wake alongside Vero's prey, no matter how sparkly.

Elle giggled from the top bunk. "He must really like you."

"Earth pets do the same thing," Cara said, backing away from the carnage. She made a mental note to have the groundskeeper dispose of the bodies. "My friend Tori used to feed a feral cat that lived in the woods by her house. It left dead lizards and mice at her front door for the next five years." She squatted down to Vero's height and ordered, "No more presents, okay?"

The way he puffed his chest and jabbered with pride promised that birds and snakes were just the beginning of Cara's bounty. She sighed and grabbed a clean uniform. At least he'd stopped peeing on her pillow.

"I'm going to practice the spinners before breakfast," Cara said. But when she tried pulling up her pants, they slouched and nearly fell from her hips. "Aw, man. I need another uniform."

This was the third time she'd had to exchange her clothes for a smaller size. Not that she was complaining. As much as Cara despised L'eihr food, she had to admit their perfectly balanced diet, combined with Satan's rigorous strength training, had made her stronger and leaner than she'd ever achieved running track at Midtown High. She only hoped Aelyx wouldn't miss the junk in her trunk. She was a lot less bootylicious these days.

"So much for the spinners." There wasn't time to hit the supply station on the fourth floor, change, practice, shower, and make it back before breakfast. "Guess I'll meet you at the nursery."

"I can't." Elle hopped down and scanned her wrist, preemptively turning off the room alarm. "My medic adviser wants me in the advanced anatomy class. To get out of it, I'll need a better excuse than being your constant alibi."

"Oh." Cara had never realized how much she'd held her roommate back. "Don't worry about it. I'll be fine."

"Are you sure?" Elle asked. "Because I can arrange to have you sit in with me."

On advanced anatomy? Cara would rather learn something useful among the kindergartners than zone out during an upper-level course. "Thanks, but I'll stick with the kids. It's not like I need someone to corroborate my every move."

"You're probably right. Aelyx tends to overreact when it comes to you." Elle ran a comb through her ponytail while gazing into empty air. "I can't blame him, though. I would have done anything for Eron."

Cara held her breath for fear of saying the wrong thing, but then she decided to stop behaving like a coward and start acting like a friend. "I'm sorry. You must miss him."

Elle didn't answer at first. But soon she gave an absent nod. "I do. I'm beginning to worry I'll never stop."

"That's normal." Cara shrugged into a clean tunic and rolled her pants at the waist. "The pain will fade with time, but you'll always remember him." Poor Elle. Like the other clones, she'd spent the first sixteen years of her life under the influence of hormone regulators, so she didn't have much experience with love or heartbreak. To her, this must feel like the end of the world. "It'll get better," Cara assured her. "And one day, you'll feel ready to try again."

"That's hard to imagine."

"You'll see." Cara wished she could give Elle a hug, but casual touches made the clones uneasy. Instead, she offered a warm smile. "But there's no rush—don't put so much pressure on yourself. Grieve as long as you need to." Cara moved close enough to deliver a gentle nudge to her roommate's shoulder. "You're allowed to be human, you know."

Elle returned the smile. "I'm glad you're here."

During rare times like these, Cara agreed.

By midafternoon, she didn't feel quite so optimistic.

"What's wrong with your hair?" asked the little boy tugging Cara's braid. "I've never seen that kind before. It's ugly, like fire."

Cara reclaimed her braid and answered in L'eihr. "There's nothing wrong with having red hair. I think it's nice."

"Why does your skin look so pale?" he asked. "Are you sick? Did you lose all your blood?"

"No." Cara placed her wrist within his coppery hand to show him the pulse in her veins. "On my planet, people have lots of different skin colors. Some humans are darker than you, and some are even lighter than me."

"But you've got spots," the boy's friend objected, pointing to the freckles splattered across Cara's nose and cheeks. "You must be sick."

"Why do we have to talk out loud to you?" the first boy asked.

She took a deep breath and counted to five, peering around the classroom for the instructor, who'd left Cara in charge during her bathroom break. "Because I can't use Silent Speech."

"I knew that," a girl bragged from her seat on the floor. "My friend Alun told me that human brains are slow. He said they go backward."

"Well, I wouldn't say that we're slow . . ."

"He said humans are savage," the girl added, eyeing Cara skeptically. "Do you really eat your young?"

Cara was tempted to say yes, that each freckle on her nose represented an obnoxious kid she'd devoured, but she took the high road. "No, your friend made that up."

"Are you going to live here forever?" the girl asked.

Before thinking, Cara spat, "No," then quickly checked herself. "I mean, yes. On the colony."

But the Freudian slip betrayed her doubts. In truth, she wasn't sure she could settle there. Not trapped on an island, devoid of any means of escape. Not with mindbenders like Jaxen and Aisly in power. Not with the clones spreading rumors that she ate babies and sported a backward brain. Why wouldn't Aelyx at least consider defecting to Earth? Why did she have to make the sacrifice?

Maybe she shouldn't think about that right now.

The young girl brought Cara back to reality with a request. "Tell us a story."

"Please," the others begged. "A human story!"

"Okay." Encouraged by the children's enthusiasm, Cara sat cross-legged and motioned for the others to form a semicircle around her. While they settled in, she decided on a simple fable that she could shorten to accommodate her limited L'eihr vocabulary: "Hansel and Gretel."

"Once upon a time," she began, "there were two children who lived with their father in the forest."

Drawing on her best theatrical skills, she spun a tale that had the children transfixed, pausing only to explain unfamiliar terms like *gingerbread* and *wicked witch*. By the time she reached the scene where the witch had captured Hansel and fattened him up for cooking, the clones' eyes were wide in rapt attention, their little bodies leaning forward to hang on Cara's every word.

Cara led them through the story's climax, ending with Gretel freeing her brother from his cage and pushing the witch to a fiery death. "And then," she concluded, "they found their father and lived happily ever after."

But instead of applauding as she'd expected, the children gasped in horror. Then the questions came flying from all directions.

"Do all human fathers abandon their children?"

"Why did they destroy that woman's home?"

"Did they really burn her up? How barbaric!"

"See, I told you! Humans *do* eat their young!"

Cara tried corralling their imaginations, but the damage was done. The children backed away shrieking, as if she might spring on them and begin nibbling their eight tiny toes, Vienna sausage–style.

"Miss Sweeney . . ." The instructor stood in the doorway, scanning the chaos. "Why don't you offer your assistance in the seclusion room?"

Cara's heart sank. The seclusion room—a padded enclosure where the Terrible Twos went to scream it out. The nursery workers dodged that assignment like a jury summons. L'eihr eardrums were more sensitive to the assault of temper tantrums, likely because the spoken word was used so infrequently.

"Yes, ma'am."

Head low, Cara slunk down the hall to her post, bracing for the worst. From the earsplitting wail that greeted her when she opened the seclusion room door, she expected to find a dozen toddlers inside. But a single child was the source of the clamor. Not quite two years old, by the looks of him, but man, the kid had a pair of banshee lungs.

Cara greeted the teenager in charge of supervising the child. "I can sit with him awhile if you'd like to take a br—"

"Oh, thank the Mother!" The girl tapped her throat twice in a sign of gratitude, then bolted from the room before Cara had a chance to ask the child's name.

She observed the boy, taking in the wispy brown locks plastered to his cheeks by tears, tiny hands clenched into fists, his quivering chin slick with drool. During the brief moments he stopped crying, his breath hitched so badly he could barely catch it. Cara didn't know much about kids, but this didn't look like a temper tantrum. The boy seemed genuinely miserable.

She sat beside the toddler and pulled him into her lap, then pressed a hand to his forehead to check for fever. "You don't feel warm," she said. "What's wrong, bud?"

He rested his head against her chest and cried out again, seeking comfort by clinging tightly to her tunic. Cara rocked from side to side while patting the boy's back. Over the next ten minutes, she hummed and bounced and cooed, using every soothing technique she knew, but nothing worked.

He was hurting—she sensed it.

After ensuring nobody was watching from the window,

she took his face in her hands and peered into his eyes, opening her mind to him.

"Where does it hurt?" she asked aloud in L'eihr.

Hurt, he mentally repeated, which didn't help much. Using Silent Speech with toddlers was a challenge because they couldn't form coherent thoughts. Instead of dialogue, they shared snippets of desire or emotion in a jumble that often didn't make sense. This time was no exception.

Cara wanted to help the boy, but she didn't know how. She rested her fingertips against his belly and locked gazes with him in desperation. *Hurt?* She moved her hand to his head. *Hurt?* After repeating the query at his ears and throat, she touched his legs. *Hurt here? Where is the hurt?*

He understood—she felt it within his consciousness. He opened his mouth and pointed inside, then told her, *Hurt here*, and projected a sensation she recognized at once. She'd known that pain at sixteen, when her wisdom teeth had pushed a jagged trail to the surface of her gums. This baby was cutting teeth—probably his two-year molars.

Anger flared through her, flushing her cheeks and making her hot all over. Teething was a common issue among young children, so why hadn't the nursery workers checked for this? How long would they have let the boy cry before realizing he was in pain?

And they had the audacity to call *her* slow.

First, she was going to treat his sore gums with an analgesic swab. Then she was going to tear someone a new L'asshole. Holding tightly to the boy, she pushed to standing and stalked across the room. But when Cara threw aside the door and stepped into the hall, she came to a sudden halt.

Wait a minute.

Had she used Silent Speech with this boy? With words and everything?

Cara's lips parted and spread into a smile. She'd really done it!

Her anger evaporated, morphing into triumph. After tireless hours of practice, she'd finally discovered the part of her brain required to share complete thoughts. Now that she'd isolated it, the region felt like a muscle she'd never known existed. She flexed it while gazing into the boy's eyes. *We'll fix the hurt*, she told him.

It was easier now!

Hurt, was all he said. He didn't understand anything more.

She carried him to the first-aid station and strapped him into the counter seat, then fished in the cubby for a plastic swab. She showed it to the boy and opened her mouth to model what she wanted him to do. *Open big.*

When he obeyed, she snapped the tip off the medicated end and dabbed thick, syrupy liquid over the back of his gums, where bits of white bone had begun to poke through the flesh. She massaged the medication into the swollen tissue and opened her mind to him. *No hurt?*

Bad taste, he complained, but his pain was gone. *Give drink.*

"Okay." She spoke aloud in L'eihr after noticing Gram, the nursery director, striding into the room with an infant on her shoulder. "Let's get you some water."

The boy tugged Cara's cheek with his sticky palm, initiating eye contact. *No water. Reed-milk.*

"Or milk," she said for the director's benefit. "Would you rather have that?"

Milk, he silently repeated.

Use your words, she told him. *Say it loud.*

"MILK!"

Gram laughed from the changing station. "He knows what he wants."

Cara left him buckled in his seat while she fetched a glass of reed-milk, which was similar in taste and consistency to soy. In other words, totally nasty. But the little guy loved it. She helped him finish his drink and told Gram his caregivers had mistaken teething pain for a temper tantrum. Gram promised to have a word with his instructor.

Cara guided the boy back to the toddler room and left him with a kiss on the cheek, which he promptly scrubbed away with his fist. That was gratitude for you. But no matter. Nothing could bring her down. Cara's accomplishment had her beaming like a new quarter. She couldn't wait to tell Aelyx tomorrow—he would be so proud.

Since the seclusion room was empty and she doubted the preschool instructor wanted any more of her help, Cara decided to sneak off to the intermediate course to blow off some steam. Besides, she was on a roll today. She'd managed to get Elle to open up about her grief, then she'd unlocked the next level of Silent Speech. If good things came in threes, she'd conquer those wily spinners before dinner.

Vero greeted her in the lobby and followed along to the obstacle course, chattering animatedly in his language of chirps and howls. Occasionally, he'd freeze, ears cocked on high alert, and dart into the trees to hunt another prize, but the daytime serpents were too quick for him. Cara strolled at an easy pace, enjoying the warmth of the sun and the citrusy scent of *ilar* leaves on the breeze. The only sounds were rhythmic percussions of insect calls and birdsongs, both foreign and familiar to her ears. While mating calls varied from one planet to another, love was universal, and it was in the air today.

"It's beautiful here," she said to Vero, even though he didn't understand. "I miss the green leaves, but the bushes and trees back home are dormant now, anyway."

She wished she had more time to enjoy the outdoors. She wanted to wander deep into the woods, where thick trees blocked the sun, and see what fuzzy wonders grew in the shadows. She wanted to shuttle over the great city wall and catch a glimpse of the beasts there, to discover whether the barrier protected the animals or if the reverse were true. It seemed criminal to overload her schedule to the point where she couldn't explore this lush place.

The intermediate course was still and silent when she reached it. Even the spinners lay motionless, which gave her a chance to inspect them more closely. Each rotator was constructed like a record player, a round disk raised slightly above its foundation held in place by a central bolt, which turned with the apparatus instead of remaining fixed.

She crouched down and grazed the pebbled surface with her palm. Good traction, a clue that she wasn't meant to skid from one to the other. She pushed against the outside edge, feeling it give an inch beneath her weight. Common sense told her she could use the bounce to her advantage, but she didn't know how.

She jogged to the solar panel that powered the course's moving elements and turned it on. In response, a soft hum arose, breaking the tranquility. Time to get down to business. She set off at a slow run and approached the first spinner, determined to crush the obstacle.

Fifteen minutes later, the only thing she'd effectively crushed was her own butt.

She rubbed her aching bottom and muttered a few swear words while the rotating disks mocked her in a steady *whir* that resembled demonic laughter. Why couldn't she figure this out?

"As if I need another reason to feel like a loser here." Glaring at the nearest spinner, she drew back and gave the base a hearty kick. It felt so good that she stomped the disk with her boot heel, not caring that the act would probably land her on her backside.

But that's not what happened.

The impact caused the disk to stall ever so briefly . . . just long enough to gain purchase and leap to the next spinner, had she been standing on it.

That was it—the secret to navigating the spinners was to land as hard as possible on each disk. Cara laughed aloud, startling Vero, who'd begun to doze in a patch of sunlight.

"Eureka!" she shouted, rubbing her palms together. "Now watch me own this course."

It took a few tries to perfect her technique, but by the fourth attempt, she had it down to a science. When she leaped from the final spinner across the finish line, she pumped her fists into the air and shouted a victory cry sweeter than any chocolate bar. She couldn't believe the rush of adrenaline surging through her veins. If besting the intermediate course felt this good, she'd probably need to change her pants after mastering the proficient track.

Satan was going to be so impressed. She couldn't wait to show him.

"Sweeeeeney!" Speak of the devil, she turned to find him waving to her from the courtyard. It was hard to tell from this distance, but he seemed upset. His already broad shoulders were hunched halfway up to his neck as he ran to meet her, a trio of lines creasing his typically smooth forehead.

Had she done something wrong? Maybe once the equipment had powered down for the day, students weren't supposed to turn it back on. L'eihrs were pretty stingy with energy.

"Sorry," she said as he approached. "I was practicing. But wait till you see—"

"Why you ignore summons?" he asked, his eyes wild. She'd never seen him so upset. "Look much bad when you refuse answer."

"What summons?" Cara checked her tunic pocket to make sure she hadn't lost her com-sphere. It was right there, but she hadn't received a message. "Did you call me?"

"No." He backed toward the Aegis, motioning for her to follow. "Headmaster and guard. Come now."

A sick, sinking feeling settled in the pit of Cara's stomach. If the headmaster and house guard had both summoned her, that meant bad news. Her mind flashed to Troy. She hadn't heard from him since he'd left for Earth. What if his ship had crashed into a rogue meteor? That had happened once, years ago, when a transport's thrusters had failed. Cold sweat collected along the back of Cara's neck as she sprinted past her fitness instructor, across the courtyard, and up the front steps of the main dormitory.

She halted at the doors only long enough to extend her wrist for the security scanner. The doors parted and she bolted into the lobby, stopping short in time to avoid a collision with Odom and Skall, the seniors who'd fought with her brother.

They moved aside to let her pass, revealing a small crowd that had gathered in the lobby. The house guard shouted for everyone to return to their classes. When the man's gaze landed on Cara, his eyes narrowed, mouth tight in a way that warned she was in trouble. An unexpected rush of relief washed over her. As long as Troy was safe, nothing else mattered.

At least that's what she thought until she saw the blood.

A slick smear of burgundy stood in stark contrast against the tile floor, winding a macabre trail that led from the far hallway to the lobby.

What had happened in here?

"Try it," Skall said in L'eihr as he brushed past her. "I'll be ready for you."

Try what? Before she could bring the question to her lips, he strode away with his friends. The clones stole glances at her over their shoulders. Fear darkened their gazes, despite the fact that each of the boys outweighed her by fifty pounds of solid muscle. They were scared of her, though she couldn't imagine why.

"Sweeeeeney." Satan had caught up with her. "Please to say you not do this."

Cara recalled the stolen tablet beneath her pillow and the false accusation in the dining hall. She had a feeling Dahla had framed her for something a lot more serious than tampering with her food this time.

"Do what?" she asked, glancing at the blood. "I don't know what happened here."

Instead of telling her, the guard demanded to know her whereabouts as of thirty minutes ago. Cara told him the truth—that she'd spent most of the day in the nursery before practicing on the outdoor track. Then he asked if she'd seen Dahla today.

"I see her every day," Cara said. "In the washroom and in our classes."

Satan interrupted the interrogation and took her gently by the shoulders. "You have much fights with this girl, yes?"

"Is that what she told you?" Cara swallowed a lump. She reminded herself that L'eihrs couldn't lie through Silent Speech, so there was no way Dahla could hurt herself and blame Cara for it. "Because I think she's been trying to get me in trouble. Whatever she said—"

"She tell us nothing," Satan said. "Girl is barely alive, getting new blood from clinic."

Cara stopped breathing.

"There you are." Aisly strode in the front door with Jaxen and the headmaster at her heels. "We've been searching for you. Why didn't you answer your sphere?"

Still in a daze, Cara stammered a few times before getting the words out. "It never rang. Or buzzed, or whatever." She pointed at the bloody trail and tried not to let her voice crack. "I didn't do that."

"Of course you didn't," Jaxen said. But he dropped his gaze to the floor and puckered his brow. "Now that you're here, you can help us understand."

"Understand what?"

"During the last class change," Aisly said, "two clones found Dahla brutally stabbed, along with a message scrawled in blood." Her gaze flickered to Jaxen's. "It said, *I'll come for you next.* But it was written in English."

"That doesn't prove anything," Cara argued. "Lots of people here speak English."

Jaxen hesitated twice before telling her, "The boys claim they had a feud with your brother—and that you and Dahla have had several altercations."

Cara closed her eyes and tried to think. Someone was still trying to frame her, but it couldn't be Dahla. Maybe Odom and Skall were to blame. Both boys had access to Dahla's breakfast that day in the dining hall. "I'll bet one of them attacked her and wrote that message."

"But the guard searched your room," Aisly said. "And found a bloody kitchen blade."

"Along with several decapitated animals and a *h'urr* blossom," Jaxen added softly.

"No," Cara whispered. She didn't even know what a *h'urr* blossom looked like, let alone how to extract a neurotoxin from it. "I swear I didn't do it."

Jaxen took a tentative step toward her, holding both hands forward like a crossing guard. "You've been under a lot of pressure, *Cah*-ra. You're alone and worried for your people. If you feel hopeless or depressed, perhaps you require . . . help. We can provide that for you."

So now they thought she was criminally insane? "I don't need help," she cried. "Someone planted the knife and blossom, and Vero put dead animals in my room as a present."

Apparently, that was the wrong thing to say if she wanted to avoid sounding crazy.

The group exchanged worried glances and began using Silent Speech to cut her out of the conversation. A vise tightened around Cara's lungs. She could use Silent Speech to clear her name, but her instincts begged her not to let Jaxen and Aisly find out she could communicate with her mind.

But what choice did she have? The siblings were in control here. One word from either of them would deem her innocent beyond reproach. As members of The Way, their decree was law.

Wait.

There were *ten* members of The Way, and even Jaxen and Aisly answered to a higher power. Cara had one other option to save herself. It meant putting her trust in an Elder she barely knew, but she'd gladly take the risk. Cara licked her lips and stood tall, faking a confidence she didn't possess.

"I held a *Sh'ovah*," she declared. "I'm a citizen and I have rights."

Aisly tipped her head in confusion. "Of course you do."

"Then I request a private audience with Alona," Cara said. "And only her. I want to go to the capital."

Chapter Fifteen

Aelyx couldn't stop thinking about the probe—and more specifically, who'd sent it. When the Voyagers had discovered Earth, they'd descended in a cloaked shuttle to explore the landscapes and urban centers. After determining a reasonably low safety risk, a crew of twelve had integrated with the human population, altering their eye color with medicated drops and wearing street clothes to observe human culture. Later, they'd reported their findings to The Way and received authorization to make official contact.

But that wasn't happening on L'eihr.

The fact that an advanced race had launched a fleet of scouting devices meant one of two things: either the society lacked the capacity for interplanetary travel—which Aelyx doubted based on the probe's extensive language database—or the senders didn't wish to establish personal contact. If the latter were true, he had to consider the possibility of an invasion.

Had The Way kept the probes a secret for fear of alarming the citizens? Was L'eihr covertly preparing for war? No, that couldn't be the case. The Aegis would train the clones for combat if an outside force posed a threat, and from what Cara had told him, the routine hadn't changed.

Curse it all, what was going on?

He wanted to ask Stepha, but then Aelyx would have to explain how he knew of the probe's existence. And Syrine was no help. Her mind was so clouded by infatuation that Aelyx had refused to engage in Silent Speech with her until she regained control of her libido. He wished she would simply bed David and be done with it. The tension inside the hotel penthouse was thick enough to spread on toast.

Aelyx leaned back in his leather armchair and watched Syrine, who in turn ogled David from her place on the sofa. Their bodyguard had taken Aelyx's advice of giving Syrine space, and it had worked too well. She wanted David so badly she'd begun daydreaming torrid fantasies about him . . . which was a disturbing thing to glimpse through Silent Speech.

In the interest of figuring out what was going on, he needed to clear Syrine's mind so they could work together. Which meant giving her "relationship" a little nudge. "David," he said. When his friend glanced up from his magazine, Aelyx suggested, "You should show Syrine that card trick you did for the guards last night."

David made a show of considering the request, then waved it off. "She doesn't want to see that."

"Yes, I do," she said in a rush. Aelyx could practically hear Syrine mentally chiding herself for answering so quickly. She faked an unaffected shrug. "I mean, there's nothing else to do while we're trapped in here."

David continued playing hard to get. "Nah. You'll figure out the trick and call me a stupid human."

"No, I won't."

"That's what you say every time you beat me at back-gammon."

"Because you deserve it," she criticized. "You make careless mistakes. Sometimes I think you're losing to me on purpose."

Aelyx rolled his eyes. "Let's make it interesting," he said. "Syrine, you pick a card, and if David guesses it correctly, you give him something. But if he can't guess it—"

"A bet?" she interrupted.

"Exactly."

She thought for a moment, then gave a decided nod and nudged David's leg with her socked foot. "What shall we wager?"

Though David maintained a disinterested expression, his eyes brightened. "I don't know. What do you want?"

Aelyx knew exactly what she wanted. "How about this," he said. "The loser has to bring the winner supper in bed tonight." If getting them alone in a bedroom while the ambassador was away didn't set something in motion, nothing would.

Syrine smiled as if she'd already won. "Perfect. I'll have a turkey club sandwich from the hotel deli—on freshly baked rye, no condiments and no tomatoes."

"That's what you think," David said as he threw his

magazine on the coffee table and pulled a pack of cards from his back pocket. "I'll have a calzone from the deli, and then you'll feed me grapes while I lounge on a stack of pillows."

"You'll feed *me* sliced pears," Syrine countered. "Drizzled in cinnamon and honey."

"Honey?" David's throat bobbed. "I love honey, especially . . . drizzled on stuff."

Sacred Mother. Aelyx was going to be sick. "Just do it already."

"Patience, my friend." David collected himself and shuffled the deck. "I don't want to give Syrine a reason to accuse me of cheating when she loses."

And she *would* lose. Aelyx had watched David stump his fellow soldiers a dozen times last night when he'd stepped into the hall to put out the recycling. Afterward, David had confided that the deck was marked. He'd bought it from a specialty store in New Jersey. The cards were decorated in an intricate—and deftly coded—design that only David could interpret.

He offered Syrine a chance to cut the deck and then fanned out the cards so she could choose one. When she made her selection, David told her to hold the card in front of her face and study it closely. The pretense was that he would try to read her thoughts, but in reality, it gave him a clear view of the encrypted symbols in the upper right-hand corner.

"Do you have it memorized?" David asked.

"Mmm-hmm."

He handed her the stack. "Then put it back in the deck."

Thinking she was clever, Syrine slipped her card on top of

the pile and snatched the deck to shuffle it. "I know how this trick works," she boasted. "You positioned a key card in the deck when I wasn't looking. But now it's out of order." With a beaming smile, she handed him the stack. "You'll never guess my card."

Aelyx held back a laugh while David searched the deck, pretending to seek a card he'd already identified. David held one up and announced, "The jack of clubs."

"No, it was the five of hearts!" Syrine bounced in her seat, clapping wildly. "I win!"

Flashing a wry grin, David wrapped a rubber band around the deck. "Yep, you beat me fair 'n' square. Guess I'll be feeding you pears and honey tonight." He peeked up at her. "Hey, any chance you're hungry? Dinner's not for a while, but I spotted a fresh pear in the fridge. If you want, you can go get comfy and I'll bring it to you."

Aelyx hid a smile. He should be taking notes, because David was a damned genius.

Syrine was too busy gloating to realize she'd been played like a game of sticks. "Okay. Make sure you slice them extra thin, and don't forget the cinnamon." She practically skipped to her room and left the door open for David to follow her into paradise.

"And that, my friend," David said, pointing at Aelyx, "is how it's done."

Needless to say, Aelyx spent the rest of the afternoon alone.

At dinnertime, he prepared a bowl of lo mein noodles and settled at the dining room table with a data tablet he'd borrowed from the ambassador. While Aelyx ate, he scanned the Voyager archives for information about the life-forms they'd discovered. He'd read most of these files in past years, but perhaps he'd overlooked a crucial detail that would lead him to the identity of whoever had launched the probes.

To shorten the possibilities, he sorted the list by intelligence, which left eleven sentient species. He eliminated ten of those because their technology hadn't advanced beyond the use of basic gear systems. The remaining race of beings had gone extinct fifty years ago from a lethal pandemic.

After an hour of research, Aelyx was no closer to solving the mystery. All that remained to explore were various academic theories on the existence of interstellar travelers. It was worth a try. His first search yielded a thesis by Larish, who believed aliens called "the Aribol" had abducted a legion of ancient humans from the Black Sea region and relocated them to L'eihr, where the soldiers had perpetuated Aelyx's entire race. Other scholars argued that humanity traced their lineage to L'eihr. But what none of these dissertations told him were any details about the Aribol.

Did the society truly exist? And why would the Aribol send probes to investigate L'eihr if they had already been there, thousands of years ago, when they'd allegedly seeded the human battalion? Aelyx was more confused than ever. He wondered if it would seem suspicious to contact Larish for more information.

He was still debating whether to message the scholar when Syrine's bedroom door clicked open and she drifted into view as if floating on air, an intoxicated grin dimpling her cheeks.

She stopped in the kitchen to fill a glass with water, then sat opposite Aelyx at the long wooden table and rested her chin in her hand.

She sighed dreamily. "That was an amazing pear."

"Oh?" Aelyx laughed and checked his watch. "Then why did it take three hours for you to finish it?"

Instead of blushing or stammering as he'd expected, Syrine widened her smile with a contentment that said nothing in the world could provoke her tonight. Aelyx noted the sheen in her eyes. This was no mere infatuation—she was completely smitten.

"When each bite is that heavenly," she said, "you want to savor it as slowly as you can."

Aelyx wrinkled his nose. "I'll take your word for it."

"We probably shouldn't use Silent Speech for a while," she added with a giggle.

"I appreciate the warning."

He'd never seen Syrine so happy. The perpetual smile on her mouth made his own lips curve in response. He'd wanted this for her—a morsel of normalcy and comfort in the wake of Eron's death—but still, Aelyx couldn't stop the tentacles of envy from gripping his chest. Until today, Syrine had never kissed a boy, and now even *she* knew more about physical love than he did. Sometimes he worried it would never happen for him, that he and Cara were jinxed.

Syrine must have read his heart. "Only one month until you see your *Elire*." Her gaze was sympathetic, even as she teased, "If you're nice to me, I might give you some pointers."

Laughing, Aelyx grabbed the nearest object he could

reach—a cloth napkin—and threw it at Syrine's head. "You can shove your pointers!"

David strode into the dining area, refastening a gun holster around his hips. "What's so funny?" When he stood behind Syrine and rested both palms on her shoulders, she reached up and covered his hands with her own, not the least bit ashamed to show him affection. Aelyx attributed the uncharacteristic behavior to the rush of dopamine in her system. A post-sex haze.

"Nothing," Aelyx said. "Did you tell Syrine the secret to your card trick?"

David dropped a kiss on top of Syrine's head. "Nope. A magician never reveals his secrets. Besides, I might want to raise the stakes and win a bet with her someday."

"I already know your trick," Syrine said. "And you owe me a sandwich."

"This is true. I never flake out on a bet." David smoothed his hands over Syrine's upper arms, clearly reluctant to leave her. Gods, this was going to be a long, awkward month. "I'm supposed to stay with you," David said. "I'll call in the order and have one of the guys in the hall pick it up." He glanced at Aelyx. "You want anything?"

Yes, he wanted Cara—alone on their colony, free from the worries of alliances and assassinations and probes. "No. Already ate."

David started to speak, but the phone rang from his pocket, and he stepped back to answer it. At once, the smile fell from his face and he reflexively touched his arm. As the seconds passed, it became clear that the caller had delivered unpleasant

229

news, and Aelyx suspected it had to do with David's medical condition. He wondered if his friend had confessed his health problems to Syrine. He made a mental note to talk with David later.

"I've got to take this," David said, covering the mouthpiece. "Be right back."

After a brief kiss, David left Syrine to continue the call from his room. From the way she gazed longingly at his retreating form, you'd think they were parting for eternity instead of five minutes.

"You love him," Aelyx said.

Syrine didn't argue.

"Will you invite him to the colony?" Until now, he thought he'd known the answer. But perhaps he'd underestimated her level of attachment for the young man.

She shook her head and lost an inch as she sank into her chair. "No."

"Why not?" Aelyx asked. "He's not like other humans."

"Yes, he is," she said. "And this feeling"—she pressed a palm to her chest—"won't last for him. I know how humans love. Their passion burns like a lump of sugar—quick and hot. And when the fire dies, they seek a new flame. They chase sparks instead of collecting the warmth of old embers."

Aelyx understood her concern. He'd once read a study claiming the average American had seven mates during a lifetime. But there were always exceptions. Cara's parents, for example. They'd married young and had never parted. And if their constant kisses and touches were any indication, their flame burned more like a centennial bulb than a sugar cube.

"You barely know him," Aelyx said. "Why not keep an open mind?"

"I'll keep a *clear* mind and enjoy the time we have left."

Aelyx had once shared the same opinion—that pairing with a human would never last—but now he couldn't imagine his future without Cara in it.

"I'm back, so quit talking about me." David rejoined them and took the seat next to Syrine. He attempted a smile, but it didn't reach his eyes. "Because that's what I always think when you're speaking L'eihr."

"He's onto us," Aelyx said in English, sliding Syrine a mock-serious look.

Syrine grinned at her new boyfriend. "Then I suppose he's not as stupid as I thought."

David didn't laugh at her joke, instead choosing to lead her to the sofa, where they gazed soulfully at each other.

Bleeding gods. It truly *was* going to be an awkward month.

David's cell phone rang again. When he sat back against the cushions and tapped his screen to answer the call, Syrine nestled against him, draping an arm across his chest as if it were the most natural thing in the world. In response, he rested his cheek atop her head and pulled her tightly against him. Aelyx was no relationship expert, but they looked like a perfectly mated pair. Syrine was delusional if she thought she could enjoy the next four weeks and then simply cut ties and return home.

"Private Sharpe," David said into the phone, followed by some indeterminate *uh-huh*s and *mmm-hmmm*s. He ended the call with an abrupt, "Okay, then," and tapped the screen.

"That was quick," Syrine said.

"Our food's here, but the sergeant won't bring it to us. Something about not leaving his post. Maybe one of the guys at the door will run down and grab it."

"I'll ask them." Aelyx opened the front door, expecting to find two armed soldiers flanking the entrance, but the only thing greeting him was a half-full Starbucks cup sitting by the floor mat. That was unusual. He'd never seen the men away from their station. He peered for them in both directions but the hallway appeared empty.

"Nobody's out here," he called to David.

"Probably a shift change," came the reply. "Let's just wait a minute."

"I'll check the stairwell," Aelyx said. "There's always someone posted in there."

The front door was set to lock automatically, so Aelyx left it propped open when he stepped into the hall. As he strode down the corridor in his socks, he made a mental note to change into a clean pair when he returned to the penthouse. The sidewalks of Los Angeles were littered with contaminants, and though the carpeted hallway appeared freshly vacuumed, he knew the residents and guests tracked in all manner of filth on the bottoms of their shoes. Which was disgusting. He'd never had to worry about this on L'eihr.

He was still grumbling to himself about the city's poor sanitation when he pushed open the stairwell door and came face-to-face with a uniformed soldier.

Only the man wasn't a guard.

Aelyx recognized the pink keloid scar that bisected the

male's forehead, his familiar brown eyes widened in surprise. Aelyx knew this man. When someone fired a gun at your chest, you committed that face to memory.

L'eihrs were quicker than humans, but not fast enough to outrun a bullet. There was no way Aelyx could make it back to the room in time, and the soldier stood too close for him to shut the stairwell door and call for help. Luckily, the man seemed just as unprepared for this meeting as Aelyx, something he intended to use to his advantage.

While the soldier fumbled for his gun, Aelyx charged him, doing his best to build momentum as his socked feet skidded against the smooth concrete floor. When the man realized Aelyx's plan was to knock him backward down the stairs, he released the butt of his pistol and braced for impact.

Their bodies collided with a hollow *smack* that told Aelyx his enemy wore a Kevlar vest—another detail that gave him an edge. The leaden vests were heavy and bulky—great for stopping a bullet, but not the best choice for hand-to-hand combat. Aelyx balled his fist and struck the sensitive area above the man's groin, eliciting a grunt of pain. He pushed with all his strength, but his slippery socks afforded him no traction.

To keep from falling, the man gripped the metal stair rail, and Aelyx did the same. With his newly gained leverage, Aelyx drew back his head and butted the soldier's face. He couldn't see what he'd struck, but the crunch of bone indicated he'd broken the man's nose. That was a good start, but the soldier didn't need his nose to fire a gun. Aelyx had to disable him long enough to get back to the suite.

He struck the soldier inside his elbow, slackening the man's grip on the handrail and sending him stumbling down a few stairs. Aelyx saw a way to use their sudden height difference to his advantage. Gripping both handrails, he lifted his legs and kicked the man squarely in the chest, sending him careening backward down a flight of concrete steps. Without hesitating, Aelyx turned and threw open the stairwell door, then sprinted down the hallway and back to the room.

Heart hammering against his ribs, he darted inside and slammed the suite door. He bolted the lock and shouted, "Call the guards!" to David in the next room. When Syrine came running into the foyer, Aelyx grabbed her around the waist and towed her back into the living area. "Stay away from the door." He locked eyes with David while trying to catch his breath. "The shooter from Christmas—he's in the stairwell. I fought him off, but he's still armed."

David dialed a number and tossed his cell phone to Aelyx. "When my CO picks up, tell him what you told me." He drew his pistol. "Stay here with Aelyx," he told Syrine. "Don't open the door for anyone unless they say the password."

Syrine held tightly to Aelyx's arm. "What's the password?"

"Pear."

Before Aelyx could try talking him out of it, David disappeared into the hall.

They knew the gunman's identity by midnight, but not because anyone had apprehended him. The ex-infantryman— Anthony Grimes, if the military reports were correct—had once again disappeared like smoke on the breeze. By the time

David had searched the stairwell, all he'd found were the bodies of three guardsmen.

No one was sure how Grimes had managed to infiltrate the building, but he appeared to have killed the stairwell guard first, then ambushed the penthouse guards during their shift change. Grimes had just dragged the bodies into the stairwell when Aelyx had surprised him. Five minutes later, and the man might have gained entry to the penthouse.

A chilling thought.

Aelyx had summoned a mental image of the gunman's countenance and shared it with Syrine. Together, they'd composed a sketch for Colonel Rutter to scan into the facial recognition system. The search yielded a few dozen possible matches, and Aelyx had easily singled out Grimes by his jagged scar—which had resulted from the same drunk driving incident that earned the man a dishonorable discharge three years earlier.

But what Aelyx found most interesting was that Grimes wasn't affiliated with HALO. He began to wonder if Isaac Richards had told the truth when he'd denied responsibility for the attacks.

But if the Patriots of Earth didn't want Aelyx dead, then who did?

"I hate to say this." David shifted forward in his seat, resting both forearms on his knees. "But I think Grimes has someone on the inside. How else would he know the shift change schedule?"

"Maybe it was a coincidence that he showed up when he did," Aelyx said. "Sheer luck."

David shook his head. "I don't believe in luck."

"Okay then," Aelyx countered. "Call it chance. Regardless, it's the reason I'm alive." Because if he'd stepped out of the penthouse any later, Grimes would've met him in the hallway with his weapon at the ready.

"I don't know . . ." David rubbed his jaw, eyes trained on the floor. "It's fishy how that soldier wouldn't bring up our food."

Syrine looped an arm through David's and clung to him. This latest attack hadn't shaken her as badly as the letter bomb, but she'd still needed to retreat to her room for an hour of *K'imsha* after dinner. "I agree," she said. "It's like he wanted us to come out."

Aelyx had found that suspicious from the beginning. "What's the man's name?"

"No clue. All I caught was *Sergeant*. He mumbled the rest."

If there were a "mole in the ranks," as the saying went, Aelyx had an idea to draw out Grimes and finally capture him. "Let's have Colonel Rutter feed false information to the unit—tell them I'm going someplace easily accessible to Grimes."

"And have a trap waiting for him," Syrine finished. "I like that."

"Me, too," David said. "I'll talk to the colonel about it in the morning." He checked his watch. "Which is technically now, since it's past midnight. Guess we should turn in." Then he and Syrine rose in unison from their seats.

Aelyx had a feeling somebody's bedroom would be vacant

tonight. "Be careful," he warned. The ambassador had returned from his meeting, and he wouldn't approve of their bodyguard mixing business with pleasure. "It won't help if you get reassigned."

Syrine stood on tiptoe to glance toward the ambassador's bedroom, then lowered her voice to a whisper and produced a tiny key from her pocket. "I locked my room from the inside, just in case he decides to check on me."

"And I'm up hours before he is, anyway," David said. "If you need anything, text me or knock twice on my door."

As the pair strode hand-in-hand to David's room, a familiar surge of envy churned inside Aelyx's stomach. He did his best to tame the sensation, but it wasn't easy. Maybe talking to Cara would help. He couldn't share his fear that Grimes would eventually succeed in killing him, not without worrying her. But simply hearing her voice would make it easier to sleep tonight. He returned to his room, hoping to catch her between classes.

But when he summoned her, she didn't answer—a fitting end to a terrible day. Aelyx slumped on his bed and tossed aside his com-sphere. He missed Cara more than ever, and the thought of spending another month apart made his insides feel raw.

He wondered what she was doing right now. Was she thinking of him, too?

Chapter Sixteen

Cara paced the waiting area to Alona's private-audience chamber, wishing more than anything that Aelyx were here. He'd know what to do. He'd remind her of the eleventy dozen rules for proper behavior during a hearing with an Elder—when to sit and stand, whether to pick up the speaker's baton for a one-on-one meeting, how to ask sensitive questions like, *You're not going to execute me for this, are you?* Aelyx would demonstrate the slight nuance in pressure and timing that marked the difference between a greeting and a grope when touching the left side of the throat. And more importantly, he'd hold her close and kiss the sweet spot behind her ear and whisper, *Don't worry,* Elire. *You can do this.*

Cara wasn't sure she could do this.

She'd only been here fifteen minutes, and already she'd stained the front of her tunic with her sweaty palms. The Aegis guard was inside with Alona right now, no doubt filling her head with tales of Cara's sociopathic hijinks. Silent Speech could save Cara, but what if she opened her mind and all her secrets came flooding out? She'd harbored some traitorous thoughts against The Way, especially about Jaxen and Aisly. Cara hoped Alona wouldn't punish her for that, but she didn't know what to expect.

The chamber door whispered open.

"Come," the Aegis guard said, waving Cara inside the small, dim chamber. He narrowed his eyes and touched the *iphal* holstered at his side.

Message received. He didn't trust her alone with the head Elder, which kind of stung. Cara had never hurt anyone. Well, except that one time she busted Marcus Johnson's knee with a baseball bat, but that didn't count. He'd aimed his rifle at Aelyx's chest, and she'd had to skew his shot. Besides, he'd used that same rifle to smash her face. Under normal circumstances, Cara wouldn't even bait a fishing hook because she found it cruel to the worm.

"It's all right," Alona's droning voice called from inside. "Come and be heard."

Cara crept into the chamber, flinching when the door shut behind her. Unlike the vast hearing room aboard the transport, this enclosure wouldn't accommodate all ten members of The Way. Only two seats stood on the beige-carpeted floor: a plush ottoman Alona occupied and a simple stool about five paces from her. A slender skylight provided the only illumination, casting a beam over Alona as if she were a deity. Which she was, in a way. No one on L'eihr wielded more power than this graying slip of a woman.

"Sit," she instructed, and Cara obeyed. The warmth—for lack of a better word—Cara had detected in Alona's gaze on *Sh'ovah* day was gone, replaced by cold indifference. It seemed the guard had succeeded in blackening Cara's name. With a *hurry up* motion, Alona ordered, "State your grievance."

Cara swallowed a lump of fear. "I'm here to defend myself from false accusations. Someone at the Aegis has committed a series of crimes and made me look like the guilty party."

"The evidence against you is damning," Alona said. "How do you refute it?"

This was it. Time to bust out the big guns.

But Cara had never used Silent Speech from so far away. She wasn't sure she could project from her seat to Alona's. She lifted her stool and scooted nearer, practically giving the guard a stroke in the process. He gasped aloud and moved to draw his *iphal*. Alona seemed startled, too, stiffening in her seat.

"It's okay," Cara assured Alona with raised palms. "I just want to look you in the eyes."

Alona regained her composure, but her voice darkened with irritation. "My vision is unimpaired. I can see you quite well from here."

Cara nodded and latched her gaze on to Alona's faded chrome irises. She isolated the region in her brain she'd discovered that morning and told the Elder, *I'm innocent*, then closed the connection between them and waited for a reaction.

Alona's response didn't disappoint. Slowly, her eyes widened in perfect conjunction with her mouth. If the lighting were better, Cara could've performed a dental exam. Alona flicked a glance at the guard and ordered, "Leave us."

The man drew a breath and hesitated a beat, but he didn't argue. Within moments, he was gone, and Cara reopened her mind to the head Elder.

How did you do that? Alona asked, her feelings of shock and amazement bleeding into Cara's mind.

Aelyx taught me what he could, Cara said. *And Elyx'a has been helping me practice. No one else knows, and I'd like to keep it that way.* She tried her best to focus on words alone, but an image of Jaxen and Aisly materialized in Cara's head, along with a fear that they'd try other methods of brainwashing if they knew their memory control hadn't worked on her.

Alona fell silent awhile before claiming, "Mind control is impossible, *Cah*-ra."

It didn't escape Cara's notice that Alona had spoken aloud instead of using Silent Speech. Apparently, they both had secrets to keep.

"But," Alona continued, "I'm intrigued that your human brain can process mental dialogue. This lends credence to the theory that we share a common lineage."

Ancestry was the last thing on Cara's mind. "I'm just glad I was able to convince you I'm innocent. A few weeks ago, someone stole an instructor's tablet and hid it in my room, and then they poisoned Dahla's breakfast. I thought she was doing it, but I was wrong. Whoever it is wants me expelled."

Or executed.

It occurred to Cara that the criminal could have simply killed her, which would be easier than framing her for a capital crime. Maybe her death wasn't the only goal.

"Allow me to apologize on behalf of the guilty party." The slight inflection in Alona's tone might not have seemed significant to the average human, but it told Cara the Elder was majorly pissed. "Rooting out the culprit will be simple. I'll order the guards to perform a mental interview with every clone in your Aegis until the individual is found." With a nod, she added, "And then neutralized."

Cara didn't like the sound of that. "You mean killed?"

"Of course. It is our way."

Cara folded her hands and tried to keep her voice from shaking. "Can I request another form of punishment? I don't think I could stand it if someone died because of me."

"The individual in question would perish because of his or her poor choices, not because of you."

Cara widened her eyes and opened her consciousness, allowing her Elder to feel the dread that crawled over her skin like a wet frost. *Execution would punish me, too. Along with anyone who cares for the criminal. Dahla and I deserve justice, but there must be another way.*

You humans and your sentimental notions of rehabilitation. Alona sighed. *However, I suppose this is what we wanted—to infuse our progeny with a breath of humanity.* She closed her mind and reflected for a moment. "I will give it some thought."

At least that wasn't a no.

"In the meantime," Alona droned, "I'm ordering a change in your schedule. Your talents, as much as they're appreciated, are wasted in the nursery. Each day after your morning calisthenics, I want you to report here and join the colony development panel. As our resident human, I believe your input will prove useful in creating a charter."

Cara drew a hopeful breath. "You want me to help form a government?" Her world studies teacher back home would be so proud.

"Yes." Alona studied her. "I sensed hesitation within you—a disruption in your resolve to join the colony."

Heat infused Cara's cheeks as she wondered what else she'd let slip during Silent Speech. Hopefully nothing too embarrassing.

"The choice is yours, but it is my hope that you'll stay." Though it was hard to tell with the older generation, Alona sounded sincere. "I can't promise a governing body akin to your America, but I give you my word that your concerns will be heard and addressed."

"Thank you," Cara said, and meant it. Democracy didn't exist here, and for The Way, who'd ruled with an authoritative hand for thousands of years, this was a big step. "I'm honored by this opportunity."

"Your morning notification will tell you where to report." With a two-fingered salute, Alona dismissed her. "Please send in the guard on your way out."

Cara returned the gesture and did as she was told. Uncertain of whether she should return to the Aegis, she scanned her wrist at the station by the front doors.

"*Cah*-ra Sweeney," the computerized voice said. "You have no notifications."

Business as usual, then. But after the bloody scene in the

Aegis lobby, it was probably best to lay low until the guard announced her innocence and began an investigation. She walked back to the Aegis and snuck inside her room only long enough to retrieve her com-sphere, then jogged into the woods to call Aelyx.

She wouldn't normally bother him at three in the morning, but she couldn't wait to tell him what had happened. They talked for nearly an hour about everything from her breakthrough in Silent Speech to her close call at the Aegis. When they said good-bye, she felt lighter by five pounds.

Late that night, energized by fresh optimism, she uploaded a new blog post.

Subscribe [Archive] [Recent Entries] [About Me]

Invaded

MAY THE SOURCE BE WITH YOU

TUESDAY, FEBRUARY 4
The Lone Invader

Well, it's official. Now that my brother's gone, I'm the only human in this galaxy.

But don't cry for me, earthlings. It's kind of empowering to go it alone. I'm like a one-woman Lewis and Clark, scoping out this foreign terrain and reporting back to you in digital glory. If you're considering joining the colony, think of me as your personal trailblazer. In fact, I've just been appointed to the colony development panel! What does that mean? That I'm doing important work here—representing your interests and advocating for the best lifestyle possible.

I want you to know what to expect, so here's what I've learned so far:

• The colony is set on a lush, balmy island with fertile soil for growing crops. It's fairly isolated, but don't worry—I'm negotiating for access to the main continent by way of shuttle.
• Not sure what to do with your life? The L'eihrs will give you an aptitude test, then supply your ideal job. I'm still working on more personal choice, but if nothing else, know that your occupation will likely suit you to a T.
• If you can't stand too much idle time, you'll enjoy the highly structured way of life here. Everyone on the colony will contribute to its success, which means you'll be a part of something larger than yourself. Hard work has its rewards.

Stay tuned for more tidbits about colony life. I'll collect as much data as possible before I come home to visit. Only fifty-ish days to go! ☺

Posted by Cara Sweeney

In the days that followed, a fleet of guards began interrogating every living being over the age of ten inside the Aegis. But halfway through the campaign, Dahla awoke from her coma and pointed her finger at Professor Helm, who promptly confessed to the attack. Since then, he'd been detained in the guard barracks, since prisons didn't exist on L'eihr and The Way hadn't quite decided what to do with him.

The entire Aegis was perplexed by the news . . . including Cara.

She knew Helm wasn't her biggest fan, and yet she couldn't picture the mild-mannered professor wielding a blade like a common street thug. Then there was the issue of Dahla's poisoning. Helm had been nowhere near the dining hall the morning she'd collapsed. Maybe he'd snapped . . . or maybe someone had used mind control to orchestrate the confession.

If that were the case, only two suspects remained—the only students capable of manipulating a mental query. Jaxen and Aisly. But for the life of her, Cara couldn't figure out a motive. Neither of them had a reason to want her expelled or dead, and thanks to their positions in The Way, accusing them of the crime would amount to treason.

So with her hands figuratively tied, she avoided them like a bikini wax and focused on her duties as Chief Human Consultant—her official title, not that she was bragging or anything.

Cara was a halfway decent politician, if she did say so herself. So far, she'd convinced the panel to allot the colony six shuttles for emergency use and establish one full day of rest per week. Not perfect, but a Kong-size leap in the right direction. When she'd mentioned the democratic method, the Elders had practically broken out in hives, but she would wear them down. She just needed more time.

However, Cara was on a different mission today—one Aelyx had assigned her—which explained why she was currently standing outside the front doors of the capital's reference building, repeatedly scanning her wrist to gain entry. No matter how many times she thrust her nano-chip beneath the dancing gray beam, the doors refused to part. Likely because the system knew she didn't belong there.

Her failed attempts at entry must have set off an internal alarm, because a guard ambled up from the front walkway.

Without offering a greeting, he motioned for her wrist while pulling a handheld scanner from his pocket.

"*Mahra*," Cara said, offering her hand, palm up.

He nodded a return hello and swept his device over her skin. A tinny voice from the speaker informed him, "*Cah*-ra Sweeney. Resident of the first Aegis, *l'ihan* to Aelyx of the first Aegis. Chief Human Consultant. No alerts."

Cara perked up at the mention of her title. "I'm here to see Larish," she told the guard in L'eihr. "He's a scholar in this building, but I can't seem to get inside. Can you help?"

He didn't seem enthused about the prospect of letting her in, but he opened the doors and led her to an office on the second floor.

The room looked more like a reading lounge than a formal workspace, with several deep-cushioned chairs positioned around a data table, its surface displaying multiple windows of text and images. A middle-age man—Larish, she presumed—bent over the screen, tapping it to enlarge a photograph of a red planet.

"Larish," the guard said, extending two fingers in greeting. "*Cah*-ra Sweeney requests congress with you. Do you accept?"

Congress? That sounded dirty, like a line from a Victorian romance novel. Cara lifted her data tablet toward Larish, who stared at her in obvious bewilderment. She smiled brightly and bounced on her toes in her best fan-girl impression. "I absolutely *loved* your thesis on the primate connection," she said in L'eihr. "If it's not too much trouble, I'd like to ask you a few questions." Being human, her interest in the topic of shared lineage shouldn't raise any red flags.

Like many of his generation, Larish's eyes betrayed little emotion, but his posture lifted in tandem with the corners of his mouth. It told Cara she'd hit the bull's-eye. Academics loved nothing more than discussing their theories—especially with those who agreed with them.

"Please," he said in meticulous English, indicating the chairs opposite him. "Be my guest."

Cara thanked the guard for his assistance and took a seat. "I can't believe I'm sitting across from *the* Larish. Your work is brilliant."

He waved her off, his smile widening. "I wouldn't say that."

"Thanks for making time for me."

"Anything to assist an eager young mind." Larish sat back and crossed his legs at the ankles. "How can I help you?"

Cara didn't want to alarm him by leading with questions about the Aribol, so she started small. "When did you realize the old legend was wrong—that your ancients were actually human?"

"As soon as we made contact and accessed your electronic databases," Larish said. "Humans have unearthed fossils of *Homo Erectus* that date back more than a million years. On L'eihr, we've found no remains that predate the ancients. Some of our anthropologists argued that L'eihr's mild climate and predominant water mass were to blame—"

"Because remains decay faster in warm temperatures," she

interrupted. "Plus, weren't storms a big problem before you controlled the weather?"

"Yes," he said, sounding impressed. "Which would have destroyed even more evidence . . . but surely not *all* of it."

"Totally." She had been on board from the beginning. Now to get to the good stuff. "I'm also curious about the Aribol—you know, the aliens who kidnapped all those ancient soldiers and carried them here?"

"A name I assigned to them based on hearsay, you understand . . ."

"Of course."

"What would you like to know?" he asked.

She leaned forward and caught her bottom lip between her teeth for a moment. "I can't stop thinking about them. I mean, if they had the technology to abduct a whole legion of warriors thousands of years ago, what's stopping them from doing it again—here or on my planet?"

Larish lifted a shoulder. "Nothing, I suppose. But they haven't, which is telling."

"What do you mean?"

He shifted in his seat, pausing for a moment while folding both hands in his lap. "I don't have any evidence to support this, but I believe the Aribol are tinkerers. Behavioral scientists on an intergalactic scale. They like to seed species across multiple galaxies to see how each one develops uniquely in a new environment. I don't think they wish us harm. But before I can convince you, I need to explain something about our ancients."

She nodded for him to go on.

"To say they were merely brutal would be a flagrant understatement," he told her. "I've studied human history, and the ancients who ruled our seas rivaled that of your most savage societies. Men and women fought alongside one another while the injured and elderly remained with the younglings. Even children were trained in combat. I've read stories of boys and girls as young as ten doing battle."

"Wow."

"Indeed," he said. "Even rulers occupied the front lines. In fact, one of our most infamous queens died in a bloody battle, along with her consort. It was rumored she was with child at the time of her death, and several years ago, scientists confirmed it."

"Oh, I heard about that. Their tomb was on the colony, right?"

"Very good." He gave an approving tip of his head like a proud teacher. "The remains were brought to our genetics labs when I was a youngling, but as my path didn't follow a scientific bend, I wasn't able to study the data. Anyway, the queen was in her second trimester when she perished."

"I had no idea the ancients were so hard-core."

"And it stands to reason their ancestors were just as savage when they were abducted from Earth. Imagine what the Aribol faced when they teleported these warriors aboard their craft." He sniffed a dry laugh. "It must have been utter bedlam."

Cara imagined the scene: dirty, blood-streaked warriors

wielding primitive weapons against their kidnappers, fighting to the death to regain their freedom.

"The fact that those ancients survived," Larish said, "implies the Aribol are not a violent race. Otherwise, they would have simply terminated the legion instead of re-homing them."

Cara supposed Larish had a point, but just because the Aribol were originally lovers and not fighters didn't mean they were passive today. Look how much the L'eihrs had changed during that time. "What if they got curious and decided to check up on L'eihr?" she asked. "How do you think they'd go about it?"

Larish let out his version of a hearty laugh, more like a snicker by human standards. "Very carefully, I imagine."

Cara didn't want to use the term *probe*, so she chose her next words carefully. "Do you think they might send a robotic device to gather information about us?"

"Like a probe?" he asked.

So much for avoiding red flags. "Yeah, I guess." She shrugged casually. "If you want to call it that."

"Anything is possible. They certainly have the technology to manage it." He cocked his head to the side and considered her in a way that warned he'd grown suspicious. "Are you worried for your safety or that of your kind?"

"Uh . . ." She thought fast. "Yes, a little. Until a couple of years ago, I didn't know life existed beyond Earth, and it's scary to think an advanced race might swoop in and kidnap me."

Larish offered a comforting smile. "You needn't be concerned. The odds of a repeat abduction are infinitesimal. The Aribol have lain dormant for thousands of years, so I doubt they pose any threat to us."

That was because he didn't know about the probes. Someone—either the Aribol or another advanced race—had taken an acute interest in this world, and until L'eihrs discovered otherwise, it was a good idea to assume the worst and hope for the best.

"Does anyone know what the Aribol look like?" she asked, pointing to the data table. "Are there any sketches or photographs of them?"

"Only about a hundred." He tapped the screen and spoke some cryptic commands, bringing into view dozens of animated sketches that depicted everything from furry purple monsters to green-tentacled squid. "The only accounts we have of the Aribol are verbal in nature—stories handed down from one generation to the next. As you can imagine, each report varies widely."

"Like a game of telephone," Cara said.

"Pardon?"

"Never mind." She flapped a hand. "It's a human thing."

"Anyway," Larish continued, "I believe they have the psychic ability to project a variety of physical appearances, to make us see what they want us to see. Besides, if L'eihrs can change our features, it stands to reason the—"

"Wait," Cara interrupted. "You can change your appearance?"

"Well . . ." Larish ducked his head. "Perhaps I exaggerated.

We can lighten or darken our skin, and of course alter our hair and eye color. It's how our Voyagers infiltrated the human population before making contact."

Something he'd said piqued her interest. "How do you change the color of your eyes?"

"With cosmetic drops. It's quite simple."

Cara thought back to the day Aisly had applied drops to her eyes, which seemed to darken to a slightly smokier shade of chrome afterward. Those drops were cosmetic, not medicinal. But what was the point in darkening Aisly's eyes . . . unless they weren't silver to begin with?

Which would mean Aisly wasn't a clone.

The tiny hairs on Cara's forearm prickled, standing on end. Her instincts told her she was right. Jaxen and Aisly were different—she'd always sensed it. Nobody seemed to know the siblings personally. What if they weren't L'eihrs at all? What if they were something else entirely—like an advanced alien race with the ability to alter their appearances?

Could Jaxen and Aisly hail from Aribol?

There was just one hole in her theory: as brilliant as the Elders were, one of them would have known if outsiders had compromised The Way. If nothing else, Silent Speech would reveal the impostors' true nature.

"Miss Sweeney?" Larish said, jerking her back to present company. "Are you all right?"

She flashed a quick smile. "Fine, just thinking. But I should probably get back to the Aegis." She stood and held two fingers toward him in a good-bye, and he did the same. "Thanks for your time."

"My pleasure," he said with sincerity. "Come back whenever you like."

Good thing he'd extended an invitation, because Cara needed all the help she could get. "I'll take you up on that."

Chapter Seventeen

Aelyx heard a knock at his door and set down his interview script. "It's unlocked."

The door flew open and David poked his head into the room, apologizing with his eyes. "Hey, I know you're studying lines and stuff, but do you have a minute? Syrine just hopped in the shower, so this is the only time I can talk."

To hear David explain, you'd think he never left Syrine's side, which was only partially true. The two parted for public relations visits, bathroom breaks, and the occasional foray into the living room when the ambassador was home.

"Sure, the notes can wait." Aelyx tried not to sound bitter, but truthfully, he resented the fact that Syrine had commandeered his only friend on Earth. Aelyx would never admit it, though. Not after he'd confided his feelings to Cara, who had then giggled and accused him of having a "bromance" with David.

The bed jiggled when David took a seat on the other side, but instead of initiating dialogue, the boy picked at his cuticles.

"You okay?" Aelyx asked. Bitterness aside, he hoped there wasn't trouble in paradise. He wanted to see his friends happy, even if they had abandoned him in favor of each other.

"Yeah, it's no big deal. I just wanted to talk. You know, guy-to-guy."

"Is something the matter with you and Syrine?"

"No. Maybe. I don't know." David bowed over, cradling his blond head in both hands. "I need to process what's going on, but I can't talk to any of my buddies about this or it might get back to my CO. He'd have my balls for paperweights if he found out about Syrine and me."

"Talk about ugly paperweights," Aelyx said.

David gave a throaty chuckle, but his shoulders remained clenched. "The worst."

"So talk." Aelyx sat back against his pillows and folded both hands behind his head. "But you'd better make it quick. Syrine takes short showers."

David nodded as if to get down to business. "I'm all mixed up."

"About what?"

"How I feel. Where this is going." David pointed toward the hall bathroom, where Syrine hummed off-key over the spray of running water. "I thought I was in love once before—senior year with this girl named Beth. I wanted her all the time and I couldn't stand to see her talk to other guys. But this is different." He grimaced. "This is painful."

Aelyx didn't quite follow, and it must have shown because David gave a sad shake of his head. "Syrine's all I think about. And when I imagine her leaving in a few weeks," David said, palming his chest, "it hurts. Like it *really* hurts, right here under my ribs."

Aelyx understood now. His own chest had perpetually ached since he'd left Cara's side. David may have thought he was in love before, but this sounded like his first experience with the real thing.

"And when we're together," David said, "you know . . . *alone* . . . I feel like I'm a living puzzle, and she takes a piece of me every time. The more I'm with her, the more I lose of myself. It's like I only feel whole when we're together because she's got all of me." He smacked his own forehead in disgust. "God, that sounds cheesy."

"No, it doesn't." Aelyx hadn't been physically intimate with Cara, so he didn't know with any degree of certainty, but it made sense that consummation would lead to a greater level of attachment. "I think what you felt for Beth was infatuation. But this time, it's love. And yes," he said with a sympathetic nod, "it's equal parts excruciating and wonderful."

"That's what I was afraid of."

"Don't worry. The crushing despair won't actually kill you." Aelyx laughed without humor. "Though occasionally you'll wish it had."

"Sometimes I think she loves me, too," David said. "But then she'll push me away or say something mean, and I second-guess myself." He thrust forward an index finger. "Like last night—we were getting ready to go to sleep, and everything was fine. Then I tossed out the idea of joining the colony."

Uh-oh. Aelyx imagined that hadn't gone over well.

"She shot me down so fast my head spun," David said in a wounded voice. "What am I supposed to think when she sends me mixed messages like that?"

Aelyx was torn between keeping Syrine's confidence and helping his heartsick friend. He wanted to give them both the push they needed to find happiness. "Remember when I told you why Syrine hates humans?" he asked. "How her negative experience during the exchange colored her view of all mankind?"

David nodded.

"One of her observations was that human love is fleeting. That your kind is never satisfied with a single mate."

"Not everyone is like that," David argued. "I'm always getting dumped, not the other way around."

"Then show her."

"That I'm different?" David pondered the advice for several long seconds. "I can do different."

"It worked last time."

"I have to find out if she loves me," David said, staring at his hands. "Or it's not worth it."

"What's not worth it?"

For a long time, David didn't answer. "You know, going to the colony."

"What about your health issues?" Aelyx asked. It was none of his business, but Syrine deserved to know, if the relationship went any further. "Have you told her?"

"Not yet, but soon."

"Why wait?" Aelyx asked. "Even if the experimental drug you're taking doesn't work, something else will." L'eihrs had the technology to keep David alive. He wouldn't be allowed to pass on his genetic material, though. Maybe that was the problem. "Do you think Syrine will be upset when she finds out she can't breed with you?"

"No, nothing like that. I just don't want her to see me as weak."

"There's nothing weak about—"

A sudden buzzing alerted Aelyx to an incoming comsphere transmission in Cara's unique frequency. A jolt of excitement ricocheted up and down the length of Aelyx's torso as he dug in his pocket and retrieved his sphere. He whispered his passkey and set it on the bed between David and himself.

Cara's image appeared, this time standing in front of the communal washroom mirror as she combed her dripping-wet locks. When her blue gaze found his, her entire face broke into a smile so radiant it sucked the breath from his lungs and made him tingle all over.

To hell with the pains of love. This was worth it.

"Sorry for the lack of ambiance," she said, gesturing at the lavatory stalls in the background. "I'm running late."

"Your timing is perfect," Aelyx told her. "I'm leaving in a few minutes for another promo piece." He recalled what she'd told him about Professor Helm's bizarre confession. "Are you all right? Any more attacks?"

"I'm fine. It's business as usual around here." She shrugged. "I didn't think Helm was guilty, but maybe I was wrong.

Nothing weird has happened since they locked him up."

Aelyx had some lingering doubt, but he was glad to hear that she was safe, at least for now. He motioned for David to move into view. "I want you to meet someone. Say hello to David."

David stood from the bed and circled around to kneel on the floor. "Hi, mini-Cara."

She gripped one hip and pointed at him with her comb. "So *you're* the guy bromancing my clone."

"Huh?" David asked.

"Nothing," Aelyx said. "She thinks she's funny."

"Yeah?" she taunted. "Well, guess what this funny girl is getting ready to do."

"Lose your breakfast on the intermediate course?" he supplied with a grin.

"Good guess, but no." She turned her hand into an imaginary gun and fired it at him, then blew pretend smoke from her index finger. "Target practice. They've added a new class to the curriculum—advanced weaponry. Sounds kind of fun. Midtown used to offer enrichment classes in archery, and I always . . ."

Her words flew to the periphery of Aelyx's mind as he reeled with fear. "They're training the clones to fight?"

"No, it's just target practice." She furrowed her ivory forehead. "That's not something they teach most L'eihrs?"

No. It most certainly was not.

The majority of his people lived and died without ever touching an *iphal*. Weapons were carefully controlled and wielded only by members of the guard. If The Way had decided to train the clones in combat, it meant they were preparing for war.

Suddenly all the loose pieces clicked into place—the probe, the weapons class, Alona's refusal to end negotiations despite repeated attempts on Aelyx's life. He now understood the true purpose behind the alliance: L'eihr possessed the technology, and Earth, the numbers. Put them together, and you had a formidable fighting force.

Aelyx asked David to give them some privacy. Once he and Cara were alone, he told her, "Take the sphere back to your room and make sure no one can hear us. There's something you need to know."

Target practice wasn't as fun now that Cara understood the real reason for these impromptu lessons. She glanced at the mock *iphal* in her palm, satiny-smooth and feather-light. When she studied its metal form closely, she noticed a slight difference from the model the guards wore on their hips. This version was smaller, sleeker, fitted to a magnetic holster on her forearm so she could snap it in place and run for cover. She might not have made the connection before, but now that she knew the truth, she realized this model was designed for combat.

Which terrified her.

She glanced over the class to the targets in the distance, no longer seeing the bags as marks but as beings—living, breathing creatures with families and goals and challenges, just like her. Cara didn't think she could kill anyone. As much as she'd enjoyed archery at Midtown High, she felt sick at the idea of honing her aim for the sake of taking lives.

"Sweeeeeney," Satan called, waving her to the head of the group. "Help me demonstrate."

Cara shouldered her way to the front of the class, dragging her boots. She wanted no part of this, but the logical side of her brain—the survivor within her—whispered, *This might save you someday.* Her inner soldier was probably right. She should at least pay attention to the lesson, even if she disagreed with it in principle.

Satan spoke to the class in L'eihr and used Cara as his personal mannequin. He lifted her hand, palm up, to show how she cradled the *iphal* with her fingers. "It should feel like a natural extension of your arm. Think of the *iphal* as part of you. You need to mentally connect with it in order to fire. When you identify your target"—he raised her arm toward the first mark—"squeeze your weapon, tell it to fire, and the synapses in your brain will trigger the required biological reaction to discharge the energy burst."

Instead of gawking at the incredible technology in her hand, Cara marveled at how intelligent Satan sounded in his native language.

"You must lock your eyes on your target," Satan said. "This will direct the energy beam to the right spot and avoid collateral damage." In other words, they wouldn't fill the air with a heart-stopping electrical pulse and cause dead birds to rain from the sky. "Go ahead and try it," he told Cara.

"You can't miss. Just visualize your target, lift your weapon, squeeze, and will it to fire."

Cara nodded, then drew a fortifying breath and reminded herself she wasn't doing anything wrong. She peered at her target, contracted her hand around the *iphal*, and thought, *Fire.*

But nothing happened.

"How hard do I have to squeeze it?" she asked.

"Not hard at all. But it won't fire unless you want it to," Satan explained. "It's a safety feature."

Impressive safety mechanism. Cara tried again, but the *iphal* lay powerless in her hand. "I'm sorry," she said. "I'm nervous, so it's probably picking up on that."

Satan clapped her on the back, sending her stumbling forward. "Not to worry. It takes practice."

It didn't take practice for anyone else.

One by one, each clone in her class stepped forward, extended an arm, and fired a burst of energy as naturally as a kid squirting a water pistol. Cara glared at her arm holster and the uncooperative weapon nestled within.

Whatever. She didn't need this class anyway.

Cara's day didn't improve once she joined the colony development panel later that morning. She was beginning to sympathize with the senators and congressmen she'd once disdained in Washington, because bickering with bureaucrats all day was a real downer.

"With all due respect," Cara said to the six geriatric faces staring blankly at her from their seats, "even some of the most oppressed humans on Earth have more freedom than you're offering. Can we at least give colonists some input on choosing their own jobs?"

They'd argued this point for days. As state debate champion, Cara never expected to feel so mentally exhausted defending a position, but L'eihrs really knew how to wear a girl down. If stubbornness were an Olympic event, they'd win the gold. Each time she broached the subject, they countered with the same statement . . .

"Our methods have served us well for several millennia," said the lead councilman.

Yep, that one.

Their reliance on the age-old credence "If it ain't broke, don't fix it" made Cara want to give herself a concussion by way of rubber mallet. She pressed her lips together and counted backward from ten to one, then offered a placid smile. "I understand. But if I'm not mistaken, The Way wants to emulate a more humanistic lifestyle on the colony."

A chorus of disagreeable grunts said she was right, but the group didn't like it. No surprise there.

"And in order for that to happen," she continued, "we have to let go of the old ways."

"But what rational human wouldn't want to be matched with his ideal occupation?" asked one man. "Our functional job assessment ensures the greatest measure of success for each citizen. And success leads to contentment."

"How about a compromise?" Cara said, smooth as cashmere. She'd catch more flies with honey than vinegar, and even more with manure, which was the very essence of politics. "Let's keep the skills inventory to identify everyone's strengths, but allow colonists to choose a specific job based on the findings. Like multiple choice."

There. They couldn't say no to that.

With pursed lips and furrowed brows, the members peered at one another in silent conversation. Cara cleared her throat and said, "Excuse me." When they glanced at her, she reminded them of the Sweeney Rule. "Out loud, please, so I can follow the discussion. It's only fair."

The head councilmember set his jaw, looking even more constipated than usual. "We cannot agree," he said. "I was about to suggest seeking guidance from The Way."

Of course they couldn't agree. *Politicians.* How did anything get done around here? Maybe these Elders were so accustomed to The Way dictating their every move that they'd never learned to make decisions for themselves.

"I'll do it," Cara volunteered. "I already requested an audience with Alona, so I'll discuss the matter with her while I'm there."

She didn't share the reason behind the request—that she'd decided to come clean about her knowledge of the Aribol threat. This wasn't an Aelyx-sanctioned act, but Cara couldn't stand another moment in limbo, wondering whether her dual citizenship would result in her deployment to an alien planet for a battle she stood no chance of surviving.

She checked the digital clock above the door, a series of dots and dashes she'd finally begun to decipher, and figured she might as well leave now.

Two guards stood outside Alona's chamber door. One

scanned Cara's wrist while the other stepped inside to confirm the appointment. They allowed her to enter, and Cara took her place on the stool in front of the Elder. Once alone, they opened the connection between their minds.

Right away, Cara felt Alona's irritation, which stunned her for a beat and caused her cheeks to grow warm. Apparently, requesting an audience with The Way was intended for emergencies, something most citizens never exercised. Alona believed Cara had abused her privilege by returning so soon.

I wouldn't have come unless it was urgent, Cara insisted.

Alona wasn't convinced. She nodded, her expression blank. *State your grievance.*

I know about the Aribol probes, Cara said. *L'eihr is preparing for an attack, and that's why you want an alliance with Earth. You have the technology but not enough soldiers for a solid defense. You want to arm humans with* iphals *and use them in battle in exchange for decontaminating our water supply.*

Alona's irritation morphed into surprise and eventually resignation. Instead of blocking her thoughts, she widened the mental stream and revealed the truth.

In the span of a few seconds, Cara learned that the Aribol *had* sent probes—dozens of them landing all over the planet. Linguists had been studying the orbs for weeks, first deciphering their requests, then feeding false information to the foreign database. The Way hoped to stave off further interest by inflating their numbers and exaggerating the scope of their weaponry systems. The Aribol had made no direct threat or done anything to warn of an invasion, but despite that, The Way was nervous. But not nervous enough to blindly agree to an alliance with Earth. If negotiations failed, they'd press humans into service.

We're taking precautions, Alona assured her. *Nothing more than that. There's no need to panic.*

But Alona's fear betrayed her. Cara felt the knot in the woman's chest as if it were her own. It was Cara's concern for the future of L'eihr that had her sharing her suspicions of Jaxen and Aisly, specifically her fear that the pair might belong to an outside race.

The subject caught Alona off guard, and she surprised Cara by quickly scrambling to block her thoughts. Not quickly enough, though. In the nanosecond she'd left her mind open, Cara saw an image—a memory—in which younger versions of Jaxen and Aisly blinked up at Alona with blue eyes. Vivid blue eyes. Before Cara had time to grasp the significance behind that juicy tidbit, Alona opened her mouth to chastise her.

"I assure you the pair is very much L'eihr. And members of The Way, which, if you've forgotten, you have vowed to obey in all matters."

Cara blushed more deeply at the reproach. "Yes, ma'am."

"Do not tell anyone what you know of the Aribol," Alona ordered. "And instruct Aelyx to do the same."

"I will."

"And don't worry." Alona's gaze seemed to warm by a few degrees. "I have no intention of deploying you to the front lines of battle, should that day ever come."

Cara offered a hesitant smile. "Good, because I'd shoot the wrong person."

"The *iphal* makes friendly fire virtually impossible."

"Trust me, I'd find a way," Cara said flatly. "But allow me to change the subject. The colony development panel needs your input." She explained the impasse they'd reached regarding the occupation program. "I'd like to allow colonists some freedom in choosing their jobs."

"No."

The instantaneous response was surprising, and pure instinct had Cara drawing a breath to argue her case.

"Do you require further assistance?" Alona asked, cutting her off.

Cara got the impression she should shut up, so she shook her head.

"Then you may depart at your leisure."

The defeat brought Cara down a few notches, leaving her more conflicted than ever about colony life. Just when she'd begun to feel the slightest bit of optimism, Alona's snap judgment had made her doubt the future. It was like emotional whiplash, and Cara didn't know how much longer she could keep this up.

But she put the defeat behind her and paid a visit to her favorite academic scholar. Cara had a theory about the Wonder Siblings' blue eyes, and she needed it confirmed. If nothing else, she would leave here knowing the truth about Jaxen and Aisly.

"During the exchange," Cara said to Larish while relaxing into her plush seat, "Aelyx told me the Elders had gone too far with organized breeding, so they backtracked and began cloning from the archives." When Larish nodded in confirmation, she continued. "But why didn't they go *way* back and clone the ancients? Then they wouldn't need human DNA to diversify the gene pool."

"That's a good question." Larish sipped the steaming *h'ali* Cara had brought to butter him up and loosen his tongue. "Genetic material loses its integrity after about two thousand years, even under the ideal storage conditions of the archives. It's possible to clone from older samples, but not without manipulating the genetic code."

"Manipulating it?" she echoed. "How?"

Larish set down his mug and tapped the data table that stood between them. An illustration appeared of the double helix structure. He used an index finger to swipe at the chains, forming cracks and breaks in the DNA. "This is what time does to an archived sample in perfect, sub-frozen storage." With the side of his fist, he took it further, scrubbing out entire rungs of the helix ladder. "And this is what you'd face if you wanted to clone the ancients—assuming you could find their remains."

"But it could be done?" Cara asked.

"In theory. We could use artificial material to fill in the missing links. But it wouldn't be a true clone. Odds are, the replicates would be . . ." He searched for the right word, then settled on the very definition of Jaxen and Aisly. "*Different* from the original."

Cara parted her lips in mock fascination, trying to appear innocent. "Different how? Like, could scientists give the replicates special powers and stuff?"

Mind control, for example.

Larish's countenance brightened and a sly grin curved his mouth. He leaned in, lowering his voice as if to share a secret. "Many years ago, a rumor was circulating that The Way had commissioned just such a project."

Cara mirrored his position, resting both elbows on her knees and summoning her most trustworthy face. "Really?"

He flashed a palm. "Just hearsay, you understand."

"Of course." She gave a solemn nod, silently willing him to spill it.

"Remember the remains taken from the colony?"

"The bodies of the pregnant queen and her consort?"

Larish nodded. "Supposedly, the true reason The Way exhumed the remains was because they'd exhausted their supply of ancient DNA. They transported the bodies here, to the capital's genetics laboratory. According to rumor, the lead geneticists were instructed to clone the pair and heighten the replicates' abilities with alien DNA."

"Aliens?" Cara asked. "Like the Aribol?"

"Maybe. It could have been any species. The Way had uncovered alien genetic material on a primitive blood-crusted weapon, and scientists salvaged just enough usable DNA to fill in the missing genetic code from the ancients."

"How long ago was this?" she asked.

Larish darted a quick gaze at the ceiling to crunch the numbers. "About twenty years ago, if I'm not mistaken." Shaking his head, he corrected, "No. I'd just relocated to the new barracks, so it would have been twenty-two years ago."

Which would make the first alien hybrid twenty-one, like Jaxen. Aelyx was right when he'd said the oldest clones were barely twenty. Jaxen wasn't a true clone. The geneticists must have used him as a guinea pig before they created Aisly.

"What about the fetus?" Cara asked. "Do you think they tried to clone it?"

Larish waved a dismissive hand. "If they did, I can't imagine they were successful. The embryonic tissue would have decayed beyond use."

If that were the case, then Aisly wasn't Jaxen's sister. In another life, thousands of years ago, she'd been his queen and the mother of his unborn child. They were probably *l'ihans* now. Cara recalled the day she'd sat beside Jaxen in his room. When she'd asked about his partner, he had said the girl was his perfect match. It had to be Aisly.

But wait.

What if there were more of these Super Ancients running around? On L'eihr, they'd never stand out if they used cosmetic drops, and on Earth, they'd blend into the blue-eyed population with no more than a trendy haircut and a change of clothes.

"Do you know how many hybrids the labs tried to create?" Cara chilled at the idea of a whole generation of mindbenders loosed upon the galaxy.

"I have no idea." Larish retrieved his mug and took a leisurely sip. "Assuming the project existed, it would've been kept highly classified, which means the lead geneticists would have lived sequestered from the general populace."

Cara started to ask why, but then the answer came. "Ah. So the scientists didn't accidentally leak information through Silent Speech."

"Exactly." Larish gave her that proud-teacher smile. "You're very intelligent, *Cah*-ra."

She waited for him to add the disclaimer *for a human*, but he never did. Her heart swelled with pride. "That means a lot coming from you."

She decided that Larish was pretty awesome—for anyone, not just a L'eihr.

CHAPTER EIGHTEEN

Subscribe [Archive] [Recent Entries] [About Me]

Invaded

MAY THE SOURCE BE WITH YOU

SATURDAY, APRIL 12
Homeward bound!

Everyone knows there's no place like home, and if you listen closely, you just might hear the *click-click-click* of my booted heels as I make like a wizard and fly.

Ever the multitasker, I'm posting from the spaceport while I wait to board the transport to Earth. If all goes according to plan, I'll arrive at the customs checkpoint in Manhattan within a week, then spend the day catching up with Aelyx before heading to Midtown for a weekend with my family and friends. After that, it's back to New York for the alliance ceremony. I hope you'll turn out to celebrate the marriage of our worlds. L'eihrs and humans have a lot to offer each other, and I'd love to see a show of support from my fellow earthlings.

I'm not granting any interviews at this time, but if you see me, make sure to say *hello*. It should be easy to spot me. I'll be the one double-fisting Reese's Cups with a chocolate malt chaser. (Shh . . . don't tell my nutrition counselor.)

Posted by Cara Sweeney

Cara waited for her post to upload to the satellite before shutting down her laptop and tucking it inside her shoulder bag. With her blog updated, she stood and scanned the bustling terminal to gauge how much time she had before boarding.

The luggage carts had vanished since she'd sat down to type her post, along with the dozen or so crates bearing the nanotechnology to neutralize Earth's prolific algae blooms—a long-awaited *Happy Alliance Day!* gift to mankind. Crew members worked in near-perfect unison to fit passengers with travel bands and haul supplies through the tunnel leading to the cargo hold.

When the metal-grated ramp descended from the boarding corridor, Cara knew it wouldn't be much longer before her travel band started buzzing. The crew was probably waiting for The Way's private shuttle to arrive. The head Elders always boarded first, kind of like business-class-elite passengers back home.

That was fine by Cara. Let them go ahead of her. She was in no hurry to entomb herself inside a hotel-size tin can and hurtle through invisible wormholes. Light speed made Cara toss her cookies—or *l'arun*, as it were.

A flicker of sunlight from the nearest spaceport window caught Cara's eye, and she strode toward the thick glass pane for one last look at L'eihr. How had three months flown by so quickly? She still remembered the thrill she'd felt when shuttling down, the wonderment of glimpsing this alien world for the first time. She'd been so desperate to capture more of the landscape's beauty that she hadn't blinked. It was stunning now, even from a distance—the planet a muted cornflower blue with swirls of caramel and cream.

But the exchange had taught her that beauty wasn't enough. Cara hadn't told anyone, but she was 99 percent sure she wasn't coming back.

Contrary to what she'd once posted on the blog, her *important work* for the colony was anything but. In truth, Cara had quit trying to make the development panel see reason. The past two weeks had been a constant battle, and when the council refused to budge on the colonist requirements—lest humans "taint L'eihr progeny with inferior genetic material"—she'd issued a silent retreat. Mentally, she was tired: of fighting to preserve her basic human rights, of dodging leaders she'd sworn to obey, of hostile strangers framing her for capital offenses, of pretending it would get better with time.

Cara felt the pull of home like an irresistible force of gravity leading her back to where she belonged. She wanted to be a normal teenager again, to go to college and spend her nights reading and studying and watching *Doctor Who* reruns. She wanted to eat pizza and wear jeans and openly disagree with her leaders without facing an electric lash.

For the last several months, she'd carried a tremendous burden, slinging the fate of Earth across her back like Atlas—something no seventeen-year-old should have to do. Wasn't she entitled to a break?

She thought so.

But an invisible weight crushed her chest as she stared out the port window. A life on Earth meant a future without

Aelyx, something she couldn't imagine without tears rushing her vision. Stars blurred into a wet glow, and when she blotted her eyes, a distant smudge of brilliance came into view—the angel nebula, tentacles of pink and violet stretched in triumph over the darkness.

Aelyx's words rang in her head, so full of hope that it tightened the pressure around her lungs. *Every time you see it, I want you to think of me. Soon we'll stand together and watch the L'eihr sky from our colony.* Moisture welled again in Cara's eyes. Even if she were able to visit him, the life they had envisioned was gone, and the pain of that loss threatened to double her over.

Why couldn't he stay on Earth for her? Didn't he love her enough?

The travel band around her wrist buzzed an alert. It was time to board the transport and face the long, nauseating journey home. She swiped beneath her eyes and dried her tears. At least she couldn't feel any worse.

Cara was eating those words the next morning as she hugged her chamber's toilet receptacle and dry-heaved for the umpteenth time. She coughed and retched in vain, having long ago emptied the contents of her stomach.

Groaning, she wiped her mouth on her tunic sleeve, cursing herself for not visiting the infirmary yesterday. She had hoped to overcome speed sickness—supposedly, the whole thing was psychological—but to hell with it. Next time she'd ask for an injection the instant she stepped aboard the ship.

Wait.

She froze with her head above the toilet rim. There wouldn't *be* a next time, would there? Cara's stomach turned heavy and sank in a way that had nothing to do with nausea. This was her last voyage. She'd never again explore the wonders beyond Earth's stratosphere, never catalog her discoveries on the colony or learn what creatures skittered beneath the crashing waves. That was almost as depressing as losing Aelyx.

Almost.

But she couldn't think about that now, not if she wanted to survive the day. Pushing the dark thoughts from her head, she crawled to the wall, then used it to right herself. Once standing, she made her way into the hallway and hugged the corridor railing until she made it to the infirmary. She didn't expect to find Jaxen inside waiting for her.

"It took you long enough." Jaxen smiled, shaking his head at her. "A less stubborn girl would have taken the injection before departure."

Cara slogged past him and collapsed onto the steely table, grateful to find it pre-warmed. She ignored Jaxen and glanced at the medic, a senior she recognized as one of Elle's classmates. "Speed sickness," Cara said in L'eihr. "I'm deyhdr—"

"Oddly, your stubbornness has always appealed to me," Jaxen interrupted. "It shows mental fortitude." He turned to the medic and locked eyes with the girl. After a few seconds of Silent Speech, the medic nodded and began gathering supplies.

"What did you tell her?" Cara eyed him suspiciously. Knowing Jaxen, he'd ordered the medic to slip her a roofie.

"Nothing of concern." He gestured toward the girl, who filled a syringe with milky-colored fluid. "Simply to administer the standard antiemetic drug, followed by electrolytes."

The medic wasted no time in carrying out Jaxen's commands. Cara gritted her teeth when the needle pierced her skin, but relief was instantaneous and definitely worth the pain. The roiling inside her stomach stilled, allowing her to drink a vial of syrupy fluid. Within the span of five minutes, she felt human again.

Cara hopped down from the table, keeping hold of the ledge until her legs proved seaworthy. Or rather, spaceworthy. When her knees held firm, she thanked the medic and took a step toward the door, but then her brain spun a double pirouette, forcing her to clutch the wall.

Whoa.

Was it her imagination, or had the floor just tilted thirty degrees? She blinked a few times, and suddenly she was in Jaxen's arms. He scooped her up like a bride and strode into the hallway as if the ship hadn't done a reverse barrel roll.

"What just happened?" Cara rested her head against Jaxen's chest. The act was too intimate for her liking, but her neck muscles had gone slack and left her no choice.

"I also told the medic to administer a sleep aid," Jaxen confessed as he carried her toward her room. "Clearly, you need rest."

Oh, God. He *had* slipped her a roofie!

After all the years she'd waited for the right time to play her v-card, she was going to lose it to a creeper like Jaxen?

Hell, no. She tried to scream for help, but all she could manage was a garbled slur.

Think, Cara. Don't panic!

She closed her eyes for a moment to focus, and when she opened them again, she was lying on her cot with Jaxen kneeling by her side. Panic flashed through her, but a quick inventory revealed her uniform was still intact, all the way down to her boots. She released a sigh of relief. Maybe she'd overreacted.

Jaxen covered her with a blanket and sat on the edge of her mattress. "Sleep well," he whispered. She felt a pinch at her wrist and glanced down to find a flash of silver and blood. Then Jaxen swiped at the wound with something resembling a fountain pen before tucking it inside his tunic pocket.

What just happened? Had he given her another shot?

Cara didn't ponder the question much longer. Her twenty-pound eyelids slid shut, and she drifted into a dark, dreamless sleep.

Aelyx used a sweater sleeve to dry his dewy forehead. He hadn't felt this nervous since his *Sh'ovah* hearing at age fifteen, when the Aegis panel had debated for an hour before finally deeming him worthy of the sacred rite of passage. Tonight, the cool spring breeze did nothing to halt beads of sweat from forming along his upper lip. Aelyx scrubbed away the moisture while staring at the shuttle's hangar door, cast in shadows from the setting sun.

Any minute now . . .

David stood back ten paces, leaning against the armored car to give Aelyx some room when he greeted Cara. But he shook his head in sympathy and shouted, "Dude, chill. You look like your heart's about to explode."

That's precisely how Aelyx felt.

The week had practically gone in reverse waiting for Cara to arrive. Now she was here—finally—a mere twenty yards away with nothing separating them but the thin metal walls of the hangar. But he didn't know what to do when she stepped outside. Should he run to meet her and sweep her into his arms? Hold back and give her some space? These past few months, they'd spent more time apart than they'd ever spent together. Cara might need a period of readjustment. But he only had one night with her before the military whisked her away to Midtown, where she'd stay until the alliance ceremony.

And Aelyx had high hopes for tonight.

He brushed back his hair, not yet long enough for a ponytail, and smoothed the wrinkles from his sweater. He'd worn the cream-colored pullover Cara had always liked, paired with the jeans she'd once said made his posterior look "crazy hot." Ironically, she would be wearing the L'eihr uniform, their roles reversed. He didn't care if she was dressed in a hemp sack; he simply wanted her near.

The hangar door swung open and a group of passengers filed outside, mostly uniformed soldiers and the shuttle crew. Aelyx's eyes moved over them until they settled on a cap of braided red hair. He locked on to Cara's blue gaze, and his heart gave a painful leap. It took all his strength to stand in place and not bolt across the tarmac, knocking down the soldiers in his path like bowling pins.

Cara's smile was timid, her gaze unsteady as she strode toward him and fidgeted with the strap of her shoulder bag. When she reached him, she stopped just outside his personal space, blushing and clearing her throat.

Aelyx extended his hand and recited the same words he'd used during their introduction last fall. "*Cah*-ra, your name is the Irish word for friend. I hope you and I will be great friends." Funny how last year he hadn't meant it. Now Cara was his whole world.

Her lips curved into a warm smile. She placed her tiny palm inside his and gave it a hearty shake. "Your name means 'son of Elyx,' which doesn't give me much to work with, but it's nice to meet you, too."

"Get over here."

With a rough tug, he sent her colliding into his chest, then wrapped both arms around her waist to crush their bodies together. She relaxed into him and rested her cheek near his shoulder, then made a sound of contentment that was satin to his ears. Sacred Mother, she felt so good, all soft curves and heat, the sweet scent of her hair filling his space with oranges and cloves.

When she tipped her ivory face toward his, he brushed her mouth in a gentle kiss. He took her lips tentatively at first, just a light, inviting sweep that let her set the pace. She rose onto her toes and hooked her arms around his neck, then tilted her head and ratcheted up the passion by a thousand blistering degrees. She kissed him like he was a soldier heading to war, never to return. It went on for several heart-pounding minutes until their breathing turned choppy and they broke for air.

"Gods," he said with a groan. "I missed you."

Clutching his sweater, Cara panted and licked her swollen lips. "Me, too."

"Show me." Aelyx took her face in his hands, relaxing his focus to experience her rush of sentiment for him. He had to feel it; he craved it more than he could stand.

Cara shook her head, glancing around them in an unspoken message that there were too many witnesses to risk Silent Speech. Then a mischievous twinkle gleamed in her eyes. "Take me to the penthouse, and I'll show you a lot more than that."

His lips parted while a jolt of excitement lit him up inside. Did that mean what he thought it meant? Was she finally ready? He lifted his brows in a question.

"We only have ten hours together until I leave again," Cara said in a voice that made her intentions clear. "I can think of better ways to spend our time than kissing in the parking lot. How fast can you get me to your place?"

The answer: twenty-three minutes and thirty-seven seconds, a new land speed record set by David, for which Aelyx was infinitely grateful.

In an epic display of restraint, Aelyx managed to keep his hands to himself long enough to get Cara behind his bedroom door, and then it was a free-for-all as they clawed at each other in an unchecked compulsion to get closer. They stole clumsy kisses while tugging off shirts and shoes, pants and socks, tossing their clothes to the floor in a haphazard trail toward their final destination.

Once there, they fell to the bed in a tangled heap.

The sensation of Cara's body beneath him, her heated skin fused to his own, was the purest form of pleasure Aelyx had ever known. He didn't think it could possibly feel any better, but then she used her hands to explore him, sparking to life a thousand nerve endings that had once lain dormant.

He touched her, too, discovering the secret places that made her breath catch and her muscles tense. It was heaven. Lacing their fingers together, he pinned both hands above her head, then whispered against her lips, "You still have the implant, right?"

She drew a shuddering breath and nodded, so flushed and beautiful it almost hurt to look at her. "You won't get me pregnant."

"And you're sure this is what you want?" *Gods, please let her say yes.* If she changed her mind now, the pressure building inside his body might actually cripple him.

Cara squeezed their linked hands. Her face glowed with the certainty he'd hoped for. "I'm sure, and I love you. I want you to know that."

He nuzzled the tip of her nose and murmured, "Show me." He wanted to connect with her on every level, body and mind, to share their sensations and create a unified memory. Their first time together might not be perfect, but it was theirs.

But instead of meeting his gaze, Cara slid her mouth over his throat and wrapped both legs around his hips. He tried to catch her eye, but with each attempt, she arched and shifted against him while hiding her face. Aelyx kept her hands fixed on either side of the pillow and rose onto his knees, beyond her reach.

"Why won't you look at me?" he asked.

Cara squinted her eyes shut, shaking her head. "Not now. After, okay?"

Something was clearly wrong. Cara had rarely shied away from Silent Speech.

"What's the matter?" he asked. "What aren't you telling me?"

Slowly, she opened one eye, then the other, but stared at his exposed chest instead of his face. "Nothing. I just want one perfect night with you. After everything we've been through, don't you think we deserve it? Let's talk in the morning."

Aelyx didn't like the way that sounded. The desperation in her voice implied this "perfect night" would be their *only* night. He reminded her of what she'd told him months ago when he'd struggled to reveal his own secrets. "If we can't be honest with each other, we're no more than strangers."

She met his gaze, pleading with her eyes. "I want to be with you. Please? I swear I'll tell you everything after—"

"No," he insisted. "Or I won't be able to stop thinking about it." When she hesitated, he promised, "You can trust me."

She sank into the pillow as if to disappear. "I'm afraid you'll hate me."

Hate her? Fear snaked its way up the length of Aelyx's body and settled in his heart. "Did you meet someone else? At the Aegis?"

"No, nothing like that."

"*Elire*, you have to show me, or I'll imagine the worst."

After several long seconds, she gave a resigned nod and locked her watery blue eyes with his. A single tear spilled down her temple, disappearing into her hair as she opened her mind to him. Aelyx lowered to his elbows and peered deep inside, holding his breath in cold fear. When he felt the swelling of her love for him like a billow of heat inflating his lungs, he sighed in relief.

But right on the heels of relief came a chill of dread.

Now he understood what she had tried so hard to hide. Cara had changed her mind about the colony. He would return to L'eihr after the alliance ceremony, but she planned to stay behind. The certainty within her was almost tangible. Cara was no happier on L'eihr than he was on Earth.

Which meant they couldn't be together.

When Aelyx had first learned to play sticks, an older clone had knocked him flat on his back to the unforgiving ground. More than pain, Aelyx remembered the panic of not being able to breathe. He'd opened his mouth and gaped for air, his eyes bulging and face throbbing for what seemed like an hour. He felt that way now, breathless and aching and utterly terrified.

"I'm sorry," she whispered. "I really tried."

Aelyx wanted to speak, but his tongue lay dead. He knew how hard she'd fought. Her frustration was his own—he'd felt it.

"Nothing's changed." She cupped his cheek. "I still want this. I want my first time to be with you. Let's have our perfect night and figure it out in the morning, okay?" Softly, she stroked the edge of his jaw and rose up to kiss his lips. "Please?"

His mind was swimming. Drowning. He had to gain some distance and think.

Rolling to the side, he pressed both palms to his eyes and tried to force the blood flow back to his brain. His body pleaded with him to give Cara what she wanted—he'd waited so long for this—but she would take a piece of him if they went any further, and as much as he loved her, he'd never get it back. If he walked away now, he'd spend the rest of the night with a leaden cramp in his belly, but that would hurt far less than a lifetime replaying the memory of joining himself with the only girl he'd ever loved.

"We'll make it work," Cara insisted. "We'll find a way to see each other."

Aelyx finally found his voice. "How often? Once every few years?" Their relationship would never survive the distance. The slow passage of time would drive them apart—and eventually into another pair of arms. Young as they were, it was as natural and inevitable as the rising of the sun.

"I don't know, but at least *I'm* willing to try," she snapped.

He pushed onto one elbow. She made it sound like he'd put no effort into their relationship. "What is that supposed to mean?"

Another tear spilled down Cara's cheek as she jerked the blanket to cover her body. "It means I've practically turned myself inside out to make a life on your planet, but you won't even consider staying on mine. There's no compromise."

"I can't believe you think that." He'd gladly stay on Earth if humans would stop trying to kill him all the damned time. But that was beyond his control. "The colony is supposed to be the compromise."

"But it's not. The Way isn't giving humans an inch."

"You've only been on the council a month. The charter isn't even written yet." Aelyx couldn't believe she'd accused *him* of quitting too easily. "Maybe if you—"

"If I what?" she interrupted. "Work harder?"

"Yes!" He hadn't meant to shout, but panic rushed through his veins.

"Why don't *you* work harder?" she yelled back.

"What do you think I've been doing all these months?" Traveling from one city to the next, going to bed without knowing where he was. Dodging assassination attempts. Missing her like crazy. "I've been fighting nonstop for this alliance."

"Only because you're the reason it failed to begin with!"

The words stung, real as any slap. Not a day had passed since Eron's death that Aelyx didn't regret his role in sabotaging the alliance. "You think I've forgotten that I helped get my best friend killed?"

Cara bit her lip while her breath hitched, and Aelyx pinched the bridge of his nose to try and calm down. He didn't want to do this. They were fighting dirty and getting nowhere.

"I'm sorry," she whispered. "That wasn't fair."

Nothing about this was fair. "Is there a chance you might change your mind?"

"Is there a chance you might change *yours?*"

When he didn't answer, she broke into fresh tears.

Slowly, and with great deliberation, Aelyx stood from the bed and picked through the trail of clothing on the floor until he'd dressed. Cara sobbed the whole time, causing his head to ache in unison with his feverish body. He couldn't stay with her, not without breaking down. He had to escape as far as this luxury high-rise prison would allow.

"You can sleep here," he told Cara, facing away because he couldn't bear to watch her cry. "I'll take the guest room."

"Aelyx, please . . ." Her voice was thick with tears, threatening to break his slippery grasp on control. "Don't go. Not yet. Let's talk about this."

He moved toward the door, though every cell in his body weighed him down and fought against it. "I'm not angry with you." He paused with one hand squeezing the doorknob. "And I hope we can still be friends."

Friend, the Irish translation of her name. How horribly, painfully prophetic.

CHAPTER NINETEEN

Cara dragged a crumpled tissue beneath her nose and padded into the kitchen, where Mom was unloading the dishwasher while Dad pressed against her from behind. He lifted the dark curls from Mom's neck and replaced them with nibbles and kisses.

"Nice to see nothing's changed since I've been gone." Cara dropped onto the nearest chair, too exhausted to stand after the walk from her bedroom. The simple act of pulling on her bathrobe had drained her.

"Oh, honey." Mom abandoned the dishwashing to wrap Cara in a warm hug. "Are you ready to talk yet?"

Cara shook her head. She'd told Mom about the breakup, but she didn't want to rehash it. Thinking about Aelyx made her heart pinch.

"I hate seeing you like this." Mom smoothed a palm over

Cara's loose hair in a comforting sweep. "When was the last time you ate?"

"Yesterday, I think." Cara had nearly gagged on her Reese's. As if to prove she was still human, she'd choked down both peanut butter cups, but her body had punished her for it. She'd felt sluggish and queasy ever since.

"Want me to make your favorite breakfast?" Mom asked. "It'll only take a minute."

Hell must have frozen over, because the idea of Mom's triple-chocolate-chip pancakes sent Cara's stomach into a somersault. "No, thanks."

"Sweetheart, why don't you call Tori? She always makes you feel better."

"I did." The inside of Cara's nose tingled, and she grabbed a fresh Kleenex from her pocket in time for a vicious *ker-choo*. Groaning, she dabbed beneath her raw nose while sliding a glare at the empty doggie bed in the corner. Mom had boarded Linus at the kennel, but the fluffball had left behind plenty of pet dander. "She's taking me to the mall for a girls' day."

Mom arched a stern brow. "Not without your brother."

Cara huffed a sigh, but secretly she was glad to have Troy home. Colonel Rutter had done them a huge favor by assigning Troy to her security detail. This was the first time in three years their entire family had slept under the same roof, and it reminded Cara of simpler days when her biggest problems were acne and frizzy hair.

"Fine," she said. "He can come, too."

"And I want you to eat something," Mom said. "What's it going to be?"

Cara scanned the open pantry for her options: Captain Crunch, coffee cakes, fudge Pop-Tarts, Nutri-Grain bars, and sweetened oatmeal. None of it appealed to her. Maybe her nutrition counselor had been right when he'd likened sugar to a toxic drug.

"I guess I could eat some eggs," Cara said.

Mom squeezed Cara's shoulders. "Coming right up."

By the time Mom finished making breakfast, the back door swung open and Troy bounded inside from his daily jog, the pits of his SEMPER FI T-shirt soaked with sweat. Cara noticed he'd tried to maintain the bulk he added on L'eihr, but he'd begun to thin at the shoulders. He tugged his earbuds free and nodded at the frying pan. "Got extra?"

"That depends," Mom said. "Do you feel like tagging along to the mall with your sister and Tori?"

He made a sour face, which Mom took as a *yes*.

"Good. Then I've got plenty to spare." Mom dished out two plates and set them on the table in front of Cara and Troy.

They ate in silence until Cara remembered something. She glanced over her shoulder to make sure Mom and Dad were out of earshot. "Elle told me to say hi and that she misses having you as a roommate."

Troy paused with a bite of scrambled egg suspended an inch from his mouth. "For real?"

"Mmm-hmm. She said taking off her shirt feels anti-climactic now."

His focus softened and he shook his head in wonderment. "What a pair."

"You're such a pig."

Shrugging a shoulder, he crammed in the rest of his eggs and spoke with one cheek full. "Yeah, well, if this pig's gonna spend his last day of vacation following around your skinny ass, he's getting a free lunch out of it."

Cara smiled for the first time in what seemed like forever. "You think my ass is skinny?"

He rolled his eyes so hard he probably glimpsed his own brain.

"Thanks for coming to the mall," she told him. "I've missed you."

Troy watched her for a long moment before ruffling her hair. "You're welcome. Dorkus."

The inside of Tori's car smelled the same as Cara remembered—a mixture of leather, fruity hair products, and Cool Ranch Doritos. It wasn't a scent she would describe as pleasant, but it evoked happy memories of away games and summer. After giving her best friend a long-overdue hug, Cara strapped into the passenger seat and used the rearview mirror to ensure no orange strands were peeking out from beneath her blond pageboy wig. Her disguise would work if nobody looked too closely at her auburn brows or the freckles dotting her cheeks.

"Here." Tori handed her a pair of oversize sunglasses, then slung a bronze wrist atop the steering wheel, narrowing her kohl-lined eyes at Cara's sweatpants and matching gray hoodie. "If you're going for the whole 'burned-out soccer mom' look, you nailed it, babe. Nobody will recognize you like this."

Cara frowned and glanced again at her reflection. Maybe

she should have worn a little makeup, at least to conceal the redness beneath her nose. After her shower, she'd plucked her favorite cosmetics from her bag, but then the whole ritual seemed kind of pointless. Who decided freckles needed to be covered up? Who said eyelashes had to be thick and black and unnaturally long? Cara thought she looked fine without her cheeks dusted or her lips painted. Nobody wore makeup on L'eihr.

But you're not on L'eihr now.

"Hey," she said to Tori. "Lend me some gloss, will you?" When Tori produced *Gritty in Pink*, Cara smoothed on a heavy coat. Her lips shimmered in the sunlight, but they felt sticky and unkissable. Not that she had anyone to kiss.

"That's a step in the right direction," Tori said. "Now let's find an outfit to show off that hot new body of yours."

"Can we not talk about my sister's body?" Troy asked from the backseat. "A trip to the mall is torture enough."

"So put in your earbuds," Tori said.

He followed her advice, then rolled down the rear passenger window and signaled to the unmarked SUV behind them that they were ready to go. The driver flashed his lights twice, and Tori pulled onto the street.

"E can't make it," Tori said over the hum of the engine. "But he says hi and he hopes you change your mind about living among the L'osers."

Cara ignored the argument bait, relieved that Eric couldn't join them. She didn't harbor any residual feelings for her ex, but it was still awkward seeing him with her best friend. "Tell him I said hey."

"Tell him yourself tonight at Jared Lee's kegger."

Cara slid her best friend a skeptical look.

"Come on," Tori pressed. "We'll say you're staying with me, and we'll crash in Jared's basement. That way nobody has to drive."

In other words, they could get wasted. The prospect of chugging warm, watered-down beer to the point of sloppy-drunken oblivion had never appealed to Cara. What was the point? To feel buzzed for a few hours until the hangover set in? "I'll pass. It would be a security nightmare, anyway."

"Talk to me." Tori delivered a light nudge. "You sounded like death when you called, and now you're saying no to a party. What's wrong?"

Cara blew out a breath and hoped she could hold the tears inside. She didn't even know if Tori would understand.

"It's the A-licker, right?" Tori pointed at Cara's sweatpants and ratty garden clogs. "This has 'broken heart' written all over it."

"We had a fight."

"Everyone fights. It's a good thing. It means you've got fire."

Cara shook her head. "Not that kind of fight. I don't think we can come back from this. It's too—" Her throat swelled with grief until it choked her next words. All she could manage was a whisper. "It's over."

She expected Tori to say "good riddance" in her own colorful way, but that's not what happened. Instead, Tori took one hand off the wheel to clasp Cara's palm. She gave it a tight squeeze and promised, "You'll feel better after a new pair of jeans and a triple fudge meltdown. And if that doesn't work, we'll watch *Magic Mike*."

Cara laughed as tears welled in her eyes. "Let's hope it doesn't come to that."

"How about some trashy gossip?" Tori said. "You'll feel like a million bucks compared to the train wrecks at Midtown High."

As they made their way onto the interstate, Tori filled in Cara on what she'd missed since last winter: Brandi Greene got caught drinking Boone's Farm at a school dance and was thus banned from prom. Murphy Finn was banging four freshmen, but none of the girls knew about one another because they attended different schools. Principal Ferguson busted the band teacher smoking weed in the back of a school bus. The stories kept coming, but Cara didn't feel like five bucks, let alone a million. If anything, the gossip added to the heaviness inside her, though she couldn't figure out why.

They pulled into the mall parking lot, and Troy explained how the security detail would operate. He'd stay by Cara's side at all times, except in the dressing rooms, and the plain-clothes soldiers would scout each store before she was allowed to enter. If anyone recognized her, the group would have to leave right away because the unit wasn't large enough to handle a mob. Fortunately, Cara had kept her arrival date vague, so nobody knew she was here.

"Let's start at Neiman's," Tori said, her high heels clicking against the asphalt. "So you can help me pick a prom dress."

Cara pressed a hand to her heart. "I forgot all about prom." The image of frilly dresses brought a smile to her lips. Maybe she'd try one on, just for fun. An eager bounce lightened her steps as she tugged open the door to her old stomping grounds, but the vibrating wall of noise that greeted her on the other side had her twitching to run back to the car.

Holy sensation overload.

An indistinct pop tune blared through the ceiling speakers, competing with the throbbing bass of club music that wafted from the entrance to Hot Topic. With spring break in full swing, every teen in the county was here, each one laughing and shouting over the din while their fingers flew across their cell phone screens. The cloying scent of perfume leaked from the doors of Hollister in clouds so thick it forced Cara to cover her nose, and when she breathed through her mouth, the residue seeped inside to coat her tongue. How could anyone stand to go in there? Or any other store, for that matter? The shops were teeming with people rudely nudging one another aside as if their lives depended on scoring this season's trendiest belt.

The scene inside Neiman Marcus was marginally calmer, but Cara had to keep reminding herself to unclench her jaw. So much for a leisurely day of shopping. Leaning toward her brother, she said, "Can you have someone bring me a bunch of jeans while Tori's trying on prom dresses? We'll finish quicker if we multitask."

Troy didn't need further convincing. "What size?"

"Somewhere between a four and a six, I guess."

He used his phone to tap a text message. "I told him to grab a few shirts, too."

"Good thinking."

She scurried to keep pace with Tori, whose mahogany eyes locked on to the formal wear department with the single-minded determination of a girl with a raging case of Prom Fever.

"*Puta madre*," Tori breathed, gravitating as if entranced toward a backless ivory gown with a side slit cut clear to the hip. With its satiny fabric and barely there straps, it looked more like lingerie than a dress. Tori reached out with reverent fingers and held the gown in front of her. "What do you think?"

Honestly? Cara thought her friend would be very cold in that dress. "Um, the color looks great with your skin." And given how easily it'd slip off at the end of the night, Eric would love it.

"I'm gonna try it on."

Cara followed to the dressing rooms, where a young soldier balanced a stack of folded jeans on one arm. He made an apologetic face. "I did the best I could, but it's redonk over there. I didn't know if you wanted cropped, boot-cut, straight-leg, skinny, flared, low-rise, high-waist, or jegging." He leaned in, shell-shocked. "And that's just the cut. Then there's dark wash, medium vintage—"

"That's okay," Cara interrupted. "I'm sure one of these will work." She took the pile of denim into the fitting room and emerged ten minutes later with three pair of jeans that fit and one pair she could actually afford. Suddenly the L'eihr uniform didn't seem so bad.

"Ta-da!" Tori sang, opening her dressing room door. She hitched up her gown and strode to the three-way mirror, then began checking out her butt from different angles. "Nice, huh?"

She really did look nice. Overly exposed, yes, but tame compared to what some girls would be wearing. Cara gave a teasing wolf whistle and checked the price tag. Her mouth dropped open. "Did you see this, Tor?"

Satisfied with her reflection, Tori turned from the mirror and strutted back to her dressing room. "Yep."

"You're gonna drop this much on a gown you'll wear once?"

"I'll put it on my card," Tori said, as if she weren't spending real money that way. "I need shoes and a bag, too. What do you think about strappy nude heels?"

By the time they reached the shoe department, Cara thought strappy nude heels were as unnecessary and overpriced as the plastic-wrapped gown draped over Tori's shoulder. Cara lifted a butt-fugly leopard-print platform pump and gasped at the price sticker affixed to the sole. Maybe if humans didn't spend so much time and money on useless crap, they wouldn't need the L'eihrs to save the world for them.

"Cute," Tori said, nodding at the monstrosity in Cara's hand. "You should try 'em on."

"Yeah. Or not."

Tori wrinkled her brow and studied Cara over a display of sandals. "Retail therapy isn't working, is it?" She set down a glittery clutch and nodded toward the exit. "Let's go. Time for that triple chocolate meltdown."

"Dig in." From the other side of the table, Tori pointed her spoon at the plate between them. "If you let me finish this by myself, I'll never fit into that kick-ass dress I just bought." The mere sight of hot fudge pooling out from the center of a gooey chocolate cake was enough to turn Cara's stomach, but she took one for the team and shoveled in a bite. She swallowed as quickly as possible before washing out the taste with unsweetened iced tea.

"What the hell?" Tori asked. "It looked like you were chewing razor blades."

"Sweets make me kind of sick now."

Tori's black brows shot up. "You're not preggers, are you?"

"No," Cara said with a humorless laugh. "Zero chance of that, trust me."

"Huh." Tori chewed the inside of her cheek and stared at their dessert. "The mall was a bust, and chocolate isn't working. This leaves us with only one option . . ."

"Oh, no. Not *Magic Mike*."

"Then give me an alternative. Tell me what's going to make you smile."

That was a good question, but Cara didn't know the answer. She thought back to the last experiences that had brought her joy—snuggling with Vero, mastering the intermediate track, glimpsing the colony for the first time, placing her hand in Aelyx's strong grasp.

Cara sighed and poked at the cake. "Nothing on Earth."

They fell silent for a while, fidgeting with bendy straws and silverware, until Tori said what they were both thinking. "You're different now."

"Yeah, I am," Cara said. And she had a feeling things would never be the same as before the exchange. She peeked up from beneath her lashes. "But I still love you."

Tori's face broke into a bittersweet grin. She reached across the table and took Cara's hand, her touch somehow both familiar and foreign. "Right back at'cha. That'll never change."

Cara flipped open the AP physics textbook she'd found in the bottom of her closet. If she wanted to apply to Dartmouth, she'd first have to make up the work she'd missed, and what better opportunity to catch up than during spring break? As she pulled her Einstein packet from her backpack, it occurred to her that she'd probably lost her valedictorian rank when she'd fled Earth.

She supposed that douche canoe, Marcus Johnson, would graduate at the top of the class. The old Cara would have devised a plot to reclaim her title, but the new Cara couldn't bring herself to care.

"Valedictorian," she muttered to herself. "Whoop-de-friggin-do. I'm the Chief Human Consultant to the most powerful woman in the universe."

Or rather, she was.

She turned to the chapter on Einstein's theory of relativity and began skimming the text, but then she realized that the advanced physics she'd learned on L'eihr transcended her AP science class. Cara closed her textbook. It had nothing to teach her.

Her internal clock was still on Aegis time, and it seemed too early for bed. She stepped into the hall, finding no signs of life other than the subdued glow of the oven exhaust hood, which Mom had always used as a night-light. Cara recognized the sound of a kitchen chair scraping the linoleum floor and decided to see who was awake.

"Hey," she said to Troy, who sat at the table with a box of Cheerios and a bottle of Sam Adams lager to keep him company. He tossed back a handful of O's and used his bare foot to push out a chair for her. Accepting his invitation, she took a seat and grabbed the cereal box.

After munching his snack and washing it down with a swig of beer, Troy asked, "Change your mind about the party?"

"Nah." Cara shook out a pile of Cheerios even though she wasn't hungry. "Just bored. What about you? I figured you'd be hanging with your friends." She nodded toward the backyard, where soldiers stood guard around the house.

He shrugged and leaned an elbow on the table, propping his chin in one hand. "They invited me to a poker game later. I dunno. I used to like that stuff, but now it seems so . . ." He appeared to struggle with the right word, eventually settling on, "Pointless."

Cara's eyes flew wide. "I know exactly what you mean! I thought it was just me."

"Trust me, it's not." Troy smirked, more at himself than at

her, then glanced through the kitchen entry and into the living room as if to make sure they were alone. "Can you keep a secret?"

Cara hesitated a beat before nodding, not because she couldn't keep her lips zipped, but because Troy had never confided in her.

"I haven't been the same since I got back from L'eihr," he said. "My CO sent me to the head shrinker, and she said I've got an adjustment disorder."

Cara tipped her head. "What's that?"

"Failure to adapt." Clearly uncomfortable, Troy dropped eye contact and began stacking his Cheerios atop one another in a crooked pyramid. "You usually see it with special forces guys—the ones who go out on big missions. They get hooked on the adrenaline and can't cope when they come home." Troy raised his gaze to hers. "How're they supposed to go from live combat and jumping out of helicopters to grocery shopping and driving their kids to school, you know?"

"Real life is dull by comparison," Cara said.

"Exactly."

"I get that." As much as she wanted to feel like a "normal teenager" again, her time on L'eihr had ruined her for dances and shopping and all the things she used to love. "But for me, it's more than that. I'm starting to see our way of life differently."

"Like . . ." Troy prompted, seeming to perk up a little.

"Remember the gas station where we stopped on the way home from the mall?" When he nodded, she said, "They had TVs built right into the pumps." The old Cara would have thought that was cool, but the new-and-ruined Cara didn't see it that way. "Are we so overstimulated that we can't spend five minutes pumping gas without a TV or a cell phone to distract us?"

"Guess so."

"And when I went inside to buy a magazine," Cara went on, "that's when it really hit me. I stood there looking at the racks, and all the headlines seemed so trivial. I've always wanted to be a journalist, but what am I going to do? Write articles about which movie star had the fat sucked from her ass and injected into her face? Which professional athlete just confessed to shooting steroids? The latest celebrity baby names?" Cara lowered both brows in frustration. "Who cares? It's like our whole culture is built on frivolity, and I never noticed before."

Troy flicked an O into the pyramid he'd built, toppling it over. "It's the noise that gets to me. Everything sounds amplified now."

"Yeah, me too," Cara agreed before continuing her rant. "And we squander our money on the most ridiculous things. You know how much Americans spent on Halloween candy last year?" Without giving him a chance to guess, she cried, "Two billion dollars. That's *billion*, with a B." She fell silent, struck by the absurdity of it all. "We're dropping piles of cash on candy while disease research and scientific advancement go unfunded. It makes my head explode."

Troy snickered and held both palms forward. "Chill, Pepper. I believe you."

"The worst of it is I don't know where I belong." She

wasn't wholly human anymore, but she didn't feel like a L'eihr. She swept aside her Cheerios, too upset to taste anything. "Can *you* keep a secret?"

"Probably," her brother said.

She told him about her decision to remain on Earth after the alliance ceremony, including her residual breakup with Aelyx, whom Troy had never liked. But by the time she finished explaining her reasoning, Troy seemed more conflicted than relieved.

"What?" she asked. "I thought you'd be happy."

He picked at the label on his beer bottle, avoiding her eyes. "I am, if it's what you really want . . ." Then he trailed off, warning her a *but* was coming.

"But?" she asked.

"If you were going to the colony," he said, peeking up at her, then back to his bottle, "I was thinking of coming, too, when my enlistment's over."

Cara drew a breath. "Are you serious?"

"Uh-huh," he said with a slow *I know it sounds crazy, but I really mean it* nod. "I've been thinking about it since I got back."

"But you hated L'eihr," Cara reminded him. "You kept saying we didn't belong there."

"Yeah, and that's still kind of true," Troy said, locking his blue eyes with hers. "But we also don't belong *here*."

He was right—Cara knew it all the way down to the marrow in her bones. But that didn't change the fact that she couldn't be happy on the colony, not without the kinds of concessions The Way would never make. It was an impossible situation. She felt like a square peg that had been shaved into an octagon, so now she didn't fit into any hole, round or otherwise. But somehow in the next forty-eight hours, Cara would have to decide once and for all where her future lay.

No pressure or anything.

Chapter Twenty

The official first day of spring was hopelessly bleak, which matched Aelyx's mood. He shifted in bed and stared out the window, where freezing rain pelted the glass. This afternoon he would have to stand by Cara's side at the alliance ceremony and pretend he didn't feel gutted—scooped out of any happiness he'd once known. At least tomorrow he'd leave this godsforsaken planet and return home, where ice never rained from the sky. If nothing else, he had that to look forward to.

With heavy limbs, he shuffled into the kitchen, hoping Syrine had made her customary pot of tea. Aelyx didn't want to foster a caffeine dependency, but lately he'd moved as if underwater. He'd take any boost he could get. After pouring himself a steaming mug of minty-scented brew, he dragged into the living room and lowered onto the ambassador's favorite chair, simply because it was closest. Gods, he was tired.

He'd just awoken and already he wanted to go back to bed.

David and Syrine were situated near him on the sofa, but instead of saying hello, they stared at each other in what appeared to be a standoff. Syrine's hands clenched into fists while David's chin tipped up in determination. Several seconds of charged silence ticked by before Aelyx asked what was wrong.

When David spoke, he kept his eyes fixed on Syrine. "I just told your friend I'm in love with her."

"Oh," Aelyx said, wishing he'd taken his tea back to his bedroom. *Awkward.*

"And," David continued, "that I won't ever stop. That I'm not like the other guys she's known, and if she'll trust me for once, I can make her happy."

Aelyx wasn't sure how to reply. Obviously David wasn't talking to him anymore. "What did she say?"

"Nothing yet." David held up his deck of cards. "But I was just about to propose another wager."

Syrine found her voice, but it barely carried in the open room. "For what?"

"If I win," David said, "we go to the colony together. *Really* together, as a couple. No more hiding."

She swallowed hard enough to make her throat shift. "And if you lose?"

"Then I stay here." David's expression fell, his voice darkening to a deadly seriousness Aelyx had never heard from the boy. "But I've never felt this way about anyone. You're it for me."

All the color drained from Syrine's cheeks, and although

she didn't agree to the bet, David began shuffling the deck. His hands trembled with the motion, something Aelyx would have attributed to anxiety if he hadn't noticed the same thing happening all weekend. David's fine motor skills were weakening. Aelyx knew the likely cause, but he refused to dwell on it. He had to believe the experimental drug would save his friend.

David fanned out the deck and held it toward Syrine. "Pick a card."

Syrine extended her hand and pulled it back three times before she drew a card from the deck. Aelyx took a sip of his tea and leaned to the side, noting she'd picked the seven of diamonds.

"You know what to do," David told her. "Hold it close and stare at it. Really focus so I can read your mind."

While Syrine peered at the red diamonds, David studied the symbols drawn on the other side. As many times as he'd practiced this trick, he couldn't fail. He parted the deck and instructed Syrine to replace the card, then reshuffled the pack. Turning the deck over, he riffled through his options, feigning deep thought, until he held up the queen of spades.

"Is this your card?" David asked, eyeing Syrine while tremors shook his hand.

At first, Aelyx couldn't comprehend why David had chosen incorrectly. He'd long ago mastered this game. But then understanding dawned, and Aelyx saw that David had forced Syrine to choose. It was his way of ensuring she truly wanted him, refusing to allow something as trivial as a wager to determine their future.

With her mouth forming a perfect O, Syrine stared at David as the seconds passed in near-painful silence. Aelyx found himself leaning forward in his seat as if he could force the answer out of her. Finally, when the wait had become nearly unbearable, she licked her lips and whispered, "Yes, you're right. That's the one."

A grateful smile split David's face while his eyes watered. He released a shaky sigh that sounded more like a sob and threw down his cards to take Syrine into his arms. The pair held each other, exchanging kisses and whispers that made Aelyx feel like an intruder. Careful not to spill his tea, he quietly returned to his bedroom to give the couple their privacy.

Aelyx was happy for Syrine—David, too. He cared for them and knew the colony would be a brighter place for their presence, but that didn't stop a lump from rising in his throat. He continued sipping his tea, but nothing would push it down.

For months, he'd been forced to watch the romance blossom between his friends, reminding himself to be patient, that his turn would come when he was reunited with Cara. But things were different now. All the patience in the world wouldn't resurrect what he'd lost. Aelyx didn't know how he was going to stand the presence of two perfectly paired lovers and still maintain his sanity.

He'd just finished his tea when Syrine knocked on the door and stepped inside, her gaze both giddy and repentant. He could tell she empathized with him.

"You made the right choice," Aelyx said, setting his cup on the dresser.

Syrine gave a noncommittal grunt, though the glow illuminating her skin showed that she agreed. "Time will tell. He may disappoint me, but I believe it's a worthy risk."

Aelyx laughed. "Practical to a fault, as usual."

"You say that like it's a bad thing." She closed the distance between them and rested a hand on his forearm, then peered into his face, softening her focus to connect with his mind. *Let me help you.*

Quickly, he turned his head aside. "No."

"This is what I'm trained for," she insisted. "I can't erase your pain, but I can lighten the burden."

Aelyx knew full well what Syrine could do. Emotional healers were sacred on L'eihr because of their rarity. But he also knew how the session would affect her. She'd take on his suffering by proxy, feeling his heartbreak as if it were her own, and he wouldn't allow it. She was entitled to her joy. "It's just a breakup." He faced her with a manufactured smile. "I'm fairly certain I'll survive it."

"Wouldn't you do the same for me?"

"You know I would." Touched by her compassion, Aelyx took her cheek in one hand and bent to kiss the top of her head, where he paused and added, "But you wouldn't let me."

"No," she admitted. "I wouldn't."

David appeared in the doorway. His expression darkened as he jerked his head toward the foyer and mouthed, *Cara's here.*

Like a bolt of blistering electricity, painful tingles shot down the length of Aelyx's spine. His flesh chilled and his pulse lurched. The visceral reaction proved what he already knew—he wasn't ready to face her. He glanced at David in a silent plea for advice.

David seemed to understand. "Grab your coat," he whispered. "I need to make a quick call, then we'll get out of here."

"I'll come, too," Syrine said.

"No." David's curt tone surprised them all, and he compensated with an apologetic smile. "You stay and talk some sense into her."

"Her mind's made up," Aelyx told them.

Syrine patted his shoulder, slipping a hurried thought into his mind before she flitted out the door. *You underestimate me.*

"Breathe, Pepper. You look like you're choking on your own tongue."

Cara leaned into her brother and released the breath she'd unconsciously trapped inside her lungs. Tugging her coat lapels together, she shivered in the heated living room. It wasn't the freak ice storm that had her trembling. The alliance ceremony didn't begin until noon—three hours from now—and Colonel Rutter had ordered her to report to the ambassador's penthouse.

With Aelyx.

No, that wouldn't be weird *at all.*

"Jesus, pull it together," Troy whispered, wrapping a quick arm around her. "You're literally shaking in your boots."

He didn't understand—how could he? He'd never been in love, not like this.

"Hello, *Cah*-ra."

Flinching, Cara whirled around to find Syrine smiling at her with the polite detachment of a salesclerk. The last time their paths had crossed, it ended with Syrine bitch-slapping Cara and wishing death upon the human race. Now the girl extended an arm, offering to take their coats.

Cara held firm to her lapels. "I'll keep mine, thanks."

Troy yanked his arm free and shook out of his camouflage jacket while Cara snuck a few covert glances behind their hostess. Aelyx was nowhere in sight. Maybe he'd decided to stay in his room until the ceremony began. She knew she should feel relieved, but she caught herself biting her lip in disappointment.

Syrine followed the direction of Cara's gaze. "Aelyx is leaving for an errand; otherwise he'd join us."

Cara felt herself blushing. *Busted.*

When Syrine strode to the closet to hang up Troy's coat, a distant door clicked open and nearly sent Cara's heart catapulting out of her chest. She tried to play it cool, but her eyes found Aelyx the instant he entered the room.

His jaw-length hair concealed part of his face, but the visible side was breathtaking, even marred by the dark circles of insomnia. Cara hated herself for thinking it, but she was glad he hadn't been sleeping. That made two of them. His silver eyes widened when he spotted her. He held her gaze for a pregnant beat as if gauging her expression to see if she'd changed her mind. Breaking contact, she stared at the hardwood floor and gave him an answer. She hated herself for that, too.

She didn't look up again until she heard David say "I love you" in a firm voice.

The boy fastened his weapons holster around his hips while staring expectantly at Syrine. Cara didn't understand at first, but then he placed a kiss atop the girl's head, and everything made sense. Well, as much sense as Syrine dating a human could possibly make.

Syrine's copper skin darkened a few shades and she pushed at her bodyguard's chest, giving him nothing but a shy grin. "Go on."

"One of these days you'll tell me," David said, zipping his coat. He stood there watching her, hesitating to leave, until Aelyx tugged on his jacket. Then the two of them disappeared out the door.

Cara crossed the room and glanced out the window to the city block below, where a stagelike platform stood naked of the decorations and folding chairs that belonged there. If the weather didn't let up, they'd have to relocate the ceremony indoors. Two figures appeared on the sidewalk, and she recognized Aelyx and David jogging across the street and darting inside what appeared to be a vacant building.

Running an *errand*? Whatever. More like running away from her.

Syrine invited Troy to help himself to the contents of the refrigerator—an offer he didn't refuse—then waved Cara into the living room. Cara sat at the far end of the sofa, and Syrine surprised her by settling so near their thighs touched.

Leaning away, Cara scanned the girl's face for an explanation for their proximity. Syrine's impatient smile made it seem like she had an agenda and was waiting for the right time to set it in motion.

"I'm sorry," Syrine said. "For what I did to you on the transport last year."

Cara didn't want to discuss it. "That's okay."

"I wasn't myself then, but I am now."

What was Cara supposed to say to that? She and Syrine weren't friends, and this encounter was starting to creep her out. "I'm glad you feel better. What happened to Eron was terrib—"

"Did Aelyx tell you what the Aegis trained me to do?" Syrine leaned farther into Cara's space.

Holy clinger. Cara pressed against the arm of the sofa. "You mean the 'emotional healer' thing?"

"Yes. I can help you." Nodding like an eager kid, she reached out to touch Cara's hand but seemed to think better of it. "I know you're conflicted about your decision."

Assuming Cara needed therapy—which she *so* didn't—the last shrink she'd confide in was Syrine. "That's all right. I don't want to talk about it."

"We don't need to talk."

"Come again?"

"I'm not a therapist, *Cah*-ra," Syrine explained. "Think of me more as an empath."

"You can feel other people's emotions?" Cara didn't see the big deal. All L'eihrs could do that.

"I alter emotions," Syrine corrected. "I know you can use Silent Speech. If you open your mind to me, I can bring you clarity and comfort."

The word *no* took shape on Cara's lips. Her experiences with Jaxen and Aisly had left her wary of mind tricks, and she didn't trust Syrine. The girl had never liked her, so why the sudden interest? And yet Cara hesitated to turn down the offer. Clarity and comfort sounded awfully tempting.

"Please," Syrine implored. "Aelyx is hurting and this is the only way I can help him."

The desperation in Syrine's eyes reached straight into Cara's heart and softened it to the consistency of cream cheese. Syrine had her faults—big time—but she loved her best friend and Cara admired her for it. Releasing the tension in her shoulders, Cara sank back into the sofa cushions. "I guess I could use some clarity."

Syrine's mouth stretched into a wide smile. "You won't regret this."

I hope you're right. "Do I need to project my feelings?"

"No." Syrine closed her eyes, drawing a deep breath through her nose as if trying to reach her Zen place. "Just open the connection and relax. I'll do the rest." When her lids fluttered open, she warned, "I might be emotional when it's over, so don't take offense to anything I say. It's not personal."

Cara wanted to issue her own warning—*Hit me again and I'll knock you on your ass*—but she bit her tongue. If this worked, it would be worth a thousand slaps. She let go of her mind and stared through Syrine's chrome irises.

She felt the surge of energy that established their connection, followed by a sudden and delicious sense of warmth trickling over her skull like she'd tipped back her head into a stream of shower jets. Cara had to focus to keep her eyes from rolling back. She no longer cared if this was a trick—it felt too good. Tiny chills raised the hair along her scalp, and her anxiety began to leak away one drop at a time until nothing was left but peace. The sensation reminded Cara of the time she'd received a morphine injection for a dislocated knee, but that had left her mind in a fog. Right now, she could recite the periodic table if she wanted to.

The connection broke, and instantly Syrine's posture sagged while Cara's lifted—lighter by a hundred pounds of worry and doubt. "Wow," she breathed, blinking at the girl she'd once considered an enemy. "You're a walking opiate. I can't believe you did that for me."

Syrine gave a weak smile, but it didn't reach her eyes, which had begun to well with tears. "Can I ask you to repay me by listening to my advice?"

"Of course. After that, I'd give you a kidney."

When Syrine opened her mouth to speak, her breath hitched and one tear spilled down her russet cheek. It brought Cara down a few notches. If she'd known Syrine would soak up all her unhappiness like an emotional sponge, she wouldn't have agreed to it.

"You think Aelyx doesn't love you enough to stay on Earth, but that's not the case. There's something you don't know. During the tour, there were several attempts on his life. I've lost count of how many."

Cara's mouth dropped open. "Why didn't he tell me?"

"Perhaps for the same reason you hid your troubles from him for so long. He didn't want to worry you. Aelyx loves his home, but he loves you more. I have no doubt he would stay here if it were possible."

Cara remembered their argument, when she'd accused him of quitting too easily. Now she felt like an ass.

"I can feel your concerns about the colony," Syrine said. "And some of them are legitimate. But you made your choice out of fear of the unknown. Now that your mind is uncluttered, you should see the issues more clearly."

"But the lack of freedom hasn't changed," Cara pointed out.

"Not *yet*. You feel defeated by the development panel," Syrine said. "But the fight isn't over, and you're not alone."

Cara supposed she had a point. As the only human on the planet, Cara had felt isolated among the Elders. But more of her kind would come—even her brother. Maybe Alona would allow more human representatives on the panel to balance the power.

"I also sense," Syrine continued, "that you feel out of place among your human peers."

There was no point denying it.

"You've changed," Syrine said. "And your needs have changed with you. I have no doubt that you could stay on Earth and make a satisfying life for yourself. But you crave more than this world has to offer. Why settle for *satisfying* when you can have *spectacular*?"

The words turned over in Cara's mind, eventually resonating within her so strongly she felt their wisdom clear down to the soles of her boots. She drew a slow breath of enlightenment, and when she exhaled, she knew where she belonged.

It wasn't on Earth.

She was no longer Cara Sweeney, Midtown High valedictorian, two-time debate champion. She also wasn't fully *Elire*, resident of the first Aegis, *l'ihan* to Aelyx of the first Aegis, Chief Human Consultant. Instead, she fell somewhere between the two, and the colony was a fertile middle ground where she could discover her newly evolved self.

"You're right," Cara said.

Syrine's brows lifted in hope. "So you'll come home with us tomorrow?"

Home. To the majestic, muted forests where the air smelled of citrus and the faded indigo ocean stretched to meet a horizon of pure slate. To Elle and Larish and Vero. Maybe L'eihr didn't feel exactly like home yet, but she had faith that someday it would. "Yes, I want to go back."

"Excellent," Syrine said, wiping her eyes. "I can't wait to tell Aelyx."

Neither could Cara. Her legs practically twitched to run to him. "He's in the building across the street."

"I'll come with you." Syrine exhaled a shaky breath. "I need to see David. I mean . . ." She lifted a shoulder in a casual shrug that wouldn't fool anyone. "To ask what we should have for dinner. It's no big deal."

Sure, it's not. "Come on. Let's drag my brother out of the pantry."

David's steps grew sluggish as they reached the fifth-floor landing, and Aelyx noticed the boy's hand occasionally slip from the rail. "We can stop here," Aelyx said. There was no reason to continue to the top floor, no matter how "amaze-balls" the view, according to David. With the sleet thickening and gray clouds obscuring the sun, there was nothing to see anyhow. "I just needed some space. Now I have it."

David paused to catch his breath. A pained look crossed his face, and no matter how many times Aelyx tried to catch his eye, he kept his gaze averted. Why was he so intent on scaling this freezing-cold stairwell when he clearly needed a rest?

"Let's keep going," David said. "It's not much farther."

Aelyx sensed something wasn't right. He took his friend's elbow and helped support him as they resumed their climb. "The drugs have stopped working, haven't they?"

"No, they work great," David claimed, even as he strained to lift his boot. "But I ran out a couple weeks ago. Jaxen only gave me enough to last until his next visit. He's supposed to bring more this afternoon when he shuttles down."

Aelyx supposed that was good news, but it bothered him that Jaxen had withheld the treatment until today. Powerful as he was, he could have easily sent a new supply of injectables on any of the transports from L'eihr to Earth. Unease twisted Aelyx's stomach. He didn't trust Jaxen. What if he'd lied or neglected to bring the medication?

"Well," Aelyx said, trying to keep his tone light, "worst case scenario: we'll put you in cryogenic storage until we get to the colony and find more drugs, then thaw you out."

He'd expected a sniff of dry laughter, but as they reached the top floor, David clasped Aelyx's shoulder, keeping his eyes fixed on the gritty concrete floor. "I want to thank you. If it weren't for you, Syrine never would've looked at me, let alone invited me to the colony."

"I didn't do as much as you think. She's crazy about you."

With his head hung low, David tugged open the heavy door leading out of the stairwell. "I'm going to take real good care of her. I promise."

Aelyx lowered a brow as he preceded his friend into the expansive space that would someday become a penthouse. Paint-splattered plastic tarps covered the floor, crinkling beneath his boots as he made his way toward the center of the room, but he was too distracted by David's comment to notice anything more. The boy had spoken with such finality.

The steel door clicked shut with an echo, and Aelyx turned to face David, who leaned back against the door with his pistol drawn and trembling in his grasp. Before Aelyx could process what his eyes were trying to tell him, the rustle of plastic sounded from the opposite end of the room, and he caught a glimpse of an eerily familiar soldier before the man's fist slammed against Aelyx's cheek.

The force of the blow knocked him to the floor. Stars exploded behind his eyes, followed by a jolt of pain and ringing in his ears. He barely had time to blink before the soldier kicked him in the stomach, expelling all the air from his lungs with a *whoosh*.

"Enough!" David shouted.

At his command, the assault stopped. It was then that Aelyx understood his "friend" hadn't brought him here to admire the view. Anthony Grimes—the man who'd failed twice to kill him—had been expecting his arrival.

"He's supposed to look roughed up," Grimes said. "So his corpse matches that kid from Lanzhou."

"I said no more."

Aelyx sat up slowly, ignoring the ache in his gut, and swiveled his head toward David, who finally had the decency to look him in the eyes.

"I'm sorry," David said. His voice cracked and his gaze shone with unshed tears. "I'm so sorry."

CHAPTER TWENTY-ONE

Grimes shook his head in disgust and glared at David's trembling form. "Jesus, you're pathetic. You'd have your meds by now if you weren't such a pansy."

You'd have your meds by now . . .

So the pair was working for Jaxen, who wanted Aelyx dead for some inexplicable reason. That probably meant they'd choreographed the attack on Christmas morning—the one in which David had thrown himself into the path of a bullet to "save" Aelyx's life . . . thus gaining complete access to him as his bodyguard. Now that Aelyx thought about it, he realized the assassination attempts had increased once David joined the PR tour. The surprise meeting with Grimes in the stairwell, the letter bomb, the poisoned food.

Had David facilitated them all?

He stared at the boy he thought he'd known—the one

he'd visited for advice and trusted like a brother. Molten rage surged through Aelyx's veins, flushing his skin. He couldn't believe he'd pushed Syrine into David's arms. Had he ever cared for her, or was that a lie, too?

"Syrine," Aelyx said, remembering how she'd opened the tampered envelope and tried to eat from his plate—before David had stopped her. "She kept getting in the way."

"It wasn't like that," David insisted before emotion choked off his words. He swallowed hard and splayed his free hand. "Jaxen tricked me. At first, he said all I had to do was watch you, but then he changed his—"

"Shut the hell up," Grimes interrupted. "Just shoot him already." Aelyx made a move to stand, and Grimes swung at him. The man's knuckles caught the outside of Aelyx's lip, and his head snapped back while the metallic tang of blood crossed his tongue. "Stay down!" Grimes ordered.

David's face contorted in anguish. "I'm sorry," he repeated. "I wanted to tell Jaxen no, but Syrine finally gave me a reason to live. He's the only one who can get the drugs. I kept stalling, hoping the meds would cure me and I wouldn't need them anymore. But—"

"But then he'd have no power over you," Aelyx finished, then paused to spit blood onto the tarp-covered floor. "And he won't give that up."

The flash of fear behind the boy's eyes said he knew it, too. "Shoot him!" Grimes yelled.

David raised his weapon and lowered it again. Clearly he didn't want to carry out the murder, and Aelyx saw a sliver of opportunity to save himself. But he had to act quickly. Grimes was growing more agitated by the second, his breathing an audible hiss through his teeth.

"Jaxen will never give you the full cure," Aelyx said in a rush. "Not when he can keep you at his mercy with weekly injections. What will he force you to do next? When will it end?" Aelyx had to appeal to the boy's dwindling sense of integrity while offering a chance for survival. "I was only half joking when I said we could freeze you and look for a cure. You don't have to do this. You can change your mind, and nobody has to know."

While David hesitated, clearly tempted by the suggestion, Grimes pulled an ammunition clip and a pistol from his pocket. "Don't even think about it," Grimes spat. "Jaxen would kill us both, and you're not the only one he made promises to."

"He'll kill you anyway," Aelyx said. Dead men told no tales. "Or you'll die along with the whole planet when The Way ends the alliance, because your water supply is infected. You need our technology to decontaminate it."

Grimes paid no heed to the warning. He shoved the clip into his pistol, staring at David hard enough to set him aflame. "Jaxen's gonna need all the muscle he can get to stay in control after the coup. That's when governments are most vulnerable."

A coup? Aelyx refused to believe it. Jaxen was certifiable if he thought he could stage a takeover. The population of L'eihr, including the capital guard, would never support any faction other than The Way. Besides, Jaxen was already in a position of great power. What would he have to gain by throwing the planet into chaos? But despite the absurdity of it, Aelyx saw how he could use this information to his advantage.

"You could be a hero," he said to David. "If we go to Alona and tell her everything, she'll reward your honesty and execute Jaxen for treason." It would solve all of David's problems. "It's not too late," he promised, hoping some molecule of their friendship had been genuine. "If you do the right thing, Syrine will forgive you, and so will I."

Grimes cocked his pistol and pointed it at Aelyx. "Forget it. I'll kill him myself."

"No." David adjusted his aim toward Grimes in a clear message to hold his fire. The other man gaped at the betrayal before his gaze turned to stone and he aimed at David in return. "Think for a minute," David said. "It could work."

"You can't trust him!" Grimes shouted, nodding at Aelyx. "You think he's gonna let this go—just forget we've been trying to kill him for months? If Jaxen fries, we fry right along with him."

Aelyx faced David, the only man he had a chance of convincing. "I give you my word. Who do you think you can trust more—Jaxen or me?"

David didn't speak, but the set of his jaw and a nearly imperceptible nod of his head told Aelyx he'd won. The dynamic in the room shifted, and after that, everything happened in a flash. In an attempt to outmaneuver the other, David and Grimes simultaneously raised their weapons and fired.

A deafening shot tore at Aelyx's eardrums, and in the time it took him to cringe from the shock, both men lay crumpled on the splattered plastic tarp—Grimes with a disturbingly tidy hole in his forehead and David with his chest torn open like a package of raw meat.

Instinctively, Aelyx's hands flew to his coat pockets for his cell phone, but he'd left it in his bedroom along with his com-sphere. He crawled to David's side and gently patted him down for his cell, but the boy pushed away his hands, shaking his head to communicate what Aelyx knew deep inside: no medical intervention on Earth could save him.

Stammering in denial, Aelyx watched the shreds of camouflage jacket turn from green to red as blood pumped out of David's chest in time with his heart, each beat noticeably slower than the last. Aelyx had to do something. His hands moved to David's blond head and down over his shoulders in useless desperation while the boy drew a strained, wet breath.

"Please," David whispered, blood rising to his mouth and coating his teeth. "Don't tell . . ." Bubbles of air rose from inside his chest, stealing his last breath and, with it, his final words.

But Aelyx understood.

"I'll tell Syrine you died protecting me. And that's the truth."

David nodded his gratitude while tears welled in his eyes. For the next minute, Aelyx held his friend's hand as the life flowed out of him, the terror in his brown gaze fading by slow degrees until his light extinguished completely.

Aelyx gritted his teeth against the pain. His fists clenched in rage. If he had to die himself to make it happen, Jaxen would account for his crimes.

Suddenly, the heavy door flew open and Troy Sweeney stormed inside, weapon drawn, scanning the carnage. "Are there more?" he asked Aelyx while darting glances up and down the hall.

"No. This is it."

Cara ran in behind her brother and stopped short, gaping at all the blood. "Oh my God."

While Troy yelled at his sister for not staying in the stairwell like he'd ordered, Syrine drifted into view. Her eyes bulged when she found David, and she swayed on her feet. After clutching the wall for support, her face took on an eerie calm, even as she paled several shades. She didn't cry out in anguish or ask what had happened. Instead, she sank to her knees at David's side and took the boy's free hand in both of hers.

For a long minute, nobody spoke. When Syrine's strangled whisper finally broke the silence, her tormented voice tore a gash in Aelyx's heart.

"I didn't tell him," she said. "He told me so many times, and I never said it back. Now he'll never know."

While Syrine wept over her *l'ihan*'s body, Cara dropped to the floor beside Aelyx and gently took his battered face between her hands. Her blue eyes flooded with tears as she locked their gazes.

I'm sorry, she told him. *I'm sorry about David, and for everything I said before. I love you, and I want to go home—to the colony.* She must have sensed his disbelief, because she opened her mind to him and shared her conversation with Syrine. That was why they had come here, because Cara couldn't wait to tell him the news. *That might have been you,* Cara said with a nod at David. *You might have died thinking we don't belong together. I couldn't live with myself if—*

She broke into a sob, and the connection between them closed.

A conflicting surge of grief and euphoria crashed so violently over him that Aelyx stopped hearing anything. All he could do was wrap his arms around Cara and crush their bodies together while reminding himself to breathe. He rested his head against her shoulder, and they clung to each other until the wail of police sirens forced them apart.

CHAPTER TWENTY-TWO

When Cara was a sophomore, she'd won her first state debate championship by arguing against the paradox of traveling back in time to murder Hitler before his rise to power. Hers was an unpopular opinion, but she'd insisted that killing a man before he committed a crime—or even worse, during the innocence of his childhood—would be just as immoral as genocide, albeit on a smaller scale.

She didn't feel that way anymore.

Faced with the knowledge that Jaxen aimed to destroy the alliance, she would end him in a heartbeat if given the opportunity. His death would save billions—a no-brainer, even for someone like Cara who opposed capital punishment. Plus, the bastard had it coming. For someone who claimed to love mankind, he had a sick way of showing it. What kind of person forced a terminally ill boy to murder his best friend?

A twisted *fasher*, that's who.

But since he was a member of The Way, taking him down posed a challenge. Even thinking about killing him made her a traitor. And she still didn't know why he would want to kill Aelyx or try to overthrow his government. The whole thing made no sense.

"She's finally asleep." Aelyx returned to the living room, where torrential sleet pelted the windows. Judging by the smooth skin around his eyes and mouth, the L'eihr ointment had done its job. He rubbed a hand over his face and Cara noticed the remnants of dried blood beneath his fingernails. God, the blood. If she lived to be a hundred, she'd never forget it. Or the sound of Syrine's mewling cries when she'd finally broken down.

The memory made Cara's vision blurry. She blinked a few times to bring Aelyx into focus and wrapped her arms around his waist. "I hope the sedative lasts a while. It seems cruel to keep her awake."

Aelyx made a noise of agreement, resting his chin atop her head. "Once we're home, we can rotate her among the emotional healers. It will help a little."

"Hey," she said into Aelyx's chest. "Look at me for a second." When he glanced down at her, she said, "I love you." She'd already told him several times, but if she'd learned one thing today, it was never to hold back those words.

He took her cheek in his palm and gave a sad smile. "I love you, too." For a long moment he simply studied her, his thumb lightly caressing her face. "Things are different now. I didn't think we could make a home here because I still assumed the worst about your people. I never would've guessed it was one of my own kind who wanted me dead." He brushed back her hair, looking into her eyes. "If you still want to stay on Earth, I'm willing to talk about it."

The offer warmed her heart. A few days ago, Cara would have taken him up on it, but not anymore. "Not a chance. The L'eihrs are stuck with me."

"You're sure?"

"Positive," she said. "So let's get back on track."

There was work to be done. She'd never thwarted a coup before, and when it came to cunning, she was out of Jaxen's league. They still didn't understand his end goal or why he'd tried killing Aelyx instead of Syrine or the ambassador. Their deaths would have ended alliance negotiations, too. She added to the list of things she didn't know: why did Jaxen want to destroy the alliance at all? Was his apparent love for mankind just a front?

"Alona didn't respond to any of my summons," Cara said.

"Did you use priority code One?"

She nodded, hoping it wasn't too late. When rebel factions took control, they started by eliminating the old regime. Aelyx had alerted Colonel Rutter to a potential threat and requested extra security for The Way, but it might not be enough.

"We need a plan," she said. "If Jaxen pulls this off, both our worlds are toast."

Troy spoke up from his spot at the dining room table, a

sandwich nestled between his palms. "I'll bet his sister's in on it, too."

"She's not his sister." Briefly as she could, Cara told Aelyx and Troy everything she'd learned about the Aribol-L'eihr genetics program.

Aelyx swore under his breath. "So they really *can* manipulate minds?"

"They can and they do." Did he seriously think she'd made that up? "I wouldn't be surprised if there are more of them."

"Enough to replace eight members of The Way?" Aelyx asked.

Cara shrugged. "Possibly. I'm guessing that Jaxen wanted The Way to think humans murdered you so the alliance would fail. Maybe he wants to take over both our planets. Either way, he'll need a lot of support."

Aelyx swore under his breath. "I need an audience with Alona. If I can manage that, I can project what Grimes said to David about the coup."

"But that's not proof," Cara pointed out. "You can't accuse Jaxen without evidence to back it up, otherwise you'll be the one facing execution." There was also the issue of mind control. Cara didn't know if Alona was immune to it. "I have an idea, but it won't work unless I can get Jaxen alone."

"No," Troy said with a firm shake of his head. "Not happening."

"Agreed," Aelyx added.

Cara took Aelyx's hand and turned it over, studying his burgundy-stained cuticles. If Jaxen had won, it would be

Aelyx's blood beneath another boy's fingernails. But since the morning's deaths hadn't made the news yet, Jaxen had no reason to believe his plans had gone astray. Cara decided to keep it that way. "We have to try," she said.

She hoped Aelyx was good at playing dead.

It was chaos as the city scrambled to accommodate twice the capacity of the convention center, but an ice storm was the least of Cara's worries. Surrounded by her security detail, she and Aelyx waded through the crowd and made their way to the lobby elevators, where Troy planned to help them slip past the soldiers and sneak off to the emergency stairwell.

Within minutes, they'd achieved their first goal. Disappearing into the masses had been disturbingly easy. The three of them jogged up four flights of stairs, and when they reached the landing, Cara paused to prep herself—scrubbing her eyelids and nose with her fists, then squeezing a few drops of Visine along the corners of her eyes.

Troy handed over his iPhone.

"Do I look like I've been crying?" she asked.

Aelyx nodded. "You sure he's here?"

Cara was certain—just like she'd known Jaxen would answer her hysterical transmission begging him to meet her. Whatever his end goal, he'd always been weirdly drawn to her. She turned on the phone's voice recorder and slipped it in her tunic pocket so the microphone faced up.

"Remember," she told Aelyx and her brother before pulling open the stairwell door, "if Aisly tries to get inside, block her without looking her in the eyes."

"Got it," Troy said. "Pound twice on the wall if you need me."

"I'll keep watch from the elevators." Aelyx gave her a quick kiss. "Be careful."

Nodding, Cara stepped into the hallway and transformed into character—slowing her steps and slackening her face with grief. She spotted the room number Jaxen had specified, and a flicker of fear tickled her chest. There were no guards in the hall, no signs of life on this floor. What if he hadn't come? After trading a worried glance with her brother, she turned the doorknob and stepped inside the room, leaving Troy behind to stand watch.

All her doubts vanished.

Jaxen was here—along with a small army. At least a dozen guards, both L'eihr and human, lined the walls of the small boardroom. The confusion must have shown on her face, because Jaxen hurried to embrace her while shutting the door.

"It's okay," he murmured into her hair, pulling her uncomfortably close. Cara ignored the urge to ram her knee between his legs and relaxed into the hug.

"I h-h-hoped we'd be alone," she whispered, hitching her breath for effect. "I d-don't want anyone to see me like th-this."

Jaxen stroked her lower back. "Don't worry, *Cah*-ra. They can't hear us." She rested both hands on his chest and glanced up with a question in her eyes. He pointed around the room at the soldiers, who stared into empty space, arms hanging loosely at their sides. She recognized a few of them from the capital. "They're in a meditative state," he explained. "We're as good as alone."

Widening her eyes, she asked, "How'd you do it?"

"I have many gifts," he said with a wave of his hand. "But that's not important." He took her upper arms, holding her back as if checking for damage. "Are you all right?"

Cara faked her best ugly cry and crumpled against Jaxen's chest. "He's gone," she sobbed. "What am I going to do?"

Jaxen smoothed her hair, making light shushing noises. "You're going to let me take care of you. Now that the extremists have killed another of our youth, the alliance will fold. But I'll see to it that your loved ones are protected on the colony. You needn't worry."

"But what about Earth? I c-can't just—"

"Earth is ruined," he said. "Humans have made an utter mess of the planet. It's best to let the elements reclaim it."

She blinked at him in shock.

"Extinction is the natural order of things," he explained smoothly. "Weaker species die out while the fittest survive."

"But I thought you loved mankind."

"I do!" His eyes widened in rapture. "Humans are wonderfully expressive and creative. I would never let them die out. But can't you see how they need to be controlled? Look at what they did to the water supply. I plan to relocate the best of your kind—the top scientists, the most brilliant artists— and integrate our people on L'eihr."

"Only the best? What about everyone else?"

"All is not lost. I may still find a use for the remainder of your kind. If humans are obedient, I'll correct the water crisis for them—in stages."

In other words, he'd keep mankind beholden to him by withholding the permanent fix, much like he'd done to David. That must've been why he'd tried sabotaging the alliance by killing Aelyx—the one L'eihr who would fight as hard as Cara to save the human race. It was the vilest form of manipulation, but not enough to convict Jaxen of treason. She needed an incriminating admission.

"I don't know if I can go to the colony," she said in a helpless voice. "It's not just memories of Aelyx; it's the government. The Elders are set in their old ways." If that didn't hook him, nothing would. "I can't live like that."

"*Cah*-ra, listen to me." He took her by the shoulders, peering down at her with raised brows. "Change is coming. A new order will rise up and restore the glory of Mother L'eihr. The Elders have made us weak, but we—"

"Wait," she interrupted, rotating her torso to ensure her phone caught every word. "Are you talking about overthrowing The Way?" Her tone was hopeful, as if nothing would please her more.

He grinned. "Look around," he said, glancing at his drone army. "These men will set it in motion."

Will set it in motion—that implied Alona and the others were still alive. Cara released a shaky breath. She had enough proof. Now she needed to make her exit and track down The Way. "This is overwhelming," she said, backing away as she brought a wrist to her forehead. "I need a minute to think."

She'd almost reached the exit when the sound of the door

opening and closing made her jump. She whirled around and came face-to-face with a furious Aisly. The girl tore her gaze to Jaxen, and after a moment of Silent Speech between the two, Jaxen turned toward Cara with a look of utter betrayal in his eyes. In two quick steps, he reached her and plucked the iPhone from her tunic pocket.

"I wiped her brother's mind," Aisly said. "He won't remember a thing. But her?" She nodded toward Cara. "She's learned to block her thoughts. We can't risk it. You know what has to happen."

Troy must have made eye contact and unwittingly told Aisly everything. He was probably out there staring at the wall in a drool coma.

"Kill her quietly," Aisly added. "I won't do it for you." She glared at Jaxen as if to say, *I told you so.* "Your fascination with them is absurd. Let this be a lesson to you—that they should *all* die fighting the Aribol. Even the finest among humans is unworthy of the new order."

It was then that Cara understood who had framed her at the Aegis. Her instincts had been right when she'd suspected that her death wasn't the only goal. "Is that why you tried to have me discredited?" she asked. "To convince everyone that humans aren't worth saving? That you should only keep us alive so we can fight for you on the front lines?"

The girl's sick smile confirmed it. "At least your kind is useful for something."

Cara remembered Jaxen's words from moments ago. *I may still find a use for the remainder of your kind.* He would force humans to fight the Aribol, and after the war, when the survivors had outlasted their usefulness, he'd let them die out slowly. He had no intention of fixing Earth's water crisis.

Jaxen peered at her with such hurt in his eyes that she almost felt sorry for him. But not quite. She darted to the nearest capital guard and ripped the *iphal* from his holster, then aimed it at Jaxen's chest.

"Stay back," Cara ordered, eyeing Aisly, too. "Both of you."

"She can't fire it," Aisly said. "I watched **her at the Aegis.**"

Testing her, Jaxen took a step toward another guard, clearly meaning to arm himself. "Stop," Cara yelled, raising her weapon. When Jaxen chanced another step, she focused on his chest and thought, *Fire!*

But nothing happened.

"Stop," she repeated and fired again.

Nothing.

In a panic, she tried two more times without success.

Aisly laughed while Jaxen's face broke into an arrogant smile. "When we use humans in battle, clearly we'll need to equip them with simpler tools, like clubs and blades."

Cara closed her eyes to focus, and when she opened them, Jaxen was lifting an *iphal* from the guard at his side.

"I hate to do this," he said with a faint sigh. "I have the genetic material to replicate you, but it won't be the same. Your clone—she won't have the unique spark and fury I've grown to adore."

That explained why he'd taken her blood on the transport: so he could make a new version of her to bend to his will.

Over her dead body. Cara aimed at him with the fury he loved so much, and thought, *Fire!*

Nothing. Her pulse raced and her breaths came in gasps. Why couldn't she do this?

Jaxen admired the chrome weapon in his hand, slowly trailing a fingertip along the curve of its spine. "You have to mean it," he said. "Clearly, you're conflicted."

The door flew open from behind, and a large body nudged Cara aside, snatching the *iphal* from her grasp. It was Aelyx, who aimed the weapon at Jaxen. "That won't be a problem for me."

No sound escaped the chrome device and Cara never saw the air distort, but in the span of a single breath, Jaxen clutched his chest and collapsed to the floor in an ungraceful heap of limbs, his heartbeat stunned by a burst of energy.

Aisly released a scream loud enough to awaken the soldiers from their trances. They jerked upright and blinked at one another in confusion before they noticed their dead leader crumpled on the carpet . . . and the *iphal* in Aelyx's fist.

"Hurry," Aelyx said, tugging Cara's hand and towing her out the door.

As they tore down the hall, Cara darted a glance over her shoulder and discovered Aisly right behind them while Troy stood in place looking confused. Cara pumped her legs faster, but instead of giving chase, Aisly turned and sprinted down a side hallway with a mingled look of terror and determination on her face. It seemed she had a plan, maybe to head them off around the corner.

"Veer left," Cara shouted ahead.

Aelyx did as she said, and they ran down an isolated stretch of hallway. The clamor of stomping boots thundered from behind, and Cara spotted at least a half dozen armed guards closing in on them. Two of the men raised their weapons at Aelyx, so Cara positioned herself behind him as they ran, blocking their shot. But that strategy would only work in the short term. Eventually, they'd consider her collateral damage and simply fire their *iphals*.

Aelyx turned down yet another hallway and increased his speed. Cara pushed her body to the limit and kept pace with him.

"Where are we going?" she yelled.

"The stairs," he hollered. "We're almost there."

Aelyx reached the stairwell door and threw it open, then grabbed her arm and pulled her inside. After slamming the door, he grasped the handle with both hands. "While you were with Jaxen, I found Alona. Two floors up, room six thirty. Hurry, show her what you know." He nodded at the door, which had begun to buck from the outside. "I'll hold them here." When she hesitated to leave him, he shouted, "Go!"

With the echo of his voice reverberating against the narrow walls, Cara turned and scaled the stairs two at a time until she reached the sixth floor. She barreled down the hall, easily identifying the correct room by the dozens of guards stationed between her and its entrance. It seemed Colonel Rutter had taken the whole "extra security" thing seriously. She couldn't even move near the door.

"How'd you get to this floor?" demanded a national guardsman. "It's restricted."

Cara thumbed behind her and panted, "The emergency stairs. I'm Cara Sweeney. I need to see—"

"Not without clearance." He pointed back the way she'd come. "I need you to wait downstairs."

Standing on tiptoe, Cara peered over his shoulder to gauge her odds of sprinting past him and into room 630. There was no chance. Even if she slipped by this one, the next ten would snag her easily. The soldier had just started to repeat his command when Cara spotted a familiar face chatting with the guard at the door—her sadistic PE teacher. It didn't surprise her that he pulled double duty as a bodyguard. The guy was built like a tank.

"Satan!"

But he didn't take notice . . . because that wasn't his name. Damn it, Cara couldn't remember what he was really called. She shouted, "Satan!" a few more times, but all that did was alarm the American guards, who exchanged wary glances. Trying another tactic, she yelled, "It's me! Sweeeeeney!"

That got his attention.

She waved wildly at him. "I need you. It's an emergency!"

He jogged to meet her and widened his eyes expectantly.

"I'm here for an audience with The Way," she said. "They're in—"

Satan cut her off. "No to visit, Sweeeeeney. It much dangerous. The Way seal themselves inside until ceremony begin."

He started backing away, and Cara made a quick decision to stop hiding her abilities. There was only one way to prove her honesty. She locked eyes with him and said, *They're in danger—I have proof. You need to take me to them now.*

She felt his shock, followed by a sense of urgency. "Come." He told the guardsmen to allow her to pass, then escorted her through the labyrinth of security to room 630.

"Aelyx needs help two floors down," Cara said over her shoulder.

Satan nodded. "I go."

Without wasting another moment, she opened the door, and eight pairs of rheumy chrome eyes fastened on her.

"This is urgent," she said to Alona, closing the door behind her. "Jaxen's trying to overthrow The Way. I mean, *was.* He's dead now, but his followers might carry out his plan. I have proof"—she tapped an index finger to her temple—"if you'll let me show you."

Alona's mouth dropped open as she swept a hand toward the head of the table. "Come and be heard."

There were no spare seats, so Cara strode to Alona's side and knelt at her feet. She lifted her face to the old woman and opened her mind, much as she'd done with Syrine, freeing her memories and emotions without holding back. Now wasn't the time for secrets.

Unlike Syrine's warmth, Alona's presence felt cool and businesslike, a reflection of the woman herself. She probed Cara's thoughts and then shared one of her own—more like a swirling stream of consciousness. Their connection broke, and Cara sat back on her heels, reflecting on what Alona had shown her.

Understanding clicked into place, and when the link was complete, Cara saw how everything fit together. The Way had created ten hybrids as a test batch, but the embryonic survival rate was so low that scientists had abandoned the project. Of the ten hybrids, only Jaxen and Aisly had proven gifted on their childhood assessments and were elevated to positions of power. The other eight teens attended Aegises in the outside precincts. But nobody had known about their mental abilities. It seemed the hybrids had hidden their true potential.

"I imagine their genetic link to the Aribol is somehow related to our recent probe invasion," Alona said. "Perhaps the hybrids found a way to initiate contact. We will have the remaining eight collected and begin an investigation into whether or not they colluded with Jaxen."

"What about the Aribol?" Cara asked. "Jaxen made it sound like we're already at war."

"Nonsense. His preemptive attack would have guaranteed one, but for the time being, the Aribol are not a threat."

"And the alliance? It's still on?"

"I'm stunned you have to ask." Alona peered down her nose like a disapproving maiden aunt. "You are not a born L'eihr, Miss Sweeney. You owe no allegiance to The Way aside from an easily broken oath. And yet you risked your life to gather evidence to present to me. In doing so, you've proven yourself brave and unfailingly loyal."

Cara felt heat creeping into her cheeks. "Thank you, but—"

"And you doubt that I would reciprocate?"

"I'm sorry. I just didn't want to leave anything to chance. The stakes are too high."

Alona seemed to turn that over in her mind. "Yes, they are." She swept a hand, indicating her fellow Elders. "And as you see, we are now two members short of a governing body. If you're willing to serve, I would like to offer one of those seats to you."

Cara cocked her head as her ears warred with her brain, because what she'd heard did not compute. "You can't mean that."

Alona arched a brow. "Can't I? What quality do you lack?"

"Experience, for starters."

"Ah, well." Alona smiled at her peers. "With the wisdom we've gathered over the years, we easily compensate. I feel it prudent to include a representative from the colony among us. Don't you agree?"

Of course Cara did. A position of influence within the government would change not only her life but the lives of every human who settled on L'eihr. The responsibility would be great, but so would the rewards. "Yes, I agree, but—"

"Do you accept?"

Cara gulped a breath. Ludicrous as the offer seemed, she would be even crazier to turn it down. "I do."

"Then yours will be among the signatures on the alliance pact." Alona paused as if remembering something. "But first I imagine you need to see to your *l'ihan*."

"Yes, thank you." Cara pushed to standing and backed away. "Jaxen's guards are trying to—"

She was interrupted by Satan throwing open the door.

From behind him, murmurs and shouts drifted inside the room, and a creeping chill raised goose bumps along the back of Cara's neck. She darted into the hallway in time to spot Aelyx round the corner with a lone capital guard on his heels. The overhead light glinted off the man's *iphal* as he lifted it, slowing his steps to take aim.

Cara gasped so hard it stung her lungs. "Get down!"

Aelyx's eyes met hers and flickered with recognition just before they rolled back in his head. He crashed to the floor, his body bouncing twice before it rested on the shorn carpet.

Time froze while Cara's own heart seized inside her chest.

Aelyx was dead.

As if outside her body, Cara heard herself screaming. She shoved aside anyone in her path and ran to him. It was like a dream; she was so desperate to reach him, but invisible hands weighed her down. When she finally skidded to her knees by his side, she rolled him onto his back and checked for a pulse.

Nothing. He was gone.

"No!" She repeated it again and again in denial. It couldn't end like this. She refused to let him go. Straddling his lifeless body, she began a set of clumsy chest compressions. Aelyx's head lolled to the side at an awkward angle, shaking with each frenzied pump of her fists. He wouldn't come back to her.

It wasn't working.

Her vision blurred as sobs burned her throat. She heard herself pleading for him not to leave, while Satan wrestled the capital guard to the floor. Then a new voice broke through the haze.

"Keep doing that!" Troy shouted, pointing at her. "I'll

be right back!" He turned on his heel and sprinted down the hallway, yelling, "Make a hole!" to those in his way.

Cara leaned down and parted Aelyx's lips to force breath into his lungs. Grunting aloud, she resumed pumping his chest. Some deep, dark place inside warned that it was over, but she couldn't make herself stop.

The stomping of heavy boots drew Cara's gaze upward. Troy had returned, clutching a small yellow case beneath his arm. He dropped to his knees and placed the device on the floor, then pressed the *on* button and untangled a set of electrodes and wires.

"Oh my God," Cara whispered.

It was an external defibrillator. All major centers—even shopping malls—stocked them near the fire extinguishers, but she'd forgotten all about them. With new hope, her hands flew into action, lifting Aelyx's shirt so Troy could affix the adhesive patches over his ribs and collarbone.

An automated female voice from the machine's speaker advised, "Stand clear. Do not touch the patient." They obeyed, and after a brief pause, she intoned, "Shock advised. Charging. Stand clear."

Troy pressed the red *shock* button, and they watched Aelyx's rib cage lift and fall. When the machine ordered another round of CPR, Cara delivered thirty quick compressions followed by two breaths. The female's voice talked her through several more rounds as it counted down two minutes. Each second was torture. Cara felt Aelyx slipping further from her reach.

"Stop CPR," the voice ordered. "Analyzing heart rhythm.

Do not touch the patient." Another pause. "Shock advised. Charging. Stand clear."

"Please," Cara begged Aelyx, God in heaven, the Blessed Virgin, the Sacred Mother, and whoever else might be listening as she punched the flashing red *shock* button and drew back.

Please work. Please!

His rib cage lurched, and again, the woman's voice advised a round of CPR. But as Cara placed her fist over his heart, she felt a stirring of motion, a nearly undetectable hum of life beneath her trembling fingers. Moving to his throat, she closed her eyes and felt a pulse growing strong and steady. Aelyx moaned and shifted in discomfort, and Cara released a sob of pure joy while tears plunked onto his chest. He blinked up at her and rubbed a hand over his ribs, clearly sore, but very much alive.

Cara turned to her brother and threw her arms around his neck. "You're a genius!"

The machine droned, "No shock advised. You may touch the patient," so Cara took the woman's suggestion and dusted kisses over Aelyx's forehead and cheeks.

Grinning, Troy peeled an electrode from Aelyx's chest. "I can't take credit for the idea. I saw Aisly using one on Jaxen about ten minutes ago."

Cara froze. "Did it work?"

"Yeah." Troy's beatified expression showed how well Aisly had brain-bleached him. He had no idea that Jaxen's revival was bad news. "But before I could call an ambulance, they took off for the elevator. Seemed like they were in a hurry."

Aelyx and Cara shared a worried glance. On a normal day, disappearing in Manhattan was effortless, but this afternoon, with thousands of bodies, umbrellas, and tents lining the streets, finding the pair would be like a living edition of *Where's Waldo?*

"Did you reach Alona?" Aelyx croaked.

Cara nodded. "They're all safe."

He didn't speak again, at least not verbally. But she felt his gratitude mingled with love and the words inside her head, *Then it's okay. We did it.*

The rest of the afternoon was calm by comparison—odd when Cara considered the magnitude of signing her name beside the president of the United States and all of Earth's major leaders. As hard as she'd fought for this alliance, Cara expected to feel a thrill of accomplishment when the ceremony ended, but honestly, she was glad to put it behind her. She'd had enough excitement, and now she wanted to go home.

Skipping the celebratory gala and the glitzy after-parties, she and Aelyx snuck to the penthouse to rest, where they spent a quiet evening cuddled up in bed. While crowds cheered and fireworks erupted above the Manhattan skyline, Cara rested her hand over Aelyx's heart, letting its steady beat lull her into the first peaceful sleep she'd enjoyed in weeks.

Chapter Twenty-Three

Saturday, May 1

Sweet Sorrow

Well, fellow humans, I bid you adieu. In a few moments, I'll board the shuttle to my transport home. I've said good-bye to everyone I love—my friends and family who have chosen to remain on Earth, and my brother, who can't join me until his enlistment is up. It's a bittersweet day . . . for more reasons than you think.

It's not only people I'm leaving behind. It's a way of life. In choosing to settle on another planet, I'm letting go of one dream to embrace another. You won't see me roaming the Dartmouth campus in the fall. Heck, you won't even see me at my high school graduation. Mine will be the ultimate hands-on education as I shape the laws and policies of a fledgling government. That's right. Me—a politician. Who'd have guessed it? If you've applied to join the colony, essentially putting your future in my hands, thank you for your trust. I won't let you down.

As for the rest of you, I suppose this isn't *really* good-bye. You can still find me here on the blog as I recount my adventures for your amusement. Take care of each other while I'm away, and eat a Reese's Cup for me.

I've lost my taste for them.

Posted by Cara Sweeney

Cara shut down her laptop and stowed it safely inside her luggage between a stack of uniforms and the *Star Wars* Snuggie her parents had given her as a going-away present. Ordinarily, she'd keep the computer by her side, but she decided to take a vacation from blogging during the voyage home. She'd already received her antinausea medication, so once the shuttle delivered her to the main transport, she intended to spend the next week suction-cupped to Aelyx's side.

"Miss Sweeney?" said the L'eihr attendant from the other side of the luggage cart. When she glanced up, he asked, *Are you sure you won't shuttle up with The Way?*

I'm sure, she told him. *After what happened yesterday, I'm not letting Aelyx out of my sight.*

The man smiled in understanding and signaled the first shuttle to depart without her. *Once we load your cargo, we'll board the second shuttle.* He nodded toward the other end of the hangar to the steel cryogenic box holding David's body.

Cara's stomach sank an inch. Her first official act as a member of The Way had been approving Syrine's request to bury her *l'ihan* on the colony. Until now, they hadn't planned for a cemetery—L'eihrs preserved a genetic sample, then cremated their dead—but Cara couldn't say no, not when she knew how it felt to lose her whole heart. The few minutes when she thought she'd lost Aelyx had left her with a permanent mark on her soul.

She peered around the dim hangar until she found him talking with Syrine near the coffee station. His hair had grown long enough for a stumpy ponytail, but one lock slipped from its clasp, then another and another until everything spilled free in a honey-brown riot. Exasperated, he shoved his hair behind both ears. It made Cara smile. Hitching her bag over one shoulder, she strode to join him.

"How're you holding up?" she asked Syrine, offering a gentle shoulder squeeze. She'd noticed Syrine had refused to engage in Silent Speech, which made sense. If their roles were reversed, Cara would want to keep her grief private, too. "Anything I can do?"

Syrine shook her head and blew into her Styrofoam cup, peeking over the rim with unnaturally wide black pupils.

Good. She was still sedated.

"I have something for you," Aelyx said to his friend. After checking to ensure no one was watching, he reached into his pocket and pressed an object into Syrine's hand. "Hide it well, or they'll take it from you at the checkpoint."

Forehead wrinkled in curiosity, Syrine uncurled her fingers, revealing a tiny brown speck resting in the center of her palm. "What is it?"

Aelyx closed her hand and covered it with his own. "A pear seed."

Cara didn't understand, but Syrine smiled and brought that hand to her chest as if the seed were more precious than plutonium. Tears streamed down her face, but they looked like the happy kind. "Thank you," she whispered. "I'll guard it with my life."

An hour later, Cara palmed her transport chamber's security panel, retracting the door with a *hiss*. Aelyx followed her inside the closet-size bedroom, and they took a few moments to simply stand there in the darkness. Shell-shocked, maybe. So much had happened in the past twenty-four hours that it seemed surreal. So much loss—but triumph, too. Cara tried to shake off the shadow of heartache and focus on the future.

It was all any of them could do.

Aelyx took her hand and brought it to his lips. "Can you believe this is actually happening?"

"No. We're starting over from scratch. I can't wrap my mind around it."

Aelyx took her cheeks between his palms and gave her a warm smile. His molten silver eyes reflected the dim lighting from the port window, so beautiful it made her breath catch. Just when she thought the sight of him couldn't stir her any more deeply, he proved her wrong. She braided her fingers in his hair and marveled at the contrast of her pale skin against his bronze cheek. He was exquisite, inside and out. And all hers.

"True," he said. "But that's not what I was referring to."

"Then—" she began before he silenced her with his lips.

He gripped her waist with powerful fingers, his touch both gentle and possessive as he explored her mouth with the tip of his soft tongue. Her pulse jump-started and rushed to some pretty interesting places. Before Cara knew what had happened, her back was to the bedroom wall.

He didn't stop, eventually forcing her to break for air. While she tried to catch her breath, he liberated both their shirts and bit the magical spot at the top of her shoulder, the one that made her knees go weak. Holding her against the wall with his body, he pressed his fingers to her throat and counted the frenzied beats of her heart. A moment later, he murmured against her lips, "One fifteen," then gave her a downright scandalous kiss—the kind that made it clear what he wanted.

Cara rested a hand on his chest and gently pushed him away, afraid of exciting him too soon after his trip into the white light. "Whoa, there. Let's give your ticker a break, okay?"

His eyes practically glowed while one corner of his mouth lifted in a grin. "I don't want a break. I want *you*."

"But you just died."

"That was ages ago."

More like twelve hours. She gave him a firm shake of her head. "Not happening. I just brought you back from the great beyond. I'm not going to risk losing you again."

"I'm fine, really," he insisted. "And if anything goes wrong, the transport medic can restart my pulse."

"No way," Cara said with a laugh. "I'm not going to the infirmary and telling them I sexed you to death!"

Smiling, Aelyx peered at the ceiling as if picturing it. "I can think of worse ways to die."

"Well, keep dreaming." She took his hand and led him

to the bunk. Whether or not Aelyx realized it, he needed his rest. "Because all you're getting is a cuddle."

He heaved a mighty sigh but didn't hesitate to scoop her into his arms once they lowered to the mattress. She tucked her cheek against that perfectly molded spot where his shoulder met his chest, and they spent the next several minutes listening to the noises of the flight crew priming the thrusters for departure.

Soon Cara felt the gentle pull of inertia as the transport picked up speed and jettisoned them toward a new galaxy. When the rumble of the boosters died down and another minute passed in silence, she traced imaginary patterns on Aelyx's chest and wondered if he felt the same subtle tug of anxiety that she did.

"Hey," Cara said. The brush of her fingertips prickled Aelyx's skin into goose bumps, but it was a good tickle. He loved her touch. "What are you thinking?"

Aelyx buried his nose in her scarlet hair. Sacred Mother, she smelled delicious, of citrus and cloves, temptation and warmth. He couldn't believe she'd agreed to come home with him.

"Just how lucky I am," he said.

"No doubt." She placed a kiss over his heart. "If Troy hadn't been there, I never would have used a defibrillator on you. I was so hysterical that my brain kind of shut down."

"There's that," Aelyx agreed, "but I was thinking more about you."

"Me?"

He nodded against his pillow. "That you're willing to leave behind everything familiar and come with me to the colony. Sometimes I still can't believe it."

Her fingertips halted their lazy skate across his chest, her mood seeming to shift.

When she didn't respond, he asked, "Having second thoughts already?"

"It's not that . . ." she said. "I'm nervous, I guess. We're on our way to the colony, but we haven't nailed down a charter. Everything was up in the air when I left. Now that I'm the human representative, I feel all this pressure. People are depending on me, and to be honest, I really don't know what I'm doing."

Ah, yes, Cara's appointment to The Way. Aelyx hated to admit it, but he wasn't sure how he felt about that. On the one hand, he was proud of her, and she deserved a reward for her sacrifice. But her new position meant he had to obey her every command. That kind of power imbalance could lead to trouble.

"Try not to worry," he said, grateful they weren't using Silent Speech. "Alona won't give you more responsibility than you can handle. You have to trust her wisdom." Aelyx supposed he should heed his own advice.

"You're probably right," she conceded. "But then there's the failed takeover. I'll bet Jaxen had more backing than just the other eight hybrids. What if they're out there somewhere, regrouping? I'd feel better if we knew where Jaxen is."

And what he's up to, Aelyx thought, still irritated that the trail had gone cold. If he ever had another chance to kill the *fasher*, he'd make sure Jaxen stayed dead.

"And the Aribol," Cara added, shivering a moment in his arms. "We don't know if they're a threat or—"

"*Elire*, stop." He pressed a finger to her lips. "You're forgetting about the alliance. Neither of us is alone now. With human numbers and L'eihr advancement, we're stronger than any enemy I know. Whatever problems lie ahead, we'll face them together."

She considered that for a while, then intertwined their fingers and repeated, "Together."

"Yes." Squeezing their linked hands, he reminded her, "And remember, we prevented a coup and saved both our worlds yesterday. We might be superheroes."

Cara smiled against his chest. "It sounds impressive when you say it like that."

"It does, doesn't it? I think we're entitled to a break."

"Agreed," she said with a nod.

"No more worries, then," he declared. "In a week, we'll be in our new home—no roommates, no bunk beds, no classes. Just you and me and miles and miles of beach."

He sensed a thrill of energy pass through her. "I can almost smell the salt in the air," she said.

So could he. Their new life was so close that when he shut his eyes, the gentle rush of sea foam seemed to bubble over his feet. It couldn't come quickly enough. The future was uncertain, but Aelyx knew one thing—it wouldn't be dull with Cara by his side.

Acknowledgments

Many thanks to my editor, Laura Schreiber, for once again leading me through the revision process and taking this book to the next level. I value your guidance more than you know. Additional thanks to my agent, Nicole Resciniti, for the countless brainstorming sessions that contributed to this finished product. If the L'eihrs truly existed, they would clone you in an instant!

Much love to my critique partners, authors Lorie Langdon and Carey Corp, for their support, and even more for their friendship. Additional hugs to the Lucky 13s, the Class of 2k14, and the NBC Writers for providing a shoulder to lean on . . . and cry on when necessary. I'm so glad that we found each other.

As always, I'm grateful to my family and friends, who never fail to amaze me with the depth of their support for my writing. I love you!

And finally, I'd like to extend my gratitude to the readers, librarians, bloggers, YouTubers, and reviewers who have made this series so successful by simply talking about it. Believe it or not, getting a book published isn't the hardest part. The real challenge is making that book stand out among a sea of other novels in the marketplace. Nothing is more powerful than word-of-mouth advertising, and your recommendations have made an enormous impact. Thank you!

AND NOW FOR A SNEAK PEEK AT
MELISSA LANDERS'S
THRILLING NEW SERIES

MELISSA LANDERS

STARFLIGHT

"Smart, action-packed, and utterly addictive."
—AMIE KAUFMAN, NEW YORK TIMES BEST-SELLING AUTHOR

CHAPTER ONE

*W*hat if nobody picks me? Nothing can be worse than that.

Solara's pulse quickened, and her palms turned cold. She hadn't considered the possibility that no one would want her, but now, as she scanned the servants' area, she noticed only two indenture candidates standing with her behind the gate—an elderly man with more hair in his ears than on his head and a teenage boy who couldn't stop scratching himself. Of the fifty standby travelers who'd arrived that morning, the three of them were the leftovers. The last boarding call would sound in a few minutes, and if she couldn't entice a passenger to hire her in exchange for a ticket to the outer realm, she'd have to wait sixty days for the next spaceliner.

That wasn't an option.

Brightening her smile, she stood up straighter and tried to catch the eye of a woman with her shirttail untucked and a chunk of dried food in her hair. "Pardon, ma'am," Solara called.

"Are you traveling with young children? I can help. All I require is passage to the last stop."

The woman paused midstride, then tipped her head in contemplation. She chanced a step toward the servants' gate. "Do you have experience?"

"Yes, ma'am! I practically raised the little ones in my group home."

"Group home?" The woman pruned her mouth and regarded Solara with new eyes, taking in the grease stains on her state-issued coveralls and the holes in the toes of her scuffed brown boots. "Show me your hands."

Solara feigned ignorance as her stomach dropped. "What?"

"Your hands," the woman repeated. "I want to see them."

With a sigh, Solara removed her fingerless gloves and allowed the passenger to read the tattoos permanently inked across her knuckles. She didn't bother trying to explain. It never made a difference anyway.

"That's what I thought." The woman shook her head in disdain exactly like one of the nuns at the home. Then she stalked away without another word.

The old man standing beside Solara invaded her personal space and delivered a light elbow nudge. He leaned in and whispered, "I know someone who can clear your record. He's the best forger in Houston—even the new laserproof ink is no match for him."

Solara rolled her eyes. She knew a dozen flesh forgers. Finding an expert wasn't the problem. "If I had that kind of money, I wouldn't be standing here, would I?"

He flashed both palms and backed away.

Soon a group of businessmen approached the gate in search of stewards for the five-month voyage. Solara hid both hands behind her back and offered her widest grin, but it wasn't enough. They indentured the old man and the itchy teenager instead.

Panic crept over her as she scanned the vacant station and the thick metal doors leading to the boarding platform. There were no passengers left. At any moment, the shuttle would transport thousands of vacationers to the moon's space station, where they'd board the SS *Zenith* and set off for exotic destinations.

Why hadn't anyone chosen her?

She wouldn't describe herself as pretty, or charming, or even entertaining, but the calluses on her palms proved she was a hard worker. She practically slept with a ratchet in one hand and a wrench in the other. Every time the diocese shuttle sputtered and coughed, it was Solara the nuns called on to fix it, even if it meant freeing her an hour early from chapel detention, where she usually knelt in penance for peeking at her data tablet during morning prayers. And when the engine purred once again, Sister Agnes would rub her arthritic fingers and remark that she'd never trained a better mechanic.

Didn't that count more than a criminal record?

Apparently not.

The click of high heels turned Solara's attention to the lobby, where a stunning girl of about eighteen sashayed toward the gate, wheeling a tote behind her. An animal yipped from inside the bag, a lapdog from the sound of it.

The young woman brushed a bit of lint from the lapel of her designer dress, then tossed a curtain of glossy pink hair over one shoulder and called to someone out of sight. "Hurry. If we miss the shuttle, your father will make us wait an hour before sending another one, just to prove a point."

Sensing her last chance of escape, Solara rose onto her toes to wave at the girl. "Miss! Over here!" She achieved eye contact and smiled. "I'm an excellent maid. All I require is . . ."

But it was no use. The girl scowled and turned away.

A deep male voice sounded from the entrance, "I wouldn't mind missing it. I can't breathe in those tight spaces," and a tall boy strode into view.

He'd slung a tuxedo jacket over one shoulder and loosened the first few buttons of his collar. Practically oozing indifference, he moved at a leisurely pace as if the *Zenith* would wait an eternity for him.

Because it would.

Solara had never seen him out of academy uniform, but the boy was easy to recognize. He was Doran Spaulding: heir to the galaxy's largest fuel corporation, first-string varsity football star, and a complete pain in her ass. Freshman year, she'd won a day scholarship to the mechanical engineering program at his private academy—classes only, no room or board—and he'd done his best to punish her for it ever since. Especially after she'd beaten him for the Richard Spaulding Alumni Award. There'd been other tiffs, too, like the time she broke Doran's quarterback arm during a bad landing in pilot's ed class. But that had been an accident, and he'd only had to sit out for half the season. She knew the real reason for his anger had always been the humiliation of losing his father's award to a penniless girl with no family of her own. As if she'd tarnished his precious name by association.

It was clear he recognized her, too, because the instant their eyes met, he stopped and laughed. "Rattail," he called. "Fancy meeting you here."

Reflexively, Solara fingered the squiggly birthmark at the base of her throat, the one Doran had once said reminded him of a rodent's tail. That'd been four years ago, and she still hadn't managed to shake the nickname.

"You missed graduation," he said, though she didn't know why he cared. "I guess all that free education didn't mean much if you couldn't be bothered to take your diploma."

Solara indulged in a small grin, relieved that he hadn't heard the news. The real reason she'd missed graduation was because the academy had dropped her like a flaming brick the instant they learned about her felony conviction. "I tested out early," she said, which technically wasn't a lie. "With a near-perfect score."

He didn't seem to like that. Jutting his chin at the indenture band around her wrist, he asked, "Selling yourself for a glimpse of the Obsidian Beaches? Can't say I blame you. It's the only way you'll ever see them."

She opened her mouth to fire a witty comeback, but nothing came. Her best lines always arrived an hour too late. "Not that it's any of your business, but I'm headed to the end of the line."

"The outer realm?" Doran drew back. "Why would you want to go *there*?"

"For a job," she told him. "The offer came last week."

In the lawless outer realm, mechanics like Solara were hard to come by. No one would care about the tattoos across her knuckles or the grease beneath her fingernails. She'd be revered as a goddess because settlers on the fringe planets appreciated skill over beauty. That was where she belonged, far from Houston's overcrowded high-rise slums and the sweatshops that paid a few measly credits to those with the connections to get inside. She was going west, all the way to the edge of the charted territories, to a new terraform called Vega. Her benefits package included a whole acre of land, all to herself. She couldn't wait to work that soil between her fingers and know that she owned it. Freedom, wealth, and security were right there, waiting for her.

All she needed was a ticket.

"But you can't afford the fare," Doran said, mostly talking to himself. "And the next trip to the outer realm isn't for a year."

"Two months," she corrected.

"No, a year." He smoothed a perfectly manicured hand over his dark hair, then took the opportunity to study his reflection in the nearby ticketing screen. "They're scaling back because there's no demand to visit the fringe planets. Only criminals end up there." Raking his gaze over her, he added, "And vagrants."

All the blood drained from Solara's head.

A year?

Where would she live? How would she support herself? The nuns had practically danced a jig when she'd left because it freed up a bed for one of the teens sleeping on the cafeteria floor. Each day more abandoned kids appeared at the front gate, their parents having fled the scene in the world's saddest game of hide-and-seek. The group home couldn't afford to keep anyone past graduation. No exceptions. Even Sister Agnes, who'd been like a mother to Solara, had pressed a handheld stunner into her palm and shoved her out the gate. *The fringe is a dangerous place,*

Agnes had said. *Keep this in your pocket.* Then she'd told Solara to go in peace and serve the Lord.

It was clear she wasn't meant to return.

Doran brought her back to present company by tapping his chin and peering at her with new interest. "My usual valet is too sick to travel," he said. "I can see that all the proper servants are taken, but you might do." His upper lip curled in a way that made Solara want to hide her face. "I'd have to let you in my suite, but I guess I can live with that."

Before Solara could respond, Doran's girlfriend made a noise of disgust and whined, "Come on, Dory. Not that one. She's so . . . dirty."

Solara's cheeks blazed. She'd taken great care to scrub her face at the public bathhouse that morning, even paying extra to have her hair washed and plaited in the latest style. "*She* is standing right here. And I'm not dirty."

Doran snapped his gaze to hers, his black brows forming a slash above blue eyes cold enough to frost the fiery moons of Volcanus. "Let's get something straight, Rattail. If I agree to finance your passage, the only words that will leave your mouth for the next five months are *Yes, Mr. Spaulding.* If you disappoint me in any way—if my every wish is not brought to fruition—I'll drop your carcass at the first outpost. Do you understand?"

Solara held her breath while a furious pulse pounded in her ears. Five months as Doran's slave or a year on the streets. Unpleasant as it was, the decision made itself.

"Yes," she said.

"Excuse me?"

"Yes, *Mr. Spaulding.*"

"That's better. See?" he said to his girlfriend. "She can be trained." He pointed at Solara's wrist. "Where's the matching band?"

"You buy it from the machine," Solara told him, nodding at the kiosk beside her.

Once Doran transferred the credits to pay her fare, the gate opened with a beep and an *M*-emblazoned bracelet dropped into the collection tray. He slapped the band around his wrist, linking them as master and servant.

"Quit standing there," he said. "You can start by taking Miss DePaul's bag."

But the girl—Miss DePaul, presumably—gripped the handle of her pet carrier with ten red-tipped fingers. "I don't want her touching my things," she declared, and clicked toward the boarding platform.

Doran shrugged and handed Solara his tuxedo jacket. When they reached the boarding entry, he shouted, "The door, Rattail. Open the door!" She scrambled ahead of him and heaved aside the metal barrier. As Doran preceded her through the gateway, he murmured, "Well, you're off to a poor start."

Solara clutched his jacket and resisted the urge to choke him with it. Maybe there *was* something worse than not being picked.

CHAPTER TWO

*T*he beeping awoke her from a dead sleep, but in her foggy state, Solara couldn't tell where it was coming from. She scanned the darkness for the source of the awful sound until a pillow arched up from the bottom bunk and smacked her in the face.

"Turn off your band!" hissed one of her roommates.

Understanding dawned, and Solara tapped the Accept button on her bracelet. By now, she should be used to Doran's constant requests. The sadistic jerk hadn't allowed her a full night's rest since they'd boarded the *Zenith* a month ago, so he wasn't likely to start now.

"He's ruining my sleep," another roommate whispered. "Why does he keep torturing you?"

That was a good question.

Solara pulled on a pair of pants and thought about it. The obvious answer was his white-knuckled hold on a grudge from freshman year, the urge to put her back in "her place" after she'd won his father's award. But aside from that, sometimes she wondered if Doran craved attention. He reminded her of a boy in the group home who used to pull her hair. When she'd complained to the nuns, they had brushed off her concerns, claiming that the boy liked her. But she didn't enjoy having her hair pulled, so she'd put a stop to it by sinking her fist into the boy's stomach.

Maybe that was what Doran needed.

After wrapping a blanket around her shoulders, she slipped quietly into the hallway and waited for the motion-sensor nightlights to activate. Soon a thin strip glowed in the middle of the floor. She knew from experience it would take 872 steps to reach Doran's first-class suite from her position in the steerage class level, so she didn't waste another moment getting there. The last time she'd waited too long to respond, he'd fallen asleep, only to summon her an hour later to pull a clean shirt from his walk-in closet. He hadn't been kidding when he'd said he hated small spaces. It made her want to lock him inside a luggage trunk.

She knocked softly on his door. Most valets had key fob access programmed into their indenture bands, but of course Doran didn't trust her enough for that.

Once the door slid into the wall, she stepped inside his suite and immediately stopped short to survey the damage. He'd hosted another party. The empty bottles littering the carpet made that clear. Someone had overturned the sofa and rearranged the furniture in what appeared to be a tic-tac-toe grid, and naturally she would have to clean it up. But that couldn't be why he'd called her in the middle of the night.

Or could it?

She slid a glare toward his bedroom but refused to go in there. If the lingering scent of Miss DePaul's perfume was any indication, he wasn't alone.

"Did you need something?" Solara shouted.

Doran's voice was sleep-roughened when he demanded, "Excuse me?"

She closed her eyes and drew a slow breath. "How may I assist you, Mr. Spaulding?"

"I've got insomnia," he said. "So I might as well make use of it and get some work done for my internship. Come in here and take notes for me."

Solara didn't move.

It was one thing to fetch a T-shirt from his closet, but spending time with Doran inside his bedroom—in the middle of the night? Not for all the fuel in all the ore refineries in all four quadrants of the galaxy.

A rustling of blankets sounded from the other room, followed by a heavy sigh. "Stay there," he grumbled. "I'll get dressed and come to you. But for future reference, anyone who stinks like a toolshed is safe from my advances."

Frowning, Solara lifted a lock of hair to her nose. She'd spent an hour touring the auxiliary engine room yesterday, but she didn't smell like grease. At least, she didn't think so.

He padded into the living room wearing a dark bathrobe that concealed everything but his bare feet. "Feel safer now?"

She answered, "Yes, Mr. Spaulding," and meant it for once.

Doran turned an armchair upright and plopped into it, not bothering to create a seat for her. He flicked a wrist toward the opposite wall. "You'll find a tablet on the desk. I assume you know how to transcribe, considering all the years the head-master let you spend at my school."

Jaw clenched, she nodded.

"I'll dictate from my . . ." He trailed off as a trio of lines wrinkled his forehead. "Damn it. Where's my data file?" Without giving her a chance to guess, he made a shooing motion with one hand. "I'll have to find it. Wait in the hall. I don't want you to see where I keep my valuables."

Solara suppressed an eye roll. The only thing she wanted to do with his data file was soak it in hot sauce and shove it up his nose, but she obediently waited outside until he reopened the door. Then she powered on the tablet and opened a new document.

"I'm ready," she said.

But Doran had fallen silent. She glanced down and caught him staring at the felony tattoos on her knuckles, his face leaking color by the second. The whites of his eyes kept growing until he looked like he'd seen a demon, and Solara half expected him to retreat to his bedroom and pull the covers over his head. She cursed herself for leaving her room with naked hands. She should have remembered to put on her gloves.

"You didn't have those when you were at my academy," he said, tugging absently at his earlobe. "I would have noticed."

"No." Her first instinct was to look at her knuckles, but she fought it. She didn't want to see them. "They're fresh. Only a few months old."

Doran swallowed hard, his gaze never leaving her hands. She found it odd that he hadn't laughed at her yet, not that she was complaining. "That's why you didn't graduate. You were expelled."

"I still graduated," she said. "Just not from the academy."

"What did you do?"

The question made her shoulders go tense. It always did. She knew she could give him the easy answer—she'd been caught stealing. But that wasn't the half of it. As the nuns always said, the devil was in the details. It was the details that shamed her beyond any punishment a judge could hand down. The details hurt like a slash to the heart, and she would die a thousand deaths before sharing them with Doran.

"I don't remember," she told him.

"You're a liar."

"Yes, Mr. Spaulding."

"You have to tell me," he insisted. "It's my right as your employer."

No, it wasn't. She knew the law. "I made a mistake and I learned from it. I didn't hurt anyone. That's what matters."

"How do I know you're telling the truth?" he asked, and swallowed hard enough to shift his Adam's apple. He almost seemed afraid of her, which couldn't be right. Nothing scared the Great Doran Spaulding, except closets and possibly the absence of mirrors. "We've already established that you're a liar."

Solara didn't want to play this game anymore. She would clean Doran's suite and fetch his slippers, but she wouldn't give him a piece of her soul. "If you trust me enough to let me in here, you must know I'm not a threat to you."

"You're not going to tell me?"

"I don't like talking about it."

"Fine, then." He thrust a finger toward the door and ordered, "Get out."

She drew her eyebrows together. Was he serious or just jerking her around? Sometimes it was hard to tell. "But what about the—"

"I don't want your help," he said. "Be at Miss DePaul's suite before breakfast to tend to that thing she calls a dog. Aside from that, I don't care what you do."

Then he stood from his chair and turned off the light in a clear dismissal.

Solara blinked a few times before setting down the tablet and backing out of the room. She returned to her bunk expecting another summons, but she slept undisturbed until the morning alarm rang.

*   *   *

The next day, she couldn't shake the feeling that something was wrong, a sort of prickly sensation in her stomach that lingered throughout her morning routine. There was no logical reason for it. The ship traveled smooth and steady, only two hours from the next refueling post. Her roommates smiled and gossiped about their onboard crushes while braiding one another's hair. Nothing seemed out of the ordinary.

It wasn't until she reached Miss DePaul's suite that Solara realized the cause for her unease. Her wristband had remained silent for too long. Doran hadn't demanded predawn breakfast in bed. He hadn't ordered her to warm his bath towels or set the telescreen to his favorite news program. He hadn't even asked her to pull an outfit from his closet.

That definitely wasn't normal.

She knocked on Miss DePaul's door and tried to ignore the worries nibbling at the edge of her mind. The girl answered wearing nothing but Doran's T-shirt—Solara had laundered it enough times to know. After tucking a gleaming pink lock behind one ear, Miss DePaul hitched a thumb over her shoulder.

"Baby had an accident on the carpet last night. Take care of it before you walk her." She sniffed a laugh and added, "You can't miss it. Look for a reeking pile the exact shade of your hair. I'll be in the shower, so lock the door when you leave."

In that moment, Solara decided to "forget" locking, or even closing, the door. She cleaned up after the dog, then tucked it gently beneath one arm and carried it to the mezzanine, where passengers brought their animals to exercise. By the time she finished six laps around the artificial park and returned the dog to Miss DePaul, the *Zenith* had stopped to refuel and Doran finally sent instructions to meet him outside the auxiliary engine room.

An odd request, but Solara knew better than to question it.

When she slid open the door to the utility hallway, a chill of foreboding prickled her skin into goose bumps. The passage was empty and cool, illuminated by flickering overhead lights that cast menacing shadows on the floor. All engines had shut down, and without the rhythmic hum, an eerie silence hung in the air. She heard only the creak of her new boots as she strode toward the stairwell to Doran's meeting place. She saw him in the distance, but he kept his back to her while she climbed the steely stairs. Even when she joined him on the upper platform, he didn't turn to face her.

Instinct told her to retreat—something wasn't right—but she crossed both arms over her chest and asked in her sweetest voice, "How can I assist you, Mr. Spaulding?"

He turned and favored her with a glance as cold and empty as their surroundings. Wordlessly, he swept a hand toward the service door at the hull of the ship.

At first Solara didn't understand. She gazed through the porthole at the outpost station to watch attendants pump fuel into the ship's massive holding tanks. But then her gaze drifted downward, and she spotted her trunk on the floor. There was no mistaking the government-standard stenciling on the lid: BROOKS, SOLARA. CHARITABLE INSTITUTE #22573.

She was still staring at her luggage when she asked, "What's this?"

"This," he told her, "is where you get off."

She whipped her gaze to his. "You can't be serious."

"Have you ever known me to enjoy a joke?"

"But this is an outpost. There's nothing here. That's why everyone's staying on board."

His casual shrug said that wasn't his problem. "There are other ships. If you're lucky, maybe someone less discriminating than me will hire you."

Solara's mouth went dry. Would he really leave her stranded at an outpost without a single credit to her name? Surely he knew what awaited her out there. She had never traveled beyond Earth before, but she'd heard stories of what girls like her had to do in these situations. She would be at the mercy of every lonely ship hand and oily smuggler who passed through this hub.

Maybe Doran was only trying to scare her.

"This isn't funny," she said in a small voice.

"Who's laughing?" he asked. "By the way, you can keep the boots and clothes I bought for you. They're of no use to me."

She searched his face for a glimpse of kindness, the barest spark of compassion, finding none. As awful as Doran's constant insults were, she'd never believed him capable of this kind of cruelty. She still didn't want to believe it. "You're really going to do this?" she asked. "Leave me here with nowhere to go?"

By way of answer, he brushed past her toward the stairs.

"Damn it, Doran!" she yelled, enjoying a morsel of satisfaction when the echo made him flinch. "We have a contract!"

He spun on her from his place at the top step. "And I warned you what would happen if you disappointed me."

Disappointed him?

The accusation was so ridiculous that it stole Solara's voice. She'd done everything he had asked of her, completed each demeaning task without once complaining. How dare he accuse her of failing to honor her side of the bargain?

Her vision tunneled, and she thrust a finger at him. "I came to your suite in the middle of the night to bring you a glass of water when you were too lazy to walk to the bathroom. I cleaned your girlfriend's vomit off the sofa cushions." Solara's voice raised a pitch. "For God's sake, I even fetched her panties when you two left them in the elevator! I wanted to amputate my own hand after that!"

Doran's cheeks flushed bright pink, but he kept his tone cool. "I don't tolerate liars."

"Liars," she repeated, finally understanding the real issue. She'd refused to share the details of her conviction with him. Well, that wasn't going to change. She ripped off one glove and held her knuckles in his face. "So this is what it's about? You want to know what I did to earn my ink?"

His blue eyes narrowed. "I can't promise I'll reconsider my decision."

"That's okay. I want you to know." She gripped the stair rails and leaned down until she was close enough to smell his musky cologne. "I killed my last boss—buried a wrench in his brain when he tried to fire me."

Doran took one step backward down the stairs, then another.

"But the judge had mercy," she said, holding his gaze as she followed him down the steps. "Because my boss was just like you . . . a total waste of flesh."

"I don't believe you." But Doran's trembling voice contradicted his words.

"That I killed someone?" she asked. "Or that you're a waste of flesh? Because one of those statements is true."

He glared at her. "While you're hustling a ride to the outer realm, I'll be sipping champagne in bed with my girlfriend. Who's the real failure here?"

"You are," Solara said. "No doubt about it." An odd sense of calm settled over her, steadying her pulse and slowing her breath. It felt good to speak her mind, even if each word was a nail in her coffin. "I might have dirt under my fingernails and tattoos across my knuckles," she told him, "but I can fix that with a hot bath and a visit to the flesh forger. You're dirty in a place that can't be washed. You'll never change, and you'll never make a difference. When you die, no one will miss you, because your life won't matter." She followed him down the stairs until they stood nose-to-nose at the base. *"You don't matter."*

If she didn't know better, she'd think her words had stung him. "Don't pretend you're better than me," he whispered. "By the time you can afford your first bolt bucket, I'll control all the fuel in the galaxy. The Solar League would collapse without Spaulding, and they know it. If you hadn't been expelled, you would've seen the League president at graduation—to congratulate me."

She shook her head. "You still don't get it."

"You're the one who's deluded."

"You know what? I'm glad you dropped me here." She jabbed a finger toward his forehead to punctuate her final words. "You're not worth my time."

Lurching back to avoid her touch, Doran pointed at the top of the stairs. "Don't let me stop you. Your passage here is unpaid. I'd hate to see you arrested as a stowaway."

But despite her bold words, Solara didn't budge.

Couldn't budge.

Beads of sweat formed along her upper lip, because once she left the safety of this transport, there was no turning back. She would never survive out there. And if she stayed on board the *Zenith* and the crew caught her, they would show no leniency. Not with her conviction so fresh. They'd send her to one of the prison colonies, where she would spend the rest of her life mining the fuel ore that made Doran so rich.

No.

She couldn't lose her freedom over him. There had to be another way.

"Better hurry," he said with a smug smile. "I've traveled on plenty of vessels like this, and they don't take all day to refuel."

While he gloated, Solara scanned the engine room for anything she could smuggle out and barter for passage on another ship. She spotted an upgraded gravity drive, but without the tools to remove it, the device was useless to her.

Think harder, she told herself. *There's always unexpected currency to find.*

Then her gaze landed on Doran's indenture band, the one that joined them as master and servant, and the solution hit like a lightning bolt to the head. That bracelet was the most valuable hunk of metal on board, because he'd linked it to his credit account. And Doran's credit was limitless. Just last week, he'd gambled away a lifetime's fortune in the casino as if it were spare tokens he'd found in a jar. If she overpowered him and took his bracelet, she could use his money to hire a private ship.

Solara chewed the inside of her cheek and sized him up—six feet, two inches of lean, sculpted muscle. His bulk came from a gym, not a work site, but that wouldn't make him any less strong. Overpowering him was out of the question.

"What's the matter?" he taunted, leaning against the stair rail with one booted foot crossed over the other. "Afraid you'll miss me?"

She sneered at him. "The only thing I'll miss is the chance to flush you out the waste port."

He laughed. "You're not very nice for a girl raised by nuns."

Solara was about to retort, *Maybe they weren't nice nuns,* when she remembered Sister Agnes's parting gift—the tiny weapon tucked inside her pocket.

She drew a hopeful breath.

The stunner dispensed a fast-absorbing liquid drug with enough neuro-inhibitors to drop a mule. One touch to Doran's skin and he'd be out cold in seconds. Better yet, when he came to, he'd have a nasty hangover and wouldn't remember his own name. That meant he couldn't tell anyone she'd stolen his band, at least not for a day or two, which was more than enough time to put a few solar systems between them.

Solara reached into her pocket and closed her fingers around the stunner while trying to ignore the sudden guilt tugging at her stomach. This didn't make her a bad person. Doran had left her with no other options—it was life or death. Besides, the toxins wouldn't hurt him.

At least not permanently.

She reminded herself of that as she positioned the button inside her palm and flicked the tiny activation switch. "I'd better go," she said.

Doran nodded. "And soon."

"Thank you for taking me this far. And for the new clothes."

"Don't forget the boots."

"And the boots," she agreed while extending her hand to him. "No hard feelings?"

The peace offering must have surprised him, because his eyebrows twitched. But even after he recovered, he made no move to touch her. He only stood there and tugged at his earlobe while refusing to look her in the eyes. It seemed the Great Doran Spaulding was too good to shake hands with her.

Solara solved that problem by grabbing his wrist.

There was just enough time for confusion to register on his face before his body collapsed to the floor, landing with a clang. Solara dropped to her knees and immediately started working the bracelet over his hand. As soon as she slipped it free, she shoved the band around her wrist and made for the stairs. She was halfway to the exit before she realized a snag in her plan.

The bracelet couldn't be used without identity verification, which meant she would need his handprint for the scanners at the retail center.

"Oh no," she whispered, and whirled around to face his sprawling body. If she wanted Doran's credits, she would have to take him with her into the outpost.

Just how was she supposed to do that?